About the

Niobia Bryant is the award-winning and national bestselling author of more than fifty works of romance and commercial mainstream fiction. Twice she has won the *RT* Reviewer's Choice Best Book Award for African American/Multicultural Romance. Her books have appeared in *Ebony, Essence, The New York Post, The Star-Ledger, The Dallas Morning News* and many other national publications.

Award-winning author **Jennifer Faye** pens fun contemporary romances. With more than a million books sold, she's internationally published with books translated into more than a dozen languages and her work has been optioned for film. Now living her dream, she resides with her very patient husband and Writer Kitty. When she's not plotting out her next romance, you can find her with a mug of tea and a book. Learn more at jenniferfaye.com

Lifelong romance addict **JC Harroway** lives in New Zealand. Writing feeds her very real obsession with happy endings and the endorphin rush they create. You can follow her at jcharroway.com and on Facebook, Instagram, and X @jcharroway

A Christmas Temptation

NIOBIA BRYANT

JENNIFER FAYE

JC HARROWAY

MILLS & BOON

First Published in Great Britain 2024
by Mills & Boon, an imprint of HarperCollins*Publishers* Ltd,
1 London Bridge Street, London, SE1 9GF

www.harpercollins.co.uk

HarperCollins*Publishers*
Macken House, 39/40 Mayor Street Upper,
Dublin 1, D01 C9W8, Ireland

A Christmas Temptation © 2024 Harlequin Enterprises ULC.

Tempting the Billionaire © 2018 Niobia Bryant
Snowbound with the Soldier © 2013 Jennifer F. Stroka
The Proposition © 2019 JC Harroway

ISBN: 978-0-263-36259-6

This book contains FSC™ certified paper and other controlled sources to ensure responsible forest management.

For more information visit: www.harpercollins.co.uk/green

Printed and Bound in the UK using 100% Renewable Electricity at CPI Group (UK) Ltd, Croydon, CR0 4YY

TEMPTING THE BILLIONAIRE

NIOBIA BRYANT

As always, for my mama/my guardian angel,

Letha 'Bird' Bryant

Chapter 1

September 2018
Cabrera, Dominican Republic

*T*hud-thud-thud-thud-thud-thud.

Chance Castillo heard the pounding of his sneakered feet beating against the packed dirt as he ran up the tree-lined path breaking through the dense trees and royal palms. He made his way up the mountains that appeared green and lush against the blue skies when viewed from a distance. He didn't break his pace until he reached the top. His lean but strong muscular frame was drenched in sweat, and his heart pounded intensely in that way after great exertion— which for him was sex or running.

I've had way more of the latter lately.

He pulled his hand towel from the rim of his basketball shorts and wiped the sweat from his face and neck as he sat atop a large moss-covered rock, propping his elbows on his knees. As his pulse began to slowly decelerate, Chance looked around at his tranquil surroundings. He was surrounded by shades of green, from vibrant emerald to the muted tones of sage and olive. The smell of earth and nature was thick. He inhaled deeply, knowing he would miss his morning run from his secluded villa down along the white sand beach of the shoreline of the Atlantic Ocean to the surrounding mountains and cliff side.

His mother, Esmerelda Diaz, had transplanted her love of her beautiful hometown of Cabrera to him. As a kid, he had loved her stories of growing up on a small farm in the hills overlooking the coast in the northern region of the Dominican Republic. Her family members were hardworking farmers of fruits and vegetables whose livelihood depended on their crops. She spoke of days more bad than good. Plenty of struggle. Sometimes just a small meal away from hunger. Money spent on nothing more than bare necessities. Her life was filled with more coastal tranquility than wealth, but her memories were of a small family working hard in humble surroundings and enjoying the simple life they led.

Chance squinted his deep-set chestnut-brown eyes as he looked around at the higher elevation of the small town that was ripe with hills, oceanfront cliffs and mountains as green as emeralds. Fortunately, the town had not yet been overtaken by traffic and congestion like neighboring tourist traps. Still, there were a good number of people from other countries living in the town, experiencing the vivid Latino culture and enjoying the excellent exchange rate of American dollars while retaining their citizenship to their home country.

Chance chuckled. *Technically,* I *am an expat.*

He was a United States citizen, and although he had been living in Cabrera for the last eight months, he had every intention of returning to the States. *Back to my life.*

His brows deepened as he frowned a bit and turned his head to look off in the distance. The sun was setting, and he could just make out the outline of his sprawling two-story beachfront villa. It was the epitome of luxury living, with its private beach and sweeping views of the surrounding mountain ranges, tranquil waters, and azure skies.

It was the best his money could buy.

And seeing the smile on his mother's face when he purchased it two years prior had been worth every cent. Never had he seen her so proud. It was everything she worked for as an Afro-Dominican single mother with a broken heart and a low-paying job as a nursing assistant who was determined her son not get lost in the shuffle of the tough streets of the Soundview section of the Bronx, New York.

He still shook his head in wonder at the sacrifices the petite beauty had made for him to have a better life. Chance was ten when Esmerelda began working double shifts as a certified nursing assistant to move them out of their apartment in the Soundview projects to a better neighborhood. It meant taking on higher rent and a longer commute to her job, but she felt it was worth the sacrifice to be closer to the fringes of the Upper East Side because she wanted him to attend the elite Manhattan private academy The Dalton School. Although she applied for scholarships, she fought hard to pay his annual tuition and fees while keeping them clothed, fed and with a roof over their heads.

Chance's heart swelled with love for his mother. He'd never forgotten or taken her sacrifice for granted. It motivated him. Her happiness was his fuel through the tough days adjusting to being the poor kid who felt different from his classmates. He went on to finish at Dalton and graduated from Harvard with a degree in accounting and finance. While making a good living in finance, six years later he became a self-made wealthy man in his own right after selling a project management app for well over $600 million. That, plus the dividends from smart investing, was rocketing him toward billionaire status. He had purchased a home in Alpine, New Jersey, for his mother and ordered her retirement—she gladly agreed.

That was three years ago.

I'm not the poor kid from the Bronx with the two uniforms and the cheap shoes anymore.

In the distance, Chance heard the up-tempo beat of Ozuna and Cardi B's "La Modelo." He looked back over his shoulder, and at the top of the hill there was a crown of bright lights. He rose from the boulder and flexed his broad shoulders as he jumped, bringing his knees to his muscled chest with ease before racing up the dirt-packed path of the hill as the darkness claimed the skies.

At the top everything intensified. The music. The smell of richly seasoned foods being cooked in the outdoor kitchen. The bright lights adorning the wooden planks of the large pergola. And the laughter and voices of his extended family all settled around the carved wooden benches, or dancing in the center of the tiled patio. The scent of the fruit of the towering royal palm trees filled the air as the firm trunks seemed gathered around the small farming property to offer privacy.

The three-bedroom villa with its one lone bathroom and barely an acre of land was modest in comparison with his beachfront estate, but it was here among his cousins, with the night pulsing with the sounds of music and laughter, that he felt warmth and comfort.

Mi familia.

He came to a stop, just barely shaded by the darkness, and looked at his petite, dark-haired mother whose brown complexion hinted at the history of a large majority of Dominicans having African ancestry due to the slave trade of the early 1700s. She stood before a rustic wood-fired oven, stirring the ingredients in a cast-iron pot as she moved her hips and shoulders in sync to the music. He chuckled as she sang along with Cardi B's part of the song and raised the large wooden spoon she held in the air.

Everyone cheered and clapped when she tackled the rap part, as well.

Esmerelda Diaz was his mother and everyone's beloved. Although only forty-nine, she was the last of the Diaz elders. The baby girl who grew up to lead their descendants.

His mother turned and spotted him standing there. Her dark, doe-shaped eyes lit up as if she didn't have her own suite on his estate and had not fixed him *pescado con coco* for lunch. His stomach grumbled at the thought of the snapper fish cooked in coconut sauce.

"Chance!" she exclaimed, waving him over. *"Mira. Mira. Mira."*

The nine members of his extended family all looked over to him and waved as they greeted him. His cousin Carlos, a rotund, strong man in his late twenties, came over to press an ice-cold green bottle of Presidente beer in his hand as he slapped him soundly on the back in greeting.

This was the home of Carlos, his wife and four small children. He owned and operated farmlands of just three acres only a few hundred yards from the villa and was proud of his work, like many other Dominican farmers, providing locally grown fruits and vegetables and taking care of his family. Chance respected his cousin's hard work ethic and enjoyed plenty of his harvest during his time in the country. In kind, he knew his family respected him for the success he had made of his life back in the Estados Unidos.

"Tough day?" Chance asked.

Carlos shrugged one shoulder. "Same as always. And you, *primo*?" he asked with a playful side-eye and a chuckle before he took a swig of his own beer.

Chance laughed. His days of finance work and the development of his app had never been physically hard, and now that he just served as a consultant to the firm that'd purchased his app, the majority of his time was spent maintaining his toned physique and enjoying the fruits of his labor. Life was good, with his private jet, his estate in Cabrera and his permanent one in Alpine, New Jersey, and the ability to do whatever he wanted, whenever he chose. And during this time of his life, he chose to travel, enjoy fine food and wine, and spare himself nothing.

His days of struggling were over. As were his days of feeling less than for having less than.

"Excuse me, I'm starving," he said, moving past his younger cousin to reach his mother.

She smiled up at him before turning her attention back to stirring the pot.

"Sancocho de mariscos," he said in pleasure at the sight of the shellfish stew rich with shrimp, lobster, scallops, garlic, plantains, pumpkin and potatoes.

"Sí," Esmerelda said, tapping the spoon on the edge of the pot before setting it atop a folded towel on the wooden table next to the stove.

Living in a town directly off the Atlantic Ocean had its privileges. Although Chance was no stranger to traditional Dominican cooking. On her rare days off, his mother would go shopping and spend the day cooking and then freezing meals for him to enjoy while she was at work.

"Como estas?" she asked in rapid Spanish as she reached up to lightly tap the bottom of his chin with her fingertips.

"I'm fine," he assured her.

She shrugged one shoulder and slightly turned her lips downward as she tilted her head to the side. Translation? She didn't agree with him, but so be it.

The radio began to blare "Borracho de Amor" by Jose Manuel Calderon, and Chance was thankful. His mother gave a little yelp of pleasure and clapped rapidly at the sound of one of her favorite songs from the past before she grabbed the hand of her nephew Victor and began dancing the traditional *bachata*.

Chance took a seat at a wooden table and placed his beer on it as he watched his mother, alive and happy among her culture and her family. But as everyone focused on their dance, his attention was on the words of the song. As was common with traditional *bachata* music that was about heartache, pain and betrayal, it was a song of a man who turned to drinking after the heartache and pain caused by a woman's scorn. It was said that the tortured emotions displayed in the song fueled *bachata* dancers to release those emotions through dance.

Chance knew about heartache all too well.

His gut tightened into a knot at the memory of his former fiancée, Helena Guzman, running off with her lover and leaving him at the altar. In the beautiful blond-haired Afro-Cuban attorney he'd thought he found the one woman to spend his life with. She'd even agreed to give up her career as a successful attorney to travel the world with him.

But he'd been wrong. And made a fool of.

His anger at her was just beginning to thaw. His mother referred to her only as "Ese Rubio Diablo." The blond devil.

Cabrera had helped him to heal.

But now I'm headed home.

This celebration was his family's farewell to both him and his mother.

The daughter of his best friend since their days at Dalton, Alek Ansah, and his wife, Alessandra, had been born and he'd been appointed her godfather. He'd yet to see her in person; photos and FaceTime had sufficed, but now it was time to press kisses to the cheek of his godchild and do his duty at her upcoming baptism.

In the morning they would board his private plane and fly back to the States. She would return to the house he purchased for her in New Jersey, and he would be back at his estate in a house he'd foolishly thought he would share with his wife and their family one day.

Chance looked over into the shadowed trunks of the trees that surrounded the property as his thoughts went back to the day he was supposed to wed the woman he loved...

"I'm sorry, Chance, but I can't marry you," Helena said, standing before him in her custom wed-

*ding dress and veil as they stood in the vestibule of
the church.*

*For a moment, Chance just eyed her. His emotions
raced one behind the other quickly, almost colliding,
like dominoes set up to fall. Confusion. Fear. Pain.*

*"I am in love with someone else," she said, her
eyes filled with her regret.*

Anger.

*Visions of her loving and being loved by another
man burned him to his core like a branding. The
anger spread across his body slowly, seeming to in-
fuse every bit of him as the truth of her betrayal set in.*

*"How could you do this, Helena?" he asked, turn-
ing from her with a slash of his hand through the air,
before immediately turning back with his blazing fury.*

And his hurt.

That infuriated him further.

"How long?" he asked, his voice stiff.

"Chance," Helena said.

"Who is he?"

*She held up her hands. "That is irrelevant," she
said. "It is over. It is what it is, Chance."*

"Who?" he asked again, unable to look at her.

"My ex, Jason."

*The heat of his anger was soon replaced with the
chill of his heart symbolically turning to stone. He
stepped back from her, his jaw tightly clenched. "To
hell with you," he said in a low and harsh whisper.*

Long after she had gathered her voluminous skirt
in her hands and rushed from the church to run down
the stairs, straight into the waiting car of her lover,

Chance had stood there in the open doorway of the church and fought to come to grips with the explosive end of their whirlwind courtship.

Chance shook his head a bit to clear it of the memory, hating that nearly eight months later it still stung. The betrayal. The hurt. The dishonor.

Damn.

"*Baila conmigo*, Chance."

He turned his head to find Sofía, the best friend of Carlos's wife, extending her hand to him as she danced in place. She was a brown-skinned beauty with bright eyes, a warm smile and a shapely frame that drew the eye of men with ease. They had enjoyed one passionate night together a few months ago after a night of dancing, but both agreed it could be no more than that, with his plans to return to the States. And his desire to not be in another relationship.

Accepting her offer, he rose to his feet and took her hand, pulling her body closer to his as they danced the *bachata*. "You remember what happened the last time we danced?" he teased her, looking down into her lively eyes.

Sofía gave him a sultry smile before spinning away and then back to him. "I can't think of a better way to say goodbye," she said.

Chance couldn't agree more.

"Lord, help me get through this day."

Ngozi Johns cast a quick pleading look up to the fall skies as she zipped up the lightly quilted crimson running jacket she wore with a black long-sleeved T-shirt, leggings and sneakers. The sun was just beginning to rise, and the early morning air was crisp. She inhaled it deeply as she stretched her limbs and bent her frame into a few squats before jogging down the double level of stairs of her parents' five-bedroom, six-bathroom brick Colonial.

Her sneakered feet easily ate up the distance around the circular drive and down the long paved driveway to reach Azalea Street—like every street in the small but affluent town of Passion Grove, New Jersey, it was named after flowers.

Ngozi picked up the pace, barely noticing the estates she passed with the homes all set back from the street. Or the wrought iron lamppost on each corner breaking up the remaining darkness. Or the lone school in town, Passion Grove Middle School, on Rose Lane. Or the entire heart-shaped lake in the center of the town that residents lounged around in the summer and skated on in the winter.

She waved to local author Lance Millner, who was in the center of the body of water in his fishing boat, as he was every morning. The only time he was to be seen by his Passion Grove neighbors was during his time in the water, tossing his reel into the lake, or the rare occasions he visited the upscale grocery store on Main Street. In the distance, on the other side of the lake, was his large brick eight-bedroom home with curtains shielding the light from entering through any of the numerous windows. He lived alone and rarely had any guests. The man was as successful at being a recluse as he was at being a *New York Times* bestselling author.

He waved back.

It was a rushed move, hard and jerking, and looked more like he was swatting away a nagging fly than giving a greeting.

Ngozi smiled as she continued her run. With one movement that was as striking as flipping the middle finger, he confirmed his reputation as a lone wolf with no time to waste for anyone. When he did venture from his lakeside estate, his tall figure was always garbed in a field jacket and a boonie hat that shaded his face.

Passion Grove was the perfect place to come to enjoy high-scale living but avoid the bustle, noise and congestion of larger cities. Home to many wealthy young millennials, the town's population was under two thousand, with fewer than three hundred homes, each on an average of five or more acres. Very unlike Harlem, New York. She had enjoyed living in the city, soaking in the vibrancy of its atmosphere and culture and the beauty of its brownstones and its brown-skinned people—until a year ago. A year to the date, in fact.

When everything changed.

"Damn," she swore in a soft whisper as she shook her head, hoping to clear it.

Of her sadness. Her guilt.

Ngozi ran harder, wishing it were as easy to outrace her feelings.

It wasn't.

She came to a stop on the corner of Marigold and Larkspur, pressing her hand to her heaving chest as her heart continued to race, even though she did not. She grimaced as she released a shaky breath. She knew the day would be hard.

It had been only a year.

Ngozi bit her bottom lip and began jogging in place to maintain the speed of her heartbeat before she finally gathered enough strength to push aside her worries and continue her morning run. She needed to finish. She needed to know there was true hope that one day her guilt and remorse would no longer hinder her.

She continued her run, noticing that outside of the echo of her colorful sneakers pounding on the pavement, the chirp of birds and errant barks of dogs occasionally broke the silence. With the town comprising sizable estates that were all set back three hundred or more feet from the streets—per a local ordinance—the noise was at a minimum.

"Good morning, Counselor."

Ngozi looked over her shoulder to find the town's police chief standing on the porch of the Victorian home that had once served as the town's mercantile during the early days of its creation in the 1900s. For the last fifty years, it had served as the police station and was more than sufficient for the small town. She turned, jogging in place as she looked up at the tall and sturdy blond man who looked as if his uniform was a size—maybe two—too small. "Morning, Chief

Ransom," she greeted him as she checked her pulse against the Fitbit. "Care to join me?"

He threw his head back and laughed, almost causing his brown Stetson hat to fall from his head. "No, no, no," he said, looking at her with a broad smile that caused the slight crinkles at the corners of his brown eyes to deepen. He patted his slightly rounded belly. "My better half loves everything just as it is."

Eloise, his wife, was as thin as a broomstick. Opposites clearly attracted because it was clear to all that they were deeply in love. The couple resided in the lone apartment in the entire town—the one directly above the police station. It was a perk of accepting the position as chief. It would be absurd to expect a public servant to afford one of the costly estates of Passion Grove—all valued at seven figures or more.

"You have any future clients for me?" Ngozi asked, biting her inner cheek to keep from smiling.

"In Passion Grove?" the chief balked. "*No* way."

She shrugged both her shoulders. "Just thought I'd ask," she said, running backward before she waved and turned to race forward down the street.

As a successful New York criminal defense attorney, Ngozi Johns was familiar with the tristate area's high-crime places. Passion Grove definitely was not counted among them. The chief had only two part-time deputies to assist him when there was a rare criminal act in the town, and so far that was limited to driving violations, not curbing a dog, jaywalking or the occasional shoplifting from the grocery store or lone upscale boutique by a thrill-seeking, bored housewife.

There were no apartment buildings or office buildings. No public transportation. Only stop signs, no traffic lights. There were strict limitations on commercial activity to maintain the small-town feel. Keeping up its beautiful aesthetic was a priority, with large pots on each street corner filled with plants or colorful perennial floras.

Like the police station, the less than dozen stores lining one side of Main Street were small converted homes that were relics from the town's incorporation in the early 1900s. She jogged past the gourmet grocery store that delivered, a few high-end boutiques, a dog groomer and the concierge service that supplied luxuries not available in town. Each business was adorned with crisp black awnings. She crossed the street to ignore the temptation of fresh-brewed coffee and fresh-baked goods wafting from La Boulangerie, the bakery whose delicacies were as sinfully delicious as the store was elegantly decorated like a French bistro.

She appreciated the serenity and beauty as she reached the garden that bloomed with colorful fall flowers, and soon was at the elaborate bronze sign welcoming everyone to Passion Grove. She tapped the back of it with gusto before taking a deep breath and starting the run back home.

Ngozi successfully kept her thoughts filled with upcoming depositions or cases. By the time she turned up the drive and spotted her parents' sprawling home, the sun was blazing in the sky and some of the chill had left the morning air. She felt less gloomy.

Thank you, God.

"Good morning, Ngozi."

Her heart pounded more from surprise at the sound of her father's deep voice than the run. She forced a pleasant smile and turned in the foyer to find her tall father, Horace Vincent, with deep brown skin that she'd inherited and low-cut silver hair, standing in the open door to his office. He was still in his silk pajamas, but files were in hand and he eyed her over the rim of his spectacles.

"Good morning, Daddy," she said, walking across the hardwood floors to press a tender kiss to his cheek. "I just finished my run."

Horace was a retired corporate and banking attorney who started Vincent and Associates Law over forty years ago. It was one of the top five hundred law firms in the country—a huge accomplishment for an African American man—and Ngozi was proud to be one of the firm's top criminal trial attorneys.

"Ngozi!"

The urge to wince rose quickly in her, but Ngozi was well practiced in hiding her true feelings from her parents. "Yes, Mama?" she asked, following her father into his office to find her mother leaning against the edge of the massive wooden desk in the center of the room. She was also still in her nightwear, a satin red floor-length gown and matching robe.

Even in her seventies, Valerie "Val" Vincent was the epitome of style, poise and confidence. Her silver bob was sleek and modern. She exercised daily and stuck to a vegan diet to maintain her size-eight figure. Her caramel-brown skin, high cheekbones, intelligent brown eyes and full mouth were beautiful even before her routine application of makeup. She was constantly mistaken for being in her fifties, but was regally proud of every year of her age.

And she was as brilliant as she was beautiful, having cultivated a career as a successful trial attorney before becoming a congresswoman and garnering respect for her political moves.

"I know today is difficult for you, Ngozi," Val said, her eyes soft and filled with the concern of a mother for her child.

As her soul withered, Ngozi kept her face stoic and her eyes vacant. She never wanted to be the cause for worry in her parents. "I'm fine, Mama," she lied with ease.

Her parents shared a look.

Ngozi diverted her eyes from them. They landed on the wedding photo sitting on the corner of her father's desk. She fought not to release a heavy breath. The day she wed Dennis Johns, she had put on a facade as well and played the role of the perfectly happy bride vowing to love the man she'd met in law school.

Until death do us part.

After only four years.

She was a widow at twenty-nine.

She blinked rapidly to keep the tears at bay.

"We want you to know there's no rush to leave," her father began.

Ngozi shifted her gaze back to them, giving them both a reassuring smile that was as false as the hair on the head of a cheap doll. It was well practiced.

I'm always pretending.

"When we suggested you move back home after Dennis's...passing, your mother and I were happy you accepted the offer, and we hope you'll stay awhile," Horace continued.

"Of course, Daddy," she said, widening her smile. "Who wants to leave a mansion with enough staff to make you think you're on vacation? I ain't going nowhere."

They both smiled, her show of humor seeming to bring them relief.

It was a pattern she was all too familiar with.

How would it feel to tell them no?

Her eyes went to the other frame on her father's desk and landed on the face of her older brother, Haaziq. More death.

She winced, unable to hide what his passing meant for her. Not just the loss of her brother from her life, but the role she accepted as defender of her parents' happiness. Losing their son, her brother, in an accidental drowning at the tender age of eight had deeply affected their family. Little six-year-old Ngozi, with her thick and coarse hair in long ponytails and glasses, had never wanted to be a hassle or let down her parents because of their grief. She'd always worn a bright smile, learned to pretend everything was perfect and always accepted that whatever they wanted for her was the right course of action.

"Let's all get ready for work, and I'm sure break-fast will be on the table by the time we're ready to go and conquer the world," Val said, lovingly stroking Horace's chin before rising to come over and squeeze her daughter's hand.

At the thought of another meal, Ngozi wished she had dipped inside the bakery, enjoyed the eye candy that was Bill the Blond and Buff Baker, and gobbled down one of the decadent treats he baked while re-sembling Paul Walker.

Bzzzzzz.

Ngozi reached for her iPhone from the small pocket of her jacket. "Excuse me," she said to her parents before turning and leaving the office.

She smiled genuinely as she answered the call. "The early baby gets the mother's milk, huh?" she teased, jogging up the wooden staircase with wrought iron railings with a beautiful scroll pattern.

"Right." Alessandra Dalmount-Ansah laughed. "The early bird has nothing on my baby. Believe that."

Alessandra was the co-CEO of the billion-dollar conglomerate the Ansah Dalmount Group, along with her husband, Alek Ansah. Ngozi served as her per-sonal attorney, while corporate matters were handled by other attorneys at Vincent and Associates Law. The women had become closer when Ngozi successfully represented Alessandra when she was mistakenly ar-rested during a drug raid. She'd been in the wrong place at the absolute worst time, trying to save her cousin Marisa Martinez during a major drug binge.

"How's my godchild?" Ngozi asked, crossing the

stylishly decorated family room on the second level to reach one of the three-bedroom suites flanking the room.

"Full. Her latch game is serious."

They laughed.

The line went quiet just as Ngozi entered her suite and kicked off her sneakers before holding the phone between her ear and her shoulder as she unzipped and removed the lightweight jacket.

"How are you?" Alessandra asked, her concern for her friend clear.

"I'm good," Ngozi said immediately, as she dropped down onto one of the four leather recliners in the sitting area before the fireplace and the flat-screen television on the wall above it.

Liar, liar.

She closed her eyes and shook her head.

Then she heard a knock.

"Alessandra, can I call you back? Someone's at my door," she said, rising to her feet and crossing the room.

"Sure. See you at the baptism Sunday."

"Absolutely."

Ngozi ended the call and opened the door. Reeds, her parents' house manager, stood before her holding a tray with a large bronzed dome cover. She smiled at the man of average height with shortbread complexion, more freckles than stars in the sky and graying brownish-red hair in shoulder-length locks. "One day my mother is going to catch you," she said as she took the tray from him and removed the lid to reveal buttered grits, bacon, scrambled eggs and toast.

He shrugged and chuckled. "The rest of the staff wouldn't know what to do without me after all these years."

"I *know* that's right," Ngozi said with a playful wink.

"Just remember to at least eat the bowl of fruit at breakfast," Reeds said before he turned and began to whistle some jazzy tune. He stopped in the middle of the family room to glance back. "*Or* you could just tell your mother you're not vegan. Your choice."

Ngozi ignored his advice and stepped back into the room, knocking the door with her hip to push it closed.

Chapter 2

Alpine, New Jersey

*T*he day of reckoning is here.

Chance splashed his face with water and pressed his hands to his cheeks before wiping the corner of his eyes with his thumb. He stood tall before the sink and eyed his reflection in the large leather-framed mirror above it. He released a heavy breath and studied himself, rubbing his hand over his low-cut fade haircut.

Today he would face his friends for the first time since what was supposed to be his wedding day. With the last bit of pride and bravado he could muster, Chance had stood before all those people and admitted that the wedding was called off. The swell of gasps of shock and whispers had filled the church as he strode down the aisle with nearly every eye locked on his stoic expression. He would admit to no one the embarrassment he felt, and didn't allow his head to sink one bit until he left the church.

He had instructed Alek to have the wedding planner, Olivia Joy, turn the reception into a party, but he had not attended the event. The idea of being pitied or ridiculed by Helena's betrayal was too strong for him to swallow. He spent what was supposed to be his wedding night ignoring all attempts at communicating with him as he nursed a bottle of pricey Dos Lunas Grand Reserve tequila, stewed in his anger and envisioned Helena being bedded by her lover.

Early that next morning, with a hangover from hell, he boarded his private jet and flew to Cabrera with no foreseeable plans to return. His consultant work for the same firm that purchased his app could be handled from anywhere in the world with Wi-Fi. All he knew was he had to get away. So he did.

Now I'm back.

He eyed his reflection, hating the nerves and anxiousness he felt.

It took him back to his school days as a poor brown-skinned Latino kid from the Bronx trying his best not to feel less than around students who were predominantly white and absolutely from wealthy families.

He flexed his arms and bent his head toward each of his shoulders, instinctively trying to diminish those feelings from his youth. "Let's get this over with," he mumbled under his breath, removing his towel and drying his body before tossing it over the smoothed edge of the cast concrete in the center of the dark and modern bathroom.

He quickly swiped on his deodorant and lightly sprayed on cologne from one of the ten bottles sitting on a long ebony wood tray in the space between the large tray sinks atop the concrete vanity.

Naked, he strode across the heated marble floors and through the opening in the tinted-glass wall to his loft-style bedroom suite. His motorized open-front closets lined the entire wall behind his king-size Monarch Vi-Spring bed, but the suit he'd already selected was laid across one of the custom chaise longues at the foot of it. His long and thick member swayed across his thighs as he moved to pull on his snug boxers, having to adjust it to comfort before he finished dressing in silk socks, his off-white wool-silk suit and a matching open-neck shirt. The fit against his athletic frame spoke to its custom tailoring and his desire for both quality and style.

Not wanting to run late, he hurriedly selected one of a dozen watches to buckle around his wrist while slipping on shoes that were almost as comfortable as his bed.

Life was good when it came to the creature comforts. The days of squeaky rubber-sole shoes from the dollar store were over.

I hated to walk in 'em, he remembered. *Felt like everyone heard me coming.*

He rushed through his opulent two-story villa-style mansion, which sat on two gated acres in Alpine, New Jersey, styled in muted tasteful decor with vibrant pops of color that were a testament to his dynamic Latino culture. Chance lived alone in the six-bedroom luxury home, and he usually kept music or his 4K televisions on to break the silence. Hip-hop from the 1990s played from the sound system, and he rapped along to Big Daddy Kane's "Ain't No Half-Steppin'" as he grabbed his keys from beside the glass-blown structures of nude women atop the table in the center of the foyer.

Soon he was out the double front doors and behind the wheel of his black-on-black Ferrari 488 Pista, taking I-280 to Passion Grove. He drove the super-car with ease with one hand, effortlessly switching lanes on the interstate as he lightly tapped his fist against his knee to the music playing. The commute was hassle-free because it was Sunday morning, and he was grateful as he finally guided the vehicle down the exit ramp and made his way through the small town. He didn't think he could find an upscale town more laid-back than Alpine, but Passion Grove proved him wrong.

A city without traffic lights in 2018?

Chance felt bored already. He still found it hard to believe that his fun-loving best friend, Alek—who was born into a billionaire dynasty—chose the small town to live in after jet-setting all over the world.

Real love will make you do unexpected things.

His and Helena's plans had been to travel the world and explore new adventures after they were wed.

And look how that turned out.

His hand gripped the steering wheel, lightening the color of his skin across his knuckles. He was glad to finally make it to Alek and Alessandra's, accelerating up the private mile-long paved street leading to the expansive twenty-five-acre estate until he reached the twelve-foot-tall wrought iron gate with the letter *D* in bronzed scroll in the center.

Alessandra had inherited the estate upon the death of her father, Frances Dalmount, who co-owned the billionaire conglomerate the Ansah Dalmount Group, along with Alek's father, the late Kwame Ansah. When Alessandra and Alek wed last year, they'd decided to make the Passion Grove estate their main home, while maintaining both his Manhattan and London penthouse apartments, and the vacation estate they built together on their private island in upstate New York.

After getting checked in by security via video surveillance, Chance drove through the open gates and soon was pulling up to the massive stone French Tudor. He hopped out and pressed a tip into the hand of one of the valets his friends were using for the day to park the vehicles.

He jogged up the stairs and accepted a flute of champagne from the tray being held by a servant. "Thank you," he said with a nod of his head as he entered the foyer through the open double doors.

"Thanks so much."

Chance paused and turned at the soft voice. He froze with his drink still raised to his mouth as he eyed the woman over the rim of the crystal flute. His heart began to pound, and his breath caught in his throat. *Well, damn...*

She was beautiful. Tall and shapely with skin as dark and smooth as melted chocolate. Long and loose waves of her beyond-shoulder-length ebony hair framed her oval face with high cheekbones, bright and clear brown doe-like eyes, and a nose bringing forth a regal beauty similar to the women of Somalia. The long-sleeved white lace dress she wore clung to her frame with a V-neck highlighting her small but plump breasts, and a wide skirt above long shapely legs. Her gold accessories gave her skin further sheen.

As she walked past the valet with a soft reserved smile, the wind shifted, causing her hair to drift back from her face as she moved with confident long strides that flexed the toned muscles of her legs and caused the skirt of her dress to flounce around her thighs. He couldn't take his eyes off her and had no desire to do so. She was a treat, and the very sight of her as she easily jogged up the stairs made him hunger for her.

He smiled like a wolf behind his flute as his eyes dipped to take her in from head to delicious feet displayed in open-toe sandals with tassels that were sexy.

Who is she?

He felt excited with each step that brought her closer to him. When she paused to take her own flute of champagne, his hawk-like eyes locked on how the flesh of her mouth pressed against the crystal, leaving a light stain of her lip gloss on the glass.

Who is she? And does she want to leave with me later?

The prospect of that made his return to the States completely worth it.

"There you are, Chance."

With regret, he turned from his temptress. "Here I am," he agreed, genuinely smiling at Alessandra Dalmount-Ansah as she walked up to him, looking beautiful in a white light georgette dress with perfect tailoring.

She grabbed his upper arms lightly as she rose up on the tips of her shoes to press a kiss to his cheek. "Welcome home, Chance," she said with warmth, looking up at him with sympathetic eyes as she raised a hand to lightly tap his chin. "You good?"

He nodded, hating the unease he felt. *How much more of this pity will there be today?* he wondered, purposefully turning from her to eye the beauty in peach as she stepped inside the foyer.

Her eyes landed on his, and he gave that lingering stare and slow once-over that was nothing but pure appreciation and a desire to know more. Her brows arched a bit and her mouth gaped as she gave him the hint of a smile that was just enough to give him hope.

"Hey, Ngozi," Alessandra said, moving past Chance to kiss her cheek in welcome.

So, this is Ngozi? Alessandra's best friend and attorney. Brains and beauty. Just as Alessandra had said to him so many times.

Her eyes left him, and Chance felt the loss, finally

taking a sip of the champagne he instantly recognized as Armand de Brignac.

"That's right, you two have never met," Alessandra said, reaching for one of Ngozi's hands and then one of Chance's. "Chance Castillo, godfather, meet Ngozi Johns, godmother."

She pressed their hands together.

Their eyes met.

As they clasped hands, Chance stroked the pulse at her wrist with his thumb, enjoying how it pounded. It matched his own.

Ngozi felt breathless.

Her first sight of Chance Castillo as she stepped inside the house had made her entire body tingle with excitement. He was tall with an athletic frame that could not be denied in his tailored suit. His stance as he stood there eyeing her over the rim of his glass spoke of unleashed power. A man. A strong man built for pleasure. Not just handsome, with his medium-brown complexion and angular features softened by lips and intensified by his deep-set eyes, the shadow of a beard and his low-cut ebony hair...but intriguing. Something about him had instantly drawn her in. Excited her. Made her curious. Forced her to wonder, *Who is he?*

And now, as Ngozi stood there with her hand seemingly engulfed by his with his thumb gently grazing her pulse, she shivered and sought control of her body. Her pulse. Her heartbeat. Her breaths.

The pounding of the sweet fleshy bud nestled between the lips of her core. *Damn.*

All of it surprised her. Never had she had such an instantaneous reaction to a man before.

Needing to be released from the spell he cast upon her, Ngozi pulled her hand from his and forced a smile that she hoped didn't look as awkward as it felt. "Nice to finally meet, Mr. Castillo," she said, proud of her restored cool composure.

It was all a sham, and she deserved an award for the performance.

"Chance," he offered, sliding the hand she once held into the pocket of his slacks.

"Right this way, y'all," Alessandra said, leading them across the stately round foyer, past the staircase and down the hall into the family room, where the glass doors were retracted, creating an entertaining space that flowed with people lounging inside or outside on the patio or around the pool.

Alek spotted them and excused himself from a couple he was talking with to cross the room to them. It was similar to watching a politician or other public figure as he spoke to each person who stopped him while still moving toward them. The man was charismatic.

Ngozi took a sip of her champagne as she glanced at Alessandra over the rim. The look in her friend's eyes as she watched her husband was nothing but love. She'd found her happily-ever-after.

A twinge of pain radiated across her chest, and Ngozi forced herself to smile in spite of it.

"Careful, Ngozi," Alessandra said, holding out her arm in front of her. "Don't get in the way of this bro love, girl."

Ngozi looked on as Chance took a few strides to meet Alek. The men, equally handsome, confident and strong in build, clasped hands and then moved in for a brotherly hug complete with a solid slap of their hand against the other's back. It barely lasted a moment, but it was clear they were close.

As the men talked quietly to one another, Ngozi eyed Chance's profile, surprised by her reaction to him. And she still felt a tingle of awareness and a thrill that ruffled her feathers. He smiled at something Alek said, and her stomach clenched as a handsome face was instantly transformed into a beautiful one.

"He looks happy," Alessandra said softly to herself.

Ngozi glanced over at her, seeing the hope on her face that her words were true. She remembered Alessandra explaining Chance's absence because he had been left at the altar by his fiancée and was in the Dominican Republic recovering from his heartache. That had been nearly nine months ago.

What woman would leave him behind?

Ngozi had never asked for any more details than Alessandra offered, but that was before she'd seen him. Now a dozen or more questions flew to mind with ease. Her curiosity was piqued.

"I'm going up to get the baby," Alessandra said. "Be right back."

Ngozi glanced around the room, raising her flute

in toast to those she knew professionally or personally. When her eyes landed back on the men, she found Chance's eyes on her. She gasped a little. Her pulse raced.

He gave her a wolfish grin—slow and devastating—as he locked his gaze with hers. They made their way toward her, and Ngozi forced herself to look away as she felt a shiver race down her spine.

"I wanted to finally greet you, Ngozi," Alek said.

She looked up at him with a smile. "I thought I was invisible," she teased, presenting her cheek for a kiss as she pretended Chance was not standing there, as well.

"Chance told me Alessandra already made the introductions between you two," Alek said.

She stiffened her back and glanced up at Chance. "Yes, it's nice to finally put a face to the name," she said.

"Same here," he agreed. "Especially since we're sharing godparent duties."

"Right, right," she agreed with a genuine smile. "We'll rock, paper, scissors for overnight stays."

He opened his mouth and then closed it, biting his bottom lip as if to refrain himself. He shared a brief look with Alek, who then shook his head and chuckled.

And she knew—she just *knew*—Chance was going to say they could have overnights together.

"Really, fellas?" she asked, eyeing them both like a teacher reprimanding naughty schoolboys.

"What?" they both asked innocently in unison.

Ngozi was surprised to see Alek, normally severe and businesslike, standing before her with mirth in his eyes. "So, we all have that one thing or one person—a vice—that makes us different. Today, Alek Ansah," she said before turning to face Chance, "I have met yours."

Chance's smile broadened as he looked down at her. "And what—or who—makes you different, Ngozi Johns?"

She loved how her name sounded on his lips. "Oh, is there something about me that needs fixing?" she asked, forcing herself not to quiver under his intense stare as she met it with one of her own.

"From what I can see, not one damn thing," Chance responded with ease, his voice deep and masculine.

"On *that* note," Alek said, clearing his throat as he looked from one to the other, "I'll take my leave."

And he did, leaving them alone.

"Ngozi!"

At the sound of her name, Ngozi broke their stare and turned to find Marisa Martinez standing beside her. She gave the petite woman with a wild mane of shoulder-length curly hair a warm smile. "It's good to see you, Marisa," she said, her eyes taking in the clarity in the woman's eyes and feeling sweet relief.

The former party girl who lived hard and fast off the allowance she received from the Dalmount dynasty had developed an addiction to alcohol and drugs that put both her and Alessandra's freedom in jeopardy. As the head of the family, Alessandra felt it her obligation to guide and protect the entire clan made up of her two aunts, Leonora Dalmount and

Brunela Martinez, her cousin Victor Dalmount and his bride, Elisabetta, and Marisa, Brunela's daughter. That sense of duty had led Alessandra to seek out Marisa at a house party and to get caught in the middle of a police drug raid.

Ngozi was called on by her client to represent them both. The charges were dropped, but Alessandra had forced Marisa to either attend the long-term rehab program Ngozi arranged or be disowned.

Marisa chose the former, and six months later, she'd returned drug-free.

"I just wanted to thank you for everything you did to help me," Marisa said, before lifting up on her toes to give Ngozi an impromptu hug.

"Well, I thank you for not letting my hard work go to waste," she said, returning the hug. "You look good."

Marisa released her. "I feel better," she said, her eyes serious before she forced a smile and walked away with one last squeeze of Ngozi's hand.

She watched her walk over to join her mother and aunt Leonora by the fireplace. With her work as a criminal attorney who insisted on pro bono work and tough cases, Ngozi was well acquainted with thankful clients.

"I've heard you're one of the best attorneys on the East Coast."

Him.

Ngozi took a sip of her champagne as she eyed him with an arched brow. "Just the East Coast?" she teased.

He chuckled.

"I'm kidding," she rushed to say, reaching out to grasp his wrist.

His pulse pounded against her fingertips. She released him.

"La tentadora," Chance said.

The temptress.

Her entire body flushed with warmth.

Chance was Dominican on his mother's side, and like many other Afro-Latinos did appear to be what was standardly thought of as such. Much like Laz Alonso, Victor Cruz and Carmelo Anthony.

"Me das demasiado crédito," she said, loving the surprise that filled his deep brown eyes at her using his native tongue to tell him that he gave her too much credit.

"Ah! ¿Tu hablas español?" he asked.

"Yes, I speak Spanish," she answered with a nod.

"¿Pero alguna vez te ha susurrado un hombre en español mientras te hace el amor?"

Ngozi gasped in surprise and pleasure and excitement at his question of whether a man had whispered to her in Spanish while making love. She recovered quickly. "No," she answered him, before easing past his strong build and imposing presence to leave.

"Usted tiene algo que esperar," Chance said from behind her.

Then you have something to look forward to.

Chance Castillo.

She gave in to her own temptation and glanced back at him over her shoulder. He had turned his attention to greeting Alek's younger brother, Naim. She pressed her fingertips to her neck as she turned away, admitting regret that his attention was no longer on her.

In truth, she couldn't remember feeling that affected by a man in a long, long time.

She pursed her lips and released a stream of air, intending to calm herself.

Ngozi stopped a male waiter and set her near-empty flute on the tray. "Thank you," she said. Her stomach rumbled, and she looked around with a slight frown, hoping no one had heard it. Quickly, she turned and tapped the shoulder of the waiter. "Is there another one like you with a tray of hors d'oeuvres? A sista is hungry."

He chuckled and shook his head. "Not yet," he said. "The food will be served after the ceremonies."

Damn. Ngozi checked her platinum watch as he walked away.

She crossed the room and made her way outdoors. During the day, the September air was still pleasant. It was the early mornings and late nights that brought on a chill that reminded her summer was drawing to an end.

As she neared the Olympic-sized pool, she felt an urge to jump in and sink beneath the crystal clear depths to swim to the other end and back. Instead, she settled for slipping off one of her sandals to dip her toes in the water, causing it to ripple outward.

Dennis loved to swim.

She felt sadness, closing her eyes as she remembered his looking back at her over his shoulder before he dived into the deep end of her parents' pool back in some of the rare moments of free time they had during law school.

She smiled a bit, remembering how happy they were then.

That was a long time ago.

"Excuse me, Ms. Johns."

She was surprised by the same waiter who took her drink, now standing beside her with a sandwich on his tray.

"Courtesy of Olga, the house manager, per the request of Mr. Castillo," he said.

Ngozi looked up and bit back a smile at Chance standing in the open doorway, raising his flute to her in a silent toast. Her stomach rumbled again as she bowed her head to him in gratitude. She assumed he had overhead her conversation with the waiter.

"One sec, please," she said, holding the man's wrist to keep her balance as she slipped her damp foot back into her sandal.

Once done, she took the sandwich and cloth napkin from him and bit into it. Her little grunt was pure pleasure at the taste of seasoned and warmed roast beef with a gooey cheese and a tasty spread on the bread. "Thank you," she said to him around the food, with a complete lack of the decorum she had been taught by her parents.

"No problem."

As he walked away to finish his duties, Ngozi turned her back to the house and enjoyed the view of the manicured lawns to avoid people watching her eat.

"Ngozi."

Him.

Her body went on high alert. Every pulse point on her pounded. *What is wrong with me? Am I in heat?*

"Yes?" she said, patting the corners of her mouth with the napkin before turning to face him. *Wow. He's fine.*

Chance was nursing his second glass of champagne and squinting from the sun of the late summer season as he eyed her.

"You shouldn't drink on an empty stomach," she said, offering him the other half of the sandwich still on the saucer.

He eyed it and then her. "My appetite isn't for food, Ngozi," he said before taking another deep sip of his drink.

"The only thing I have for you is half of this sandwich, Mr. Castillo," she said, keeping her voice cool and even.

He chuckled.

"Akwaaba. Akwaaba. Memo o akwaaba."

They both turned to find LuLu Ansah, Alek's mother, standing in the open doorway looking resplendent in traditional African white garb with gold embroidery with a matching head wrap that was simply regal. Both the Ansah and Dalmount families surrounded her, with Alek and Alessandra beside her with the baby in Alessandra's arms. Both she and Alek looked around before they spotted Chance and Ngozi, waving them over.

They rushed to take their place, Ngozi gratefully handing the saucer and the remainder of the sandwich to one of the waiters.

"Welcome. Welcome. We welcome you," LuLu

translated, looking around at everyone gathered with a warm smile that made her eyes twinkle.

Ngozi leaned forward a bit to eye her goddaughter, who was just eight days old. She was beautiful. A perfect blend of Alek and Alessandra, with tightly coiled ebony hair and cheeks that were already round. She couldn't wait to hear her name. Alessandra had not budged in revealing it early.

"Today we are honored to officially present a new addition to our family. We will have both a religious ceremony to baptize our little beauty to ensure she is favored by God, and then an outdooring, which is a traditional Ghanaian ceremony when a baby is taken outside the home for the first time, given a name and prepared with the love and wisdom we all hope for her. Is that okay with you all?" she asked, looking around at the faces of everyone in attendance with a sweet, loving expression.

People applauded or shouted out their approval.

"And so, we welcome into our world, our community, our village... Aliyah Olivia Ansah," LuLu said with pride. "May we all pray for her, guide her and love her."

Alessandra pressed a kiss to Aliyah's head, and then Alek pressed one to her temple.

She was so loved.

Ngozi was happy for them and couldn't help but smile.

Chapter 3

Two weeks later

"Congratulations, Counselor."

Ngozi finished sliding her files inside her briefcase and then raised her hand to take the one offered by the Brooklyn district attorney Walter Xavier. She had just served him a loss in his attempt to prosecute her client, an ex-FBI agent, for murder. "You didn't make it easy," she told him, matching his steady gaze with one of her own.

With one last pump of her hand and cursory nod of his head, the man who was her senior by more than thirty years turned and walked out of the courtroom with several staff members behind him.

Ngozi allowed herself a hint of a smile as she looked down into her briefcase.

"Ayyeeee! Ayyeeee! Ayyeeee!"

"Angel!" Ngozi snapped in a harsh whisper, whirling around to eye her newly appointed personal assistant at her loud cry. She found her arm raised above her head, as if she was about to hit a dance move, which took her aback. A win in the courtroom was not the same as getting "turned up" in the club.

Angel, a twentysomething beauty whose enhanced body made a button-up shirt and slacks look indecent, slowly lowered her hands and smoothed them over her hips.

"Get out," Ngozi mouthed with a stern look, seeing that other people in the court were openly eyeing them.

"What?" she mouthed back, looking confused as she picked up her fuchsia tote from her seat in the gallery and left the courtroom with a pout.

"Precious Lord," she mumbled, thankful her client had already been taken back into the holding cell by the court officers.

Ngozi often went above and beyond for her clients, including hiring a former stripper/escort as her personal assistant to meet the requirements of the probation Ngozi was able to secure. At the firm she had her own staff, clerks, paralegals and junior associates, plus an experienced legal secretary. The last thing she needed was a personal assistant—especially one like Angel, who lacked discernment.

Two weeks down, two years to go...

Ngozi gathered the rest of her items and finally left the courtroom. As she made her way through the people milling about the hallway, Angel and her junior associate, Gregor, immediately fell in behind her. Her walk was brisk. She had to get back to the Manhattan office for an appointment with a prospective new client.

She had a rule on no walking and talking outside the offices of Vincent and Associates Law, VAL, so they were quiet. Once they reached the exit on the lobby level, she saw the crowd of reporters and news cameras awaiting her. This was another huge win for her in a controversial case. She felt confident in the navy Armani cap sleeve silk charmeuse blouse, tailored blazer and wide-leg pants she wore. She had self-assuredly and correctly anticipated the win and made sure to be camera ready—which had included an early morning visit from her hairstylist/makeup artist.

"Angel, go mannequin-style and say nothing," she mumbled to the woman.

"But—"

A stare from Ngozi ended her statement before it even began.

They exited the building and then descended the double level of stairs, with Ngozi in the lead. She stopped on the street and the crowd created a semi-arc around them. "Hello, everyone. I am Ngozi Johns of Vincent and Associates Law. As you know, I am the attorney for Oscar Erscole, who has been successfully exonerated of the charges of murder that were brought against him. After a long and tenuous fight, we are thankful that the jury's discernment of the facts and the evidence presented in the case has proven what we have always asserted, which is the innocence of Mr. Erscole, who can now rebuild his life, reclaim his character and enjoy his life. Thank you all. Have a good day."

With one last cordial smile, she turned from them, ignoring the barrage of questions being fired at her as they made their way through the crowd and to their waiting black-on-black SUVs. Ngozi and Angel climbed into the rear of the first one. She pulled her iPhone from her briefcase and began checking her email. "Back to the office, please, Frank," she said to the driver, working her thumb against the touch screen to scroll.

"Now, Ms. J.?" Angel asked, sounding childlike and not twenty-one years of age.

It wasn't until the doors were closed and their tinted windows blocked them from view that Ngozi glanced over at Angel and bit the corner of her mouth to keep back her smile. "Now, Angel," she agreed.

"Ayyeeee! Ayyeeee! Ayyeeee!" Angel said, sticking out her pierced tongue and bouncing around in her seat. "Congrats, boss."

"Thanks, Angel," Ngozi said, laughing when she saw the driver, a white middle-aged man who liked the music of Frank Sinatra, stiffen in his seat and eye them in alarm via the rearview mirror.

They continued the rest of the ride in relative silence as Ngozi swiftly responded to emails and took a few calls. When the car pulled to a stop, double-parking on Park Avenue in midtown Manhattan, Ngozi gathered her things back into her briefcase as the driver came around to open the door for her. "Thank you, Frank," she said, lightly accepting the hand he offered to help her climb from the vehicle and then swiftly crossing the sidewalk with Angel on her heels and the rest of her team just behind her.

They entered the thirty-five-story beaux arts–style building complete with retail and restaurant space on the lower levels and corporate offices on the remaining thirty-three. Everything about the building spoke to its prominence and prestige. After breezing through security with their digital badges, Ngozi and the others traveled up to the twenty-second floor, where Vincent and Law Associates had occupied the entire twenty-two thousand square feet for the last twenty years, housing nearly fifty private offices, a dozen workstations, several conference rooms, a pantry, reception area complete with a waiting space and other areas essential for office work. The offices of the senior partners, including the one her father had vacated upon his retirement, were on half of the floor of the next level up.

Vincent and Associates Law was a force with which to be reckoned. Her father had begun his firm over forty years ago with his expertise in corporate and banking law. Over the years, he acquired smaller firms and attorneys with proven records of success in other specialties to expand and become a goliath in the Northeast and one of the top five hundred law firms in the country.

To know that her father spearheaded such power

and prominence made her proud each and every time she walked through the doors. It had been no easy ride for an African American man, and her respect for her father was endless. And she was determined to rightfully earn her spot as a senior partner and claim the office that sat empty awaiting her—when the time was right.

It was one of the few goals for her that they shared.

Ngozi moved with an Olivia Pope–like stride as she checked her Piaget watch. The team separated to go to their own offices or workstations in the bright white-on-white interior of the offices. Angel took her seat at a cubicle usually reserved for law interns. "Angel, order lunch. I want it in my office as soon as my meeting is over," Ngozi said as she continued her stroll across the tiled floors to her glass corner office.

"Champagne or brandy, boss?" her legal assistant, Anne, asked as she neared.

Champagne to celebrate. Brandy to commiserate.

Ngozi bit her cheek to keep from smiling. "Champagne," she said with a wink, doing a little fist pump before entering her office and waving her hand across the panel on the wall to close the automated glass door etched with her name.

She didn't have much time to marinate on the win. She took her seat behind her large glass desk and unpacked several files, her tablet and her phone from her suitcase. After checking the online record of messages sent to her by those at the reception desk, she tucked her hair behind her ear and lightly bit the tip of her nail as she stared off, away from her computer monitor, at a beam of sunlight radiating across the floor and the white leather sofa in her conversation area.

Bzzzzzz.

Her eyes went back to the screen.

A Skype call from Reception. She accepted the video option instead of the phone one. The face of Georgia, one of the firm's six receptionists, filled the screen. "Ms. Johns. Your one o'clock appointment, Mr. Castle of CIS, is here."

"Thank you, Georgia, send him in," she said.

Ngozi turned off her monitor and cleared her desk. She glanced through the glass wall of her office and then did a double take.

Him.

All her senses went haywire as she watched the handsome charmer make his way past the workstations in the center of the office with the ease of a well-trained politician. A smile here, a nod there.

And it was clear that a lot of the women—and a few of the men—were eyeing him in appreciation.

Chance Castillo was undeniably handsome, and the navy-and-olive blazer he wore with a navy button-up shirt and dark denim were stylish and sexy without even trying.

She hadn't seen him since the festivities for their goddaughter, Aliyah.

"What is he up to?" she mumbled aloud as she settled her chin in one hand and drummed the fingernails of the other against the top of her desk.

When Angel jumped up to her feet and leaned

over the wall of her cubicle, Ngozi rolled her eyes heavenward. Especially when he paused to talk to her. Soon they both looked down the length of the walkway, at her office.

His smile widened at the sight of her in the distance.

Ngozi raised her hand from the desk and waved briefly at him with a stiff smile before bending her finger to beckon him to her.

By the time he reached her office, there were many pairs of eyes on him.

She pressed the button on her desk to open the door as she rose to her feet. "Very slick of you, using the English version of Castillo, Chance," she said, extending her hand to him as she would any client—new or old.

"I didn't want to risk you canceling to avoid me," he said, taking her hand in his.

It was warm to her touch.

She gently broke the hold, reclaiming her seat. "So, you're clear on me wanting to avoid you, then?" she asked.

"Damn, you're smart," Chance said, walking around her office.

His presence made it seem smaller.

"Um, excuse, Ms. J."

Both Ngozi and Chance looked over to find Angel standing in the open doorway.

"Yes?" Ngozi asked, noting to herself that the young'un usually avoided work (in other words, coming to her office) at all costs.

"I wondered if you were ready for lunch?" Angel asked Ngozi with her eyes on Chance.

He turned his attention back to the bookshelves lining the wall.

"Yes, I already asked you to order lunch, remember? And is there something wrong with all the communication available between us...from your desk?" Ngozi asked, pointing her finger in that direction.

Angel smiled as she tucked a loose strand of her four bundles of waist-length weave behind her ear. She used to wear her hair in voluminous curls that gave her a hairdo like the Cowardly Lion from the *Wizard of Oz*. Ngozi had requested she wear it straight and pulled back into a ponytail while at work. Thankfully, she acquiesced.

"I also wanted to ask if you or your guest wanted somethin' to drink?" Angel asked, cutting her appreciating eyes on Chance again.

"No, thank you," Ngozi said politely, as she jerked her thumb hard a few times toward Angel's workstation.

With one last look at Chance's tall figure behind his back, Ngozi's young assistant reluctantly left them alone, but not before flicking her tongue at him in a move Ngozi knew had been a hit during her former profession. She added a long talk on not flirting with clients on the long mental list of things to school Angel on.

She closed the automated door.

Chance turned to eye it before focusing his attention on her. "She's...unexpected," he mused with a slight smile.

That she is.

Some of the partners were still not fully sold on her working there.

"No pictures," Chance observed, walking up to her desk.

"Too many reminders of death," she said truthfully, without thinking to censor herself.

"Death?" he asked.

"Nothing," she muttered, sitting back in her chair as she eyed him. "I'm sure you didn't set up a fake appointment with me just to survey my office."

Chance shook his head as he folded his frame into one of the chairs facing her desk. "Fake name. Real appointment. I would like you to represent me," he explained.

That surprised her, and her face showed it. She reached for a legal pad and one of her favorite extrafine-point pens filling a pink-tinted glass bowl on the corner of her desk. The firm had every technological advance available, but she preferred the feel of a pen on paper when assessing the facts of a new case. "Typically, I handle criminal cases," she began.

"I know," Chance said, smiling at her. "Congratulations on your win this morning."

"Thank you," she said graciously, wondering if his smile had the same effect on all women the way it did on her. "You saw the news?"

He nodded. "You looked beautiful, Ngozi."

Thump-thump-thump-thump-thump.

She fought for nonchalance as her heart pounded wildly, seeming to thump in her ears. "And smart," she added.

"Of course, but beautiful nonetheless, Ngozi."

Thump-thump-thump-thump-thump-thump-thump-thump-thump-thump.

She shifted her eyes away from his. "What type of trouble are you in?" she asked, seeking a diversion from her reaction to him.

"It's a civil matter," Chance told her, raising one leg to rest his ankle on the knee of the opposite one.

Ngozi set her pen down atop the pad. "I'm sure a man of your means already has proper representation for a civil case."

"I may be interested in moving all my business here to Vincent and Associates Law…if this case is successfully litigated," he said. "That's a revenue of seven figures, if you're wondering."

She had been.

Ngozi steepled her fingers as she studied him, trying her best to focus on the business at hand and not how the darkness of his low-cut hair and shadowy beard gave him an intense look that happened to be very sexy. The news of the Harvard grad and successful financier inventing a project management app and reportedly selling it for well over $600 million had taken the business and tech sectors by storm, but it was his backstory of claiming success in spite of his humble beginnings that made Ngozi respect his hustle. He retained a small percentage of ownership with the deal and served as a well-paid consultant on top, making several large investments beyond the sale of his app to only increase his wealth and holdings.

Chance Castillo was a man to be admired for his brains. He made smart money moves that even Cardi B could respect.

The senior partners would appreciate bringing his legal interests under the firm's umbrella, and it would take the assistance of other attorneys more equipped to handle matters outside her expertise...if she won the civil case.

"What is the case about?" she asked, her curiosity piqued as she reclaimed her pen from the pad.

Chance shifted his eyes to the window wall displaying the sun breaking through the heart of midtown Manhattan's towering buildings. "I'm sure you heard about the end of my engagement last year," he began.

Her eyes widened a bit at the hardness that suddenly filled the line of his jaw and his voice. Yes, she had heard. The story held almost as much prominence in the news as the sale of his app. Although she had avoided reading about gossip, it was hard to ignore as conversation filler at dinner parties and such.

"She was having an affair the entire time she planned a million-dollar wedding on my dime. The willingness to foot the bill was mine, I admit that," he said, shifting eyes that lacked the warmth and charm they'd once contained. "But doing so after she ends the engagement to be with another man, that I can't swallow. Not on top of the cost of the engagement ring, as well."

Ngozi paused in taking notes. "And the cost of the ring?"

"A million."

"Would you like that recouped, as well?"

"I wish I could recoup every cent I ever spent on her," he said, his voice cold and angry.

Ngozi tapped the top of her pen against the pad as she bit the corner of her mouth in thought. "You understand that gifts cannot be recovered."

He held up his hand. "That's why I said I *wish* and not I *want*. I understand those things are lost to me."

She nodded. "The name of your ex-fiancée?"

He frowned as if the very thought of her was offensive and distasteful. "Helena Guzman," he said, reaching into the inner pocket of his blazer to remove a folded sheet of paper to hand to her.

Ngozi accepted it and opened it, finding her contact information. She frowned a bit at her work address, recognizing it instantly. "She works for Kingston Law?"

"She's a real estate attorney," he said, rising to his feet and pushing his hands into the pockets of his jeans as he stood before the window. He chuckled. It was bitter. "I assume once she left her meal ticket behind, she put aside her plan to stop working."

He was angry. Still. It had been nine months or more.

She broke his heart.

Ngozi eyed his profile, feeling bad for him. Gone were the bravado and charm. This was a man dealing badly with heartbreak.

"Are you sure litigation is necessary?" she asked, rising from her desk to come around it.

"Yes."

She came to stand with him at the window, their reflection showing his stony expression and her glancing up at his profile. "Why the wait, Chance?"

He turned his head to look down at her, seemingly surprised by her sudden closeness. "I was out of the country," he answered, his eyes vacant.

This Chance was nothing like the man she'd met two weeks ago, or even the one he'd been when he first strolled into her office. Which was the facade?

She gave him a soft smile.

He blinked, and the heat in the depth of his eyes returned, warming her. "With you looking up at me, I could almost believe in—"

Thump-thump-thump-thump-thump.

"Believe in what?" she asked.

He shook his head, softly touched her chin and then turned his focus back to the view splayed out before them. "Will you take the case?" he asked.

Ngozi swallowed over a lump in her throat and put the distance back between them. "Is this about anger over her not marrying you—which is breach of promise to marry and is no longer a viable defense in certain states? Or do you feel you've been wronged and would like a cause of action for strictly financial remedy?"

Chance flexed his shoulders. "The latter" was his response.

Ngozi reclaimed her seat, not admitting that she

did not believe him. "I think a case of this nature is best presented before a jury. It will be a long way to go, particularly with Ms. Guzman being an attorney herself, but perhaps she will be willing to settle this out of court."

Chance nodded.

She made several notes on her pad before looking up at him again. "I will need the details of your relationship and its breakup, and any receipts and invoices you have pertaining to the purchase of the ring and the wedding should be provided."

He nodded once more.

"Chance," she called to him.

He looked at her.

Their eyes locked.

Thump-thump-thump-thump-thump.

"During the length of this case you are going to have to relive what was clearly a very difficult time for you," she said. "It may become fodder for the news—"

"Again," he injected.

"Right," she agreed. "I just want to be *sure* you want to pursue this."

He smiled at her. "I'm sure, Ngozi."

"And you're sure you want me to represent you?" she asked, ignoring the thrill of her name on his lips.

His smile widened. "I take any business or legal matters very seriously. Even the offer to move my interests to this firm was researched first. I joke and laugh a lot. I love life, I love to have fun, but I never play about my money."

She stood up and extended her hand. "Then let's get your money back, Mr. Castillo," she said with confidence.

He took her hand in his but did not shake it, instead raising it a bit to eye her body. "We should celebrate our future win with dinner and a night of dancing, *la tentadora*," he said.

Ngozi visibly shivered, even as she looked to her right through the glass wall of her office and, sure enough, discovered quite a few eyes on them, most widened in surprise and open curiosity. She jerked her hand away and reclaimed her seat as she cleared her throat. "Please make an appointment at the receptionist's desk for us to review the details of the case," she said, paying far too much attention to the notepad on her desk. "I will need that information to complete the summons."

Chance chuckled. "Was I just dismissed?" he asked.

"Yes," she said, glancing up at him with a smile.

"Hay más de una forma de atrapar al gato," he said, turning to walk out of her office with one last look back at her.

His words lingered with her long after he was gone, while she futilely tried to focus on her work.

There is more than one way to catch a cat.

It wasn't quite the proper saying, but nothing had been lost in translation.

Chance Castillo had made his intention very clear.

Ngozi put her chin in her hand and traced her

thumb across the same spot on her chin that he had touched.

Thump-thump-thump-thump-thump-thump.

She released a stream of breath through pursed lips.

This was uncharted territory...for the last year, at least.

This attraction. This reaction. This desire.

An awakening.

Ngozi swore as the all-too-familiar pings of guilt and regret nipped at her, seemingly an integral part of her DNA.

Her brother's death. Her parents' grief. Her husband's death.

She pushed aside her thoughts and focused on work, soon getting lost in the minutiae of motions, reviewing court minutes, and at the end of the day celebrating her latest win with a champagne toast from the senior partners.

That evening, behind the wheel of her caldera red Jaguar F-Type coupe, Ngozi put the five-liter V8 engine to good use once she was on I-80 West, headed to Passion Grove. The sky darkened as she passed the township's welcome sign. She was grateful for the panoramic roof as she made her way toward her parents' estate. She slowed to a stop and looked out into the distance at the town's heart-shaped lake. Soon the chill of winter would freeze it over and the townspeople would enjoy ice skating, but tonight the stars reflected against the gentle sway of the water and she found the serenity of it comforting.

Following an impulse, she parked the car on the street and then climbed out to swap her heels for the pair of running sneakers she kept in her trunk. With her key fob in her hand, Ngozi made her way up the street around the brick-paved path surrounding the lake. She took a seat on one of the wrought iron benches, crossing her legs and leaning forward to look out at the water.

Ngozi, come on. Come skate with me.

Ngozi smiled a bit, feeling as if she could see her late husband, Dennis, before her at the edge of the frozen lake, beckoning her with his arm outstretched toward her. It was not a dream, but a memory.

Christmas night.

Maxwell's "Pretty Wings" was playing via the outdoor surround system that streamed top pop hits around the lake during the winter.

Earlier, right after Christmas dinner, the lake had been crowded with townspeople enjoying snowball fights or ice skating, but now only a few remained as darkness claimed prominence and the temperature slid downward with the absence of the sun. Snow covered the ground, casting the night with an eerie bright glow as the moon and stars reflected down upon the sheen of the ice…

Ngozi had been happy just to watch Dennis effortlessly gliding upon the ice with the skill of an Olympian, but she slid on her ice skates and made her way to him, accepting his hands and stepping onto the ice. They took off together, picking up the speed they needed before gliding across the ice with Dennis in the lead and their hands clasped together.

When he tugged her closer, she yelled out a little until he held her securely in his arms, burying his head against her neck as she flung hers back and smiled up at the moon while they slid for a few dozen feet before easing to a stop...

A tear slid down her cheek, and she reached out as if to touch the all-too-vivid memory of better times.

Bzzzzzz.

She let her hand drop as the vibration of her phone brought her out of her reverie. Blinking and wiping away her tears with one hand, she dug her iPhone out of the pocket of her fitted blazer.

"Yes?" she answered.

"Ngozi?"

Her father.

She closed her eyes and fought to remove the sadness from her tone. "Hey, Dad," she said and then winced because it sounded too jovial and false to her ears.

"Hey, congrats on the win, baby girl," Horace said, the pride in his voice unmistakable. "I thought you would be home by now. You didn't say you had a meeting or event or anything."

Her interpretation of that: Why are you late?

She was as predictable as a broken clock being right at least two times out of the day. Predictable and perfunctory.

"I'm on the way," she said, delivering a half-truth.

"Good. Your mother had a council meeting and Reeds is serving up real food for us while she's gone."

Ngozi laughed. Her father disdained the vegan lifestyle as much as she did. "Steaks simmered in brown butter with mashed potatoes and two stiff bourbons on ice?" she asked as she rose to her feet and made the small trek back to her car, guided by the lampposts lining the street.

"Absolutely," he said with a deep chuckle. "Hurry!"

"On my way," she promised, turning and taking a few steps backward as she gave the lake one last look and released the memory.

Chapter 4

Two weeks later

Chance reached inside the jar of almonds he kept on his desk, gathering a few into his hand to toss into his mouth as he leaned back in the ergonomic chair. Since he'd hit his major windfall a couple of years ago and left behind his work in finance, he rarely used his home office, but for the last couple of days an idea for a new app had been nagging at him. So he took his morning run, returned to shower and then meditate, and then headed into his office to hammer out the details floating around in his head.

The normal blare of the music was gone. He needed quiet to focus, and his estate in Alpine provided him plenty of that.

Again, the app was a labor of necessity. Although he was no longer on an 8:00 a.m.–8:00 p.m. job, he still found a need to be productive. Unlike his wealthy friends who grew up with staff, Chance preferred to do without. Many were not aware that the staff seen during his lavish dinner parties were not full-time nor live-in. He used a household staffing agency on an as-needed basis.

But for someone who preferred solitude, yet also had an active social life, traveled frequently and at times conducted business on the go, to have a virtual personal or executive assistant was as good as the real thing—or with the right analytics and algorithms, even better.

Ding.

He glanced at the email notification on the screen. It was from Ngozi's firm. Another request for an appointment.

Chance ignored it with a chuckle as he rose from his chair and crossed the wide breadth of his office to leave it and enter the kitchen. He froze and frowned at the sight of his mother stirring a bowl at the island. She was so consumed with it that she didn't even notice him. He crossed his arms over his chest and leaned in the doorway before he cleared his throat.

Esmerelda looked up and smiled at the sight of him. "Hello, Chance. I thought you were sleeping," she said, moving about his kitchen with ease.

He released a heavy breath. He loved his mother. Adored her. He was so thankful for her contribution and sacrifice to his success. He loved to gift her whatever she wished for, except…

"Ma," he said, pushing off the doorjamb with his hand extended toward her. "Come on. Give it up."

Esmerelda stared at him.

He bent his fingers as he returned her stare.

She sucked air between her teeth and wiped her hands clean with a dish towel before reaching in her designer tote bag for her key ring. She mumbled things in Spanish as she worked one of the keys around the ring.

Chance didn't lower his arm until she came around the island and pressed the key against his palm with a jerk. "How many copies did you make?" he asked, sliding the key into the pocket of his cotton sleep pants. "This has to be the tenth key I have taken from you. It has to stop. One day you're gonna walk up in here and see *way* more of me and a lady guest than you want to."

Esmerelda waved her hand dismissively. "Nothing I haven't seen. I changed your diapers," she said, stirring a spatula in the large ceramic bowl again.

"Things are not the same," he balked.

"I hope not."

Chance shook his head, walking up to press his hands against the marble top of the island. "Ma, I *need* my privacy," he said, his voice serious.

Esmerelda avoided eye contact. "You need this stew," she stressed.

Bzzzzzz.

He reached for his cell phone from the pocket of

his sleep pants. Soon he smiled and then ignored the call from Ngozi's assistant.

Will you walk into my parlor? said the Spider to the Fly.

"How is your case coming?" Esmerelda asked.

"It's still in the early stages," he said, raising his arms above his head to stretch as he watched her.

"Have you heard from Ese Rubio Diablo?"

Chance shook his head. "And I don't want to," he said with honesty. "The time for talking is over."

Esmerelda nodded and glanced at him before she turned to set the bowl on the countertop next to the eight-burner Viking stove he rarely used. "It is no easy feat to overcome heartbreak," she said. "Nothing but time can do it. Time and…forgiveness, *mi amada.*"

Chance had moved to the French door smart fridge for a bottle of water, but paused at her words and the softness of her tone. "You think I should forgive her and move on?" he asked in surprise.

Esmerelda turned from the stove. "In time, you will have to, for yourself if not for *that* witch," she said. "Trust me, I know."

He took a deep swig of the water before setting the bottle atop the island as he watched her. His mother was only in her late forties. Still young and beautiful, with an air and vibrancy that made her seem far younger than her years, but with a lifestyle of a woman twenty years her senior. As far as he knew, the only man in her life was his father, and that was a subject they rarely discussed. Yet it had not quelled his curiosity about the man he knew he favored in looks.

His mother had been just seventeen and fresh from a move to America from the Dominican Republic with her grandmother. She met and fell in love with Jeffrey Castillo, a young and handsome Afro-Cuban street dude whom she later found out to be more fabrication than truth and more lust than love. When she told him she was pregnant, he ended the relationship and began seeing another young woman who lived in the same Bronx apartment building as Esmerelda— something that caused her great pain and shame. In time, that relationship of his ended as well, and he soon moved out of their neighborhood. She never saw him again.

"¿Has perdonado a mi padre?" he asked of her forgiveness of his father, using Spanish to connect to the Latino heritage in them both—the mother he knew and the father he did not.

Esmerelda's face became bitter. "For breaking my heart? Yes," she said. "For breaking yours? *Never.*"

Chance came around the island to hug her petite frame to his side, pushing aside the pang of hurt he felt at the truth of her words. He'd never spoken of the hurt of not having a father in his life. The questions. The curiosity about him. The regrets. At times, the anger. "I'm good, Ma," he reassured her.

"You are better than good, *mi amada.*"

My beloved.

Bzzzzzz.

His phone vibrated atop the island. He moved away

from her to retrieve it as she turned back to the stove. Flipping it over, he looked down at the screen. *Jackpot.*

"I gotta take this," he said to his mother, picking up the phone and padding barefoot across the tiled floor back to his office. "Hello, Ngozi."

"Mr. Castillo, my staff has been attempting to reach out to you to set an appointment to come in and discuss the facts of the case you want to take to court," she stressed, her tone formal and indicating clear annoyance.

He held the phone to his ear with one hand and massaged his bare chest with the other as he stood at the windows behind his desk and looked out at his pool. "I apologize for that. My schedule has been hectic. In fact, I'm in the middle of something right now but I didn't want to miss your call."

"Chance," she said, in warning.

"Can we meet this evening? I know it's last-minute, but I will be flying out of the country later tonight—"

"Chance," she repeated slowly.

"Yes?" he asked.

"Where are you?"

He paused. *Should I lie? No, never lie.* "I'm home."

"Do you have the information I requested?"

"Yup," he said, eyeing the folder of information he'd had prepared for her the day after their first appointment.

"I'll be there by seven to pick it up."

Even better than his original plan to have her meet him at the airfield.

Click.

Whistling, he left his office and reentered the kitchen. "Ma, I appreciate the food," he said.

"No problem," she said. "I felt like some oxtails, and I like your kitchen better than mine."

"Do you want to have it remodeled?" he asked, always wanting to spoil her.

"No, Chance, it's a new house and I lied. I love my kitchen, but I love my son more," she stressed, giving him a stern eye to let him know she meant it.

"How long before you're done?" he asked with feigned nonchalance.

Esmerelda raised a brow and rolled her eyes. "A girl."

"A woman," he corrected with emphasis.

She shook her head. "You're kicking me to the curb for some noony-knack," she said, glancing back at him over her shoulder.

"I don't think sending you home to your four-bedroom French Tudor is kicking you to the curb," he drawled, crossing his strong arms over his chest.

"I could go get a mani-pedi at seven," she said.

"Throw in a massage and be gone by six," he bartered.

"Deal. No cash. I'll charge it," she assured him, patting her pocketbook.

"Same difference," he said.

He gave her a weekly allowance, paid her monthly utility bills and gave her an unlimited credit card—that she refused to use without his permission.

"I'm glad you're dating, Chance. You deserve to

be loved again," she said as she emptied a bowl of diced onions into a pan that soon sizzled.

He frowned deeply. "Love?" he scoffed. "No, I'm not looking for the lies of love again. You can forget about that. Helena taught me a lesson I will never forget. Trust no one. Nah."

Esmerelda pointed the tip of the spatula at him. "You're smarter than that. No one can live without love forever," she said.

"Says the woman who has only loved one man in her life," he rebutted.

Esmerelda looked at him as if he had suddenly grown a horn in the center of his handsome head. "Says the silly man who thinks his mama has only loved—or been loved—by one man in thirty years," she said, widening her eyes at him as she released a short laugh. "Silly Chance."

His mouth opened in shock.

"Just because you didn't see it, baby boy, don't mean it wasn't going down, o-*kay*?" she said, her Spanish accent thick. "I wasn't hot to trot, but I got *me*. O-*kay*? And that wasn't any of your business. O-*kay*?"

Chance frowned, shaking his head as if to clear it. "I'm done with this conversation," he said, tilting his head back to drain the last of the water in the bottle into his mouth.

"Yeah, I thought so." Esmerelda chuckled. "Ain't nothing dead on me."

"Let yourself out, Mama. Love you," he said over his shoulder as he left the kitchen.

"Bless his silly heart."

Chance pushed aside thoughts of his mother having a sex life and made his way through the massive house, then jogged up the stairs to his master suite. Standing before the walls of his closet, he admitted to feeling excited at seeing Ngozi again as he selected an outfit.

You deserve to be loved again.

He paused.

He desired Ngozi. He liked her spunk and cleverness. Being around her made him feel good.

But love wasn't in the equation.

Love—or what he thought was love—led to him being made a fool, and a public one at that.

"Nah, I'm good on that," he said to himself, selecting an outfit. "A brother's just trying to have fun with a beautiful lady. That's it. That's all."

Right?

"Right," he said, as if to reassure himself while he laid the clothes on his bed and made his way to his bathroom.

When he returned downstairs, fully dressed and subtly smelling of Creed Viking cologne, the scent of the stew permeated the lower level of the house. He headed to a large framed mirror on the wall beside the front doors, opening it to display the security monitors. He was scanning each room and both three-car garages to make sure his mother had taken leave when one of the monitors showed a red sports car pulling to a stop in front of the secured gate.

The driver's side window lowered, and Ngozi sat

behind the wheel with rose-gold aviator shades in place.

Chance smiled at the sight of her as she reached out and tapped the touch screen. *Just beautiful.*

His security system was automated, but he tapped the pad on its wall base anyway. "Come on in," he said, watching as the gate slid open, and soon she was on her way up the short driveway to him.

He closed the mirror front and then checked his appearance in it, smoothing his beard and adjusting the lightweight V-neck silk sweater he wore with linen slacks. He pushed the sleeves midway up onto his forearms before opening the door and walking down the steps to his stone-paved courtyard.

She parked at an angle before climbing from the car.

With his hands pushed into the pockets of his pants, he watched her, loving the way her hair was pulled back into a sleek ponytail that showed off her high cheekbones. The gray metallic sheath dress she wore fit her frame and complemented her shapely legs. The sun was just beginning to set, and the white uplight began to glow, casting a gleam against her deep brown complexion as she walked up to him. "Nice ride, Ms. Johns," he said. "You sure you can handle it?"

Ngozi slid her shades on top of her head as she glanced back at her vehicle and then looked up at him. "I'm not giving you an opening for a double entendre," she drawled.

He chuckled before giving her a smile. "Welcome to my home, Ngozi," he said.

"And a beautiful home it is," she said, looking around at the manicured lawn and the wrought iron accents on the French villa exterior.

"Would you like a tour?" he asked, surprised that her opinion mattered to him.

Ngozi crossed her arms over her small bosom and tapped one toe of her shoe against a stone paver. "Nope. I'm not falling for the banana in the tailpipe again, Eddie Murphy," she said. "Over the last two weeks, you have been elusive. I have suggested meetings in every *possible* location except my office."

Chance nodded.

"And yet, each and every time I have been unsuccessful," she said, undoing her arms and splaying her hands. "Do you have the paperwork and the timeline of your relationship—including its demise—with Helena Guzman?"

"Yes," he said, fighting hard not to smile because he knew her annoyance with him was genuine and understandable.

She clapped a few times and then clasped her hands together. "Thank you, Lord. Now...do you have it *here*?"

"Yes. It's in my office."

She arched a brow. *"Here?"* Ngozi stressed again. "Yes."

"Would have been so lovely if you had it in your hand to give to me right now, and send me on my way," she said.

He reached down for her hand, clasping it with his own before turning to walk up the steps. "What fun would that be?" he asked.

She followed him up the stairs and into the house, but when they stepped inside the grand foyer, she eased her hand from his. "Wow," she said, turning on her heels to look around at the elaborate metal chandelier and the towering height of the ceiling. "Nice."

He watched her as she walked up to the sculptures of the nude figures. He didn't miss when her mouth opened just a bit as she reached out to trace from one clavicle to the other on a few of the figures. Chance's gut clenched at the subtle and seemingly innocent gesture.

Damn.

"This is a lot of house," she said, glancing back at him as she withdrew her hand.

"Big house for a big man."

Their eyes met.

His heart pounded.

She looked away with a lick of her lips as if they were suddenly parched. "The...the paperwork," she reminded him gently, raising her hand to smooth the hair pulled up into her ponytail.

There were things Chance knew for sure, and other things he could only assume or guess—but his gut instinct rarely let him down. And there were two things he knew for sure over the time they'd spent together in the last two weeks. He desired Ngozi with an intensity that was distracting.

And Ngozi Johns wanted him just as badly.

The thought of striding up to her and pressing his lips against hers captured his attention at random moments throughout his day, and curiosity if her attitude in bed was as fierce as it was in court dominated his nights.

All of the telltale signs were there.

Long stares.

Little licks of her lips.

Catching her watching him.

Hunger in her eyes.

Moments where the will to resist him was seemingly weak.

But each time, she fought and won over her desire for him, leaving him disappointed and craving her even more.

But this chess game of desire between them was always her play. Her move. Her time.

Releasing a short breath that did nothing to quell the racing of his pulse, Chance pointed beyond the wrought iron stairs. "This way," he said, clearing his throat and leading the way into the chef's kitchen.

"Whatever that is smells so good," she said, eyeing the stove as they passed the massive island. "Kudos to your chef."

"My mom made oxtail stew," he said, opening the door to the office and turning on the ceiling light.

"You live with your mom?" she asked from behind him.

Chance picked up the folder and looked at her in disbelief. "I am a grown-ass man," he said as he handed it to her. "I live alone."

She held up her hand as if to say *my bad* before taking it from him and flipping through it. "I have people on staff and couriers on call to pick up stuff like this, Mr. Castillo," she said, chastising him.

He leaned against the edge of his desk, crossing his legs at the ankles. "I enjoy your company, Ms. Johns," he countered smoothly. Honestly.

Again, their eyes met.

That vibe between them pulsed, electrifying the air.

"I don't mix business and pleasure, Chance, not with clients nor coworkers," she said.

He wasn't sure if she was schooling him or reminding herself about the line she had drawn in the sand.

He eyed her, finding himself unable to stop. His eyes dropped to her mouth.

"Show me your beautiful house," Ngozi offered, turning from him to leave the office.

Her invitation to remain in his company both surprised and pleased him.

"You think I can get a to-go box of some of your mama's stew?" she asked with a coquettish smile that brightened her eyes.

"Or you could stay and have dinner with me," he offered, coming to a stop before where she leaned back against the island.

Ngozi swallowed hard as she looked up at him. "Chance," she whispered softly, her eyes dropping to his mouth as she licked the corners of her own. "Come on, help me out."

He put his hands on either side of her, leaning toward her, feeling drawn into her as he inhaled the warm scent of her perfume in the small and intimate space between them. "Help you what?"

He saw her tremble. It made him weak. That attraction—an *awareness*—throbbed between them. It was hard to resist. Passion. Chemistry. Electricity.

"Fight this," she implored, her eyes soft and filling with the heat rising in her.

"Nah," he drawled slowly and low in his throat as he lowered his head and pressed a soft kiss to the corner of her mouth.

It was softness. Sweetness.

"Chance," she sighed with just a little hint of aching in her tone.

He shook his head as he smiled and then pressed his lips against hers.

The tip of her clever tongue darted out to lick at the little dip in the center of his bottom lip.

He grunted in hot pleasure, feeling his entire body jolt with an unseen surge, a current. This power created by a connection between them had been stoked over the last two weeks, taunting and tempting them with a force that could not be ignored.

There was no woman he'd ever wanted so much in his life.

When she brought her quivering hands up to clutch at the front of his sweater, he followed her lead—her unspoken acceptance—and gripped her hips to pull their bodies close together as they deepened the kiss and gave in to the passion that could not be denied.

It started out slow, as if they were trying to savor every moment.

Chance brought his hands up to her back, massaging the small of it as he drew the tip of her tongue into his mouth and suckled it. She whimpered as she brought her hands up to hold the sides of his face.

He felt her hunger and matched it with his own, relinquishing control as he gently broke their kiss to press his mouth to her neck. He inhaled deeply of the warm scent of her perfume, and he enjoyed the feel of her racing pulse against his lips. And when he suckled that spot, she gasped and flung her head back.

"Yes," she whispered hotly, her hands rising from his cheeks to the back of his head to press him closer.

Chance felt a wildness stir in him as he suckled her deeply, not caring if he left a mark as he brought his hands down to pull her body from the edge of the island and glide his hands to her buttocks. Cupping them. Massaging the softness. Loving the feel of his hardness pressed against her stomach as he ached for her.

"Ngozi," he moaned against her neck, feeling lost in her. Her scent. Her presence. Her vibe. Her energy.

Her being. Her everything.

He grabbed her by the waist and hoisted her up on top of the island as he undid the zipper on the back of her dress. Eased the top of her dress down, moved back to take in the sight of her small but plump breasts in the black strapless lace bra she wore before he quickly jerked off his sweater and flung it away.

Chance stood there between her open thighs with

the skirt of her dress up around the top of her thighs, eyeing her. The hint of her lace bikini panties peeked out between her legs, with her chest slightly heaving as her hard nipples pressed against the barely there lace, her eyes glazed and the gloss on her swollen lips smudged from his kisses. He had never seen anything sexier.

Ngozi Johns was allure personified.

And when her eyes took in the sight of his chest and abs, and moved down to his hard curve tenting his linen pants, he saw both her appreciation and anticipation. Never had he wanted so much to live up to expectations.

One small move forward and she was back in his arms, her flesh against his as she wrapped her arms around his neck when their lips met again with one kiss and then a dozen more. Small but satisfying, and leading to more as he offered her his tongue and she touched it with her own with a hungry moan.

The sound of one shoe and then another hitting the floor echoed in the moments before Ngozi wrapped her legs around his waist. The heel of her foot dug into his buttock, and Chance couldn't care less. He kissed a trail down her body until he lightly bit the edge of her bra to jerk it down below one breast with his teeth. The first stroke of his tongue against her nipple caused Ngozi to arch her back.

"Yessss," she cried out. "Yes. Yes. Yes."

He sucked harder. Deeper. Pulling as much of her breast into his mouth as he could.

Ngozi reached down between them and began to undo his belt with rushed movements.

Chance stepped up onto the foot rail lining the island to make the job easier for her. And when she pressed her mouth to the hard ridge between his biceps, it was his turn to tremble. She kissed a trail to one hard nipple to circle it with her tongue.

That move surprised him, and the moan of pleasure he released came from his gut.

She guided her lips to the other, and this time she sucked that nipple into her mouth before lightly grazing it with her teeth as his loose-fitting pants fell down around his ankles.

He was so anxious for her that he could hardly think straight. His lengthy manhood was so hard that his loins ached to be surrounded by her, deeply stroking until satisfied. He removed his boxers, freeing his thick curving member. It lay atop the island between her open thighs, the coolness of the marble surprisingly arousing to him.

"Oh…oh my." She sighed in pleasure as she looked down at his inches and then up at his eyes.

"Look," he said, gesturing downward with his head.

She did.

With no hands, he raised it off the cool marble and brought it back down upon it with a light thud.

Her jaw slowly dropped. "You…uh…you really have great control of that," she said.

"Imagine when I use my hips," he forewarned with a sultry chuckle.

Ngozi licked her lips and swallowed hard. "Why imagine?" she asked, sliding backward along the smooth marble until she was in the center of it. She lay back, her eyes on him as she slid her pinkies inside the edge of her lace bikini panties and raised her buttocks to ease them down until they lay in a pile by her feet.

Chance quickly retrieved protection for them from his wallet and sheathed himself with it before he climbed atop the island with her, his erection leading between her open legs. As soon as he lay on top of her, her hands were on his back and then his buttocks, gripping his firm cheeks as he arched his hips and guided his hardness inside her with one firm thrust.

He looked down into her face as her eyes widened, and she gasped before she released a tiny little wail and arched her back. He could feel her walls throbbing against his hard length. He buried his face against the side of hers as his body went tense. "You're so tight, Ngozi," he said near her ear, the strain in his voice clear.

"I feel you. I... I... I feel it," she whispered with a breath. "I needed this. I *needed* this."

Her words seemed like a revelation to herself... and they were pure motivation to him.

Chance was more than ready to give her *exactly* what she needed.

He eased his hands beneath her buttocks and raised her hips up a bit as he began to stroke inside her, seeking and finding her mouth to kiss her.

"Yes, yes, yes," she panted in between kisses with an urgency.

He felt her body against him. Wet. Hot. Throbbing. Her moans of passion were a catalyst. Her hands switched between gripping or massaging his back and buttocks, pushing him closer and closer to the edge of his climax. But he was not ready for the ride to end, and so he would pause in his strokes many times as it eased.

"We're moving," she said.

He raised his head from where he was biting down on her shoulder and saw that each of his thrusts had propelled their bodies down the length of the slippery island. A few more inches and her head would be over the side. He looked down at her, and they shared a smile. "I want to make you come, not give you a concussion."

Her eyes warmed over before she lifted her head and licked hotly at his mouth as she raised her arms high above her head and gripped the edge of the island tightly. The move caused her breasts to spread and her nipples to point to the ceiling, drawing his eyes. He shifted his body to pull one and then the other with his mouth.

"Mmm," she moaned, arching her back again.

He looked up at her. "Still want it?" he asked, his voice deep.

She matched his look with dazed eyes. "Still *need* it," she stressed, working her hips so that her core glided down the length of his hardness.

Chance crushed his mouth down upon hers as he

drove his maleness in to fill her again and again and again. His pace quickened. His erection hardened. His thrusts deepened.

Her cries of wild abandon fueled him.

The sight of her breasts lunging back and forth with each hard thrust or circular motion of his hips excited him.

And the feel of her walls tightening down on him with white-hot spasms of her own release pushed him over the edge. He willingly fell into the abyss, tumbling into pleasure and excitement that blinded him to everything but the feel of her body and the look of surprise and rapture on her face.

And when he saw that tears filled her eyes as she trembled, he kissed them away and held her tightly, turning them over so that her body was now atop his and her head was nuzzled against his chest. He could feel her heart pounding as hard and as fast as his own. He looked up to the towering custom coffered ceiling as he waited for his equilibrium to return.

"I... I...have to go."

Chance jerked his head up as Ngozi rushed to rise, standing up on the island and then stepping over his legs to climb down off it. Not even the delectable sight of her bare bottom could distract him from the sudden shift in mood. "Hey, Ngozi, what's wrong?" he asked, quickly jumping down to grab a wad of paper towels from the countertop holder.

She jerked her strapless bra up over her breasts and fixed her dress so that she wore it properly but leaving the back unzipped. "This was a mistake," she said.

Oh hell.

He removed his condom inside the towels as he watched her frantically gather her discarded panties into a wad in her hand. "Ngozi," he said again, reaching for her arm as she struggled to step into her heels.

"Just let me leave, Chance," she pleaded, jerking out of his grasp and bending down to grab both shoes by the heels with one hand instead.

"What the hell happened?" he asked, confused by her behavior.

"Bye, Chance," she said, turning away with an awkward wave to leave the kitchen.

Naked and uncaring, he followed behind her. "Ngozi, at least put your damn shoes on," he said.

She stopped in the foyer, looking back at him. Her eyes darted down to his now-limp member, and she whirled away from him to hold the edge of the table as she slid on each of her shoes.

"Not exactly sure how you go from *I need this* to needing to get the hell away from me," he said.

She continued on to the door, her perfect ponytail now mussed and her makeup smeared. She opened the door and paused. "It was amazing, Chance, but a mistake," she said, not turning to face him. "You're my client. You *were* my client. I can't represent you now—"

Chance scowled. "So not only are you making me feel bad for giving you exactly what you said you needed, but you also won't rep me anymore. You know what? Unnecessary drama, Ngozi. Just…unnecessary. If that's how you want it, then fine."

She turned. "You got what you wanted, right?" she asked.

No, I got more than I asked for.

"Whatever you say," Chance said, turning to walk away.

When the front door closed, he paused, wiping his bearded chin with his hand as he shook his head. *Damn.*

Chapter 5

"*You're so tight, Ngozi.*"

"*I feel you. I... I... I feel it. I needed this. I needed this.*"

Ngozi shivered at the hot memory and then was flooded with embarrassment, raising her hands to press her palms against her cheeks. She had begged the man to please her. Making love with Chance atop that island had been so out of character for her. Not Miss Prim-and-Proper. Not Miss Perfect.

But...

It had felt so right. So good. So *necessary*.

But that didn't take away from her unprofessionalism. She had broken her one rule of not mixing business with pleasure. For that, she was disappointed in herself and ashamed.

But…

At odd moments through the last few days and each night, she had thought of him, inside her, riding her, pleasing her…and she wanted more.

"Whoo," she sighed, releasing a shaky breath as she leaned back in her chair in her office at VAL and closed her eyes, hoping to abate the steady throb of her femininity and the hardening of her nipples as her arousal came in a rush at the very *thought* of Chance Castillo and every delicious, long, curving inch—

"Mmm."

She popped up out of her chair, her eyes wide, and pressed the back of her hand to her lips, surprised by her own moan of pleasure. She looked out the glass wall of her office and was happy no one had noticed her startled reaction. She smoothed the fitted black lambskin dress with embroidered pocket she wore before reclaiming her seat with a shake of her head.

"Come on, Ngozi. Gather yourself," she said, reaching for her conference phone to hit the button for the speakerphone before she dialed an extension.

"Yes, Ms. Johns?"

"Hello, Roberta. Can Larry take a quick call?" she asked the legal secretary of Larry Rawlings.

"Sure thing. Hold on, I'll transfer you in."

Beep.

He was on the line within a second. "Yes, Ngozi?"

"Hey, Larry, I just wondered if Mr. Castillo followed up with you," she said, shifting her gaze out at the sun beginning to set beyond the towering Manhattan buildings.

"Yes, he did. Matter of fact, a messenger just dropped off a folder of receipts with a detailed outline of dates," he said. "We have an appointment to meet next to get the ball rolling."

In her haste to leave Chance's home she had left the folder of information behind.

"Good," she said, confused by her disappointment. "Thanks for picking up the ball for me, but I know you will get the job done, and hopefully the firm will be able to cover some other interests for Mr. Castillo, as well."

"I'm on it."

"Thanks, Larry. Enjoy your weekend."

She ended the call.

Chance had moved on. There had been no calls or attempts to finagle more of her time. There was no more chasing to be done.

Ngozi winced as she thought of his annoyance at her. She could understand.

So not only are you making me feel bad for giving you exactly what you said you needed, but you also won't rep me anymore.

Glancing at her watch, she rose and retrieved her black wool and lambskin belted jacket from her closet before grabbing her clutch and portfolio, as well. She quickly began packing files into the crocodile briefcase.

"Good night, Ms. J."

She glanced up at Angel with a smile. "Have a good weekend," she bid her assistant, before returning to her task. Suddenly, she looked up. "Not *too* good. You're on probation."

"Yes, I know. You remind me *every* weekend," she said. "What do you have planned? Any fun?"

Ngozi looked taken aback. "I have fun, Angel," she said.

Three days ago, I had plenty of it atop an island in the middle of a kitchen.

Her personal assistant looked disbelieving.

"As a matter of fact, tonight I am attending a charity dinner and I'm looking forward to it," she lied.

Alek and Alessandra had purchased a few tables in support of a charity benefiting inner-city youth. The odds were in favor of Chance being in attendance, as well. Their seeing each other was inevitable. They shared a godchild and friends.

What if he brought a date?

Ngozi came out from around her desk. "I am headed home to find just the *right* outfit," she said as they walked down the length of the office together to the elevator.

Chance stood at the entrance of the open brass door leading into the grand ballroom of midtown Manhattan's Gotham Hall and took in the sight of the elegant decor with bluish lighting that highlighted the gilded ceiling with its stained glass center and the oval-shaped room's marble flooring. It was as beautiful as every other gala event. Tables set. Flower arrangements centered. Candles lit. Music playing.

Gourmet food ready to be served. Drinks prepped to be poured. Attendees mingling in their finery.

He was bored.

He was better with writing the check and wishing the charity well, and didn't need the pomp and circumstance surrounding it. It all was a bit much for the boy from the wrong side of the tracks, but alas, he had long since learned to play the role. To show up. Write the check. Rub shoulders. Advance.

And then find his fun elsewhere.

He spotted Alek at the large bar and made his way toward him, weaving his way through the crowd of people filling the large room. "Good to see familiar faces," he said.

Alek turned, and they shared a handshake.

"Right," Alek said. "Thanks for coming. I know this is not your thing. Why'd you change your mind?"

Chance shrugged before leaning against the bar and looking about the room.

"No date?"

At that moment, Chance spotted Ngozi as she stepped into the open doorway of the ballroom. His heart instantly pounded at the sight of her in the floor-length illusion gown with a fringe skirt and plunging neckline lined with lace scalloped edges that made her décolletage all the more appealing. *Damn.*

Memories of nuzzling his face in that soft spot between her breasts as he made love to her came in a rush. Flashes of hot moments they shared in his kitchen replayed—the same memories that had plagued him since that evening. In that moment, she brushed her sleek hair back from her face and entered the ballroom. Any hints of the anger he once held for her faded like a fine mist.

He missed her.

He wanted her.

And it took every bit of strength contained within him not to call her. To accept that the heated moments they shared had been a mistake, just as she had said.

He didn't believe that. The energy and excitement he felt in her presence was like nothing he had ever experienced with any other woman. Not even Helena.

And the sex?

His gut clenched.

He thought he'd gone mad in those furious moments as he climaxed inside her.

His eyes were on her as she made her way across the room. He watched as she reached the table. Alessandra rose to greet her, and the two women hugged each other, exchanged words and shared a laugh.

Alek turned and pushed a double shot of tequila into Chance's hand.

"Huh?" he said, looking down at the drink in surprise before taking it from his friend.

"There's Ngozi," Alek said, sipping from his drink with one hand and holding a flute of champagne with the other. "Wow, that dress is unforgettable. I wonder who she's trying to tempt tonight."

"Me," Chance answered, looking on as both Ngozi and Alessandra looked across the room toward them.

"Huh?" Alek said, frowning. "Am I missing something?"

"Plenty," Chance said before taking a deep sip of his drink.

"Care to fill me in?"

"Nope."

"Cool," Alek said, motioning for the bartender. "Another flute of Dom, please."

With drinks in hand, Chance eyed how the blue lights reflected so perfectly against her dark complexion and highlighted her back in the low cut of the dress. "Why is she so damn fine?" he asked, accepting that his nerves would forever be shot in her presence as he neared her.

"I couldn't answer that because I got a hella fine one my damn self," Alek said, giving his wife an appreciative eye in the strapless white dress she wore with a large statement necklace of gold.

"Hello, Ngozi," he said.

She turned and looked up at him. "Chance. How are you?" she asked, accepting the flute he handed to her.

Their hands lightly grazed each other, and their eyes locked.

And there it was again. Big. Bold. Undeniable. Constant.

Chemistry.

Ngozi barely heard the live band's rendition of Minnie Riperton's "Loving You" as she tried her best not to stare at Chance, but they both seemed to be failing at it. She would look at him, he would look away. She would feel his eyes on her, like heat, but when she glanced in his direction, his attention was elsewhere.

Several times she caught both Alek's and Alessandra's eyes shifting back and forth between them. Her heart was pounding so rapidly that she feared it would outpace her and send her into a total blackout. And when Chance rose, tossing his linen napkin on his untouched food, and came around the table to extend his hand to her, she pursed her glossy lips and released a breath filled with all her nervous anxiety.

She looked up at him, down at his big beautiful hand, and then back up at his face, knowing that sliding her hand in his was much more than an invitation to dance.

"Come on," he mouthed.

She couldn't resist.

"What am I missing?" she heard Alessandra ask from behind her.

"Hush, baby," Alek suggested.

Ngozi hung her beaded egg-shaped clutch around her wrist and accepted Chance's offer. Her hand was warm where they touched as he led her onto the dance floor beneath the oscillating lights. He stopped and gently tugged her to pull her body close to his. She settled her arms across his back as he settled his around her waist. The top of her head came to his chin, and as they danced, their bodies seemed to fit. To work. To click. Like lock to key.

He dipped his head. "Still don't need me anymore?" he asked near her ear.

She leaned back to look up at him. "Chance," she whispered, her resolve sounding feeble to her own ears.

"I came here tonight looking for you," he admitted.

"Really?" she asked, acutely aware of how warm his hand was against her bared lower back.

"And you wore this dress tonight for me, *la tentadora*. Right?"

The temptress.

Yes, her dress fit that bill.

She looked away from him and licked the corner of her mouth. "In case you brought a date," she confessed, arching her brow as she tilted her head to look up at him once again.

He chuckled. It was deep and rich.

"Your hand feels good rubbing my neck."

Ngozi lowered her hand to his back once more, not even realizing she had been stroking his nape with her fingertips. It felt natural showing affection toward him.

He held her arm high in the air and slowly danced around her before pulling her back into his embrace and then spinning her out and reeling her back in to him. "You should smile more often, Ngozi Johns," he said.

"I haven't had much to smile about in a really long time," she admitted, surprised by her candor.

"Me either," Chance said. "So let's have fun together. Nothing serious. No ties. Just fun."

Why does that sound so good to me?

"Your caveat about not dating clients no longer fits, because you no longer represent me," he reminded her.

That's true.

"I don't know, Chance," she said, allowing herself to stroke his nape again.

"Okay, think about it, but let me offer this?" he began, trailing his finger up her spine.

Ngozi shivered and her nipples hardened as all of her pulse points throbbed—including the now-swollen bud nestled between the lips of her core. "What?" she whispered, her eyes falling to his soft mouth.

"Let's have fun tonight and worry about tomorrow when it comes."

Ngozi always put what was right before what she wanted. Always. With her parents. With her marriage. With her career.

Sometimes being so damn perfect was so damn tiring.

"I need it," he moaned near her ear, his breath lightly breezing against the lobe.

She feigned indignation. "Really, you're playing the need card?"

"You played it first. Remember?"

"I haven't been able to forget."

They shared a laugh that was all too knowing.

"It was *fun*," Ngozi acknowledged, her body trembling.

"Damn right it was."

"Let's go," she said, stepping back from him.

"We're gone," Chance agreed, grabbing her hand as they made a hasty retreat toward the door.

Ngozi sat up on the bed and ran her hand through her tousled hair as she looked down at Chance's nude body sprawled out beside her. The contours of his body were defined by the silver moonlight through the open curtains of the hotel suite's balcony doors. The soft buzz of his snores was thankfully muffled by the pillows over his head.

He deserves his rest.

She shook her head in wonder at his skill as she reached for her iPhone on the bedside table. She held the lightweight cover across the front of her body as she rose from the bed gently and stepped over her $3,000 gown carelessly left on the floor in their haste. As she made her way to the open balcony doors, she dialed her parents' landline phone number, tapping the tip of her nail against the rose-gold sequin as it rang.

"Hello."

"Hey, Reeds," she said, hating that she felt like a high schooler sneaking out for the night.

I am a successful over-thirty-years-old attorney—

"Is everything okay?" the house manager asked, his voice filled with concern.

"Everything's fine, Reeds. Everything okay there?" she asked, looking out at the moon shining down on the New York skyline.

"Same as always. Your parents already turned in for the night."

"Thank God. I thought they would wait up for me."

"They asked me to do it," Reeds admitted with a chuckle. "No one is roaming about this time of night but me and one of your father's Cuban cigars."

"Enjoy your cigar and go to bed," Ngozi said. "I'm staying in the city tonight."

"Okay. Be safe. Good night, Ngozi."

"Night," she said softly, hating the relief she felt that she had dodged talking to either of her parents.

"Should I be jealous?"

Ngozi whirled, causing the blanket to twist around her legs as she eyed Chance rising from the bed to walk over to her. She ran her hand through her hair, failing to free it of the tangles created during their love play. "No," she said, looking up at him as he stood before her, naked and beautiful in the moon-light. "Because this is only for the night. Remember?"

"Give me the weekend," Chance requested. "We can fly wherever you want in the world. Name it. It's yours."

Ngozi shook her head, lightly touching her kiss-swollen lips with her fingertips. "I can't."

He bent his strong legs and wrapped his arms around her waist to heft her up. She had to look down into his upturned face, and gave in to the urge to stroke his cheek. "Paris. Dubai. Italy," he offered. "Ibiza, Antigua, French Riviera, Bora Bora…"

Chance paused and smiled.

"Your life is different from mine, huh?" she asked.

He bent his head to press a kiss to her clavicle, then drew a circle there with his tongue.

Ngozi let her head fall back, the ends of her weaved tresses tickling the small of her back. "I haven't had a break in a long while," she admitted with a sigh. "And I do carry my passport in my wallet."

Chance carried her over to lay her on the bed, and then grabbed the blanket to pull off her body and fling onto the floor.

Feeling flirty, she rolled over onto her stomach and glanced back at him over her shoulder as she raised her buttocks. Her smile spread as he became erect before her eyes. *He really is all kinds of perfection.*

Chance lightly held her ankles and slid her body across the bed until she was bent over it. He reached onto the bedside table for one of the dozen foil packets of condoms. She watched him roll the ribbed latex down his length before she closed her eyes and sighed in pleasure. The warmth of his body radiated as he knelt behind her and curved his body against hers as he licked a hot trail up her spine and then lightly bit her shoulder. And when he spread her open and guided every inch of his hardness inside her, she grimaced and clutched the sheet in her fist as her body tried to conform to the fit and hard feel of him.

"Chance?" she said, looking back at him as he stroked inside her, slowly enough for her to take note of each inch as it went in and out of her.

"Yeah, baby," he said, looking down at the connection before tilting his head to the side to give her his attention.

"Not so deep," she said, closing her eyes. "I don't need all of it. I'm good."

He chuckled a little as he pulled out some. "Better?" he asked, biting the side of his tongue.

She relaxed her body with an eager nod.

He slid his hand around her body and pressed his fingertips against her moist and swollen bud, gently stroking it as he thrust inside her.

Ngozi's eyes and mouth widened.

"I thought making you come a couple times make up for it," he said thickly.

"A couple?" she asked with a lick of her lips.

"Oh *yes*," he stressed.

"Oh my."

She chose Italy.

Chance eyed Ngozi standing there on the balcony of the sprawling villa he rented in Sorrento off the Amalfi Coast. Her arms were splayed as she gripped the railing of the private balcony off their palatial bedroom as she overlooked the gardens, the grass-covered mountains and the nearby bluish-green waters of the Mediterranean Sea. Her hair was loose, and she wore a red strapless maxi dress that clung to her body when the wind blew.

He found her so breathtaking that he paused his steps as his pulse raced and his heart pounded.

She turned and smiled at him at the exact moment that the sunlight framed her from behind, bringing to mind dark chocolate lightly dusted with gold powder.

Ngozi Johns was trouble.

Forcing a smile, he continued over to her, handing her the goblet of white wine he carried. "A little fun isn't so bad, right?" he asked, leaning back against the railing as he sipped from his snifter of tequila.

"Yes, but too much is not for the best either," she countered.

"Here's to balance," he said, raising his snifter.

"To balance," she agreed, touching her glass to his.

Chance looked beyond her to the downtown area

of Sorrento in the far distance. "I still can't believe you agreed to stay through Monday," he said.

"I can't believe you made it worth the extra work I will have on Tuesday to catch up with my crazy workload," Ngozi said, moving away from him to lie on one of the lounges.

He watched her drape her hair over one shoulder before extending one leg and bending the other as she closed her eyes and let the sun toast her flawless skin a deeper shade of brown.

From the moment they had arrived in Italy on his jet, they had squeezed in as much sightseeing, fine foods and fun as they could during the days, and fell into that heated abyss they created throughout the nights. They were scheduled to leave tomorrow afternoon, and for him it was a mixed blessing.

He didn't trust how she made him feel.

The stain Helena had left on his life and his belief in his instincts was ever present.

"Can I ask you something?" he called over to her, seeking refuge from his thoughts.

Ngozi waved her bent leg back and forth as she looked over at him. "I'm a lawyer. Questions are my life," she said.

Chance took a sip of his drink, looking at her over the rim of the crystal as he closed the short distance between them to sit on the lounge beside her. "The first time, in my kitchen, why did you run away like that?" he asked. "We were both lying there caught up in a *damn* good moment, and it made you run?"

She reached for her wine and took a deep sip as if stalling for time or gathering courage.

He said nothing, patiently waiting for an answer to a question that had remained with him since the moment she fled.

"In that *damn* good moment," she began, not meeting his eyes, "I felt guilty that the first time I ever climaxed in my life was with someone other than my husband."

First time?

"It felt like a betrayal," she continued. "It felt like that *damn* good moment overshadowed my entire sex life with him. So, it was glorious and shocking and damn good and…hurtful."

"And now?" he asked, not really sure what to say.

Ngozi leveled her eyes on him. "Still damn good," she admitted with a smile, sliding her leg onto his lap.

"Still hurtful?" Chance asked as he turned to straddle the lounge chair facing her. He ran his hands up the smooth expanse of her legs, from her ankles to the V at the top of her thighs.

"I'm getting better with it," she said softly, her chest rising and falling.

He took note of her reaction to him and tossed the edge of her dress up around her hips, exposing her clean-shaven mound and her core to him. "And are you satisfied?" he asked, bending to bless each of her soft thighs with a kiss.

He felt her tremble as she softly grunted in pleasure.

"Each and *every* time," Ngozi confessed, setting her wineglass down before she reached over to smooth one hand over the back of his head.

"Then let me go for a perfect record," he said, his words breezing against her core in the seconds before he suckled her clit into his mouth.

Ngozi descended the stairs from Chance's jet, giving him a smile of thanks when he extended his hand to help her down off the last step. Hand in hand, they walked across the tarmac to the two black-on-black SUVs awaiting their arrival.

The extended weekend was over.

She could hardly believe the whirlwind of it. The shopping for clothes and undergarments, the long flight to Italy, the sightseeing, the delicacies, the lovemaking and so much more. It seemed like much longer than three days.

It was over, just as they had agreed.

At the first SUV, she turned and faced him. "Thank you for the escape. Thank you for giving me what I didn't know I needed, Chance Castillo," she said.

"Same here."

His eyes dipped to her lips.

She licked them.

"Can we say goodbye to what we shared with a kiss?" he asked.

She stepped toward him and rose up on the tip of her toes to cover his mouth with her own.

He moaned as he wrapped a strong arm around

her waist, picking her up to level their mouths as he deepened the kiss.

With regret, and a few soft touches of their lips, Chance and Ngozi ended it, both stepping away.

With one last look at him, she turned and allowed the driver to open the rear door so that she could climb onto the leather seat. With one last wave, she faced forward and was proud of herself for not looking back as the driver closed the door and drove the vehicle away.

Chance's mansion was quiet and dimly lit. He found the setting necessary as he struggled with his thoughts. From the time he was a poor kid with wealthy classmates up until the moment he sold his app, he had always relied on his guts. That all changed when the woman he thought loved him revealed her betrayal.

The last thing he wanted was another relationship. Another opportunity to be burned and betrayed. Embarrassed. Disrespected.

But I miss her already. I miss Ngozi.

He wasn't ready to pretend that nothing had happened between them. With her, there had been no thoughts of Helena and the havoc she'd wrought on his life. With Ngozi, he had felt lighthearted again. He'd had fun.

Security check. Front exterior gate.

At his alarm system sending out an alert, Chance picked up the tablet on the sofa where he sat in the den. He checked the surveillance video. At the sight of the car sitting there, he squinted even as he tapped the screen to unlock the gate.

Dropping the tablet back onto the couch, he rose and made his way across the expansive house to the grand foyer. He pulled one of the front double doors open and stood in the entrance as he watched her climb from her car and walk over to the front steps to look up at him.

"I thought maybe for a little while longer, we could have some more fun together," Ngozi said, climbing the steps to lightly trace the ridged grooves of his abdomen with her finger.

Without a word, Chance captured her hand in his and turned to walk back inside his home with Ngozi close behind him.

Chapter 6

Two months later

"Hello, Aliyah," Ngozi cooed to her goddaughter as she held her in her arms where she sat on one of the chaise longues in her nursery.

Alessandra sat in the other, smiling as she looked on at her friend and her baby daughter. "You ready for one of those?" she asked.

Ngozi gave her a side-eye. "No, I am not," she stressed, moments before she bent her head to press her face in the baby's neck to inhale her scent.

"Lies," Alessandra drawled with a chuckle.

Ngozi shrugged one shoulder before shifting the baby upward to rest against her belly. "Okay, maybe one day, but not now."

"And not Chance?"

Ngozi frowned in confusion. "What about Chance?"

"What exactly is going on with you two?" Alessandra asked.

A hot memory of her biting down into the softness of a pillow with her buttocks high in the air as he gripped her fleshy cheeks and stroked deep inside her from behind played in Ngozi's mind.

Her cheeks warmed and the bud between her legs throbbed to life.

"Just fun. Nothing serious," she said.

But I miss him even right now.

"I figured that when you two spent Thanksgiving and Christmas apart."

Truth? She had thought of him on both holidays, and their texting had not sufficed to slay her longing for him.

"And there won't be any kissing at midnight on New Year's Eve either," Ngozi said. "Neither one of us are looking for anything more than what we have, which is nice *private* fun to pass the time."

More truth? He had become a new normal in Ngozi's life.

Ding-ding.

As a notification rang out, Ngozi picked up her iPhone from the lounge to read her text. She smiled as her heart raced. *Chance.*

He'd spent the holidays with his mother and family in Cabrera.

Chance: Coming home 2night. Can I see u?

Yessss, she thought.

"Pass the time until what?" Alessandra asked.

"Huh?" Ngozi asked, pausing in answering his text with one of her own.

Alessandra arched a brow and looked pointedly down at her friend's iPhone. "You and Chance are passing the time until what?" she asked again.

Ding-ding.

"Until it's not fun anymore," Ngozi said as she opened his text.

Chance: I can send a car.

Aliyah began to stir and cry in her arms.

"It's time for her to eat," Alessandra said, rising to walk across the large room to gather her baby in her arms.

Ngozi rose with her phone in her hand and walked over to one of the bay windows. She paused at the sight of Alek's mother, LuLu, talking to Alessandra's longtime driver, Roje, in the rear garden. Her eyes widened when he pulled her body close to his by her waist, and she pressed her hands to his broad chest to resist him even as her head tilted back to look up at him.

Ngozi's eyes widened when they shared a passionate kiss that lasted just moments before LuLu broke it and wrenched out of his grasp.

Feeling small for peeking into other people's lives, Ngozi whirled from the window.

Alessandra was breastfeeding Aliyah with a lightweight blanket over her shoulder and the baby to shield herself. "What's wrong?"

"Nothing," Ngozi said, respecting LuLu and Roje's privacy even as her curiosity over the extent of their relationship shifted in overdrive.

As far as she knew, LuLu had never remarried or even dated after the death of her husband, but there was clearly something between her and the handsome middle-aged driver.

Ngozi flipped her phone over.

Ngozi: Welcome back. I can drive. Time?
Chance: 7? I can fix dinner.
Ngozi: Dinner at 7? Dessert by 8? ;-)
Chance: And breakfast in the a.m.?
Ngozi arched a brow at that.
Ngozi: See you at 7, Chance.
Chance: K.

She looked up when the door to the nursery opened and LuLu entered. Only hints of her bright red lipstick remained, with some a little smudged outside the natural lines of her lips. Ngozi bit back a smile. Passion had ruined many lipstick or lip gloss applications for her, as well.

Humph.

Throughout her marriage and for one year after the death of her husband, Ngozi had lived without the passion Chance evoked. And now, just two months into their dalliance, she hungered for him after just a week without it.

"Hello, ladies," LuLu said, setting her tote bag on the floor before heading straight to Alessandra and Aliyah.

"She's all full, LuLu. You can burp her," Alessandra said, rising to hand the baby and a burping cloth over to her mother-in-law.

"How are we doing, ladies?" LuLu asked, lightly patting upward on Aliyah's back as the baby struggled to hold her head up.

Feeling flirty, Ngozi texted Chance.

Ngozi: Panties or no?

Ding-ding.

Chance: Yes...if I can tear them off.

Hmm...

"We were just talking about finding love again after the death of a spouse," Alessandra said, readjusting her maternity bra beneath the rose-gold silk shirt she wore with matching slacks.

Ngozi froze and eyed her client and friend.

Alessandra gave her a deadpan expression.

LuLu looked at Ngozi with a sad smile. "I lost my Kwame six years ago," she began, shifting Aliyah to sit on her lap. "It felt like a piece of me died with him, so I understand how you feel."

Ngozi looked away, unable to accept her sympathy when the truth was unknown to everyone but herself, shielded by her long-practiced ability to hide imperfections and present what was palatable to everyone else. Guilt twisted her stomach as if its grips were real.

"But our stories are different because I am limited by *obligations*…to children, to the dynasty he helped create, to a marriage of more than twenty years, to class, to my age," she admitted.

Her sadness was clear, and it drew Ngozi's eyes back to hers.

"You have a freedom I do not, Ngozi," she said, raising the baby and pressing her cheek against hers. "Do not waste it."

And right then, Ngozi knew that LuLu Ansah loved Roje and wanted nothing more than to be with him, but felt she could not.

Alessandra stooped down beside where LuLu softly sang a Ghanaian song to the baby and lightly touched her knee. "LuLu," she said softly.

The older woman looked down at her.

"Your obligation as a grown woman who has successfully raised her children and mourned her husband is to yourself," Alessandra said, her eyes filled with sincerity and conviction. "You deserve to be loved again, and I *know* there is a man out there who can and will love you just as much if not more, and nothing—not children, business, class or age—should keep that from you."

LuLu's eyes filled with a myriad of emotions, but above all she seemed curious as to just what Alessandra knew of her life.

Ngozi wondered the same.

Ding-ding.

Chance: I really missed you Go-Go.

Her pulse raced. *Go-Go* was short for *Ngozi*. She had no idea why he insisted on giving her a nickname. She'd never had one.

And secretly she liked it. It was something just for them.

Ngozi: I missed you 2.
Chance: Not fun.
Ngozi: Not expected.
Chance: Not a part of the plan.
Ngozi: No. Not at all.

She awaited another text from him. None came. She checked the time. Three more hours until she was with Chance again. It seemed like forever.

You have a freedom I do not, Ngozi. Do not waste it.

Dinner was forgotten.

Food would not sate their hunger for each other.

Chance feasted on her body like it was his own buffet, kissing her skin, licking and lightly biting her taut nipples, massaging the soft flesh of her buttocks as he lifted her hips high off the bed to bury his face first against her thighs and then her plump mound, before spreading her legs wide to expose the beautiful layers of her femininity. Slowly, with more restraint than he had ever shown in his life, he pleased her with his tongue as he enjoyed her unique scent. His moans were guttural as he sucked her fleshy bud between his lips gently, pulling it in and out of his mouth as if to revive her, but it was her shivers and her moans and the tight grips of her hands on his head and shoulders and the way she arched her hips upward, seeking more, that gave him renewed life.

His body in tune with hers, he knew when her release was near and did not relent, wanting to taste her nectar, feel her vibrations and hear her wild cries. With no compassion for wrecked senses, as she was still shivering and crying out, he entered her with one hard thrust that united them, and he did not one stroke until his own body quivered and then stiffened as he joined her in that sweet chasm, crying out like a wounded beast as he clutched her body. He bit down on the pillow beside her head to muffle his high-pitched cries as he forced himself to continue each deep thrust even though he felt near the edge of madness.

Long afterward they lay there, bodies soaked in sweat, pulses racing, hearts pounding and breaths harshly filling the air as they waited for that kinetic energy they'd created to dissipate and free them.

Snores—evidence of their exhaustion—soon filled the air.

Chance awakened the moment he felt the weight of her body shift the bed. She was already reaching for her clothing. "No, Ngozi," he said, his voice deep and thick with sleep.

She paused in pulling on her lingerie to look back at him over her shoulder. "Huh?" she asked, as she clasped her bra from behind.

"Stay the night," he said, sitting up in bed and reaching over to turn on the bedside lamp.

She shook her head, causing her now-unkempt hair to sway back and forth. "No," she said.

The silence in the room became stilted.

"We haven't shared a night together since Italy," he began, finally broaching the subject he'd wanted to for weeks. "You run home to your parents like a little girl with a curfew."

Her brows dipped as she eyed him over the wrap dress she held in her hands. "What...what—what is this?" she asked, motioning her hand from him to her several times. "When did the rules change, because no one told me."

Chance eyed her, knowing she was right.

"I'm not a little girl with a curfew. I am a grown woman with respect for my parents' home," she said.

"Then maybe it's time for a grown woman to have her own home," he said, bending his knees beneath the sheets and setting his arms on top of them.

"Says the grown man who spends his days frolicking," Ngozi said, her tone hard as she jerked on her dress.

Chance stiffened at the judgment. "Frolicking?" he asked, kicking his legs free of the sheets before he climbed from the bed to stand before her.

"Yes, Mr. Italy today and Cabrera tomorrow and... and...and skiing and sailing...and not doing a damn thing else but working on your body and deepening your tan," she said, motioning with her hand toward his sculpted physique.

"Because my work doesn't look like what you think it should, then I'm just a loaf?" Chance asked. "Because I work smarter and not harder, then I ain't shit because I increased my wealth by a million dollars just yesterday. Did *you*?"

"No. Nope. I did not, Mr. Billionaire, but I spent my holidays working to get the bail reduced on a hundred different pro bono clients of nickel-and-dime crimes so they could spend that time with their families, and for those whom I failed, I paid their bail out of my own pocket," she said, her voice impassioned as she looked up at him. "So, you tell me, Mr. Million-Dollars-in-a-Day, what the hell are you doing with your wealth—and your time and your brilliance—besides creating more opportunities to play and have fun?"

"You have no idea what I do because we don't share every aspect of our lives with each other," he spouted, feeling insulted and belittled.

Ngozi raked the tangles from her hair. "Right."

"And when your life is exhausted and time flies because you are so busy working your nine-to-five—excuse me, your six-to-eight—that you haven't lived, then what?" he asked. "You spend the last years of your life with damn regrets. Well, no thank you. I will live and let live."

"You know what, you don't have to justify your life of leisure to me. Just don't judge me for how I choose to color within the lines," she said, dropping down on the edge of the bed to pull on her heels.

Chance turned from her. "All we do is either fuck or fight," he said, wiping his hand over his mouth.

"Then maybe this has run its course," she said.

He looked at her over his broad shoulder. Their eyes locked. "Maybe it has," he agreed.

Ngozi finished gathering her things. "Goodbye, Chance," she said softly, moving to the door.

He followed behind her, saying nothing but feeling so many things. At the front door, he reached out past her to open it for her, even though the chill of December sent goose bumps racing over his nude form. He stood there looking down at her. "It was fun," he began.

"Until it wasn't," she finished.

He bent his head to press a kiss to her forehead and her cheek. "Goodbye, Go-Go," he whispered near her ear.

And with that, she left his home without looking back.

He stood there until she was safely in her car and had driven away from him.

"Five...four...three...two...one! Happy New Year!"

Ngozi took a sip of her champagne from the second floor of her parents' home as all of the partygoers began to either kiss their mate or join in singing "Auld Lang Syne." The charity dinner/silent auction was an annual event for her parents, and Ngozi had attended for many years with Dennis by her side. Now she turned away from the festivities and the emotions it evoked, making her way to her bedroom suite and gratefully closing the door.

She crossed the sitting room to her bedroom, setting the flute on the eight-drawer dresser. The maid staff had already cleaned her room and turned down the bed. She could barely make out the sounds of the party down below as she stepped out of her heels and unzipped the black sequin dress she wore to let it drop to the floor around her feet.

After washing the makeup from her face and wrapping her head with a silk scarf, she sat on the edge of the bed. Soon the quiet was disturbing. Her thoughts were varied. She shifted between grieving the loss of Dennis and feeling guilt over missing Chance.

Needing an escape from her own thoughts and emotions, Ngozi turned off the lights and snuggled beneath the covers. Her line of vision fell on her iPhone sitting on her bedside table. She snaked her arm from under the thick coverlet to tilt it up. No missed calls or texts.

She rubbed the screen with her thumb, fighting a small inner battle over whether to reach out to Chance or not.

The latter won.

There was no happily-ever-after for her and Chance, so why be with someone you were so very different from? It would be fine if their different outlooks on life didn't cause conflict, but Chance wanted to fly out of the country on a whim and would expect her to be able to do the same. And when he drove them somewhere, his lack of respect for the speed limit was another point of contention. Ngozi Johns the attorney most certainly was not a rule breaker testing the boundaries and risking wasting money on speeding tickets.

Their moments together were either filled with passion or skirmishes.

It was tiring.

She returned the phone to its place and released a heavy sigh as she closed her eyes and hoped that her dreams were a distraction from Chance and not filled with memories of him as they had been over the last week since their divide.

"Five...four...three...two...one! Happy New Year!"

Chance pressed a kiss to the mouth of a woman he'd met just that night at the multilevel Drai's Nightclub on the Las Vegas Strip. He couldn't remember her name, and her mouth tasted of cigarettes and liquor that had soured on her tongue. *Serves me right.*

He turned from her just as the fireworks shot off from Caesar's Palace across the street began to echo around them as they lit up the sky. When he felt her tugging at his arm, he gently disengaged her, closed out his tab with the bottle service girl and made his way out of his own section, leaving her and her friends to have at the abundance of liquor he'd already ordered.

Bzzzzzz.

He paused on the dance floor of the club as his

cell phone vibrated against his chest from the inner pocket of his custom black-on-black tuxedo.

Ngozi?

Chance looked down at the screen. "Mama," he mouthed, accepting his disappointment as he answered her call and made his way to the elevator.

"Feliz Año Nuevo, hijo!" Esmerelda exclaimed.

He smiled. "Happy New Year to you, too," he replied, pressing a finger in his ear to help hear beyond the music and noise of the club and the commotion coming through from his mother's boisterous background. She had remained behind in Cabrera after the Christmas holidays.

Chance looked down at his polished shoes. He'd planned to do so as well, but he'd traveled back to the States because he longed for Ngozi. *And then we fought.*

"I'll call you tomorrow," he said, ending the phone call.

He stood there with the colorful strobe lights playing against his face and the bass of the music seeming to reverberate inside his chest, looked around at the gyrating bodies crowding the space and accepted that it would take more than that to make him forget Ngozi.

Two weeks had passed since Ngozi last spoke to Chance. Fourteen days. Three hundred and thirty-six hours. Twenty thousand one hundred and sixty minutes.

She shook her head and rolled her eyes at her desk

in her office as she looked out at the snow falling down on the city.

She'd been so steadfast in her avoidance of the dynamic Dominican that she'd avoided Alessandra and Alek's estate. She was determined to get Chance Castillo out of her system.

And she was failing at it miserably.

Chance increased the speed and incline on one of the three treadmills in his state-of-the-art exercise room. He picked up the pace as he looked out of the glass wall at the snow steadily piling high on the ground and weighing down the branches of the trees in his spacious backyard. He'd spent the last two weeks cooped up in the house, alternating between exercising and working on his app.

Nothing worked to keep Ngozi out of his thoughts.

Or memories of her out of his bed.

With a grunt and mind filled with determination, he picked up the pace, almost at a full sprint now.

It did absolutely nothing toward his outrunning his desires to have Ngozi Johns back in his life.

"Ngozi."

"Chance."

They shared a brief look before moving away from each other after exchanging stilted pleasantries at a charity art exhibit. She hadn't expected him to be there, and from the look on his face when he first spotted her, he had been just as surprised by her appearance. Her heart felt like it was trying to push its way out of her chest.

Wow. He looks sooo good.

Ngozi gripped the stem of the glass of white wine she sipped, fighting the nervous anxiety she felt. She barely focused on the exhibit as she moved about the gallery. Her eyes kept seeking Chance out. And several times, she'd found his gaze on her already.

That thrilled her beyond measure.

Why are we mad at each other again?

That familiar hum of energy and awareness she felt in his presence was still there. Across the room. Across the divide. When their eyes met, it seemed no one else was in the modern gallery.

Not a soul.

She released a breath into her glass as she trailed her fingertips across her collarbone and turned from the sight of him. She soon glanced back. He was gone. She took a few steps in each direction as she searched for him.

What if?

What if they never argued?

What if they were not so intrinsically different?

Then what?

Sex, sex and more sex. And fun.

She couldn't deny that Chance had brought plenty of joy into her life. With him, she had laughed more and done a lot more *things*.

Her clit throbbed like it agreed with her naughty thoughts.

Humph.

Ngozi shook her head. "Where did he go?" she mouthed to herself.

She could clearly envision herself walking up to him and requesting that he take her home. And then staying there with him for days on end, whether making love or watching those 1990s action movies they both enjoyed or jogging together or cooking together. Anything. Everything. With him.

Maybe I should go.

Her longing was so strong, and she wasn't quite confident in her willpower.

She took a final sip of her wine and stopped a uniformed waiter to set the goblet on his tray with a smile of thanks. Tucking her gold metallic clutch under her arm, she turned and walked right into a solid chest. "Sorry," she said as a pair of hands gripped her upper arms to steady her.

Warm masculine hands.

She inhaled the scent of cologne.

Both were all too familiar.

Chance.

She knew it before she tilted her head back and looked up into his handsome face.

Chance couldn't remember Ngozi ever looking so beautiful to him. She was stunning in the winterwhite jumpsuit she wore with her hair pulled back into a sleek ponytail. The contrast against her skin was amazing.

He hadn't been able to take his eyes off her.

Nor could she him.

Finally, he had to close the distance between them. Now he hesitated to take his hands off her.

And he knew in his gut if he pulled her into a dark secluded corner and pressed his lips to that delicate dip above her collarbone—her spot—that she would not resist him. Once again, she would be his. But for how long? A few stolen moments? One night?

"We can't avoid each other," Chance said, finally dropping his hands from her arms as his heart beat wildly.

"We spoke," she said, taking a step back from him as she smoothed her hand over her head and dragged it down her waist-length ponytail.

Chance nodded. "We did."

They fell silent.

"I thought this wasn't your type of thing?" Ngozi said.

"Art?" Chance asked.

"No, charity," she said with a sly lift of her brows and a "so there" look.

Chance frowned. "Still throwing jabs, huh?"

"Yes, that was childish, Chance. My bad," she admitted.

"As a matter of fact, I am sponsoring this event," Chance said, trying his best not to sound smug or give her the same "so there" look.

She looked perplexed. "Did the Ansahs know about that?"

He nodded. "Yes. I wish they could be here. Alek helped me arrange the connection."

"Well, they claimed they couldn't make it so I was

pressed to use their ticket…with no mention of your involvement, of course."

Chance rocked on his heels and looked up at the well-lit ceiling as he chuckled. "Scheming, huh?" he asked, looking back at her.

Their eyes locked before she looked away with a bite of her bottom lip that stirred naughty thoughts in him.

"It seems so," Ngozi said, her nervousness clear.

"You were right," he said.

"About?"

"Me needing to do more. Care more. Focus more on what's right," he admitted, his eyes searching her face for a sign that she understood this shift in his thinking was due to her.

She looked surprised. "You did this for me?" she asked.

He shook his head. "No, I didn't know you were coming, remember, *but* I took your advice, Ngozi, and it feels good to give back more, Mrs. Pro Bono."

Her shoulders slumped a bit as she looked up at him in wonder.

Chance balled his hands into fists behind his back to beat off the temptation to stroke her face. "What's that look about, Ngozi?" he asked.

Tears filled her eyes, and his gut felt wrenched. She tried valiantly to blink them away before turning to quickly stride away.

He fell in step with her and placed an arm around her shoulder to guide her into an office. "Ngozi," he said softly, wanting her to open up to him.

She shook her head. "I feel silly, but… I appreciate your taking my advice and listening to me even though I voiced it out of anger. Outside of my career, what I care about, what I think…what I *feel*," she stressed, letting the rest of her words fade as she pinched the bridge of her nose and closed her eyes.

Chance could no longer resist, stepping close to pull her into his embrace. When she allowed him to do so and rested her forehead against his chest as she released a long breath before her body relaxed, he enjoyed being someone she could rely on for comfort and support.

"You just don't know, Chance," she admitted softly.

He set his chin on her head lightly. "Tell me. You can talk to me about anything, Ngozi. I promise you that," he swore, surprised by the truth of his own words.

He wanted so badly, in that moment, to inquire if her husband had been that for her. Her protector. Her warrior. Her shoulder to lean on.

But he did not.

"Chance Castillo, I don't know what to do with you," she professed.

The same struggle he felt between what he wanted and what he needed was there in her voice. "Help me become a better man."

She looked up at him. "And what will you do with me?" she asked, her hands snaking around his waist to settle on his back.

"Help you color out of the lines a little bit more."

She smiled. "And somewhere in the middle—"

"We have amazing sex."

"Chance," she chided softly.

"Ngozi," he volleyed back.

She chuckled.

He looked down at her, studied her, enjoyed the beauty of her. *She is not Helena.*

The truth was Ngozi Johns was not the type of woman built for frivolity. She was "it"—fun, brilliant, sexy, loyal, reliable, empathetic...

He could go on and on.

But what if I'm wrong?

"Let's stop fighting this, Ngozi," he implored, touching his index finger to the base of her chin to lift her head high as he bent his legs to lower himself and touch his lips down upon hers.

Her answer, he was pleased to note, was to tightly grip his shirt in her hands as she kissed him back with the passion he had craved and missed.

Chapter 7

Ngozi was exhausted.

From the moment they left the art gallery together, she and Chance hadn't been able to keep their hands—or anything else—off each other.

In the office at the gallery.

In the car.

Against the wall of the living room.

On the bench of his nine-foot Steinway grand piano in the music room.

In the shower.

And the bed…where he held her nude body closely as he united them with deep intense strokes and whispered to her how much he missed her until they climaxed and cried out in sweet release together.

And she was spent as she straddled Chance's

strong thighs as he sat in the middle of his bed with his back pressed against the headboard. Her sigh was inevitable when he gripped her thighs to massage them. She rested her hands on his shoulders, gently kneading the muscles there.

"We're really doing this?" Ngozi asked, pressing kisses to his brow as he lowered his head to her chest.

"I don't think we can resist," Chance said, turning his face from one side to the other to plant a warm kiss to each curve of her breasts.

She eased her hands from his shoulders and up his neck to grip his face to tilt upward until he was looking at her. The room was dimly lit by a corner lamp across the room, but the light of the moon and the brightness of the white snow reflected a light in his eyes that she felt herself getting lost in. He met her stare and she lost her breath, feeling something tugging at her heart and claiming a piece of her soul.

She kissed him lightly. "Chance," she whispered, her eyes searching his as she felt a lightness in her chest.

Bzzzzzz.

They both looked to his iPhone vibrating on his bedside table.

Ngozi was thankful for the intrusion. She had started to feel spellbound.

Chance held one of her butt cheeks with one hand and reached for his phone with the other.

She felt his body stiffen. "What's wrong?"

"The attorney notified me that Helena has been officially served her summons," Chance said, his voice hard as he turned the phone to show her.

Ngozi winced. *Helena.*

She moved to rise up off him, but he wrapped his arm around her waist and held her closer. "Don't answer that, Chance," she advised, putting on her attorney hat.

She visualized the blonde Cuban with whom he'd been ready to share his life. Ngozi, educated woman and accomplished attorney, had looked up the woman's Instagram account weeks ago. She was gorgeous. J-Lo level.

"Helena," he said, his tone chilly enough to make her wish for a sweater.

"You have got to be kidding me, Chance. Are you serious? Suing me?" she railed.

He had her on speaker.

Ngozi successfully freed herself from his hold and rose from the bed, not interested in eavesdropping on their conversation.

"Racking up a million dollars' worth of bills for a wedding while screwing another man? Are *you* serious?" he countered, his anger and annoyance clear.

Ngozi paused in the entrance to his bathroom and looked back at him over his shoulder. Something in him needed this moment with Helena.

She squinted as he began to slash his hands across the air as he rose from the bed and paced, and they began arguing heatedly in Spanish.

Her entire body went warm and she leaned against

the frame of the doorway as she accepted what she was feeling. Jealousy. Pure and simple.

And she knew that when she looked in his eyes and saw the moonlight in the brown depths, that the emotion that took her breath was the same one that made her warm with envy.

Her heart pounded so loudly it felt like it thudded in her ears.

Ngozi gripped the door frame tightly and released a long, shaky breath as the truth of her feelings settled in…and scared her.

I love him. I love Chance.

"Go to hell!" Helena screamed.

Ngozi refocused her attention on them.

"I will see you there," Chance returned coldly, holding the phone close to his mouth.

Ngozi stiffened her back and pushed off the door frame to walk across his expansive bedroom and calmly slip the phone out of his hand to end the call. She turned and tossed it onto the middle of his bed. "It is hurtful to your case to argue with Ms. Guzman," she said, turning away from him so he couldn't see how hurtful it was to her, as well.

How did I let this happen?

"You're right," he said.

She glanced at him as she gathered her clothing, taking note with a critical eye that he stood before the floor-to-ceiling windows with his hands on his hips as he looked out at his backyard. His back was to her, but in his reflection in the glass, she took in both his nudity and the pensive look on his face.

He looked lost in thought.

She was tempted to dress and walk out, leaving him lost.

Instead, she set her clothes down on the edge of the bed and walked over to him to press her body against his back and wrap her arms around him as she pressed a kiss to his spine.

Chance brought one hand up to cover hers as he looked down at her over his shoulder. "I'm glad you're back," he said.

Ngozi eased her body around his to stand before him with her bare bottom, her upper back and head against the chilly glass as she looked up at him. "You sure?" she asked, reaching up to stroke his low-cut beard.

Chance cupped her face with his hands, tilting her face up as he bent his head to kiss her. "Honestly?" he asked, as his eyes searched hers just as hers had searched his earlier.

She wondered if he felt the same breathlessness that she had in that moment. "Always," she finally answered, her voice whisper soft.

"I wasn't looking for anything serious and…and I'm not sure I'm ready," Chance admitted. "In fact, I don't think either of us are."

She nodded with a slight smile. "True," she confessed, enjoying the feel of his hands.

Chance stroked her lip with his thumb. "But I don't know how to be without you, Ngozi. I've tried and failed. Twice."

More truth.

The hour was late. Later than she'd ever stayed at Chance's home, but when their simple kisses filled with heat and passion, she didn't dare to resist. Once she stroked him to hardness, in tune to her soft sucking motions of his tongue, the chill of the glass against her body faded as the heat of their passion reigned. She wrapped her arms around his neck and her legs around his waist after he hoisted her body up, centered her core above his upright hardened length and lowered her body down on each inch until they were united fully.

Ngozi gasped and released a tiny cry as she arched her back, pushing her small but plump breasts forward. Chance licked at each of her taut brown nipples with a low growl as she rotated her hips in an up-and-down motion like a rider on a mechanical bull. She kept looking at him, enjoying the glaze of pleasure in his eyes, the grimace of intensity and the quick shallow breaths through pursed lips as he fought for control.

"Ahhhh," she sighed, her eyes still locked on him as she released his neck to press the back of her hands against the glass and slid them upward as she continued to wind her hips.

Chance's grip on her hips deepened, and she felt him harden even more inside her.

"Yes," she sighed with a grunt of pleasure, closing her eyes as she tilted her head back.

Never had she felt so bold, so sexy, so powerful as she did with Chance. The look in his eyes, the strength of his hold and his reaction to her moves pushed her beyond her normal limits with her sexuality. It was new and refreshing and satisfying in every way.

With him there was no shame. No inhibitions. No denial of her wants and desires.

With him she was free.

With the strength of her thigh muscles from her daily runs, Ngozi gripped his waist tighter and lowered her body down the glass until they were face-to-face. They locked eyes and shared what seemed to be a dozen small kisses as he took the lead, alternating between a deep thrust and a circular rotation of his hips that caused his stiff inches to touch every bit of her feminine core and drag against her throbbing bud.

And there against the chilly glass, with the heat they created steaming away the frost, Chance stroked them to another explosive climax that shook Ngozi to her core with such beauty and pleasure that it evoked tears.

She felt like she was free-falling.

It was amazing.

Still shivering, she clung to Chance and buried her face against his neck as he walked them over to his bed. She relaxed into the softness of the bed and snuggled one of the down pillows under her head. She closed her eyes as the exhaustion of her emotions and her climax defeated her.

"You're staying?" Chance asked, his surprise swelling in his voice.

She nodded as he curved his body to hers and

wrapped a strong arm around her waist after pulling
a cool cotton sheet over them.

Ngozi snuggled down deeper on the bed, content
that she didn't have the will or the energy to leave
him.

It was early morning before Ngozi made the short
trip home from Alpine to Passion Grove. She entered
her security code on the side entrance in the massive
kitchen, pushing it open as a yawn escaped her mouth.
Chance had gifted her another mind-blowing, energy-
sapping, eyes-crossing orgasm before she left him.

"No sleep last night?"

Startled, she paused in the doorway at her father
sitting at the mahogany island, still in his plaid robe
and pajamas, drinking from a cup of what she pre-
sumed to be coffee from the heavy scent of it in the
air. "Sir?" she asked, by way of stalling as her nerves
were instantly rattled.

"We're not trying to heat the outdoors, Ngozi."

Her head whipped to the right to find her mother
at the breakfast nook, also in her nightclothes as she
drummed her clear-coated fingernails atop the round
table.

Double trouble.

Ngozi turned to close the door, pausing to lick her
lips as she furrowed her brows. She felt like a child
about to be scolded.

"Reeds was kind enough to let us know you called
and told him you were staying in the city for the night

at the firm's apartment," her father began, ever the attorney—retired or not.

Late last night, she had dug her phone out of the pile of clothing on the floor and texted Reeds to cover for her yet again. "Good, I wouldn't want you to worry," she said, striding across the kitchen at a pace that could have won a speed-walking race with ease.

"Ngozi," her mother said, all simple and easy.

Deceptive as hell.

Ngozi paused and turned, uncomfortable with her face makeup-free and her hair disheveled, dressed in the same white outfit she'd worn to the art gallery the night before.

"Your father is retired from the firm but he's still the majority owner, my daughter," Val said, turning on the padded bench to fold her legs and look across the distance at her daughter. "And that includes the firm's apartment—"

Oh damn.

She was a gifted attorney as well and knew exactly where she had made a wrong calculation. Her eyes shifted from one to the other. Her father took another drink, and in that moment, Ngozi wished he would stir his spoon in his cup so the floor would open and send her to her own special sunken place.

They know I wasn't there.

"Who is he?" Horace asked, setting the cup down on top of the island.

Ngozi opened her mouth to lie. When it came to her relationship with her parents, subterfuge was her first line of defense.

Val held up a hand. "Let's remember that anything less than the truth is disrespect," she advised before shifting her focus back to her husband.

"Who is he?" Horace repeated.

I don't want to lie. I don't want to deny Chance. I don't want to.

"Chance Castillo," she said, physically and mentally steeling herself for a long list of questions and reminders of obligations to Dennis even beyond his death.

Silence reigned.

Their faces were unreadable.

"Invite him to dinner," her mother said.

Ngozi grimaced. "But—"

"Soon," her father added before returning his attention to his coffee.

"Horace, we better go up and get ready," Val said, rising from her seat. "We have that breakfast meeting with possible donors for my upcoming campaign."

Ngozi looked from one to the other, her mouth slightly ajar. She couldn't hide her shock, even as they eased past her to leave her in the kitchen alone.

Chance carefully steered his silver Bentley Bentayga SUV over the busy New Jersey streets, being sure to stay focused with all of the snow and ice on the ground. As he pulled the vehicle to a stop at a red traffic light, he looked over at Ngozi sitting beside him in the passenger seat. He smiled at all the nervous gestures he spotted. Swaying her knee back and forth.

Twisting the large diamond-encrusted dome ring she wore on her index finger. Nibbling on her bottom lip.

He had picked her up from work, fresh off yet another trial win, and she was dressed in a claret ostrich feather coat with a turtleneck and pencil leather skirt of the same shade that was beautiful against her mocha complexion, particularly with the deep mahogany lipstick she wore.

"Mi madre no muerde, sabes," he said, giving her thigh a warm rub and squeeze as he steered forward under the green traffic light with his other hand.

"She doesn't bite, huh?" Ngozi said, translating his words. Inside the dimly lit interior of the SUV, she glanced at him with a weak smile. "I told you my parents want to meet you as well, so let's see how easy-breezy you are when I finally get the nerve to serve you up to them."

"I'm ready," Chance said with a chuckle as he turned onto the short paved drive of his mother's two-story brick home just a few miles from his estate. He pressed the button to open the door of the two-car garage and pulled into the empty spot next to her red convertible Mercedes Benz she called "Spicy."

"And the deposition tomorrow—are you ready for that?" Ngozi asked.

Chance shut the SUV off and looked over at her. The overhead motion lighting of the garage lit up the car, offering him a clearer view of her face. "Yes, I am."

"That's good," she said. "Just be sure to keep your cool."

He frowned. They rarely discussed his lawsuit against Helena. "My cool?"

Ngozi reached for the handle to the passenger door. She looked nonplussed. "Same advice I would give if you were still my client," she said matter-of-factly with a one-shoulder shrug.

"But you're not my attorney, you're my woman," he reminded her.

Ngozi relaxed back against the seat. She stroked the underside of his chin, letting the short beard hairs prick against her hand. "Your woman, huh?" she asked.

He smiled as he leaned in and pressed his lips to her own as he reached down to use the controls to lower her seat backward.

"Don't…start…something…we…can't…finish," she whispered up to him in between kisses as her eyes studied his.

"Who says we can't—"

"Chance! Are you coming in?"

They froze before they sat straight up in their separate chairs again.

Chance looked through the windshield at his mother standing in the open doorway leading from the garage into her kitchen. She was squinting as she peered into the car with a frown.

Ngozi covered her face with her hands, feeling the warmth of embarrassment that rose in her cheeks. "Oh God," she moaned.

Chance chuckled before he opened the driver's side door. "We're headed right in," he called out to her.

She turned and walked back into the house, leaving the door ajar.

"Great first impression," Ngozi drawled, before he climbed from the car and strode around the front to open the passenger door.

"No worries, *mi tentadora*," he said, closing the door when she stepped aside.

"Your temptress?" she asked, looking back at him as she climbed the brick staircase.

Yes, you are.

A relationship had not been in the cards for him after Helena, but Ngozi had drawn him in from their first meeting and he hadn't been able to shake his desire for her ever since. She was his temptation. His temptress.

And in time, his acceptance of that truth shook him to his core.

"Ready?" he asked, seeing the nervousness in her eyes as she waited for him to pull the glass door open for her.

She nodded before stepping inside.

Chance eyed his mother as she turned and walked across the spacious kitchen with a wide, warm smile.

"Welcome, welcome," Esmerelda said, grasping Ngozi's shoulders as she kissed both of her cheeks. "It's nice to meet you."

Chance eyed Ngozi as she returned the warmth, and her shoulders relaxed.

Their exchange pleased him.

"We can go in to eat since you were running a little behind," she said, with a meaningful stare at Chance.

He gave her a wide smile. Her disapproval vanished.

"What do you want me to carry, Ma?" Chance asked.

"Nothing, just go on in."

Chance led Ngozi out of the kitchen and through to the dining room. The large wood table, covered with a beautiful lace tablecloth that looked out of place among the modern design of the home, was set for three with his mother's favorite crystal drink ware and a large floral arrangement. "She went all out," he said as he pulled back the chair for Ngozi at the table.

She took the seat, smiling up at him when he stroked her neck before moving around the table to take the chair across from her.

"Relax," he mouthed as his mother began carrying in large ceramic bowls in bright colors to set on the table.

The smell of the food intensified, and Chance's stomach rumbled.

"I'm too nervous to eat," she admitted.

"Nervous? Why?" Esmerelda asked, setting down a bowl of white rice and a pitcher of amber-colored liquid with fresh fruit pieces.

"Nothing, Ms. Castillo," Ngozi said.

Chance fought not to wince as his mother gave her a stiff smile. "It's Ms. Diaz," she said with emphasis. "Castillo is the name of his father, who didn't choose to share it with me by marriage."

Ngozi remained silent, giving Chance a pointed

stare as his mother took her seat at the head of the table.

"She didn't know, Ma," he said, reaching to remove the lid from the bright turquoise tureen. "*Tayota guisada con longaniza.* I love it."

"This is a popular dish from my country," Esmerelda said, scooping a heaped spoonful of rice into each of three bowls stacked by her place setting. She handed each bowl to Chance to ladle the sausage and chayote cooked in tomato sauce, onion, garlic, cilantro and bell peppers. "I hope you don't find it *too* spicy. Sometimes the palate of those not raised in our culture is delicate."

Chance frowned. Traditionally, there wasn't much heat to the dish.

"I'm sure it's fine. Everything looks delicious," Ngozi said, using both of her hands to accept the bowl he handed her.

He picked up his spoon and dug in, enjoying the flavor of the food. There was a little bit of a spicy kick that tickled even his tongue.

Ngozi coughed.

He glanced across the table at her. Sweat beads were on her upper lip and forehead. Her eyes were glassy from tears.

She coughed some more.

Chance rushed to fill her glass with his mother's homemade fruit juice, standing to reach across the table and press it into her hands.

Ngozi drank from it in large gulps.

"I'm so sorry, Ngozi. Perhaps I can fix you something else if that is too much for you," Esmerelda said, sounding contrite.

Ngozi cleared her throat. "No, this is delicious," she said, setting the glass down before dabbing her upper lip with the cloth napkin she'd opened across her lap.

Chance shook his head. "You don't have to—"

"This is fine," she said, giving him a hard stare and his mother a soft smile before taking a smaller bite of the dish from her bowl.

As their meal continued in silence, Chance eyed Ngozi taking small bites of food followed by large sips of juice. It was clear she didn't want to offend his mother.

"Ngozi, Chance tells me you're an attorney," Esmerelda said, covering her nearly empty bowl with her cloth napkin as she placed her elbows on the table and looked directly at Ngozi.

"Yes, I'm a junior partner of the firm my father established," she answered.

"My Chance seems to have a soft spot for attorneys," she said.

Ngozi licked her lips as she set her napkin on the table.

"Helena and Ngozi are nothing alike," Chance offered into the stilted silence.

"Espero que no, por tu bien," Esmerelda said. *"Ella debería estar llorando a su esposo y no buscando uno nuevo. Los buscadores de oro huelen el dinero como tiburones huelen a sangre."*

"Ma," he snapped sharply as he sat up straight in the chair and eyed her in surprise and disappointment.

He could hardly believe her words and could only imagine how harsh they sounded to Ngozi: *"I hope not for your sake. She should be grieving her husband and not looking for a new one. Gold diggers smell money like sharks smell blood."* Ngozi rose to her feet, looking down at his mother. Chance rose, as well.

"Se equivoca acerca de mí, Señora Díaz," Ngozi said.

His mother's jaw tightened, and her eyes widened in surprise to find Ngozi speak in fluent Spanish to proclaim that she was wrong about her.

Chance shook his head. He agreed with Ngozi that his mother was mistaken about her.

"I am not a gold digger nor am I on the prowl to replace my dead husband with a new one," she said in his mother's native tongue, her voice hollow.

Chance eyed his mother in disbelief. He could tell she felt his stare as she avoided his look.

"My apologies if I offended you," Esmerelda said, reverting to English.

"Thank you for dinner," Ngozi said before quickly turning to walk into the kitchen. Soon the alarm system announced the opening and closing of the side entrance door.

Chance's eyes continued to bore into her.

"What?" she asked.

"You have never taught me or shown me the example of how to be rude and mean to anyone," he began. "I'm just trying to figure out who is sitting before me."

Esmerelda turned in her chair and looked up at him. "I watched you recover from heartbreak by Ese Rubio Diablo for almost a year, so what you see now is a mother willing to fight to make sure you don't go through that heartache again," she said, her voice impassioned and her eyes lit with the fire of determination.

"I know you mean well, but Ngozi should not have to suffer for what Helena did to me," Chance insisted, forcing softness into his tone. "All I ask is that you give her the same kindness you give strangers. Even a dog deserves respect, Ma."

She shrugged and turned her lips downward.

He stepped near her and bent at the waist to press a kiss to the top of her head. "Thank you for dinner," he said and then frowned deeply as he rose to look down at her again in skepticism. "Did you spice the food on purpose?"

Esmerelda sucked air between her teeth and threw her hands up. "It didn't kill her," she said.

"Ma!"

"What?"

"I'll see you later," Chance said, walking around her chair. He paused. "Do you need anything?"

"Just for you to be happy," Esmerelda said.

"I'm a grown man. My happiness is in my hands now," he said. "You don't have to work double shifts to take care of me and send me to private school. I will love you and spoil you because of your sacrifice, but your time putting me before yourself is over. I got it from here."

She remained quiet and studied her nails.

He could tell she was hurt, but the truth of his words could not be retracted to save her feelings. He gave his mother the world, but he was a man who had no desire to be babied and coddled by his mother.

"Te amo, Ma."

"I love you, too, Chance."

With that he took his leave.

Ngozi was sitting in the SUV. He eyed her through the windshield as he made his way over to the driver's side door. He climbed inside. Unspoken words swelled between them.

Chance licked his lips and reached over to take one of her soft hands in his. "Say it," he urged. "I'm listening."

"It's nothing. I'm fine," she said, looking to him with a smile as fake as the plastic one pinned onto a Mr. Potato Head toy.

"Don't ever deny your feelings for the sake of anyone—not me or anyone else—because they matter," he said.

She smiled again. It was soft and genuine. "I wouldn't know what it feels like to put myself first," she admitted.

Chance leaned over to press kisses to the side of her face. "Try it," he whispered into her ear.

"I want you to know that I am not looking to replace Dennis," she said, turning on the seat to face him. "Hell, I don't even feel I have the right to move on and be happy when he's dead."

Chance took a moment to properly frame what he said next. "I never expect you to let go of Dennis."

She began to stroke his hand. "Not of him, of my guilt," she acknowledged before closing her eyes and releasing a breath.

He wondered if talking about him was like releasing steam to dissolve the buildup of pressure.

"We've never spoken of his death," he offered, being sure to tread lightly to avoid stepping on or disrespecting her feelings.

"I've never talked about it with anyone."

Her sadness was palpable, and his gut ached for her. "And do you want to talk now?" he asked.

Ngozi shook her head. "Not yet, but thank you for letting me know that someone is there to finally listen to me."

"Sounds like a lot to unload from that clever brain of yours," he said, his eyes searching his.

"It is. Think you can handle it?"

With a final kiss, he turned his attention to starting the car. "For you I will do anything," he said, letting the truth of his words settle in his chest as the engine roared to life.

Chapter 8

No, Ngozi. No.

Determined not to give in to her own curiosity, she pushed back from her desk and crossed her arms over her chest. Her eyes stayed locked on her computer monitor, though. She had to tighten her fingers into a fist, hoping to stop herself from reaching out and pulling up the video recording of the deposition of Helena Guzman in Chance's lawsuit against her.

No.

Ngozi had been in court all morning and missed when Helena and her attorney arrived. She considered it a mixed blessing.

Grabbing the edge of her desk, she rolled the few inches forward and picked up her pen. Even as she reviewed the case file in front of her, her attention kept shifting to her monitor. *To hell with it.*

Ngozi reached for the keyboard.

"Ms. J."

She jumped like a startled deer, rising and then dropping back down in her seat. Angel looked at her in bewilderment. She cleared her throat and pressed her palms down on the desk. "Yes, Angel?" she asked, thankful for the black shirt and simple wide-leg slacks the young lady wore.

She'd really been making an effort of late to tame her wild ways and boisterous unprofessional behavior. Ngozi took note, appreciated it and was proud of her.

Angel walked in the room, looking nervous as she set an envelope before her.

"What's this?" Ngozi said, opening the flap to find a check.

"I finally saved enough to repay you for my fine and the bond that you paid," Angel said with a wide smile. "And that's the first check I ever wrote from my new checking account, ya heard me."

Ngozi was stunned and she sat back in her chair, letting the check and the envelope drop to the desk as she pressed her fingertips to her lips. There was no denying the pride on Angela's face. And it was the reason she fought just as hard for her pro bono cases as all her others. The hope of giving someone a second chance to better their lives. To find a better way. And in truth, out of all the clients she went above and beyond her attorney duties for, she wouldn't have guessed that Angel would be such a success story.

"If it wasn't for you, I would still be stripping and tricking. Now I'm looking up to you, and I ain't gonna never be no lawyer or nothing, but I want to go back to school…because of you. So thank you for seeing something in me 'cause it taught me to see more in myself, Ms. J.," Angel said.

Ngozi felt emotional, but she kept her face neutral. Maintained her professionalism.

Stuck to her routine—her facade.

Don't ever deny your feelings for the sake of anyone—not me or anyone else—because they matter.

Taking a breath, she rose from her seat and came around the desk to pull Angel into a tight hug. "I'm so proud of you," she said, letting her emotions swell in her tone. "Keep it up."

"I will, Ms. J. I won't let you down," she promised.

Ngozi nodded, releasing her as she stepped back. "I believe that. Thank you," she said, turning to reclaim her seat behind her desk.

Angel took her leave with one last little wave.

"Shut the door, please," she requested, already turning her attention back to her wireless keyboard.

Ngozi was left with her curiosity about the deposition still nagging at her. With a bite of her bottom lip, she logged on to the company's server and searched for the video file of the deposition. She stroked her chin and released long steady breaths at the sight of Chance and his attorney, Larry Rawlings, entering one of the three conference rooms in the offices of Vincent and Associates Law.

Her heart raced at the sight of Chance. The night before, they had lain naked together in front of his lit fireplace as she worked on a new case and he read a book. Leaving him to return to Passion Grove had not been easy, especially because she knew his deposition was the next day.

Now here she sat looking on like a Peeping Thomasina at his ex, a blonde and beautiful golden-skinned Afro-Cuban, entering the room with her attorney. She was rattled. She and Helena were completely different in looks, and although Ngozi was a confident woman, it would be hard to deny Helena's stunning beauty...or the way Chance stared at her with such livid intensity.

Ngozi's heart was pounding as she looked on.

"Ms. Guzman, were you actively involved in a relationship with Jason Young while planning your wedding to my client, Chance Castillo?" Larry asked, looking across the table at the woman over the rim of his horn-rimmed glasses.

Larry's slightly disheveled appearance and his brilliance didn't align, which caught most people unfamiliar with him off guard.

Helena conferred with her attorney before giving Larry a cool look. "No. It was not a relationship," she said, her accent present.

Chance loudly scoffed.

Helena continued to ignore him.

Ngozi nibbled on her bottom lip.

Larry made a note on his notepad. "Were you and Mr. Young intimate during that time? Did you share meals? Did you vacation together? Did you have conversations about life? Did you ever discuss your future with him?"

Helena again conferred with her attorney, a tall silver-haired woman with an olive complexion. "Per the advice of my counsel, I am invoking my right under the Fifth Amendment not to answer, on the grounds I may incriminate myself."

Ngozi winced when Chance jumped up out of his seat. "If I were you, I wouldn't admit to being a scheming two-timing—"

Larry rose to his feet and whispered in Chance's ear.

Both men took their seats.

Ngozi barely heard the rest of their words because of her focus on how Helena barely glanced in Chance's direction, but he never took his eyes off her. His hostility toward Helena seemed to swell and fill the room. Long after the deposition ended and the video faded to black, Ngozi couldn't forget the look in his eyes or the tense stance of his frame.

Sadness and jealousy stung with the sharpness of a needle. His demeanor gave credence to Helena's response that the motivation for Chance's lawsuit was irrational hurt brought on by a broken heart, and even more, injured pride.

His anger was immense, and she felt his hurt was equal to it. As was the love he'd once had for her.

Love he doesn't have for me.

His anger leaves no room in his heart for anything else.

For a long time, she sat staring out the window with that thought foremost in her mind.

The dry heat of the sauna radiated against their nude frames as Ngozi sat astride Chance's lap on one of the cedar benches lining the large infrared sauna. The red light cast their bronzed bodies with a glow meant to be therapeutic, but which also gave the warm interior a vibe that was sexy.

"Talk to me, Ngozi."

Chance was stroking her back. He felt her stiffen for a millisecond before her body relaxed against his again. They'd decided to enjoy a sauna while a three-star Michelin chef who now worked exclusively as a private chef prepared them a romantic dinner. It was clear to him that her mind was elsewhere from the moment she had arrived at his estate.

As much as he enjoyed the feel of her soft body pressed against the hard muscles of his frame, it was clear that a conversation was more needed than another session of fiery sex in a steamy room beneath a red light.

She took a large breath that caused her chest to rise and fall as she sat up straight to look down into his face with serious eyes. "I don't think I have a right to ask, because I know that I'm not where I should be with the death of my husband...and who am I to expect something from you that I can't seem to claim for myself?"

Chance felt lost in her gaze. "And what is that?" he asked, massaging her buttocks.

"Moving beyond. Letting go," she admitted with several soft nods as if to reaffirm her words to herself.

He remembered the moment they shared in his SUV the night he brought her to dinner at his mother's. "About your guilt?"

She looked unsure. "Yes...my guilt about Dennis... and whether you could drop your lawsuit against Helena?" she asked, forcing her words out in a rush because of the courage it took for her to finally voice her worries.

Chance frowned, and his hands paused on her bottom. "You want me to drop the lawsuit?" he asked, his surprise clear.

Ngozi looked away from him as she nodded.

He gently touched her chin and guided her face forward so that their eyes were locked once more. "What's going on? Do you think I'll lose? Is this about us? What...what's going on?" he asked, his tone soft.

Ngozi gave him a soft smile, looking up at the red light before glancing back at him. "Did you mean it when you said I could tell you anything?"

"Absolutely, Ngozi. Anything," he emphasized, as a dozen or more questions about the legal validity of his case raced through his head.

"I have never told anyone that my marriage was not at all what it appeared to be," she began, withdrawing her hands from his body as she bent her arms and pressed her hands to the back of her neck. "I think we were meant to be friends rather than spouses, because in the end this person with whom I had once enjoyed spending time began to feel like an...an...adversary."

Ngozi tilted her head, exposing the smooth expanse of her neck as she closed her eyes and released a long breath.

He remained quiet, wanting her to unload her feelings.

"In law school we worked together to study, pass tests and graduate, but soon our careers seemed to take us in two different directions, and all of a sudden, we were cold and distant with each other, and the only heat was in arguments, but then we would put on the greatest show alive like circus monkeys and pretend in public. All smiles. All kisses. All lovey-dovey bull. Nothing but icing covering up shit."

She looked off into the distance, but the pain in her eyes was clear. "We were in our apartment one Sunday and we were both preparing for cases the next day. He was in our office, and I was in the living room on the floor in front of the fireplace. I was feeling weary and decided to make coffee. I made him a cup just the way he liked, black and sweet, in this huge Superman mug that he'd had since like high school," she said softly, as if back in the moment. "I took the coffee in to him and he didn't look up at me or say thank you. I don't know, in that moment I was so sick of the silence and the distance and the way we were with each other. I missed my friend and I *felt* like I hated my husband—and they were one in the same man."

Chance noticed she was raking the tips of her fingernails against her neck, and he reached up to take her hand into his. She seemed so lost in her thoughts that he wondered if she even noticed.

"In that moment I just wanted him out of the apartment, out of my sight. Just gone," she said, her expression becoming pained. "I asked him to go get lunch, just to get him out…and…and he *never* came back."

Her body tensed, and she winced as a tear raced down her cheek, quickly followed by another and another.

Chance's heart ached for her. "What happened, Ngozi?" he asked, his voice tempered.

"A car crash," she said. "I wished he was gone. I wanted our marriage over. I sent him out. And he never came back. And I have never told a soul," she admitted in a harsh whisper.

"Oh, baby, you can't put the weight of his death on your conscience or your shoulders like that," Chance said, pressing his hands to her face.

She nodded. "My brain understands that, but I still feel like I don't deserve to be so happy."

"With me?" he asked.

Ngozi looked at him. "You were the last thing I was looking for, Chance Castillo," she admitted. "And now I wonder just what I would do without you."

His heart swelled and filled with an emotion for her that had become familiar of late. An emotion he was still hesitant to claim but was finding hard to deny.

I love her.

His heart pounded furiously.

"Do you still love Helena?"

His brows dipped. "No," he said unequivocally.

I love you.

"Then why the lawsuit, Chance?" Ngozi asked. "It keeps you connected to her. It keeps you angry at her."

He stiffened, feeling uneasy. "I'm not—"

"I saw the video of the deposition, Chance."

He swallowed the rest of his denial, closing his eyes to avoid her gaze on him. Yes, Helena had infuriated him earlier in the deposition. That was undeniable. "It was my first time seeing her since she walked out on me before the wedding," he admitted, giving her the same glimpse into his vulnerability that she'd given him. "All I could think about when I was looking at her is how much she'd fooled me. Made a fool of me. It took me back to being the poor kid at school with the rich kids, with girls who looked a lot like Helena, who wouldn't give me the time of day."

Damn.

The thought that childhood issues still affected him stung like crazy.

Ngozi stroked his face and he turned his head toward her touch, enjoying the warmth, care and concern he felt there.

"I'm not dropping the case, Ngozi," he insisted, waiting for her touch to cease.

It didn't.

But she released a heavy breath. "Chance?"

"I don't want her back. I am glad that she didn't marry me and have me financing her side relationship, but it was wasteful and vindictive to push for a huge wedding on my dime when she knew she wasn't all-in, Ngozi. She doesn't just get to walk away with no consequences. She left me holding the bag regarding that wedding."

Ngozi said no more as she rested her forehead against his.

He knew she still held her doubts about his feelings for Helena, and he wanted nothing more than to admit that she had captured the heart he swore he would never entrust to another woman again. But the moment didn't call for it. It would seem more of a ploy than a revelation of his true feelings, so he held back, admitting that he needed time to adjust to the truth himself.

I love Ngozi.

The sound of utensils hitting against flatware echoed into the quiet of the stately dining room as Chance, Ngozi and her parents enjoyed their dinner of prime rib, potatoes au gratin and sautéed string beans.

It was *so* awkward.

Ngozi took a sip of plum wine—a deep one.

"So, Chance, tell me more about your work?" Horace asked, settling back in his chair as he eyed the man sitting to his right.

Ngozi went tense. *Work? Chance spent his downtime planning what to do during his free time.*

"Once I sold my app, I shifted away from finance full-time, and now I have a few different irons in the fire," he said, sounding confident and proud. "I'm a consultant and minority owner of the firm that purchased the app I developed. I do freelance investing for several clients that insisted I continue to work on their portfolios. And I'm currently finishing up a new app to help productivity for businesspeople on the go."

Ngozi sputtered the sip of wine she just took, her eyes wide in surprise. Was he lying to impress her parents? *Why don't I know about any of this?*

All eyes shifted to her as she grabbed her cloth napkin and cleaned up the small splatter she had made on the tabletop.

"Ngozi, since you don't drink alcohol much, maybe you should take it easy on that wine," Valerie said.

Chance frowned deeply. "She drinks—"

Ngozi kicked his shin under the table, silencing him.

He grunted as he eyed her with a hard stare.

"You're right, Ma. I better stick to water," she said, setting the goblet of wine aside as she avoided Chance's confused stare.

Their conversation continued, and the air became less tense as the questioning of Chance subsided. Ngozi sat back and observed her parents and her man as the conversation switched to politics. She had *never* imagined introducing her parents to a man other than Dennis—and definitely assumed they would resent him because of their fondness of her deceased husband.

This isn't bad. Not bad at all.

"So how long have you been interested in my daughter?" Valerie asked, before sliding a bite of food in her mouth.

Ngozi sat up straight. *What now? Weren't they just talking about the president?*

"Not long, really," she said, purposefully vague.

Chance gave her another odd expression. "From the first day we met, I wanted to know more about her other than her beauty," he said, resting his eyes on Ngozi.

She swallowed a sudden lump in her throat, finding herself unable to look away from him.

"I have discovered that she is as brilliant, caring, empathetic, loyal and funny as she is beautiful," he added.

Her entire body warmed under his praise. It was hard to deny that in time she had not felt appreciated or respected in her marriage. It was as if the success in her career had to be diminished to soothe the ego of a man used to being in the lead.

With Chance, it was different. He was her biggest champion.

After dinner and some more polite conversation over coffee and drinks, Ngozi looked on as Chance shook her father's hand and offered her mother a polite hug. "It was good to meet you both," he said.

"Same here," her father said with a nod, turning his attention to his nightly ritual of smoking a cigar and reading the local newspaper, *The Passion Grove Press*, which was mostly news and tidbits about the small town and the achievements of its residents.

"See, I survived," Chance said as they walked together to the front door.

Ngozi nodded, wrapping both of her arms around one of his. "Yes, you did," she said, looking up at him.

At the sound of footsteps, she quickly released him, but relaxed when she turned to find Reeds carrying Chance's leather coat. "Thank you, Reeds," she said.

"No problem," he said, undraping it from over his arm and handing it to Chance with a warm smile. "Drive safe, sir."

"Thank you."

Ngozi looked up at Chance but was surprised by the troubled look clouding his handsome features. "What's wrong?"

"Nothing," he said, outstretching each arm to pull on his fur-lined coat to defeat the arctic northeaster snow still dominating the March weather. "Are you coming back to Alpine with me?"

Her hands paused in smoothing the collar of his coat. "No, not tonight."

"You haven't stayed over except that one time," he said, his brows dipping as he brought his own hands up to cover hers.

Ngozi forced a smile, remembering her parents' ambushing her that next morning. "I will again," she said, conciliating him.

"Not with me, Ngozi," he said. "No, ma'am. Save the show for those who purchased a ticket. Me? I want nothing but the real. So, no, not with me. Never with me."

Ngozi withdrew her hands from his and rubbed them together as she looked into his eyes. "You're the only one who makes me feel like I can be me, whatever that may be. Shit show and all," she said, moving to take a seat on the bottom of the staircase.

Chance walked over to stand in front of where she sat, his hands now pressed into the pockets of his coat.

"I just would prefer my parents not know we've... uh...we're...intimate," she said.

He frowned as he looked up at the large chandelier above their heads. "Or that you drink. Or how long we've been together. Or a dozen other things I saw you outright lie or skirt the truth around tonight," he said.

"Really, Chance?" she asked, leaning to the side a bit as she gave him a stare filled with attitude.

"Really," he affirmed, looking down at her. "It was quite a performance."

Ngozi rose and moved up two steps so they were eye level with each other. "Don't judge me, Chance," she warned.

"Like you did about the lawsuit?" he asked, his voice chiding.

Wow.

"I'm wrong for making sure I'm not wasting my time trying to build something with you?" she asked.

"No, definitely not. Just like it's okay for me to now be skeptical about moving forward after seeing you so willingly—and so easily—present yourself as whatever is needed in the moment," he countered.

"You don't trust me, Chance?" she asked, her feelings hurt by the thought of that.

He shook his head. "I didn't say that," he insisted.

"But I do wonder if you even trust yourself to be who and what you truly want to be, if you are so busy playing the role of Ms. Perfect."

Ngozi arched a brow. "That's not playing perfect—it's providing respect," she countered.

"And who were you respecting by staying in an unhappy marriage—"

Ngozi held up both hands with her palms facing him as she shook her head vigorously. "No, you don't get to focus on issues you think I have and ignore the emotional baggage sitting on your own doorstep."

They fell silent. The air was tense. Gone was the joy they usually had just being in each other's company.

"It seems we both have some stuff we need to fix," Chance finally offered.

She nodded in agreement. "Maybe we should work on that before trying to complicate each other's lives further," she said, unable to overlook her hurt and offense at his words.

He looked surprised, but then he nodded, as well. "Maybe," he agreed.

What are you doing, Ngozi? What are we doing?

She descended the few steps, moving beyond him to stride across the space to open the front door. The chilly winter winds instantly pushed inside. She trembled as goose bumps covered her.

Chance looked at her over his broad shoulder before he turned with a solemn expression and walked over to stand before her. "We never can seem to get this right," he said, wiping away a snowflake that blew in and landed on her cheek.

Ngozi had to fight not to lean into his touch. "Maybe one day we'll both be ready for this," she said, sadness filling her as she doubted the truth of it.

They had taken a chance on each other and failed.

"Maybe," Chance agreed.

With one final look shared between them, he turned and left.

Ngozi gave not one care about the brutal cold as she stood in the doorway and watched him walk out of her life at her request.

A warm hand touched her arm and pulled her back from the door to close it. She turned to find Reeds just as a tear raced down her cheek. Her feelings were not bruised because he had pointed out what she knew about herself—she flew under the radar in her personal life by putting on a facade to make everyone but herself happy. Having it presented to her on a platter by the man she loved had been embarrassing, but the true hurt was his inability to release Helena from his life and move on. That stung like crazy, and she'd be a fool to risk her heart when she wasn't sure his wasn't too bruised by another woman to love her in return.

"It's just a mess, Reeds," she admitted, wiping away her tears and blinking rapidly to prevent any more from rising and falling.

"You've been hiding your tears since your brother's death, Ngozi," he said, his wise eyes searching hers. "Shrinking yourself. Denying yourself. You were a child taking on the role and responsibility of an adult by trying to adjust her life for grown people. Now you're grown, and you're still doing it. And I'll tell you this—I'm glad *somebody* finally said it."

Ngozi was startled. "Say what now?" she asked.

"Listen, my job around here is to make sure the house operates well and the staff acts right. It's not to cross the line and interject myself between the people who pay me and their daughter whom I adore, but I will tell you this—since your young man opened the door. They feel they are protecting you just as much as you feel you're protecting them, and I think you're all wrong for the way you're going about it. Avoidance is never the answer."

And now Ngozi was confused, because she knew Reeds wouldn't speak on personal family matters—especially if he wasn't sure about his opinion.

"Well, since it's clear you overheard my conversation with Chance," she said, kicking into attorney mode, "why should I risk my heart for a man who won't let something go for me?"

Reeds smiled. "And if he did? If he readily agreed to drop this lawsuit you're so worried about, would you have been prepared in that moment to be the woman he is requesting of you—to stand up for yourself and demand your happiness in whatever way *you* see fit?"

Ngozi quickly shifted through emotions. *How could I love someone when I haven't learned to fully discover and love myself?*

"I believe you have just put me at a rare loss, Reeds," she admitted as he chuckled.

"Now that is high praise, Madam Counselor," he said, reaching over to squeeze her hand before he turned and walked away toward the dining room, presumably to ensure the staff had cleaned the area.

She crossed her arms over her chest and rubbed the back of her upper arms as she made her way back to the den. Her parents were lying on the sofa together watching television. Her eyes shifted to the spot on the floor in front of the polished entertainment center. An image of her and her brother, Haaziq, sitting cross-legged replayed in her mind. They were dressed in nightclothes and laughing at some TV comedy as their parents snuggled.

It was a memory that was hard to forget because of its regular occurrence in their life as a family.

In the image, he slowly faded away and she was left alone.

God, I miss my brother. I miss him so much.

"Ngozi? What's wrong?" her mother asked, rising from where she had been resting her head against her father's chest.

She smiled and shook her head, falling into her all-too-familiar role. "Nothing," she lied, sounding fine but feeling hollow.

"Okay," Valerie said, reclaiming her spot. "You had an odd look on your face."

And just like that, a hiccup in their life, a spot of imperfection, was corrected.

"Is your friend gone?" her father asked.

Maybe forever.

Ngozi nodded, feeling overwhelmed. *When do my feelings matter?*

"Mama," she called out, wringing her hands together.

Valerie looked over at her. "Yes?"

"I lied before," she admitted.

"About what?" her mother asked, rising from her husband's chest once more.

"I was thinking about...about...how we all sat in here every night, me, you, Daddy and... Haaziq, and watched TV before you would send us to bed," she admitted, wincing and releasing a harsh gasp as one tear and then another raced down her cheek. "And how much I miss him."

Her parents shared a long, knowing look before her mother rose to come over to her and her father used the iPad to turn off the television.

And at the first feel of her mother's arms wrapping around her body and embracing her, Ngozi buried her face in her neck and inhaled her familiar scent.

"We knew this was coming, we just didn't know it would take so long," her father added, coming close to massage warm circles on her back.

Ngozi enjoyed the warmth of their comfort, and cried like she had never cried before.

Chapter 9

Three months later

Chance leaned against the wall of the hospital with his hands pressed deep into the pockets of the dark denim he wore. As hospital personnel moved past him in completion of their duties and he ignored the scent of illness and antiseptic blending in the air, Chance eyed room 317.

On the other side of the closed door was his father. Jeffrey Castillo.

He'd never seen him. Never met him. Never known anything about him except he was his father.

Over the last ninety days, he had made his life one adventure after another. Helicopter skiing in Alaska. Diving with sharks on the Australian coast off a megayacht. Shopping at the House of Bijan in

Beverly Hills. Kayaking in Norway. Watching the grand prix in Monte Carlo. Skydiving in Dubai.

And then he'd received an inbox message on Facebook from a woman introducing herself as his father's wife and letting him know his father was terminally ill and wanted to finally meet his eldest son. That was the day before, and now here he was. Chance hadn't even told his mother.

I don't know why I'm here.

Pushing up off the wall, he walked down the length of the corridor to the window, looking out at the cars lined up in the many parking spots and at the traffic whizzing past on the street.

He froze when he spotted a tall dark-skinned woman climb from a red car and make her way toward the hospital's main entrance. His gut clenched until the moment he realized she was not Ngozi.

"Chance?"

He turned from the window to find a pretty round-faced woman with a short silvery hairdo paused at the door to his father's hospital room. It was his father's wife, Maria. She gave him a warm smile as she walked up to him.

"You came," she said.

"I haven't gone in," he admitted.

Her eyes showed her understanding of his hesitation. "If you decide not to, I won't tell him," she said. "The man he is today is not the man he was before. Life has caused him to change, but that will never top how you must have felt growing up without his presence in your life."

Chance liked her. Empathy was always a bridge to understanding and respect.

"Does he know you reached out to me?" he asked, looking down the length of the hall to the closed door.

She shook her head. "No, I didn't want to disappoint him if you—or the others—chose not to come."

Chance went still with a frown. "Others?"

Maria nodded, bending her head to look down as she opened her purse and removed a folded, well-worn envelope with frayed edges. She pressed it into his hands.

Chance allowed his body to lean against the wall as he took in the list of three names in faded ink—his and two more. "And these are?" he asked, looking at the woman.

"Your two brothers," she said, offering him a gentle smile.

Chance deeply frowned. When he was younger, he was optimistic enough to wonder if he had sisters and brothers. Age and the passing of time with no such knowledge had led to him not caring and then not wondering about it all.

"Jeffrey and I also have a daughter, Chance," she said gently. "Her name is Camila."

His father. A stepmother. And three half siblings.

Chance shook his head, not quite sure of anyone's intention and whether he was ready for a new family. "I need time," he admitted, folding and shoving the envelope in his back pocket.

"I understand," Maria said. "Please keep in mind that your fath—that Jeffrey is very ill, and this may be your last opportunity to see him alive."

He nodded as his emotions whirled around like a tornado.

"Ma?"

He looked down the hall at a tall, slender woman in her midtwenties, with short jet-black hair and a shortbread complexion, standing in the open doorway to room 317. He knew from the lean beauty of her face and the similarities in their look that she was his sister, Camila. Camila Castillo.

"I'm coming," Maria said, giving him one more smile filled with her desire for him to meet his father before she turned and walked to her daughter.

"Who is that?" Camila asked, swiping her long bangs out of her face as she eyed him in open curiosity.

"Someone who knows your father," Maria said, offering a hint at the truth but successfully evading it.

Both women gave him one final look before entering the hospital room and closing the door behind them.

Quickly, Chance strode down the middle of the hallway, his height and strength seeming to make the space smaller. He felt pressure filling his chest as he pressed the button for the elevator with far more vigor than necessary. Coming there had become more than he bargained for. Once on the elevator, he pulled the frayed envelope from his back pocket and lightly rubbed the side of his thumb against the faded block lettering that he assumed to be that of his father.

A name on an envelope wasn't much, but it was more of a thought than he'd ever imagined his father to have spent on him.

Chance stopped the elevator doors from closing

and stepped off, making his way back down the hall to room 317. The door opened, and Camila exited. He stepped out of her path, but she stood there looking up at him even as the door closed behind her. "Excuse me," he said, moving to step past her.

"You look just like my father. Are we related?" she asked in Spanish.

Chance froze and then stepped back, causing a nurse to have to swerve to avoid bumping into him. "My bad," he apologized.

The pretty blonde gave him an appreciative look. "No problem," she stressed before continuing on her way with a look back at him over her shoulder.

The door opened again, and Chance's eyes landed on the gray-haired man lying on the hospital bed. He had but a brief glimpse as the door closed. He was surprised his heart pounded with such vigor.

Maria eyed Chance and then her daughter.

"Camila, I thought you went down to the café," she said, reaching to press a folded bill into the younger woman's hand. "Bring me something sweet to nibble on."

"But, Ma—"

"Adios, Camila," Maria said, gently nudging her daughter on her way.

With one last long look at Chance, she turned and walked down the hall to the elevators.

"You came back," Maria said, squeezing his hand. "Come, Chance. Come."

Gently, he withdrew his hand, but he followed her into the room.

"Mi amor, mi amor," she said gently in a singsong fashion. "Look who is here, *mi amor*. It is Chance, your son."

Chance stood at the foot of the bed and looked at the tall and thin man whose gaunt features could not deflect that he looked like a younger, fuller version of his father. Jeffrey opened his eyes. They were slightly tinged with yellow and glassy, but he couldn't deny when they filled with tears.

Jeffrey reached out his hand to Chance and bent his fingers, beckoning him.

For so long, when he was younger, he wondered about the moment he would meet his father. Never had he imagined it happening on his deathbed with cancer winning in the fight for his life. His hesitation was clear as Maria eyed him and then her husband. His father's hand dropped some, as if the effort exhausted him.

That evoked compassion from him, and Chance moved to the side of the bed to take his father's hand in his own. His grip lacked strength. The scent of on-coming death clung to the air around him.

"Forgive me," Jeffrey said, his Spanish accent present even in the weakened state of his tone.

Chance remained stoic even as he looked down into his father's face. He didn't know if his heart could soften to him. His mother had worked double shifts to make up for the help she did not receive from him. Even now, he didn't know if she would feel betrayed by his coming to his father's bedside.

"Forgive me?" Jeffrey asked this time.

Chance glanced across the bed to find Maria had

quietly left them alone in the room. He shifted his gaze back down to his father. It was amazing that he could look so much like a man he had never met. His imprint was undeniable.

Chance released a breath and looked up at the ceiling as the emotions from his childhood came flooding back to him. He clenched his jaw.

The grip on his hand tightened.

Chance looked down. "Why?" he asked.

Jeffrey squeezed his eyes shut, and tears fell as he shook his head.

Chance hoped to be a father one day. He knew he would do better than his own sire because he would be present, scolding when needed and loving always, but *if* he made a misstep, he would hope on his deathbed he would be forgiven. He believed you had to give what you hoped to receive for yourself.

"Te perdono," Chance said, offering this stranger the clemency he requested.

His father pulled his hand to his mouth to kiss the back of it and then made the sign of the cross as he gripped it. *"Gracias,"* he whispered up to him.

He had learned through the loss of the woman he loved that vengeance was a drawback he refused to let hinder his life again.

Passion Grove was truly home.

Ngozi adjusted the large oil painting she'd hung above her fireplace and then stood back to observe her handiwork. The artwork was alive with the vibrant colors and matched the decor of her new home in the affluent small town. It was a rental, but the Realtor said the owners may be interested in selling the four-bedroom, four-bathroom Colonial early next year.

Regardless, for the last month it was home.

"When did you get so Afrocentric?"

Ngozi sighed at the sound of her mother's voice behind her. "I don't know, Ma, maybe my name inspired me," she said as she turned and eased her hand into the pockets of her oversize coveralls.

Her father chuckled from his spot relaxing on her bright red leather sofa.

Valerie gave him a sharp eye that only made him laugh harder. "With the new hair and all this art-work everywhere, you really are taking us back to the motherland," she said, touching a large wooden African ceremonial mask that hung on the wall by the door.

Ngozi touched her faux locks, which were twisted up into a topknot. "My house, my way, Ma," she said, coming close to kiss her cheek before moving past her to close the French doors and unfortunately cut off the breeze of April air drifting in from outside.

"You know, this new and improved Ngozi is a lot chattier," Valerie said.

"Well, I like it," Horace said, rising from the sofa.

"Me, too, Dad," Ngozi agreed, looking around at the spacious family room, which had been the last of the areas she decorated.

For the first time in a long time, longer than she could remember, Ngozi had the same confidence and tenacity that made her a conqueror in the courtroom in her personal life. She enjoyed living her life by her gut instincts and not just by what she thought others wanted her to do or to be. Not living to please others was freeing.

Her parents, particularly her mother, were adjusting to discovering just who their daughter truly was.

Valerie winked at Ngozi. "If you like it, I love it," she said.

Ngozi had discovered over the last ninety days that her parents weren't as strict and judgmental as she'd thought growing up. She'd never felt so close to them.

The night she'd opened up about Haaziq, they'd discussed the impact of his death on their lives. She'd discovered that they tiptoed around her just as much as she placated them. In the end, they were a family trying to cope with a death and just didn't know how to do it.

Now if a memory of Haaziq rose, no one shied away from the thought, and instead they would share a laugh or just reminisce on the time they did get to have him in their lives. And if they were moved to a few tears, that was fine. They grieved him and got through the moment.

"Horace, you ready?" Valerie asked, reaching for her designer tote bag sitting on one of the round end tables flanking the leather sofa. "The town council is cutting the ribbon on the Spring Bazaar, and I do not want to be late."

He eyed his wife as she smoothed her white-gloved hands over the skirt of the pale apricot floral lace dress she wore. It was beautiful and fit her frame well, but it was completely over the top for a local bazaar being held on the grounds of the middle school that offered the works of artists and crafters with plenty of vendors, good food, rides and live music.

"Has she always been so extra?" Ngozi whispered to her dad as her mother reapplied her sheer coral lip gloss.

"Yes, and I love every bit of it," he said with warm appreciation in his tone.

Ngozi looked at him, clearly a man still enthralled by his wife.

I want someone to look at me that way.

Not someone. Chance.

Ngozi pushed thoughts of him away.

"I never wanted to marry until I met and eventually fell in love with your mother," Horace said, walking over to wrap his arm around his wife's waist and pull her close. They began to sway together as they looked into each other's eyes.

"Right," Valerie agreed. "And I was so career driven that at thirty-nine I began to assume I would never find love and have a family of my own...until your daddy put on the full-court press for my attention. I never assumed this man I competed with in the courtroom for so many years would turn into the love of my life."

"Same here," he agreed, doing a little shimmy and leading them into a spin.

"I tamed that dog," she teased.

"The dog tamed himself," he countered.

"So I guess your always loving that Vincent and

Associates Law also spells out VAL isn't proof enough that you're sprung?" Valerie stroked his nape.

"And you're not?" he asked, with a little jerk that pulled her body closer.

They shared an intimate, knowing laugh.

"Respect your elders, Horace," she said. "You're lucky I don't make you call me Mrs. Vincent."

"Two whole years older than me. Big deal," he said.

Ngozi looked at them with pleasure at their happiness and a bit of melancholy that she didn't have that, as well.

Her parents were in their early seventies but lived life—and looked—as if they were far younger.

"You're going to wrinkle my dress, Horace," Valerie said, not truly sounding as if she cared.

"Wait until you see what I do to it when I get you home," he said low in his throat before nuzzling his face against her neck.

Ngozi rolled her eyed. "*Helllllooo*, I'm still here. Daughter in the room," she said.

"And? How you think you got here, little girl?" Valerie asked, ending their dance with a kiss that cleared her lips of the gloss she'd just applied. "Your conception was *not* immaculate."

"But it was spectacular," Horace said.

"Don't you make us late," she said in playful warning.

Ngozi walked across the spacious family room. "Okay, let me help mosey y'all along," she said over her shoulder as she left the room and crossed the foyer to open the front door.

They followed behind her.

"Any chance you're going to change?" Valerie asked, eying the overalls.

In the past, Ngozi would have found a pretty spring dress to wear to please her mother, complete with pearls and a cardigan. "No, ma'am."

"Leave her be, Val," Horace said before leaving the house and taking the stairs down to his silver two-door Rolls Royce Wraith sitting on the paved drive.

Valerie quietly made prayer hands in supplication as she left.

"See you later at the bazaar, Ma," Ngozi said, closing the door.

She turned and leaned against it, looking at her home. She was proud she had taken a large space and infused it with warmth and color. Not even the apartment she'd shared with her husband had her personal touch. She had chosen what she thought he would like.

No, this is all me.

Ngozi closed her eyes and just enjoyed being in her own place and her own space for the first time in her life.

Ding-dong.

The doorbell startled her. Ngozi's heartbeat was racing as she turned to open the door. She smiled at Josh, one of the high school kids who served as deliverymen for The Gourmet Way, the grocery store on Main Street that specialized in delicacies.

"Hello, Ms. Johns, I have your weekly delivery," the tall freckle-faced blond said with a smile that showed off his Invisalign braces.

"Come on in," she said, closing the door when he obeyed and then leading him with the heavy black basket he carried through the family room, which opened into the gourmet kitchen.

Josh set the basket on top of the marble island.

"Are you going to the Spring Bazaar?" Ngozi asked as she removed a twenty-dollar bill from the billfold sitting with files and her laptop on the large kitchen table before the open French doors.

"As soon as my shift is over," he said, accepting the tip with a polite nod.

"See you there," she offered as he turned to leave.

"Bye, Ms. Johns."

Ngozi opened the basket and removed the perishables to place in her fridge or freezer, deciding to leave the little things like chutneys, a canister of caviar, bottles of cordials and black garlic. She did allow herself a treat of thinly sliced *soppressata*, broke a small piece off the ball of fresh mozzarella and wrapped both around a garlic-stuffed olive.

"Vegan who?" she said before taking a bite.

Mmm.

After popping the last bite into her mouth, she cleaned her moist fingertips on a napkin before reclaiming her seat at the table. She had an office upstairs in one of the spare bedrooms, but the light was the brightest and the breeze from outside the best at the kitchen table. It was Saturday, but she had a court case to prepare for in defense of an heir charged with murdering his parents.

The Skype incoming-call tone sounded from her tablet.

Ngozi eyed it, reaching over the open files with pen in hand to tap the screen and accept the video, then propping the tablet up by its case. She laughed as her goddaughter's face filled the screen and she released a spit bubble that exploded. "Hello, Aliyah," she cooed.

"Hewwoo, Godmommy!"

Ngozi arched a brow. "Really, Alessandra, I thought you were a co-CEO of a billion-dollar corporation, not offering voice characterizations for the cutest baby in the world," she drawled.

Alessandra sat Aliyah on her lap in her office and smiled into the screen over the top of her reading glasses. "I do both. I'm complex," she said with a one-shoulder shrug.

"A woman's worth," Ngozi said.

"Right...although Alek is pretty hands-on with her. I can't really complain. In the boardroom, bedroom and nursery, we are getting the job done together."

"Why can't we all be that lucky?" Ngozi said wistfully.

"*We* all could," Alessandra said with a pointed look.

Chance.

Her friend had thankfully agreed not to mention him, but it was clear from the way Alessandra stopped that his name almost tumbled from her lips.

Ngozi looked out the window at the trees neatly

surrounding the backyard without really seeing them. At a different time in their lives, what they shared could have blossomed into that lifetime of love her parents had. She smiled at the thought of Chance— older, wiser and more handsome—lovingly teasing her as they danced to their music no one else heard.

"I thought we could ride to the bazaar together," Alessandra offered.

"I'll probably walk. The school isn't that far from here," she said.

"Alek and Naim, his brother, are in London on business...so you won't be third-wheeling, as you call it."

Ngozi smiled.

"I'm on the way."

She ended the Skype call and rose to close the French doors before she grabbed her wallet and bill-fold. She dropped those items into the bright orange designer tote bag sitting on the half-moon table by the door. She used the half bath off the foyer to freshen up before sliding her feet into leather wedges and applying bright red lip gloss.

On the security screen, she saw the black 1954 Jaguar MK VII sedan that had belonged to Alessandra's father. Ngozi slid her tote onto the crook of her arm and left the house. Roje, Alessandra's driver, climbed from the car. The middle-aged man with a smooth bald head and silvery goatee looked smart and fit in his black button-up shirt and slacks as he left the car to open the rear door for her.

The scent of his cologne was nice, and Ngozi bit

back a smile as she remembered the private moments he had shared with Alessandra's mother-in-law. She could easily see how the man was hard for LuLu to resist.

"Thank you," Ngozi said to him before climbing in the rear of the car beside Aliyah's car seat.

"Soo...does Alek know about his mother and your driver?" Ngozi asked as she allowed six-month-old Aliyah to grip her index finger.

Alessandra gasped in surprise.

Ngozi gave her friend a look that said *deny it*.

"I plead the fifth."

"You can plead whatever. I *know* what I saw," Ngozi said, eyeing Roje coming around the front of the vintage car through the windshield mirror.

"What?" Alessandra asked.

Aliyah cooed as if she, too, was curious.

"You tell what you know, and I'll tell what I know. Then *we'll* keep their secret," she said.

Roje climbed into the driver's seat and eyed the women in the rearview mirror before starting the car. "Ready?" he asked, his voice deep and rich.

They both nodded and gave him a smile.

Roje eyed them oddly before pulling off down the driveway.

They rode in silence until they reached Passion Grove Middle, a stately brick building with beautiful ivy topiaries and a large playground surrounded by wrought iron finish with scrollwork. Like most community events in the small town, attendance was high, with those from neighboring cities attending the annual affair, as well.

"The elusive Lance Millner is doing a book signing?" Ngozi asked after reading the large sign as Roje pulled the car to a stop before the open gate.

"That's a first around here," Alessandra said.

"Hell, I have never seen him without that damn hat on," Ngozi said. "I have got to see this."

"Ladies, you go in and I'll search for some parking on the street," Roje said, climbing from the driver's seat to open the rear door and then retrieve the folded stroller.

"Good idea. Thanks," Alessandra said, unsnapping Aliyah from her car seat.

Ngozi climbed from the car and looked at the crowd milling around the artwork and crafts on display, the vendors selling their wares, food trucks offering tasty treats, live music offering entertainment, and a few carnival rides on the athletic fields for the children.

"Roje, I'm sure you don't want to hang around for this, so you can go and come back for us in a few," Alessandra said.

Ngozi turned just as Roje smiled and inclined his head in agreement.

"I would like to run a quick errand," he admitted.

"To Manhattan?" Alessandra asked.

LuLu Ansah lived in a beautiful penthouse apartment on the upper east side.

Roje's expression was curious as he pulled mirror shades from the front pocket of his shirt and slid them on his face. "Would you like me to pick up something for you in the city?" he asked, sidestepping her question.

"A little happiness for yourself," Alessandra said.

"I wish," he admitted. "Sometimes life gets in the way."

Ngozi thought of Chance. Her love had not been enough to stop life from getting in their way.

Chance sat on his private plane, looking out the window at the clouds seeming to fade as darkness descended. In the two weeks since he'd met his father, he hadn't returned to see him again. Instead, he had continued his tour around the world. Paris. London. China. And now he was headed to his estate in Cabrera.

He pulled his wallet from his back pocket and opened it to remove the well-worn envelope.

More than anything, it was his siblings he was avoiding. He wasn't ready. Chance was well aware that he was a man of considerable means, and he had no idea what Pandora's box of problems he was setting himself up for with the inclusion of so many new people in his life. Suddenly. And perhaps suspiciously.

Was his father's sudden need for reconciliation more about his guilt as death neared, or his discovery of his sudden billionaire status?

I'd be a fool not to consider that.

He was just as aware he was in a position to help people who were his family by default. By blood.

I'd be an asshole not to consider that.

Chance put the envelope back in its safe spot inside his wallet before rising from his ergonomic reclining chair to walk to his bedroom suite. He was exhausted from his quests and ready to settle down in one spot to rest and relax. Nothing spoke more of relaxation to him than being on his estate in Cabrera.

Except making love to Ngozi.

He thought of her. Moments they had shared in fun or in sex. Her smile. Her scent. Her touch.

Damn. When will I get over her?

He flopped over onto his back and unlocked his iPhone to pull up a picture of her in his bed, her body covered by a sheet as she playfully stuck her tongue out at him.

When will my love go away?

He deleted the picture and dropped his phone onto the bed, wishing like hell it was that easy to erase her from his thoughts and his heart.

"Congratulations on another win, Ngozi."

"Do you even know what an L is?"

"Congrats."

"Ngozi, good win."

"District attorneys hate to see you coming, Counselor."

Ngozi kept her facade cool, like it was just another day at work, accepting each bit of praise as she made her way through the offices of Vincent and Associates Law. She smiled, thinking of her parents' inside joke about the acronym. This was the house Horace

Vincent had built, and his love for his wife was in the name.

And now I'm making my mark.

Instead of heading to her office, Ngozi turned and rode the elevator up one story to the executive offices of the senior partners. "Good afternoon, Ms. Johns," the receptionist for the senior partners greeted her.

"Good afternoon, Evelyn," she said, always making sure in her years at the firm to know the name of each staff member.

To her, that was one of the true signs of leadership.

"Can I get anything for you?" Evelyn asked.

"Not a thing but thank you. I just want to hang out in my dad's office for a little bit," she said softly, moving past the reception desk.

"Actually, he's in today."

Ngozi paused and looked back at her in surprise. "Really?" she said, unsure why she suddenly felt nervous.

Evelyn nodded before turning her attention to the ringing phone.

Large executive offices were arranged in a horseshoe pattern around the reception area, but it was the office dominating the rear wall of the floor toward which she walked. Her briefcase lightly slapped against the side of her leg in the silk oxblood suit she wore with matching heels. Reaching the white double doors, she knocked twice before opening the door.

"Getting my office ready for me, Pops?" she quipped, but the rest of her words faded as all five managing partners of Vincent and Associates Law turned to eye her.

Ngozi dropped her head abashedly. "My apologies, I thought my father was here alone," she said, moving forward to offer her hand to each partner.

"It will be yours one day, Ngozi," her father said as she came to stand beside his desk. "Just as soon as you're ready."

She nodded in agreement. Her father offered her no shortcuts to success, and she never expected any. She would become the principal partner of the firm her father started by consistent wins and proven leadership, bringing in high-level clients with strong billable hours. She was just thirty, and although she was making good headway, she had a long journey ahead of her.

Ngozi didn't want it any other way.

"More wins like today definitely doesn't hurt," Angela Brinks, a sharp and decisive blonde in her early sixties, offered.

"Thank you," Ngozi said, holding her briefcase in front of her. "It was a tough acquittal, but my staff pulled it out and the client is heavily considering moving some other corporate business our direction."

"I understand you played a role in Chance Castillo putting VAL on retainer to oversee his corporate and business matters," Greg Landon said.

Chance.

Her heart seemed to pound against her chest.

She hadn't known that. She made it her business to avoid even discovering the outcome of his case.

"Everything okay?" her father asked.

Get it together, Ngozi.

"Yes," she said. "Actually, I'm going to leave you all to the meeting I interrupted. I actually have another case to prep."

"Federal, right?" Monique Reeves asked. She was the newest managing partner—and the youngest, at forty-five.

Ngozi found the woman smart, formidable and tenacious—her role model, particularly as an African American woman.

"I would offer you my expertise in that arena... but I don't think you need it. Still, the offer is on the table," Monique said.

"Thank you, Monique, that's good to know," she said before moving toward the door. "Have a good day, everyone."

As soon as she exited and closed the door, Ngozi dropped onto the long leather bench against the wall, letting her briefcase land on the floor as she pressed one hand to the side of her face and the other against her racing heart.

Chance. Chance. Chance.

Just when she had a nearly complete day without his invading her thoughts and creating a craving... BOOM! Nearly four months since their breakup and she was not over him.

Not yet.

Ngozi cleared her throat and stood with her briefcase in hand as she stiffened her back and notched her chin a bit higher, then made her way down the long length of the hall.

But I will be...one day.

I hope.

Chapter 10

One month later

Ngozi brought her swift run to an end as she came to Main Street of Passion Grove. She released puffs of air through pursed lips and checked her vitals and mileage via her Fitbit. She waved and smiled to those townspeople she knew as she continued to move her feet in place while she waited for her heart rate to gradually decline.

Feeling thirsty, she walked down the block toward the bakery, pausing a moment at the display in the window of the high-end boutique, Spree, that offered the latest trend in designer clothing. A beautiful silver beaded sheath dress with a short hem caught her eye, and she knew if she wasn't still sweaty and hot from a run, she would have gone into the boutique to try it on. "Another time," she promised herself, continuing on her way.

The large black metal bell sounded as she opened the door to La Boulangerie. The scent of fresh-brewed coffee and decadent sweets filled the air. There was a small line of customers awaiting treats in the pastry shop decorated like old-world Europe, with modern accents and brick walls. It was a warm Saturday in June, and the townspeople were out and about, milling around their small downtown area.

She checked incoming messages on her phone as she waited her turn. Soft hairs seemed to tickle her nape and she kept smoothing them with her free hand, also aware that she suddenly felt a nervousness that made her wonder if she'd caught a flu bug or something. When the hairs stood on end, she turned but didn't recognize any of the people in line behind her.

"Welcome to La Boulangerie. How may I help you?"

Ngozi faced forward. Her eyes widened to see Alessandra's cousin and her former client behind the counter. "Marisa, you work here?" she asked, her surprise clear.

Alessandra's family, the Dalmounts, was a super-rich family of prominence. She doubted her salary matched the weekly stipend Alessandra allotted her entire family, following the tradition her father had started when he was the head of the family.

Marisa, a beautiful young woman in her late twenties with a massive head full of natural curls that rested on her petite shoulders, smiled and shrugged one shoulder. "I've never had a job and I have to start somewhere," she said, her voice soft and raspy as if she could bring true justice to a soulful song. Although Ngozi recalled that her deceased father was Mexican, there was no hint of a Spanish accent.

"That's true, but I'm surprised Alessandra couldn't get you something entry level at ADG," Ngozi said, taking a small step back to eye the desserts on display in the glass case.

"I'm just starting to think a handout from your rich family isn't the best way for me," she said, sounding vague.

"Not many young women would feel that way," Ngozi said, pushing aside her curiosity. "I'm proud of you," she offered, feeling odd giving praise to a woman not far from her own age.

"Thanks," Marisa said.

"Hey, Bill," Ngozi said, smiling at the man with shoulder-length blond hair pulled back in a ponytail. As always, his black apron with Bill the Pâtissier embroidered on it was in place.

"Afternoon," he said, his tone appreciative as he gave her a slow once-over in her pink form-fitting running gear.

Bill wants some chocolate in his life.

"Marisa, I'll take a bottle of water and a fresh fruit cup for my walk home," she said, politely ignoring his flirty look. She was used to it. Bill had long ago let his intentions be known, and she had always turned him down gently.

He just chuckled at her deflection before heading back to the rear of the bakery.

"Coming right up," Marisa said, using the back of her hand to swipe away a long tendril that escaped from her top knot before pulling on gloves.

Ngozi was tempted to purchase a mini walnut Danish ring, able to tell it was packed with cinnamon sugar. She wasn't ever going vegan, but she did try to fit in healthy eating when she could. *Still...that Danish is looking like a treat.*

"Let me get a walnut Danish ring, too," she said, pulling her credit card from the zippered pocket on the sleeve of her running jacket.

Marisa gave her a knowing smile as she used tongs to slide the treat into a small brown paper bag with the bakery's logo. She took the card and handed Ngozi her treats and a small foil packet with a wet wipe for her hands. Soon she returned with her receipt. "Thank you and come again," she said.

"Bye, Marisa. I will," Ngozi said, turning away with a smile.

She tucked the water bottle under her arm and the Danish in her pocket before opening the wet wipe packet to wipe her hands.

"Ngozi."

Her body froze, but her heart raced a marathon, and those hairs on her nape stood on end. Now the nervous energy was familiar.

Chance.

Turning toward his voice, she spotted him sitting at a bistro table in the corner of the pastry shop with Alek. She hadn't even noticed them there. Chance unbent his tall frame—his tall, well-proportioned, strong frame—and waved an inviting hand to an empty chair across from him.

Ngozi hesitated.

They had done so well avoiding each other for all these months. And now, just like that, out of the clear blue sky, here they were.

Fate?

Perhaps.

Finally, she moved toward him, and it was as if everything else in the bakery outside of her line of vision on him blurred. With every step that brought her closer to him, her nerves felt more and more frayed.

Alek tossed the last of his powdered doughnut into his mouth before wiping his hands with a napkin and rising. "Good to see you, Ngozi," he said.

She just nodded, never taking her eyes off Chance.

Alek looked between his friend and his wife's best friend before walking out of the pastry shop as if he knew his presence was suddenly forgotten.

Chance reached around her to pull the chair out.

"Still the gentleman," she said, offering him a polite smile before she sat down and crossed one leg over the other.

"Of course, of course," Chance said, offering her a charming smile as he sat back down.

Ngozi set her water and the plastic container of fruit on the table as she eyed how good he looked in a navy tracksuit with one of his dozen or so Patek watches on his wrist. "You look good, Chance," she admitted, picking up the bottle to open and take a sip.

"So do you," he said, eyeing her before shifting his gaze out the window of the storefront.

They both fell silent.

Then they spoke at once.

"Ngozi—"

"Chance—"

They laughed.

"Our goddaughter is growing up fast," Ngozi said, searching for a neutral topic.

Chance nodded. "I got her a baby Lambo car. She'll be driving around their courtyard in no time."

"Only you would buy a baby a mini-Lambo," she said. "Is it pink or bright red?"

His smile widened. "Fire red, of course."

"Of course," she agreed.

More silence.

So many questions were sitting on the tip of her tongue, ready to tumble out.

"You're still running?" Chance asked.

Ngozi looked pensive. "Running from what?" she asked, instantly nervous an argument would ensue.

Chance shook his head. "No, I meant running. Exercising. Jogging," he said, making back-and-forth motions with his fists as if he were running.

"Oh," Ngozi said. "My bad. Yeah. I'm still running, addicted to the high of it. You?"

He nodded. "I did ten miles this morning," he said.

"I did like five around the lake and then came here for a little snack before I head back to my house," she said.

"Your house?" he asked.

Their eyes met.

Ngozi looked away first, opening the container to pop a grape into her mouth. "I moved out of my parents'," she said, lifting the container toward him in offering.

He picked it up and poured a few grapes into his hand. "How is it?"

"The house?" she asked.

"Living alone for the first time."

They shared another look.

"Necessary," she admitted. "It was time to trust myself to be who and what I truly want to be. Right?"

Those were the words he had given to her that night they'd ended their relationship. She could tell he caught the reference instantly.

"I only wanted the best for you," he explained.

Ngozi leaned forward to grasp his hand atop the table. "No, I'm not throwing shade. I needed to learn to want the best for me, too," she said.

He looked down at their hands clasped together and stroked her thumb with his.

Ngozi shivered, feeling a rush she could only guess was like an addict getting their first hit of drugs after a long break of sobriety. Not wanting to stir up the desire for him for which she was still in recovery, Ngozi gently withdrew her hand.

Chance instantly felt the loss of her touch. He looked down at his empty hand for a few beats before closing it into a fist.

He hadn't expected to run into Ngozi today. Even

with sharing godparent duties for baby Aliyah and each of their best friends being married to each other, they hadn't crossed paths. When she walked into the bakery, he'd watched her, but he wasn't even sure he wanted to make his presence known to her. They had moved on from each other. Survived the breakup.

He was so intent on letting her go about her day that he never let Alek, who had his back to the door, know that she was there. But he never lost sight of her. Never took his attention off her. He couldn't deny that he was pleased to see her again. And the jealousy sparked by Bill the Surfing Dude flirting with her could not be denied.

And when she reached for the door handle to leave, he had to stop her.

Now she pulled away from his touch.

"I saw they did a news story on your pro bono work," he offered, shifting away from sensitive subjects.

Ngozi nodded. "Recently, I've been doing more of that, but I think it's necessary. Not everyone is as privileged as we are to afford proper legal representation."

"People forget I grew up in the hood, but I have never forgotten, and I remember young dudes getting locked up for small crimes but staying in jail for months or longer because no one could afford bail or owned property to put up as collateral," he said.

"Maybe you could donate to help the underserved with that issue," Ngozi offered, tearing the label off the water bottle. "I'm thinking of setting up a non-profit to do just that."

Nervous?

The thought that he still affected her made him anxious.

"Yes, or you could refer such cases to Second Chances, the nonprofit I've already set up to do that," he said, remembering all of her urgings for him to give back more with his wealth.

Remember, to whom much is given, much is required, Chance. God didn't bless you so that you can buy thousand-dollar burgers and million-dollar cars.

She looked taken aback. He gave her a wide smile, enjoying it. "Growth," he pointed out.

"Right," she agreed. "I will definitely send some referrals your way. Maybe I could talk to the partners about making an annual donation. It would be a good look for the firm."

Chance looked around the busy little pastry shop to avoid getting lost in her deep eyes. "So, we're teaming up?" he asked.

"For a noble cause? Definitely," she said without hesitation.

His heart hammered, and he could hardly believe that this woman still had the power to weaken him at the knees. "And more?" he asked.

Now, that caused her to noticeably pause.

"You know what, forget it," he said, shifting in his seat as he took a sip of the cup of Brazilian coffee he'd purchased. "You may have met someone."

"I haven't."

He cut his eyes up at her over the rim of his black cup. She didn't look away.

Chance set the cup down as he wrestled with the myriad feelings now swirling inside him, creating their own little storm.

"Have you?" she asked, her voice soft.

He shook his head. "How could I? When I *love* you, Ngozi," he confessed.

Her eyes widened, and she covered her mouth with her hand that trembled.

"I dropped the lawsuit when I realized that not having you in my life hurt far more than losing a million damn dollars on a stupid wedding I shouldn't be having anyway because she was *not* the love of my life," he said with such passion, leaning forward to take her free hand in his.

"You are, Ngozi. You are the love of *my* life."

Her grip tightened around his hand.

"I have tried to forget. Tried to move on. Tried not to dream about you. Tried like hell not to miss you. And until I saw you today, I convinced myself that I succeeded, but I didn't," he said, licking his suddenly dry mouth as his breaths quickened. He pressed a hand to his chest over his pounding heart, patting it. "You are in here. All of it. And I don't know what to do but love you. To have you. To fight for you. To take care of you. To make love to you. To be happier than I have ever been…with you."

Again, she tugged her hand, freeing it of his clasp as she rose, gathered her items and strode away.

His heart ached at her denial of his love. He clenched

his jaw and curled his fingers into a fist to fight the regret that filled him as he watched her walk away from him. She tossed the water bottle and the fruit cup in the trash can before walking back over.

He stiffened his spine and cleared his throat, preparing for another of their epic arguments—those he did not miss. *Especially in public.*

"Let's go," Ngozi said, extending her hand.

His confusion showed on his face. "Where?"

"To my house, to show you just how much I *love* you, Chance Castillo," she said with a sassy and tiny bite of her bottom lip.

His desire stirred in an instant.

As he grabbed his keys and took her hand to follow her, he was thankful that his heated blood didn't rush to his groin and leave him to walk out of the shop with a noticeable hard-on.

They barely made it through the front door.

Ngozi gasped as Chance pressed her body against it with his, holding her face with his hands as he kissed her with unrelenting passion that left her breathless and panting. And when he lowered his body against hers, layering her with hot kisses to her neck and the soft cleavage he revealed as he unzipped her jacket, she spread her arms and foolishly tried to grasp the wood of the door, looking for something to cling to as her hunger for him sent her reeling.

With each press of his lips or lick of his tongue against her skin—the valley of her breasts in her lace sports bra, her navel, the soft skin just above the edge of her undies—she lost a bit of sanity.

And cared not one bit.

Chance stripped her free of her clothing and her undergarments, leaving her naked and exposed to his eyes and his pleasure. And he enjoyed her long neck, rounded shoulders, long limbs, both pert breasts with large areolae surrounding her hard nipples and clean-shaven vulva with plump lips that only hinted at the pleasures it concealed.

With his hard and long erection pressing against the soft material of his pants, Chance hoisted Ngozi's naked body against his and carried her the short distance to the stairs, laying her on the steps and then spreading her smooth thighs as he knelt between them.

"I'm sweaty," she protested, pressing a hand to his forehead when he dipped his head above her core.

Chance looked up at her. "I don't give a good god-damn," he said low in his throat before brushing her hand away and dipping his head to lightly lick and then suck her warm fleshy bud.

He ached at the feel of it pulsing against his tongue, and when she cried out, arching her hips up off the steps as she shifted her hands to the back of his head, he sucked a little harder. Feeling heady from the scent and taste of her, Chance stroked inside her with his tongue.

"Chance," she gasped, her thighs snapping closed on his shoulders as she tried to fight off the pleasure.

He shook his head, denying her, not caring if he pushed her over the brink into insanity as he pressed her legs back open and continued his passionate on-slaught with a deep guttural moan.

"Please...please," she gasped.

He raised his head, his eyes intense as he took in hers brimming with pleasure, and her mouth gaped in wonder. "Please what? Please stop or please make me come?" he asked, his words breezing across her moist flesh.

The sounds of her harsh breathing filled the air as she looked down at him. "Make me come," she whispered. "Please."

Chance smiled like a wolf as he lowered his head and circled her bud with his tongue before flicking the tip against the smooth flesh with rapid speed meant to tease, to titillate, to arouse and to make his woman go crashing headfirst into an explosive orgasm. He had to lock his arms around her thighs to keep her in place as she wrestled between enjoying the pleasure and being driven mad by it.

And while she was deep in the throes of her cli-max, he rose from her just long enough to shed his clothes and sheathe himself. To be as naked as she. To relieve his aching erection. He hungered for her and could not wait one more moment to be inside her.

Chance thrust his hard inches inside her swiftly. Deeply.

Ngozi reached out blindly and gripped the wrought iron railing of her staircase, not caring about the hard edge of the step bearing into her lower back or how each of his wild thrusts caused her buttocks to be chafed by the wood.

Chance lifted up his upper body to look down at her as he worked his hips back and forth. Each stroke caused his hardness to slide against the moist ridges of her intimacy. She was lost. To time. To place. To reason.

"Here it comes," he whispered down to her.

She gasped as his inches got harder right as he quickened his thrusts and climaxed inside her, flinging his head back, the muscles of his body tensing as he went still and roughly cried out in pure pleasure.

Wrapping her ankles behind his strong thighs, Ngozi worked her hips in a downward motion that pulled on the length of him.

Chance swore.

Ngozi had a devilish little smile, taking over as she worked her walls and flexed her hips to send him over the edge into the same mindless pleasure he brought her. And when he gave a shriek similar to the falsetto of an opera singer and tried to back out of her, she locked him in place and continued to work every bit of his release from him.

"Please," he begged, wincing and biting his bottom lip.

"Please what? Huh? Please stop, or please make me come some more?" she asked, her tone flirtatiously mocking in between hot little pants of her own.

"*Please* stop," he pleaded.

She stopped her sex play, but with him still inside

her, she sat up and pulled his face down to kiss his mouth a dozen or more times. "Don't you ever forget that I love you, too," she whispered against his lips, searching his eyes and seeing that all her doubts of his feelings for her had been for naught.

The next weeks for Chance and Ngozi seemed to fly by. Happiness and being in love had a way of snatching time. And they were happy. Their time apart had brought on changes both needed to be able to love someone properly.

Life was good.

Ding-dong.

Ngozi was lounging on her sofa reading through briefs. She picked up her tablet and checked the security system, frowning at the sight of Chance's mother, Esmerelda, standing on her front doorstep.

Well, life was almost good.

She dropped the tablet and the back of her head onto the sofa as she released a heavy sigh. *What could she possibly want?*

Ngozi avoided Esmerelda at all costs. Although she and Chance had reconciled, they'd never discussed his mother or her clear dislike of her son's choice for love. "Hell, I'm not the one who left him at the altar," she muttered, rising from the sofa to pad barefoot out of the room and over to the front door.

Ding-dong.

Ngozi paused and frowned with an arched brow. "A'ight now," she warned.

She allowed herself one final inhale and exhale

of breath with a prayer for patience before opening the door with a smile that felt too wide and too false. "Hello, Ms. Diaz. How can I help you?" she said.

Esmerelda was a beautiful woman of just her late forties. Having had Chance at such a young age, she physically did not look that much older than him. She stood there in a strapless red dress with her hair in a messy topknot. Ngozi couldn't deny that she was beautiful.

"May I come in?" she asked, looking past Ngozi's shoulder.

"Chance isn't here," she immediately explained.

"Yes, I know," Esmerelda said. "He's at the offices for Second Chances."

Very true. Yes, he was. Of course, she would know that. Esmerelda and Chance were very close, Ngozi knew, but she also felt they were too close. *Hell, does she think anyone is good enough for him?*

"So, may I come in?" Esmerelda asked again.

Ngozi nodded and stepped back, pulling the door open along with her. "Right this way," she said, closing the door and leading her into the family room.

"That is a beautiful painting," Esmerelda said, moving to stand in front of the fireplace and look up at the artwork Ngozi had hung there the day of the Spring Bazaar.

Three svelte women in floral print dresses with large wide-brimmed hats that covered their faces sat in a field of flowers. "It is *The Gossiping Neighbors* by—"

"Juan Eduardo Martinez," Esmerelda provided,

turning to offer her a smile. "I am very familiar with his work."

"Chance introduced me to him and some other Dominican painters with the art he has at his house," Ngozi said, crossing her arms over her chest in the strapless woven cotton jumpsuit she wore.

"Yes, *I* introduce *him* to our culture any time we are back in Cabrera," she said with pride.

Ngozi nodded. "We flew there last weekend and it really is a beautiful city, Ms. Diaz," she said.

Esmerelda looked around at the room, taking in the vibrant colors and artwork. "Do you mean that or are you just saying it?" she asked.

"I mean it or I wouldn't have said it," Ngozi said, feeling offended.

Esmerelda looked surprised by Ngozi's push back. "I don't know," she said with a shrug and downturn of her ruby red lips as she dragged a finger across the edge of the wooden table.

The hell...

"Ms. Diaz, I love your son. I r*eally* do. I mean, I thought I would never be blessed with happiness after losing my husband. At first I didn't know what I did to deserve a second chance. I actually thought I didn't, but now I know I am just as good and decent and caring as he is. We are *good* for each other," Ngozi stressed. "And if you can't see that I make your son happy, then you just don't want him to be happy with me or maybe anybody else. I just really wished you had been this vigilant with Helena and saved him the heartache and shame."

Esmerelda's eyes lit up and she rubbed her fingers together, like she was excited by Ngozi's spunk and candor. "Hello, Ngozi Johns, it's nice to finally meet the *real* you," she said, extending her hand.

Ngozi looked down at it guardedly. "Huh?" she asked.

"I thought you were a phony blowhard like the Blonde Devil, and it's good to see a difference in you," she explained, her hand still offered. "I fed you the spiciest meal I have ever cooked, and you still swallowed it down to avoid angering Chance's mother. You wouldn't even speak up for yourself. I saw you as docile and weak. That is not the type of woman my son needs."

Ngozi was surprised at the woman's discernment. They'd met just once, and she saw right through the facade.

"I told him this and my Chance kept insisting that you were fiery, strong and had no problem telling him when he was wrong. I wanted to see this for myself and I didn't...until just now," Esmerelda said, actually offering Ngozi a smile. "I know my son. Sometimes, not all the time, but *sometimes* he needs to be challenged and pushed. Push him to be the best man he can be, and then my job can be done, Ngozi."

She nodded, feeling relief as she finally took Esmerelda's hand into her own. "I will because he does the same for me."

"Good," Esmerelda said, releasing her hand and turning to open her tote to remove a teal canister with delicate flowers. She handed it to Ngozi. "Recipes of my son's favorite Dominican dishes. Learn to feed him something besides sex. *Bueno?*"

Ngozi took the can and laughed. *"Si,"* she said, holding the canister to her chest.

Esmerelda reached for her purse and headed out of the room, pausing at the entrance. "The only two secrets I want you to keep from Chance are that you have those recipes and that I was here today," she said before turning and leaving.

Ngozi didn't have a chance to walk her to the door.

Instead, she opened the canister and sifted through the recipe cards. They were photocopies of the originals Esmerelda obviously wasn't ready to part with.

Feed him something besides sex.

Ngozi could only laugh.

Chance was watching television as they lounged in Ngozi's master suite, having decided to spend the night at her home in Passion Grove instead of at his in Alpine. He glanced over at where she had been reading Colson Whitehead's *Underground Railroad*. The book was lying on the lounge chair in front of the window, and she stared outside at the late summer night.

"Something wrong?" he asked.

Ngozi glanced over at him with a soft smile. "Today would have been my brother's birthday," she said.

Chance used the remote to turn the television off and then rolled off the bed in nothing but his sleep pants to walk over and straddle the lounge as he sat closely behind her. He pressed a kiss to her shoulder and then her nape. Finally, she had shared more with him about her brother's death and its impact on her family's life, just as he told her about meeting his father and discovering he had three half siblings—none of which he was prepared to deal with in the manner it called for. Ngozi had made sure he knew that she wanted him to reach out and meet his siblings sooner rather than later. It was clear her longing for her deceased brother intensified her feelings on his relationship, or lack thereof, with his siblings.

"If he was here, what would you give him for his birthday?" he asked, redirecting his thoughts back to her as he leaned to the side to watch her beautiful profile.

"Oh wow, I never thought about it," she said, looking reflective. "He used to love comic books, so I would've bought out a whole theater and watched *Black Panther* with him," she said, nodding. "He would've loved that movie."

"Or you could have just brought him over to my theater at the house," Chance reminded her, massaging her upper arms.

"True," she agreed. "Sometimes I forget you're a billionaire."

"And that's one of the reasons I want to marry you," he said, meaning to surprise her with his admission.

He felt her body go stiff before she turned on the lounge to face him.

"Chance," she said.

"Ngozi," he returned, digging into the pocket of his pants and removing the box he had placed there.

The plan had been to slip it under the pillows and propose after making love to her, but the moment seemed perfect.

"Whoo," she exclaimed as she caught sight of the large diamond solitaire atop a band of diamonds.

"Are you saying yes?" he asked, feeling so much love for her and no fear of laying his heart on the line once again.

"Are you *asking* me?" she said gently with a pointed look at the floor.

"Right," he agreed, chuckling as he rose from the seat to lower his body to one knee and take her hand in his.

"Marry me, Ngozi, and love me just the way I need you to, and I promise to love and to cherish you just as you need to be loved and cherished. I want nothing more than to create a family with you. To love and be tempted by you for the rest of my life," he said earnestly, hiding none of his love for her.

Ngozi nodded. "I will love you forever and always, Chance Castillo," she swore as he slid the hefty ring onto her finger.

"Mi tentacion," he whispered to her as he rose and pulled her body up against his and kissed her with enough love and passion to last a lifetime.

Epilogue

Three months later

Ngozi felt sexy as she came down the stairs of Chance's mansion in Alpine in the beautiful silver beaded sheath dress she'd seen in the window of Spree the very same day she reconciled with Chance. She had returned to the upscale boutique and purchased the dress the very next day. She now finally had just the right opportunity to wear it.

A celebration.

She looked over at Chance, looking ever so handsome in his black-on-black tuxedo as he awaited her. *Life is good.*

Chance's foundation, Second Chances, had just received a multimillion-dollar grant to help fund its philanthropic efforts toward underserved and sorely underrepresented lower-income defendants unable to afford bail or bond. With Ngozi's involvement as cochair of the board, the foundation's efforts would also expand to recruit skilled attorneys for pro bono work, including helping innocent men serving time for crimes they did not commit. Together, Chance and Ngozi were determined to effect change with the unfair treatment of people of color within the judicial system.

"Ready?" Ngozi called over to him, striking a pose.

Chance turned, and his eyes instantly went to the short hem lightly stroking her legs midthigh. "Worth the wait, Ngozi," he said, now looking at her face as he came over to her.

They shared a brief but passionate kiss.

When his hands rose to grip her buttocks, she reluctantly shook her head. "We have a whole party and all our family and friends waiting for us at Alek and Alessandra's," she reminded him, using her thumb to rub her crimson gloss from his lips.

"To *hell* with that party," he growled low in his throat.

"Don't you want to celebrate the sale of your second app, Mr. Tech King?" she teased.

He smiled, and it slowly broadened. "Tech King, huh?"

She shrugged one bare shoulder. "*Forbes'* words, not mine," she said, accepting his hand as they crossed the foyer together.

"Not bad for a kid from the projects?" Chance asked as he opened the front door for her.

She glanced up and stroked his cheek as he passed. "Not bad at all," she assured him.

The sun had disappeared, but the summer evening was still warm as they made their way to Chance's new white Lamborghini—a celebratory gift.

He deserves it.

She looked around at the beautiful grounds of his estate before climbing inside the car. "You sure you're not going to miss all this?" she asked him once he was behind the wheel in the driver's seat.

"We're building from scratch. I'll be fine," he assured her.

Ngozi covered his hand on the stick shift with her own. "Good, because I really want our home base to be in Passion Grove," she said as she eyed the ornate bronzed for-sale sign just outside his exterior gate.

She had gladly given up her rental. Its purpose in her newfound independence had been served.

Chance chuckled. "Can you believe I used to make fun of Alek for moving to a small town?" he asked, accelerating the sports car forward.

"Yes, but Passion Grove is no ordinary small town," she said, thinking of the ability to maintain its charms but still perfectly blend with luxury.

"Damn straight it's not."

Chance pulled the car to a smooth stop at a red light. His hand went to one of her exposed thighs.

She released a little grunt of pleasure. "I can't wait to let everyone in on our secret, Mr. Castillo," she said.

Chance smiled as he looked over at her. "Me either, Mrs. Castillo," he said.

Just that morning they had followed their impulses and flew to Vegas to get married. Neither longed for a huge event after their past experiences with such—his nuptials never happened and hers led to anything but marital bliss.

They chose to focus on their marriage and not the wedding.

"My *tentadora*," Chance said, indulging himself with a kiss.

"Will I always be your *temptress*?" she asked, her voice and her eyes soft with her love for him.

"Until death do us part."

"Now *that* sounds tempting."

* * * * *

SNOWBOUND WITH THE SOLDIER

JENNIFER FAYE

This book is dedicated to the real life Sly. A beautiful, sweet black cat who crossed my path and stole my heart. She was my muse for this heart-touching story.

Sly, you passed through our lives far too quickly. You are missed.

CHAPTER ONE

OLD MAN WINTER huffed and puffed, rattling the doors of the Greene Summit Resort. Kara Jameson turned her back on the dark, blustery night. She didn't relish heading out into the declining weather to navigate her way home after a very long day at work.

She took a moment to admire the massive evergreen standing in the lobby of what had once been one of Pennsylvania's premier ski destinations. The twinkling white lights combined with the sparkling green and red decorations would normally fill her with holiday cheer, but not tonight. Not even the rendition of "Jingle Bells" playing softly in the background could tempt her to hum along.

The resort had been sold. The somber thought weighed heavily on her shoulders. It didn't help that rumors were running rampant that all the management positions were being replaced. Why did it have to happen with Christmas only a few weeks away?

Everything will work out. Everything will work out. She repeated the mantra over and over in her mind, anxious to believe the old adage. But something in her gut said nothing would ever be the same again.

"Kara?"

The deep baritone voice came from behind her. She froze. Her gaze remained locked on a red bell-shaped ornament as her mind processed the sound. Even in the two syllables of her name, she knew that voice, knew the way her name rolled off his tongue as sweet as candy.

Jason Smith.

It couldn't be. He'd sworn he would never come back.

"Kara, won't you even look at me?"

Her gaze shifted to the glass doors that led to the parking lot. Her feet refused to cooperate, remaining cemented to the swirled golden pattern on the hotel carpet. Seven years ago, she'd bolted out those exact doors after Jason had broken their engagement. Back then she'd been unsure and confused by the depth of her emotions. Since then life had given her a crash course in growing up. Running was no longer her style.

She sucked in a deep breath, leveled her shoulders and turned.

Clear blue eyes stared back at her. A slow, easy grin lifted the tired lines around Jason's eyes. She blinked, but he was still there.

This couldn't be happening. The overtime and lack of sleep must be catching up with her.

"Are you okay?" He reached out to her.

She jumped back before he could touch her. Words rushed up her throat, but clogged in her mouth. She pressed her lips together and willed her heart to slow. Her pulse pounded in her ears as her fists clenched at her sides. A breath in. A breath out.

"You're so pale. Sit down." He gestured to one of the overstuffed couches surrounding the stone fireplace. "You look like you've seen a ghost."

She didn't move. This surreal moment struck her as a clip from a movie—a visit from the ghost of Christmas past. Only, this wasn't a Hollywood soundstage and he wasn't an actor.

She studied the man before her, trying to make sense of things. The dark scruff obscuring his boyish features was a new addition, as was the two-inch scar trailing up the right side of his jaw. His hardened appearance was a visual reminder of the military life he'd chosen over her. Her fingers longed to reach out and trace the uneven skin of his jaw, but instead she gripped the strap of her tote even tighter. A bit older and a little scuffed up, but it was most definitely Jason.

Just pretend he's a mere acquaintance from years ago, not the man who threw your love back in your face and walked away without any explanation.

"Jason Smith. I can't believe you're here," she said, trying her best to sound casual.

"Actually, I go by Jason Greene these days...."

The fact he now used his mother's maiden name came as a surprise, but Kara supposed she shouldn't find it too shocking, knowing the stormy relationship between him and his father. The name change had presumably contributed to her inability to track him down and notify him of his father's failing health. A question teetered on her tongue, but she clamped her lips shut. Playing catch-up with Jason was akin to striking a match near fireworks. One wrong move and it'd blow up in her face. Best to stick to safe topics.

His gaze implored her for an answer, but to what? She'd lost track of the strained conversation. "What did you say?"

"How are you?"

He wanted to exchange pleasantries as though they'd parted on good terms? She didn't have time to beat around the bush. She should already be home, getting dinner for her daughter before they went over her homework.

"When you left Pleasant Valley, you swore you'd never

return. So what happened? What finally changed your mind?"

His expression hardened. If he'd been expecting a warm welcome, he'd been sadly mistaken.

He shrugged. "Things change."

Well, most things did, and generally not for the better, but not in Jason's case. He hadn't gained so much as a beer gut or a receding hairline. Even the jagged scar on his face added to his sexiness.

Kara's gaze rose to meet his. At first glance, she thought his intense blue eyes were the same as she remembered, but a closer inspection revealed a hard glint in them. He no longer resembled the warm, lighthearted guy she'd dated for nearly four years. Or had he been that way all along? Had those rose-colored glasses she'd been wearing back then obscured his real character? Had she ever truly known him at all?

Jason hitched his thumbs in his jeans pockets. "I'm sorry about what happened between us. I handled it poorly."

"You certainly did."

"If I could explain, I would, but I can't—"

"Don't." She held up a hand, stalling his too little, too late explanation. "Nothing you say will change what happened."

Her pride refused to let on that his presence affected her, that even after all this time she longed to know what had changed his mind about marrying her. She reconciled herself to the fact that she was better off not knowing—not prying open that door to her past.

Jason shifted his weight from one foot to the other. "I guess it was too much to hope that you'd be willing to put the past behind us."

She lifted her chin, drawing on the strength she'd used

to manage this place in the recent absence of her boss, who also happened to be Jason's father. "I've moved on."

It'd taken time—lots of time—but she'd gotten over him and the way her life had unraveled after he'd dumped her. She refused to let him get under her skin again. Besides, she had enough on her plate already.

After working her way up through the ranks, to now be dismissed from her hard-earned position would be utterly demoralizing. She'd like to think she was needlessly worrying, but the rumors said the new owners wanted their own people running the show—people with more education and experience.

She went to step around Jason, but he snagged hold of her arm. "Wait. I need to apologize."

Even through her coat she could feel his warmth radiating into her body. She yanked at her arm, to no avail.

"Let go," she said with a hard edge. He couldn't just worm his way past her defenses with an empty apology. She refused to let him off the hook that easily. "If you were truly sorry, you'd have said something before now. You wouldn't have ignored me all these years or returned your father's letters unopened."

His hand slipped from her arm. "You know about that?"

She tightened her hold on the strap of the tote bag slung over her shoulder, which held the red scarf she was knitting for Jason's father for Christmas. "Yes. He told me. After you left, he was never quite the same. Not knowing if you were dead or alive seemed to age him overnight."

Jason's body visibly stiffened. "I think you've mixed my father up with someone who cares."

"He's sick, Jason. Real sick. I've done what I can to help him, but he needs you."

"I don't want to discuss him."

She should turn away and walk out the door before the

snow grew any deeper, but her feet wouldn't cooperate. There was one thing she needed to know—one nagging question that demanded an answer.

She licked her dry lips. "If it isn't because of your father, then why have you suddenly returned home?"

"Do you really care?" His gaze never left hers.

"No. Never mind. I shouldn't have asked."

Her pulse quickened. Heat scorched her cheeks. Even though it was a lie, she refused to let him think that she cared anything about what he said or did. He was part of her past...nothing more.

"I have to go." She needed space to make sense of things.

"Kara, I know we can't go back to the way things used to be, but it doesn't have to be this awkward. We were friends for years before we dated."

They had been the best of friends. She'd told him everything about her life, but apparently that openness had been one-sided. She wouldn't make the mistake of trusting him again.

"Does this plea of friendship mean you're planning to stay in Pleasant Valley?"

"Yes."

The blunt response lacked any telling details of what had prompted his unexpected return. Her errant gaze strayed to his bare ring finger. Still single. Still available. Been there, done that. She glanced away.

"Welcome home." She buttoned her black peacoat. "I really do need to go."

"Be careful. The snow's picking up." His gaze moved to the glass doors. "It looks bad out. You should spend the night at the hotel."

She shook her head. "The resort's closed for renovations. You shouldn't even be here. Who's been showing you around?"

They weren't the only ones there late. With the new owner, GSR Inc., arriving on Monday, a number of people were working late even though it was a Friday evening. Everyone had gone above and beyond their duties, hoping to make a good impression on the new owner. Though Jason had been away for years, a number of employees knew him and would have volunteered to give him a last look around the place.

She glanced up at him, waiting for a response. His lips were pursed as though he was about to say something, but had refrained.

"I don't have all night," she stated.

"I don't need an escort."

Kara squared her shoulders. "Since I'm in charge around here, I'm telling you that either you have an escort or you must leave. Now."

This close to the new owner's arrival, she wasn't taking any chances. The last thing she needed was for anyone to get hurt on her watch.

Jason's brows arched. "You like being the boss, don't you?"

"I do whatever needs to be done to keep this place going."

"Good. I hope all my employees are so devoted."

"Your employees...?" Alarm tightened her throat, smothering her next words. Surely she hadn't heard him correctly. Or she'd misunderstood.

"Yes, my employees."

This nightmare couldn't be unfolding right before her eyes. "You...you're GSR?"

"I've gone in with a couple of investors. This place needs to be reorganized. A lot of cutting needs to be done, but I think it's possible to turn the business around with the right management."

A lot of cutting? Right management? The implication of his words shattered her dream of keeping her job. Fragments of her hopes scattered over the freshly laid carpet. Finding an equivalent job would not be easy without a college degree. She inwardly groaned.

She might even have to move. Her thoughts turned to her parents, who had been involved in their only grandchild's life since the day she was born. To tear her daughter away from them now would devastate not only them but her little girl, as well. But Kara wouldn't have a choice. She would have to move wherever she could find reasonable employment.

"Time to start job hunting," she muttered under her breath.

"What?"

"Nothing. I have to go before the snow gets too deep to drive in." She yanked on her gloves. "Good night."

Kara forced herself to take measured steps, training her gaze on the glass door. She hadn't run away when the locals had clucked their tongues and shaken their heads at her youthful mistake. Now she wouldn't give Jason the satisfaction of witnessing how he could still shake her to the core.

Jason Greene clenched his hands. He'd heard enough of her mumbled comment to know she had no intention of working for him. He couldn't leave things like this. Her assistance and knowledge over these next several weeks were essential to the resort's success. He'd risked everything he owned on restoring the Greene Summit. And he couldn't afford to lose it all now.

He started for the door. Large snowflakes fell, adding to the several inches of accumulation on the ground. He'd forgotten how fast the weather could deteriorate in the Laurel Highlands. An overwhelming urge settled in his chest to stop her and convince her to stay over in one of the hotel rooms, where she'd be safe and warm during this stormy night.

His steps grew quicker. Damn, he still cared about her. This was bigger than when they'd grown up together— back when Kara was 100 percent tomboy and he'd protected her from the school bully. The emotions brewing inside him now had an adult edge.

He lingered at the glass doors, staring out into the stormy night. He couldn't tear his gaze from Kara's petite figure as she braved fierce winds while crossing the snowy parking lot. Her appearance had changed, from jeans and snug T-shirts that nestled against her soft curves, to casual business attire. A short haircut replaced her ponytail. Everything combined to give her a mature, polished persona. He certainly wasn't the only one who'd changed.

Was she worried about her trip home? Or was she doing the same as him and reliving the past? He still had time to stop her. He pushed the door open. The bitter wind stung his face as he followed her footsteps. She would demand once more to know the sordid details behind his seven-year absence. His pace slowed. Could he bring himself to explain that dreadful night?

He stopped. No. No way. If he knew the words to make everything right between them, he'd have said them years ago. As the cold cut through his coat and over his exposed skin, he realized he'd played out all the scenarios in his mind thousands of times. Each ended with her looking at him with repulsion. No way could he put either of them through that experience.

Jason rubbed the back of his neck, trying to ease the

stiff muscles. His return to the Summit was going to be just as rough and bumpy as he'd imagined, but he'd get through it. He turned and limped back to the lobby. Only one day on his feet, with the cold seeping into his bones, and already the wound in his thigh throbbed.

He exhaled a weary sigh. The last time he'd worked at the resort, Kara had been his priority. Now, with no significant other in his life, he could sink his dreams into restoring this place without all the emotional entanglements of a relationship and raging teenage hormones. His experience in the military had forced him to grow up. He now realized what was important and why.

He shoved his fingers through his hair, hating the selfish boy he'd once been. This time he'd prove himself worthy of the trust others placed in him. He wouldn't repeat the mistakes of his past.

Muffled footsteps drew his attention. He glanced over his shoulder to find his childhood friend Robert Heinze approaching him. He looked every bit the professional in his navy suit, and definitely fit the part of a distinguished attorney.

"Jason, what are you still doing here?"

"While I was walking the grounds, I came across some maintenance men working on a problem with the towrope for the bunny hill."

"And from the grease stains on your jacket and jeans, I'm assuming you couldn't just let the staff handle it on their own."

Jason shook his head. "I'm not good at standing around watching when I could pitch in and lend a hand."

"You'll have plenty of time to play Mr. Fix-it after tomorrow. By the way, I heard the roads are getting bad. If you don't leave now, you might find yourself riding out the storm right here."

"Before I go, I want to thank you for finalizing this sale with my father. Without you going back and forth between us, I don't think an agreement would have ever been reached."

Robert flashed a small smile. "I think you give me too much credit. You were the mastermind behind this whole venture. I hope it turns out the way you planned."

"It will." He'd returned a couple of days ago, and until the deal had become official, he'd intentionally kept a low profile. "By the way, I just ran into Kara Jameson."

He didn't know why he'd mentioned it. Maybe he just wanted someone to talk some sense into him. After all, before Robert had moved away to be an attorney in downtown Pittsburgh, he'd grown up right here with Kara and Jason.

"Did you tell her you bought this place?"

He nodded.

Robert shrugged on his coat. "How'd it go?"

"The news took her by surprise."

"Seems like an understandable reaction. You've been gone for years." His old friend paused and looked intently at him. "What else is bothering you? Did she quit on the spot?"

"Not exactly."

"Then why do you look like you just chugged a carton of sour milk?"

"Kara lit into me about ignoring my father. He must have fed her some kind of lies to gain her sympathy." Jason didn't bother to hide the loathing he felt.

Robert let out a low whistle. "Boy, you didn't exaggerate about the rift between you two."

If anything, he'd understated the distance between himself and his father. Every muscle in Jason's body grew rigid at the thought of their insurmountable differences. He refused to dwell on something that could never be fixed.

With the help of a couple of investors, he'd at last gained ownership of his heritage—the resort his grandfather had founded. His gaze moved around the lobby, taking in its splendor.

"I've thought of nothing else for the past year but of making this place mine, of restoring the Greene Summit back to its former glory, like when my grandfather was alive. I'll make him proud. No matter what it takes."

Robert patted him on the shoulder. "Then you might want to start by being honest with Kara. I've talked with her and she's bright. When your father's health started to decline, he leaned on her to keep this place running. By now, she must know where each and every skeleton is buried. You're going to need her."

"I know. I'll tell her everything Monday." Well, not everything—just the parts pertaining to the Greene Summit.

Robert's brow furrowed and he began patting his pockets. "I must have left my phone in the office. I'll run back and grab it."

"Okay. I'll see you in the morning."

"Get some sleep. We've got work to do."

Jason turned to the lobby doors and gazed out at the parking lot. He rubbed his thigh, trying to ease the persistent throbbing. He had a business to rebuild and no time to slow down.

The grand reopening in three weeks had to go off without a hitch. All his investors would be on hand to take part in the festivities, and their approval was of the utmost importance, especially if he wanted more capital to undo the years of neglect.

He knew he could never again be the man in Kara's life.

Still, he had to find a way to get her to stay on at the resort. He needed her knowledge to make this a smooth transition.

But when she preferred braving a snowstorm to staying safe here with him, how in the world would they be able to work side by side?

CHAPTER TWO

THE HYPNOTIC SWIRL of flakes made it difficult for Kara to focus on the winding mountain road. The cascade of snow hit the windshield harder and faster with each passing minute. She flicked on the wipers. The built-up ice on the rubber blades made an awful ruckus. *Swish. Thunk. Swish. Thunk.*

The knowledge that Jason was now her boss haunted her. She'd thought that, with the resort sold, any lingering ties to him would be severed. How could she have been so wrong?

A bend in the road loomed ahead. Her foot tapped the brake a little too hard and the car lost traction. Her fingers tightened on the steering wheel as she started to skid.

Stay calm. You know how to drive in this weather.

Thoughts of Jason vanished as she turned into the skid. Like a pinball shot into action, the vehicle slid forward. Trees and the guardrail whizzed by in a blur. In an attempt to straighten the car, she spun the wheel in the other direction. Her throat constricted. At last, she came to a stop in what she hoped was the middle of the road.

That was way too close.

The pent-up air whooshed from her burning lungs. She

rested her forehead against the steering wheel, trying to calm the frantic thumping of her heart. She silently sent up a thankful prayer.

On her way to work that morning, the radio announcer had mentioned the possibility of light snow flurries this evening but never alluded to a foot of snow. And it still continued to fall.

She let off the brake and crept forward, anxious to put as much distance between herself and Jason as possible. Would she ever be able to sweep away the tangled web of attraction, woven tightly with strands of resentment? She sure hoped so, because as long as she lived around here, they were bound to run into each other. After all this time, she'd expected to feel absolutely nothing where he was concerned. So why did she let him get to her?

She exhaled a frustrated groan and glanced down to crank up the heater. When she looked up again, a brief flash caught her attention. Her gaze focused off to the side of the road, where her headlights reflected off a pair of eyes staring back at her. A millisecond later, a deer darted into her path.

A screech of terror tore from Kara's throat as she tramped the brakes, braced for the inevitable collision. Like a skater on a sheet of ice, the car careened over the slick pavement. At the last second, the deer jumped over the hood, just as the front tires dropped off the pavement.

Kara's foothold on the brake slipped, sending the car off the road. She pitched forward, but the seat belt jerked her back, slamming her into the door. With a thud, her head careened into the driver's side window. Pain splintered through her skull. The sound of ripping metal pierced the inky darkness.

At last the car shuddered to a halt. The air bag thumped hard into her chest, sending the breath whooshing from her lungs. She clung to the memory of her daughter's sweet smile.

With newly attached chains on the SUV's tires, Jason drove cautiously down the curvy mountain road. Soon he'd be home, enjoying a piping-hot bowl of leftover stew. His stomach rumbled in anticipation.

He stared out the windshield at the dark, desolate road. When he was a kid, there would have been a string of headlights passing him as anxious skiers flocked to the resort to try out the fresh snow. Tonight, the only evidence of another soul on this road was the faint outline of tire tracks.

Was it possible they belonged to Kara?

The thought of making peace with his childhood sweetheart weighed heavily on his mind. He didn't blame her for still being angry with him. She had every right to be furious over the way he'd walked out on their engagement. He'd probably act the same way if their roles had been reversed. No, he'd have been worse—much worse.

If only there was a way to make her understand that even though he'd handled it poorly, his leaving had been the only answer. But he had no idea how to convey that to her without going into the details of that fateful night, and that was not something he was willing to do. Not even to save the Summit, his birthright.

The wipers were beginning to lose their battle with the thickening snow. He turned on the vehicle's fog lamps, hoping they'd give him a better idea where he was on the road.

The tire tracks he'd been following suddenly veered to the right. His stomach muscles tightened. Trying to get a rescue squad out for an accident during this storm would take hours. He'd best go investigate first. He gently applied pressure to the brakes. The tires fought for traction, sliding a few yards before the SUV stopped. He glanced around, not spotting anyone standing next to the road. Not a good sign. They could be injured or worse.

He grabbed a flashlight from the glove compartment and flicked the switch, sending a light beam out the window. He squinted, trying to see through the thickening snow. At last he spotted the tracks. They led off the road into a gulley. Concern sliced through him. *Please don't let it be Kara.*

He threw the SUV into Park, switched on the flashers and jumped out. Wet snow tossed about by the biting wind stung his face. If Kara was out here, he'd find her.

With his hand shielding his eyes, he marched forward. Piercing pain shot down his thigh as he forced his way through a drift. He gritted his teeth and kept moving. From the edge of the road, he shone the light down at what appeared to be a ten-foot drop. At the bottom was a car with its front end smashed against a tree trunk. Whoever was in it was in need of help.

He'd just started down the embankment when his foot slipped. Hot pain shot through his knee and up his thigh, and his eyes smarted as he choked back a string of curses. Beads of perspiration ran down the sides of his face. But he couldn't stop now. He had a mission to complete.

His fingers curled around a branch and, using his good leg, he regained his balance and sucked in an unsteady breath. He massaged his knee, hoping he hadn't just undone the surgeon's long hours of reconstructive surgery, and weeks of physical therapy. Cautiously Jason flexed the joint. A new wave of agony swept up his body and socked him in the gut. It might hurt like the dickens, but it still worked. That had to be a good sign.

When he reached the two-door coupe, he tapped on a snow-covered window. "I'm here to help. Open up."

The window inched down, letting the buildup of flurries spill inside. Jason flashed his light into the dark interior. A hand immediately shot up, shielding the occupant's eyes from the glare.

"Jason?"

"Kara?" He leaned down, trying to see her better. "Are you all right?"

"I don't know. I think so." Her breathy voice held an eerie squeak. "There was a deer. Then the car skidded off the road. The door's stuck and my phone won't work."

"Okay, slow down. First thing we've got to do is get you out of there."

She started pushing on the door with her palms. He tried pulling on the handle. Without warning, she slammed her shoulder into the door. A grunt followed, but she pulled back, ready to repeat the process.

"Stop!" He used his drill sergeant voice, hoping to gain her attention. "Sit still."

"But I smell gas."

The mention of a gas leak shot a dagger of fear through his chest. Jason surveyed the area with the help of the flashlight, soon spotting the reason the door was stuck. The bottom was jammed against the embankment. The passenger door was pressed against a tree trunk.

"I need out!"

"Wind down your window the whole way."

"It's stuck." Her eyes grew round as her palms pressed against the glass. Her fingertips slipped through the opening and curled over the edge. "Help me."

The frigid wind continued to throw snow through the opening. With these low temperatures, he needed to get her out—fast. He kicked the ground, hoping to find a rock beneath the white blanket of frozen moisture.

At last, armed with a decent-size rock, he used his drill sergeant voice again. "I've got to break the window to get you out. Turn away. And cover your head with your coat."

She did as he instructed, and soon he was assisting her through the opening. When her foot sank down into the deep snow, she lost her balance and pitched to the side. He caught her, hugging her slight form to him. Her hands clutched at his shoulders, pulling him closer. When her head came to rest on his chest, he breathed in the faint scent of strawberries. The feel of her body next to his and the enchanting smell of her all came together, jumbling his senses.

Unable to resist the temptation, he ran his fingers over her golden locks. "It's okay," he murmured. "You're safe now."

Her weight shifted fully against him. Warmth filled his chest. After all those long, lonely nights in different towns and countries, Jason felt as if he'd finally found his way home. He never wanted to let her go.

A gust of wind threw wet snow in his face, bringing him back to his senses. He shouldn't be holding her. It was wrong to enjoy their closeness. He'd sacrificed that liberty years ago. And he was no longer the same man she'd once known.

He held her at arm's length. "You're bleeding."

"I am? I don't feel a thing."

He cupped her face in his hands. A crimson streak trailed from her forehead to her cheek. *Please don't let it be serious.*

"Are you sure? No headache? No double vision?"

"Nothing."

Ever so gently he wiped away the blood with his thumb.

When he found only a minor cut, he breathed a little easier. "Tell me if you start to feel bad."

She nodded.

He pulled his phone from his pocket, punched in the numbers for help and held the device to his ear. After a few seconds, he moved, positioning the phone in front of him. "I can't get a signal. Looks like we're on our own."

She shivered, wrapping her arms around her midsection. "How will I get my car out of there?"

He gave her a quick once-over. Aside from the small cut, he didn't see any other signs of trauma. "The car's not going anywhere tonight. And if you smelled gas, we aren't taking any chances. The tow truck people can deal with it tomorrow."

Her body shook and her teeth chattered. "Now…what… am I going to do?"

He worried about shock settling in. He was certain the accident had been horrific enough, but then to be trapped, even for a brief time, might have been too much for her.

"My SUV's up on the road. We need to get you warm."

He ushered her up the short embankment to his vehicle, which still had the engine running. After she climbed in, he reached behind the seat and pulled out a blanket. "This should warm you up."

He was about to close the door when she said, "Wait. I need my stuff from the car."

She started to climb back out, but he placed a hand on her shoulder, holding her in place. "I'll get your stuff. You wait here and turn up the heater."

"My purse is there…in the backseat…and my cell phone."

Jason closed the door and yanked his gloves from his pocket. He hobbled along, doing his best not to stumble on the uneven ground. The coldness seemed to freeze all but one of his thoughts: *Kara*. He'd missed her much more than he'd been willing to admit to himself. Between her pouty lips and soulful eyes, it was tempting to forget the demons that lurked in his past.

But that couldn't happen. He couldn't let himself go soft in the brain. It wouldn't be fair to her. Soon they'd be off this mountain, he assured himself. Once he gathered her belongings from the car, his only agenda was to deliver her safely to her doorstep and leave.

He limped to the wrecked vehicle and ran the flashlight's beam from trunk to hood. A sour taste rose in the back of his throat. In the military he'd witnessed the tangled metal wrecks and human carnage caused by IEDs, so this accident scene shouldn't evoke a reaction—certainly nothing like the wave of nausea washing over him. But he couldn't escape the fact that Kara could have died here tonight.

He blocked the awful thought from his mind. She was safe, he assured himself. All he had to do now was retrieve her belongings and drive her home.

Long minutes ticked by before Jason reappeared in the glow of the headlights. *Thank goodness he's back.* Soon she'd be home, snug and warm, with her family. Still, something struck her as not quite right. She gazed through the window, giving him a second, more intense inspection. She noticed he moved with a limp. The knowledge that he'd been hurt while rescuing her gave her pause.

When he yanked the back door open, she asked, "Are you all right?"

"I'm fine."

After placing her belongings on the backseat, he closed the door with a loud thud and climbed in beside her. It'd been a long time since they'd been together, but as close as they were physically, they'd never been so far apart in every other way. And it would remain that way. It was for the best.

But that didn't mean she could ignore his physical pain. "You aren't fine. You were limping."

"Don't worry. I'll be fine after I rest my leg for a bit."

The lines etched around his eyes and mouth said the pain was more severe than he'd admitted. Once again he was holding back the truth.

"Can I do anything—for your leg?"

He shook his head. "The, uh, weather—it's getting worse. We better get moving. Are you ready?"

"Definitely. I'm anxious to get home. I don't want my family to worry."

He yanked off his snow-covered hat and tossed it in the backseat. When he unbuttoned his coat, a fluff of pink fur poked out. Kara gaped at him. Nothing about him either in the past or now screamed pink fuzzy anything.

He withdrew the object. "I found this on the floor in back when I was searching for your purse."

"Bubbles." Her daughter must have forgotten the stuffed animal that morning, when Kara had dropped Samantha off at her grandparents' house before school.

"Huh?" Jason's gaze darted from the teddy bear with Baby Girl embroidered on its belly to her. "Bubbles? Really?"

Kara reached for the stuffed animal. "Something wrong with the name?"

"Uh...no." He tossed her the ball of fluff. "Not at all."

"Hey, it's the color of bubble gum—hence the name Bubbles."

"Logical. I guess."

She glanced at him, expecting to find humor easing the tense lines marring his face, but his expression hadn't changed. What had happened to the old Jason, the one with a thousand and one fast comebacks and an easy grin? Sadness burrowed into her chest. She mourned the boy who had always made a point of making her smile, even during the worst teenage crisis.

She hugged Bubbles to her chest. "Thanks for rescuing him."

"The bear is really yours?" Suspicion laced every syllable. "You carry a baby's toy around in your car?"

She stared down at the bear. It had been her daughter's very first stuffed animal. Even though Samantha had accumulated an army of plush toys over the years, she still reached for Bubbles when she was tired or upset.

Kara considered pretending she hadn't heard the question. However, she recalled how Jason had been worse than a hound dog rooting around for a bone when he wanted information. He would continue to hunt and dig until he found exactly what he was after.

Maybe a glib answer would suffice. She did know one thing: she certainly wasn't prepared to blurt out the entire truth about her daughter. So she'd give him the basics, and hopefully, he wouldn't ask any more questions.

"The bear belongs to my daughter."

CHAPTER THREE

SERIOUSLY, COULD THIS night get any worse?

Kara didn't say anything more, hoping he'd get the hint that she didn't want to talk. Her daughter was off-limits to him. She turned her head and stared out at the starless night, which mirrored her dismal mood.

"So you're a mother?"

The astonishment in his voice set her on edge. This was the very last topic she wanted to discuss with him. After all, she didn't owe him any explanations. She didn't owe him a single thing. Her daughter was no secret, but that didn't mean she had to share the circumstances of her birth with him.

"A lot changed after you left."

"Obviously. So who's the lucky man in your life?"

Kara suddenly hated her single status. The thought of lying tiptoed across her mind, but she'd never been any good at it, even as a kid. Best to stick with the truth. "There is no man."

"Thought you'd have guys lined up, waiting to take you out."

"And you'd be wrong."

She smothered a sigh. After he'd dumped her and she'd found out she was pregnant, it was a very long time until she was willing to trust any man. When she finally did dip her toe in the dating pool, finding a man with the right personality, who was ready to take on a young mother, was a challenge. Most of the guys she met simply didn't want the hassle of a ready-made family. And they certainly weren't thrilled about having their social calendars dictated by whether or not Kara could secure a babysitter.

Not that she'd become a nun or anything. She'd dated here and there. The evenings out were nice, but that's all they were—nice. She shielded her daughter from her dating life. She didn't want Samantha getting attached to someone, only to lose him when things didn't work out.

Sensing Jason giving her periodic glances, Kara refused to meet his gaze. Instead, she continued to stare into the night. The thickening snow kept her from spotting the pond where they used to skate as kids. In those days, they'd been practically inseparable. Did Jason ever think about the good old days? Did he even regret his abrupt departure from her life and this community? Was that why he'd finally come home? To make amends?

She sneaked a glance at him. His long fingers clenched the steering wheel, fighting to keep the vehicle on the road. When he turned his head to glance at her, she jerked her gaze away, focusing on the hypnotic swish, swish of the windshield wipers.

A loud crack echoed through the night as a tree limb fell onto the road. "Watch out!"

He cut the wheel to the left. The driver's side tires dropped off the snow-covered pavement. Kara's upper body jerked to the left, where firm muscles pillowed her and held her steady. Jason's body was rock hard. The kid she'd planned to explore the world with was long gone, and in his place was this man she barely recognized. The army life had transformed him into a human tank. And in that moment, she knew he'd protect her.

Thankfully, the vehicle slowed to a stop. With some effort, Jason eased it back on the road. "Sorry about that. You okay?"

Realizing she was still leaning against his arm, she pulled herself upright. "I'm fine."

But was she? Her heart continued to palpitate faster than a jackhammer. The blood pounded in her ears. It was the near miss with the tree limb that had her all riled up. She was certain of it. She settled back in her seat and took a calming breath.

"Hang on tight." Jason released the brake and the vehicle crawled forward. "The weather's getting worse. I can barely make out the road."

The tires crunched over the snow blanketing the pavement. The wind created white sheets that draped over the vehicle. All the while, the wipers worked furiously to clear the windshield for a second or two at a time. How in the world was she going to get home tonight? It'd be dawn before they got down the mountain at this inchworm pace.

"What are we going to do?" She didn't bother to hide the quaver in her voice.

Jason patted her leg. "We'll be okay. Trust me."

He was the very last person she should trust, but in these extreme circumstances, she didn't have much choice. Heat emanated from his lingering touch and radiated outward, sweeping through her limbs. Her gaze zeroed in on his fingers gripping her thigh. She should pull away, at the very least shove his hand aside. Before she could act, he withdrew it himself, to grip the steering wheel.

"Kara, why are you still there—at the resort? Working for my father?"

Not exactly a subject she wanted to broach with him, but at least it kept him from asking about her daughter. "You mean why didn't I leave him like you did?"

"That isn't what I meant." A note of bitterness wove through his tone. "Why haven't you moved on with your life? Gotten away from here? You always dreamed of traveling the world. Why give it all up for an old drunk who ran my grandfather's dream into the ground?"

She straightened. "Don't you dare judge me. Your father and I did our best to keep the resort up and running. Maybe if you'd been here, you could have helped."

"I was busy at the time, getting shot at while defending our country." He turned to her, his eyes glittering. "And recovering from a bomb blast."

Her brain stuttered, trying to imagine the dangers he'd faced. "I had no idea."

"You weren't supposed to. I shouldn't have mentioned it."

"What happened? Are you okay now?"

"I'm fine."

"If you're so fine, why are you here and not still overseas?"

A muscle flexed in his cheek. "They gave me a medical discharge."

She realized abruptly that something awful had happened to him. For all she knew, he might have come close to dying. A shiver washed over her body. Common sense said she should let the subject drop. After all, he was no longer part of her life, and she couldn't afford to let him back in.

But the tense silence set her frazzled nerves on edge. Maybe some light conversation would ease her anxiety about the weather. "Your father must be so relieved to know you're home. That you're safe."

"I haven't seen him. And I don't know if I will."

Shocked at his admission, she paused. It wasn't right that these two men, who had only each other, should be so distant. She fiddled with the blanket's satin binding while staring out at the storm. Time was running out for his father. She felt compelled to try to help them.

"You have to go to him," she insisted. "His liver is failing. I tried to put him on the transplant list, but with his history, he isn't a candidate."

"You can't expect me to act surprised. No one can drink at breakfast, lunch and dinner without paying for it in the end."

"Jason!" She glared at him.

In all the time she'd known him, he'd had a strained relationship with his father. Kara surmised it had started with the death of Jason's mother, but none of that explained why Jason had turned his back on his dad after so many years. She couldn't imagine ever cutting herself off from her parents. They didn't have a perfect relationship, but her folks were always there when she needed them, and vice versa.

Refusing to believe Jason could be so cold, she said, "The next time I stop by the nursing home, I'll let him know you're in town."

"Don't interfere. That man and I took care of everything we had to say to each other years ago. There's nothing left between us."

Jason's rigid tone told her she was pushing her luck, but she couldn't help herself. "But he's changed. He's sober—"

"No more." Jason's hand slashed through the air, as though drawing an imaginary line she shouldn't cross. "I can't argue with you. I need to focus on the road."

She sagged back against the seat with a heavy sigh. He was right. Now wasn't the time to delve into the situation with his father. At best, Jason would be only partially listening to her while he worked to keep them out of a ditch. At least she'd had a chance to make her point about his father's condition. There wasn't much more she could do now. She just hoped Jason would come to his senses and make peace with his dad before it was too late. Regrets were tough to live with. She should know.

She reached for the radio, then paused. "Do you mind if I turn on some music?"

"Go ahead."

At the press of a button, an ad for a local grocery store resonated from the SUV's speakers. Kara turned the dial, searching for her favorite country station. The headline news greeted her. She glanced at the clock on the dash. With it being the top of the hour, news would be on most every station.

"This bulletin is just in from the National Weather Service," the radio announcer said in a somber tone, garnering Kara's full attention. "The arctic express is supposed to dump twenty-four inches of snow in the higher elevations by tomorrow."

"Two feet," she said in horror.

"We'll be okay." Jason reached over and gave her hand a reassuring squeeze. An army of goose bumps marched up her limbs. She assured herself it was just a reaction to the dire forecast and had nothing to do with his touch.

The radio crackled as the announcer's voice continued to ring out. "That isn't even the worst of the storm. Sometime this evening, a blast from the south will raise the temperature, only to have the thermometer quickly sink back below freezing. I know you're thinking this is a good thing, but let me tell you, folks, those pretty little flakes are going to change into an ice shower, and with a wind advisory due to kick in at midnight, it's going to get dicey, resulting in downed trees and power lines...."

After another advertisement, strains of "Let It Snow" began to play. Someone at the radio station had a sick sense of humor. Outside, the flakes were continuing to come down hard and fast. A glance at Jason's squinted eyes and the determined set of his jaw told Kara the conditions were already beyond dicey.

Minutes later, when the vehicle skidded to a stop next to an old elm tree, outside a modest log home, she turned to him. "What are we doing here?"

"The roads are too dangerous. We'll hunker down here until the storm passes."

"Here?" A half-dozen snow-covered trees surrounded them. "In the middle of nowhere?"

"This isn't the boonies. There's heat and shelter. You'll be fine. Trust me."

There he went again with that line about trust. The words grated across her thinly stretched nerves. What in the world had she done for Fate to conspire against her?

"I can't spend the night with you," she protested, even though she knew her daughter would be safe with her parents.

Jason leveled a frown at her, as though he wasn't any more pleased than she was about the situation. "You aren't scared of being alone with me, are you?"

"Don't flatter yourself," she said a little too quickly, refusing to meet his intense stare. "I grew up a long time ago."

Her lips pressed into a firm line as she surveyed the sprawling log structure. Being snowed in with Jason, of all people, would be more stressful than sliding down the slick mountain road. Her hands clenched. She and Jason had too much history, and she hated how he still got under her skin, evoking a physical awareness she hadn't experienced in ages.

"Do you even know who lives here? Or are we about to commit an act of breaking and entering?"

"This is now my home. Don't you remember it? I

brought you here a couple of times to visit my grand-mother."

Her gaze moved past him to the covered porch, with its two wooden rocking chairs. She searched her memory. At last she grasped on to a vague recollection that brought a smile to her lips. "I remember now. She fed us chocolate chip cookies fresh from the oven. I liked her a lot."

"She liked you, too." His lips quirked as though he'd been transported back in time—back to a life that wasn't so complicated. "I inherited this place from my grandpar-ents, along with a trust fund my father couldn't squander."

Glowing light from the dashboard illuminated Jason's face, highlighting the discomfort he felt when mention-ing his dad, as he opened the door, letting the frigid air rush in. "Wait here. I'll leave the heat on while I shovel a path to the porch."

She refused to let him overexert his injured leg again on her behalf. With a twist of the key, she turned off the engine and vaulted out of the SUV. She sidled up next to him as he limped along.

He frowned down at her. "Don't you ever listen?"

"Only when I want to. Now, lean on me and take some pressure off your leg."

He breathed out an exasperated sigh before draping his arm over her shoulder. She started to lean in closer, but then pulled back, keeping a respectable distance while still assisting him. She refused to give in to her body's desire to once again feel his heat, his strength. She had to keep herself in check. This was simply a matter of he'd helped her and now she was returning the favor—that was all.

On the top step, they paused. Her eyes scanned the lengthy porch. Her gaze stopped when she noticed a freshly cut pine tree, all ready to be decked out in colorful orna-ments and tinsel. She remembered as a child accompanying her father and grandfather to the local Christmas-tree farm to cut down their own tree. The fond memory left her smiling.

"I'm so jealous," she said as Jason pulled away to stand on his own. "You have a real Christmas tree. All I ever have time for is the artificial kind. I remember how the live trees would bring such a wonderful scent to the whole house."

"A neighbor asked to cut down a tree on my property, and thanked me by chopping one for me, too. The thing is, I don't do Christmas."

"What do you mean, you don't do Christmas?" Her eyes opened wide. "How do you not do Christmas? It's the best time of the year."

"Not for me." His definite tone left no doubt that he wanted nothing to do with the holiday.

Her thoughts strayed to her daughter and how her eyes lit up when they put up the Christmas tree. Even in the lean years before her promotion to office manager, Kara had managed to collect dollar-store ornaments and strings of lights. With carols playing in the background, they would sing as they hooked the decorations over the branches.

The holiday was a time for family, for togetherness. A time to be grateful for life's many blessings. Not a time to be alone with nothing but your memories for company. The thought of Jason detached from his family and friends during such a festive time filled her with such sorrow.

"I haven't celebrated it since...my mother was alive." His last words were barely audible.

Kara recalled when they were dating how he'd always have a small gift for her, including the silver locket at home in her jewelry box. But he'd always made one excuse after another to avoid the Christmas festivities.

"Surely after all these years you've enjoyed Christmas

carols around a bonfire, driven around to check out the houses all decked out in lights or exchanged presents with various girlfriends?" Kara didn't want to dwell on that last uneasy thought.

He shook his head.

"What about the military? Didn't they do anything for the holidays?"

He paused by the front door. His back went ramrod straight.

"I always opted to be on duty," he said, his tone clipped. "I'll get rid of the tree the first chance I get."

"How could you possibly throw away such a perfect tree? You're home now. Time to start over. A chance for new beginnings..." Her voice trailed off. She didn't want him to misconstrue her words—to think she wanted them to have a new beginning. Not giving him time to ponder her statement, she continued, "You should try joining in the fun. After all, it's the most joyous time of the year."

Kara forced a smile. She couldn't believe she was trying to talk him into celebrating the exact same holiday during which he'd broken her heart. If he wanted to be an old, cranky Scrooge, why should she care?

Jason didn't say anything as he opened the door and stepped aside, allowing her to enter. In the narrow opening, her arm brushed against him, and even through the layers of clothing an electrical current zinged up her arm, warming a spot in her chest.

Staying here wasn't a good idea.

Being alone with her new boss was an even poorer idea.

This whole situation constituted the worst idea ever.

CHAPTER FOUR

ALARM BELLS CLANGED loud and clear in Kara's mind.

There had to be a realistic alternative to staying, but for the life of her, she couldn't come up with anything reasonable. One hesitant step after another led her across the threshold and into the log house. Warmth enveloped her in an instant.

"It's getting really bad out there." Jason slammed the door against the gusting wind before stomping the caked snow from his boots. "Let me get some lights on in here."

He moved past her to a table and switched on a small antique lamp with little blue flowers painted around the base. The soft glow added warmth to her unfamiliar surroundings.

"Thanks." She clasped her shivering hands, rubbing her fingers together.

When her eyes adjusted to the lighting, her curious gaze meandered around the place Jason called home. Worn yet well-kept maple furniture stood prominently in the room, with a braided, blue oval rug covering a large portion of the oak floor. Nothing flashy, but not dingy, either—more like cozy and comfortable.

Jason favored his leg as he made his way to the fireplace and arranged some kindling. He struck a match, and soon a golden glow gave his hunched figure a larger-than-life appearance. What would it be like to curl up with him on that leather couch with a hot mug of tea and a fire crackling in the stone-and-mortar fireplace? To sit there and discuss the day, or make plans for the future?

She gave herself a mental shake. This wasn't a romantic vacation. Nor was she interested in curling up with him now or ever. She'd keep out of his way and wait out the storm. Once the weather broke and the plows cleared the roads, she'd be gone. And it couldn't be soon enough.

She tugged her soggy jacket tighter, trying to ward off the chill that went clear through to her bones. All the while, she continued to examine her surroundings. A wadded up pile of white sheets lay on one of the armchairs, as though Jason was still in the process of making himself at home. Her attention moved to the oak coffee table with a folded newspaper and a tidy stack of what appeared to be sports magazines.

"Something wrong?" he asked.

"You mean other than being snowed in here with you?" She couldn't resist the jab. She didn't want either one of them to get too comfortable in this arrangement and forget about all the problems between them. "Actually, I'm surprised to find this place so clean. I guess I just don't think of men as being neat freaks. Unless, of course, you're living with someone...."

The thought hadn't occurred to her until then, and it annoyed her that it even made a difference to her. Yet the presence of a girlfriend would assure their past remained in the hazy shadows, along with the snarled web of emotions.

"I'm not involved with anyone." The flat statement left no doubt in her mind about the status of his bachelorhood. "I learned to clean up after myself in the military. You've got to be prepared to move out on a moment's notice, and you can't be ready if your gear is in a jumbled heap."

The tension in Kara's stomach eased. Instead of examining her worrisome response to finding out he had no one special in his life, she chose to stick to safer topics.

Glancing up, she said, "I love the cathedral ceiling and how the chimney rises into the rafters."

"Wait until you see this place with the morning sun coming in through the wall of windows on the other side of the room."

Preferring not to dwell on the idea of watching the sunrise with him by her side, she pointed past the fireplace. "What's over there?"

"My grandfather used the area as a study, and I didn't feel a need to change things."

She glanced around, taking in the winding stairs. "Where do those go?"

"To the loft. When I was little my grandparents used it as a bedroom for me. I'd spend hours up there playing. Now the space is crammed full of junk. Maybe this summer I'll get around to throwing it all out."

"Why would you want to do that? There are probably heirlooms up there that you'll one day want to hand down to your children."

His thick brows puckered. Storm clouds raced across his sky-blue eyes. "One man's treasure is another man's junk. And since I'm not having kids, I don't need the stuff."

Not having kids. The knowledge knocked the air from her lungs. He made it sound so final, as though he'd already given the subject considerable thought. She'd never heard him say such things when they'd been dating. In fact, they'd discussed having a boy and a girl. A little Jason and a little Kara.

In that instant, she realized a stranger faced her. *What could have changed him so drastically?* She bit back the question. None of her business, she reminded herself.

Dredging up these old memories stung worse than pouring rubbing alcohol over a festering wound. Her judgment concerning men seemed to be made up of one painful mistake after another.

"I'll get us something warm to drink," he said, ending the conversation. "You can get out of those wet clothes in there." He pointed to a door on the opposite end of the great room.

"I don't have anything to change into. Besides, I need to call my family."

"You need to get warmed up before you come down with pneumonia. Then you can phone home. It's not late, so they shouldn't be too worried yet."

She hoped he was right.

When Jason bent over to untie his boots, he groaned in pain. She grabbed his arm, tugging him upright. He started to pull away, but she tightened her grip, noticing how his muscles rippled beneath her fingertips. In spite of her awareness of his very muscular build, she dragged him over to a wooden chair beneath the picture window.

"Sit," she commanded, in the same tone she used when Samantha was being uncooperative. "You don't need to put any more pressure on your sore leg."

His startled gaze met hers. Then, ignoring her words, he once again attempted to loosen his laces. She swiped his hand away.

"I'll do it," she insisted, kneeling before him.

Her cold fingers ached as she dug her short nails through the chunks of ice, trying to loosen the laces.

"So this take-charge woman you've become, is it part of being a mother?" he asked, startling her with the intimate question.

"I suppose so." The mention of her daughter, combined with his nearness, flustered her. Her fingers refused to cooperate. "I almost have your boots untied. There's just this one knot…"

She bit down on her lip, forcing her attention to remain on the frozen tangle and to ignore how easy it'd be to end up in his capable arms. With one last pull, followed by a solid yank, she loosened the laces. And none too soon. This proximity was short-circuiting her thought processes.

She jumped to her feet and strode over to the fireplace. Why did this log home have to be so small? She supposed *small* wasn't a fair description, as this all-purpose room was quite spacious. But it didn't allow for any privacy, any breathing space away from Jason.

Her gaze shot to the two doorways off to the side, below the loft. Maybe she could wait out the storm in one of those rooms.

"I'll find you something to wear." Jason got to his feet. "Come on."

He led her to the nearest bedroom. Before he even opened the door, she guessed it was his. Definitely not her first choice for accommodations. She couldn't imagine sleeping in his bed, surrounded by his things.

"What's in the other room?"

"Wall-to-wall furniture. My grandmother had the great room loaded with so much stuff you could hardly get around."

So much for that great idea.

She stepped into his room. It wasn't spacious, but roomy enough for a dresser and a double bed. Her gaze lingered on the bright colored scrap quilt covering the mattress. The thought of being here alone with Jason had her lingering at the doorway.

Her mind reeled back to the summer of her sophomore year in college. Jason had told her that he wanted to leave Pleasant Valley, that he was joining the army. In the very next breath, he'd proposed to her. He wanted to elope with her after she earned her journalism degree. The answer had been a no-brainer—a very definite "Yes!" But she hadn't wanted to wait. She'd planned to drop out of college and earn her degree via the internet while following Jason around the world. She'd been so certain she could make it work.

She recalled how they'd made love over and over, celebrating their impending nuptials. At the time, she'd thought her heart would burst from the abundance of love. Never once had they been bold enough to come together in the luxury of a bed. Their special spot had been a remote pasture near a creek at the back of the resort, where the warm rays of the sun had kissed their bodies. The place hadn't been important, only that they were alone to talk, laugh and love each other.

When Jason abruptly left Pleasant Valley—left *her*— seeing the world was no longer an option. As the only child of two loving parents who worked manual labor jobs to get by, Kara realized as soon as she learned she was pregnant that she couldn't burden them with another mouth to feed. The day after she'd finished her junior year of college, her job at the Greene Summit Resort went from part-time to full-time.

Youthful endeavors and girlish dreams were lost to her. With the most sweet, well-behaved baby counting on her, Kara grew up overnight. Her parents were supportive, but the bulk of the responsibility for child care fell to her, whether she'd been up half the night for feedings or exhausted from a strenuous day at work. It was a lot to adjust to, but she would do anything for her daughter— then and now.

The dresser drawer banged closed, jarring her back to the here and now. When Jason handed over a pair of gray sweatpants and a flannel shirt, their fingers briefly touched, causing her heart to skip a beat.

"Thank you." She jerked her hand away.

"The bathroom is just through that door." He pointed over his shoulder. "I'll go get you something warm to drink."

"You should rest your leg," she protested.

"I'm fine. But you won't be if you don't get out of those wet things."

Before she could utter a rebuttal, the door thudded shut. Irritation niggled at her. Did that man always have to have the last word?

She rushed over to the door, only to find it lacked a lock. Nothing like feeling utterly vulnerable. With a sigh, she turned and leaned back against the door. She stood there for countless minutes with his clothes clutched to her pounding chest. She inhaled deeply and Jason's manly scent assailed her senses. She couldn't resist burying her face in the soft flannel. Even though it had obviously been laundered, spicy aftershave clung to the material. He wore the same brand as he had years ago. Okay, so maybe not everything about him had changed. She smothered a groan of desire.

After everything that had happened, why did she still have a weakness for him? But no matter how many memories bombarded her, they couldn't go backward. What was broken between them couldn't be undone. The only thing for them to do now was to take a step forward—in opposite directions.

Determined to stave off her lingering attraction to him, she rushed off to the bathroom. The pulsating water eased her achy muscles and the billowing steam soothed her anxiety. She refused to let the crush of memories overwhelm her. She just had to treat Jason in the same gracious manner she would anyone else who rescued her.

Minutes later, dressed in the warm clothing, she glanced in the oval mirror mounted above the chest of drawers. Kara didn't need to inspect her reflection to know she looked ridiculous, as though she'd just fallen out of a Salvation Army donation bin. She cinched the baggy sweats around her waist so they didn't slip down over her hips, and rolled up the dangling sleeves.

That left dealing with her hair, which was an absolute mess. She attempted to finger-comb the waves, but it didn't help. Surely there had to be a brush or comb around here. She scanned the dresser top, taking in the papers and envelopes haphazardly dropped in the middle. She noticed how there were no photos of people from his past or ones currently in his life. It was as if he was a clean slate just waiting to be written on, but she knew that was far from the truth.

A small, flat box sticking out from beneath the papers snagged her attention. Though she knew it was none of her business, a longing to learn more about this man from her past had her reaching for the box. It creaked open. Suspended from a red-white-and-blue ribbon was a gold five-point star with a laurel wreath surrounding a silver star in the center. Her heart swelled with pride for Jason. Her eyes grew moist as she realized he must have put his life on the line to receive such a great honor.

With her thumb, she lifted the medal and read the engraving on the back: For Gallantry in Action. A tear dripped onto her cheek. Jason was a bona fide hero. Just not *her* hero.

A brief knock at the door drew her attention. "Uh… coming."

She repositioned the medal and snapped the lid closed.

Just as she was about to return the box to its original spot, the door squeaked open.

Heat swirled in her chest before rushing to her cheeks and ears. Nothing like getting caught red-handed, snooping. Still, part of her was glad she'd learned this important detail of Jason's life. Knowing their country had taken time to recognize him for risking his life touched her deeply. Before her stood a rock-solid hero with broad shoulders, hefty biceps and a chest any woman would crave to be held against—except her.

Kara refused to let his gallant acts or obvious good looks change what she knew about him. When a relationship got too serious or hit a snag, he'd rather skip town than talk out their problems. She refused to get involved with someone she couldn't trust.

His blank stare moved from the box in her hand to her eyes. "I have the water heated up. I just need to know if you want tea or coffee."

"Tea." Her mouth grew dry and she struggled to swallow. Giving herself a moment to suck down her embarrassment, she took her time returning the box to the dresser top. At last she turned. "I didn't read about your heroism in the paper."

He leaned against the doorjamb and crossed his arms. His eyes needled her. "Snooping, huh?"

She didn't know if her face could get any hotter without catching fire. Unable to deny his accusation, she went with a different tack. "Such a great honor shouldn't be kept a secret."

"And that justifies you going through my things? Digging up unwanted memories?" The roughness of his voice spoke of a deep emotional attachment to the memories.

"Why were you honored?" she asked, needing to understand what had happened to him during those missing seven years.

"I did what had to be done. End of story."

"Does everything have to be some sort of deep dark secret? Or is it just me that you refuse to be honest with?"

Pain reflected in his eyes, but in a blink, it was gone—hidden behind an impenetrable wall. Regret for snapping at him rolled over Kara. She hadn't meant to make him defensive. She truly cared about what had happened to him.

"I'll get you some tea."

"You don't need to bother." She didn't want to be even more of an imposition. "I can just wait in here, out of the way, until the snowplow digs us out."

"I don't think that's a good idea."

"It's for the best. This way we don't have to get in each other's way. You can go about your business like I'm not even here."

"This room isn't very warm. You'll be a lot more comfortable in front of the fireplace."

"I could just bundle up in a blanket."

Why was he being so difficult when she was trying to make this awkward arrangement as tolerable as possible for both of them? Surely he wasn't any more interested in spending time with her than she was about spending it with him.

"Suit yourself." He shrugged. "But you should know that as soon as I get your tea, I'll be in to get my shower. And with the bathroom being a bit cramped, I tend to strip down in the bedroom."

Heat scorched her cheeks until she thought for sure her hair would go up in smoke. So much for her idea about keeping distance between them.

"I'll be out in a minute," she said. "You wouldn't have a comb handy, would you?"

He pulled one out of his rear pocket and tossed it to her before walking away.

She turned back to the dresser, catching sight of the box containing his medal. She hated that he refused to open up to her. But he wasn't the only one keeping secrets. She had things in her past that she preferred not to discuss—especially not with him. Maybe he was right. Nothing good would come of them opening up to each other.

After doing what she could with her hair, she walked into the living room to find the fireplace crackling with a decent-size blaze. The glow of the burgeoning flames filled the room with dancing shadows.

A movement on one of the chairs drew her attention. A black cat stood and stretched, arching its back. Kara stepped forward. The cat poised at the edge of the chair, ready to scamper away.

"It's okay. I won't hurt you."

The cat sent her a wide-eyed stare, as though trying to make up its mind about her. Finding her not to be an immediate threat, it sat down.

"Well, aren't you a cutie? I'm surprised you'd live here with Mr. Scrooge. You know, he wasn't always so grouchy."

Kara glanced around, making sure they were alone. A clank followed by a thud assured her Jason was still in the kitchen. Now would be a good time to contact her family.

"I'll be back," she told the cat, whose golden eyes followed her every movement.

With her outerwear wet, Kara borrowed Jason's far-too-large boots and a dry blue coat that was hanging on a wooden peg by the door. She rushed out into the driving snow to retrieve her belongings from the SUV. She hoped and prayed her cell phone hadn't been damaged in the accident. Once back on the covered porch, she dropped her stuff on one of the rockers. A quick search of her tote revealed her phone had survived the accident. The lights twinkled across the screen and displayed a weak signal. It'd have to do.

Her parents would be anxious to hear from her. She always called when she was going to be late, and she refused to take advantage of their generosity. Only tonight, there was no way she was going to make it home. She hit the speed dial and pressed the cold plastic to her ear.

Crackle. Crackle. Ring.

By the fourth ring, she began to worry. Surely her parents hadn't done anything foolish, like heading out in this storm to hunt for her. She paced back and forth. *Please let them be safe.*

As though in answer to her prayer, her father's voice came over the line. "Kara? Is that you?"

"It's me, Dad."

Crackle. "...been so worried."

"Dad? I can hardly hear you."

"Kara..." *Crackle.* "...and Samantha are all right. Where are you?"

"I'm at the resort." The answer was close enough to the truth without having to get into the sticky explanation about spending the night with her ex-fiancé. "The roads are impassable. I'll be home tomorrow."

"Okay, be..."

Crackle. Crackle. Silence.

Time to deal with Jason. What in the world would they discuss? Her mind raced as she rushed back inside to warm herself by the fire. There had to be some sort of casual conversation they could make to keep the tense silence at bay.

The weather? A mere glance outside pretty much summed up that depressing subject.

The resort? It was bad enough being snowed in with

the new owner. If firing her was part of his reorganization plan, she didn't want to find out tonight.

The past? The mere thought soured her stomach. That subject was best left alone.

Perhaps in this case silence truly was golden.

Jason reached into the far corner of the cabinet above the stove. Luckily, a neighbor had presented him with a welcome basket containing some tea bags. Not knowing what to do with them, he'd stashed the bags in the back of the cabinet. He never imagined he'd be serving Kara, of all people, some chai tea.

His mind was still reeling from the news that she was now a mother. As he placed the mug of tea on an old tray, an image of her with a baby in her arms filled his mind. Uneasiness settled in his gut. Years ago, when he'd proposed marriage, he'd been too young to think much about kids, other than someday they'd have two. A boy and a girl.

Even though he'd wanted her to move on, he'd never thought he'd be around to see her again. And he'd certainly never imagined she'd end up a single mom. A fiery rage slithered through his veins and burned in the pit of his stomach. The guy who'd abandoned Kara and her little girl better hope Jason never crossed his path.

Jason opened the fridge, removed a jug of milk and banged it down on the counter. What excuse did this man have for walking away from Kara? Sure, he himself had done the same thing, but there hadn't been a baby involved. He'd left in order to protect Kara from what he'd learned about himself. At the time, he'd been in shock, and repulsed by the ugly words his drunken father had spewed at him. Emotionally wounded and in trauma, he'd needed to get away from everyone he knew, including Kara.

The memory of the tears streaking down her cheeks,

dripping onto her new green Christmas dress, still bowled him over with self-loathing. His jaw clenched. He'd totally botched the entire situation. Now he deserved her contempt, and anything else she could throw at him. He was a mature man, a soldier, he could shoulder her wrath. Besides, she couldn't say anything about him that he hadn't thought at some point.

"Do you need any help?" she called out from the other room.

"I'll be right there."

He gathered his thoughts while retrieving a big bag of sugar from the cabinet. With everything balanced on the tray, he headed back to the living room, expecting to find Kara on the couch, snuggled under one of his grandmother's quilts. When he found the cushions empty, he paused.

"Hey, sweetie," Kara's soothing voice called out.

The tray rattled in his hands. Sweetie? Every nerve ending stood on high alert. Had he heard her correctly?

"Come on over here," she crooned.

His heart careened into his ribs with enough velocity to leave a big bruise. Where was she? In the bedroom? A flood of testosterone roared through Jason's eager body, drowning out the pleading strains of his common sense.

"Hey, big boy. You know you want to. I promise I won't bite."

CHAPTER FIVE

JASON SNAPPED HIS gaping mouth closed. His jaw clenched, grinding his back teeth together.

The tray in his hands tilted. The tea sloshed over the rim of the cup, while the sack of sugar slid to the edge. He righted the tray before the contents could spill onto the floor. In haste, he safely deposited the armload on the table.

"Kara?" He cleared the hoarseness from his voice. "Where are you?"

"Over here."

He scanned the couch and the two easy chairs, but saw no sign of her. "Quit playing games."

"I'm down here."

His gaze fell to the floor, and in the corner, behind the easy chair, he spotted the most enticing derriere sticking up in the air.

"Come on, sweetie," she coaxed. "A little closer."

His heart rate shot into the triple digits and showed no signs of slowing down. He reached for the back of the couch to anchor himself. His ears must be playing tricks on him. She despised him...didn't she?

"Please," she crooned. "I promise to be gentle."

"Kara," he said. "What are you doing?"

"There's the sweetest kitty under this chair."

"You're talking to the cat?"

She raised her head to look at him. Amusement danced in her green eyes. "You thought I was talking to you?"

Her lips bowed and a peal of laughter danced through the room, making him all the more uncomfortable.

"It's not funny!" The air grew uncomfortably warm and he yanked at his shirt collar. He shouldn't have built that fire up so much. "Leave the cat alone. She'll come out if she wants to. Your tea's on the table. I'm going to grab a shower."

He headed for the bedroom, needing a cold, cold shower to set him straight. On second thought, he'd be better off to go outside and roll around in the mounting snow. He could just imagine the steam billowing off his body. How was it possible that woman could still drive him crazy, like some hormonal teenager?

With the door firmly closed, he raked his fingers through his hair. He sucked in a ragged breath. The cat. He shook his head in disbelief. Wow, he'd been alone way too long.

Maybe once he got the resort back in operation, he'd consider spending an evening or two with a cute snow bunny. The problem was when he closed his eyes and sought out the ideal woman to spend time with, his mind automatically conjured up Kara's image.

Jason groaned. Boy, he was in deep trouble. If he couldn't keep his feelings for her in check for this one evening, how in the world would they work together?

Kara got to her feet, giving up on her attempts to befriend the cat, for now. Still chilled, she grabbed the red-white-and-blue patriotic quilt from the back of the couch and draped it over her shoulders. She made her way to the scarred oak table, where her now lukewarm tea waited.

A smile pulled at her lips as she thought of Jason preparing her tea.

She pulled out one of the ladder-back chairs and made herself comfortable. The table was strategically placed in the room, giving the occupants somewhere to dine while admiring the landscape, which at this moment was hidden beneath a fluffy white blanket of snow. Coldness radiated through the windowpanes, sending goose bumps cascading down her arms. She clutched the quilt tighter.

Some hot tea would help warm her up. She dug a teaspoon into the five-pound sack of sugar and ladled out three even spoonfuls. All the while, her mind replayed the moment when Jason thought she'd been calling out to him and not the cat. She couldn't help but notice the flame of desire that had burned in his eyes. Knowing he was still interested in her unfurled a ribbon of excitement within her. Long-ignored needs swept over her, making her weak in the knees.

The spoon clanked against the mug a little too hard, jarring her attention back to stirring the tea without making a mess. They weren't meant to be, she reminded herself. She'd learned that unforgettable lesson the hard way. She didn't need a repeat. Someday she'd find the right man. He was out there somewhere.

Still, she was intrigued to know that beneath Jason's grouchy, war-hardened veneer was a kind, caring heart—one capable of opening up his home to a stray cat and an old love. She thought of mentioning her observation to him—but what was she thinking? She needed to stop dwelling on her sexy host. But being stuck with him in this cozy log home, she had no way to avoid him.

What she needed to do was keep herself busy. But doing what? She couldn't remember the last time she'd been faced with having to find something to occupy her time. Usually there weren't enough hours in the day, to help Samantha with her homework, do the laundry, cook dinner...the list went on and on. But here in Jason's home, Kara felt out of sorts.

She had just lifted the warm mug to her lips to savor that first sip of tea, which was always infinitely better than the rest, when Jason entered the room with his hair still damp from the shower. His scowl was firmly in place. In fact, the only time he'd appeared the slightest bit at ease was when he'd thought she was flirting with him. *Not going there,* she reminded herself.

"When did you get a cat?"

"I didn't."

She glanced across the room, finding the aforementioned feline sitting on the coffee table. Kara couldn't help but smile as the sleek feline let out a big yawn, showing off its pink tongue. "Are you going to try to tell me there isn't a black cat sitting across the room, staring at us?"

His forehead creased. "Of course there's a cat. But I didn't get her. She just made herself at home."

"So it's a girl. And let me guess, she was hungry and you started feeding her."

He shrugged a shoulder. "Something like that."

So the curmudgeon wasn't as hard-hearted as he wanted to let on. "What's her name?"

"Sly."

A kitty with a name was a kitty with a permanent home. "Sly? Hmm...what kind of a name is that for a girl cat?"

"For a person with a stuffed bear named Bubbles, I wouldn't be casting any stones."

Kara, feeling childish, stuck her tongue out at him. His blue eyes grew round and his pupils dilated. All the blood swirled in her chest and rushed up her neck. Obviously, that wasn't the right move to make around a man who'd just moments ago thought she was flirting with him. She inwardly groaned, wondering if she'd ever figure out how to act around him.

"Do you think Sly will ever let me pet her?"

"The way to make nice with that cat is through her stomach. If you feed her, you'll be friends for life."

Kara paused at the mention of friends for life. She wouldn't be around after tonight. In fact, she had no idea where she'd be this time next year, after Jason replaced her at the resort. Not that she intended to give him any reason to fire her. When she left she wanted it to be on her terms—with a stable job waiting, to support her and her daughter.

"How about I fix us some food?" she asked, anxious to do something—anything.

"Dinner's already taken care of," he said, getting to his feet while keeping his gaze averted. "You'll have to make do with leftover stew."

If he was anticipating an argument, he wouldn't get one. "Sounds good. Anything I can do to help?"

"No, it only needs to be warmed. Shouldn't be long. Then you can feed Sly. She eats when I eat. Keeps her occupied so she isn't stealing my food."

Kara laughed, trying to imagine such an innocent-looking thief. "Just call if you need me."

Of course he wouldn't *need* her. He'd made that abundantly clear seven years ago.

His plan was working. He'd made it through that conversation like a true host. No errant thoughts or overtly awkward moments. He just had to keep his cool a bit longer.

With the bread buttered and the stew ladled into bowls, Jason returned to the living room. He couldn't help but notice how Kara looked at home. Her hair was in disarray, and her cheeks were rosy, as though they'd just spent a lazy afternoon making love. His gaze drifted downward, catching sight of his plaid shirt with just enough buttons undone that when she leaned toward the cat he caught a glimpse of her lacy white bra. His mouth grew dry.

In some distant part of his brain, Jason knew he shouldn't be staring, but the sight was too delicious to turn away. He never would have imagined that old flannel shirt could look sexy on anyone, but he doubted Kara could look bad in anything.

Every muscle in his body grew rigid and he swallowed hard. This wasn't right. She shouldn't be here. It would be way too easy to slip back into an old, comfortable routine with her. His gaze continued to drink in her beauty, impressing it upon his memory, because that was as much of her as he'd allow himself.

When she cleared her throat and straightened her top, his gaze jerked upward, meeting her jade-green eyes. He resisted the urge to tug on the collar of his T-shirt to let out the steam coming off his heated body.

"Here, take this," he said, his voice gruffer than normal. He held out a bowl of hot stew. "I'll— It'll warm you up."

"Thank you. Smells good." She sat up, tucking her feet beneath her and reaching for the bowl and plate. "Is this homemade bread?" She sniffed it and ripped off a healthy chunk.

He nodded. "Just bought a bread machine."

Sly leaped onto the sturdy coffee table and plopped down in front of him. Her piercing gold eyes seemed to question him about why she didn't have her dinner, too.

"You'll get yours in a sec," he muttered, before leaning over and holding out a spoon for Kara. "Here."

"The stew smells so good. I can't wait to try some."

She lifted a steaming spoonful, her full lips puckered.

He couldn't turn away as she blew on the spoon, then devoured the stew. He waited, wondering what she thought of his culinary skills. When she moaned in approval, his mind spiraled in a totally different direction. His hand tightened at his side. He needed to concentrate on anything other than this infernal effect she was having on him.

He glanced back at her. Her eyes were lit up, and his chest warmed at the sight. He struggled to maintain his outward composure. Then the tip of her tongue slipped out and licked her lips. His mouth grew dry as his mind filled with the most sizzling images. A frustrated groan swelled deep inside him as he continued to stare, mesmerized by her sensuous act. Thankfully he had just enough functioning brain cells to squelch the sound before Kara realized how much power she could still wield over him.

"This is excellent," she said. "Aren't you going to eat?"

An indignant meow sounded, drawing him back to reality. He glanced down at the annoyed feline. "I'll go get yours."

He strode past the glaring cat. Right now, food was the absolute last thought on Jason's mind. The only thing he hungered for was Kara. This was going to be the longest night of his life.

If he intended to stick with his plan, his sole focus had to be on reopening the resort. Playing the friendly, considerate host was only going to get him in trouble. After all, he'd rescued her, sheltered her—heck, he'd even given her clothes to wear and a warm meal. No one could expect him to do more.

He needed to distance himself. He couldn't let his desires run unchecked, because Kara wasn't a casual-fling kind of girl. Of that he was certain. And with his past, marriage and children weren't in the cards for him. Not with Kara, not with anyone.

He had to break this spell she had over him, for her sake as much as his own. Thinking of her as just another old friend wasn't cutting it. Time for a new plan. When he returned to the living room, he'd start by reminding them both that their relationship was a professional one now... should she agree to stay on at the resort.

CHAPTER SIX

WITH THE STRAINED dinner over, Jason turned to Kara. She wasn't paying the least bit of attention to him. Instead, she was crooning over the silly cat, which was lapping up her attention as it would warmed milk.

"Kara, it's time we talked."

She scratched behind the cat's velvety ear. "With us stuck here, now probably isn't the best time to get into something serious."

"Might as well get it out of the way. There's really no time to waste."

She shot him a puzzled glance. He thought she'd have guessed he'd be extending her a job offer. After all, she'd worked her way up in the company and though he would have preferred it if things were different, she was a vital employee.

"Since you're determined to talk," she said, "get it over with."

"I want you to stay on at the resort." Her pencil-thin brows shot upward, but not giving her a chance to turn him down before he finished, he rushed on. "I want you to work for me as my assistant."

Her mouth opened, but only air came out. Why did she look as though he'd just handed her a life sentence? Couldn't she be the least bit happy, or appear interested?

"Say something," he demanded, getting to his feet to put another log on the fire.

"I...I don't know what to say. I thought you'd be replacing me, and I'd be moving on. A new town. A new job. A new life."

Did he detect a hint of regret in her voice? Was she upset because he'd messed up her plans to get out of Pleasant Valley? Was this her chance to escape, and he was standing in her way?

He knew what it was like to want to move away. Sure, when he was a little kid, things had been good at home. Back then he couldn't imagine ever leaving the Greene Summit. But his entire life had changed the day his mother died. His father's drinking had increased. The yelling and fighting quickly escalated. Nothing Jason did was right. His waning ego craved a chance to prove himself as a man. Yet he couldn't leave behind the one woman who loved him—Kara.

Swept up in his need to show the world he wasn't the screwup his father accused him of being, he'd convinced Kara to become his army wife. When she'd suggested dropping out of college and starting their adventure right away, he'd agreed. Even then he knew he wasn't being fair to her, but he'd convinced himself he'd find a way to make it up to her.

Looking back now, he realized how wrong he'd been to attempt to drag her into his messed-up life. After learning Kara had dropped out of college anyway—she'd never finished her degree—he felt awful. Another of her dreams dashed. The guilt on his shoulders doubled. Holding Kara back now wouldn't be fair to her. If moving on was important to her, he wouldn't stand in her way.

But above all, he was a businessman. The success of the resort had to be his priority. He had employees relying on him for a paycheck. And more importantly, he wasn't the only investor in this endeavor. He had people to answer to if he didn't produce a profit.

When he glanced up, the worry in her green eyes ripped at his gut. He needed to come up with a solution that would work for both of them. That would leave Kara with an out.

"Work for me at the Summit until after the New Year. Just until I get a handle on everything," he offered, even though he'd much rather have her and her wealth of knowledge on hand for a lot longer.

She eyed him. "What's in it for me?"

He couldn't resist smiling at her resilience. She would definitely land on her feet, no matter where she ended up. "How about three months' severance?"

"And?"

"And...a glowing recommendation. Do we have a deal?"

"Maybe."

"Maybe?" He jumped to his feet and turned toward his home office. "Fine, you think about it. I have work to do."

"While you're working, what do you expect me to do?"

He paused and faced her. "There's got to be something around here to amuse you. Maybe check the stash in the loft. You should find some of my grandmother's books. Feel free to bring down whatever you want. I don't have any use for that junk."

He strode away, disappointed that she hadn't jumped at the chance to stay on at the resort. Still, the worry over whether she'd accept his offer was a welcome distraction from his continual battle with his blasted attraction to her.

In hindsight, he had to concede that she was right to weigh her options. He certainly would if he were in her shoes. Now he just hoped she came to the conclusion that would benefit them both.

* * *

Kara watched until he disappeared into the shadows. He wanted her to work for him—well, temporarily. The fact he wanted her input for the reopening had her straightening her shoulders as a tiny smile tugged at her lips. The knowledge that he recognized her accomplishments was quite satisfying.

But even with this recognition, was it possible for her to set aside the past and work closely with a man who could melt her insides with one heated glance?

She'd tried so hard to put the past behind her. She couldn't let him tear down all her defenses. The surest means of doing that would be to turn down his offer. No pondering. No wondering. Just a simple "no."

Oh, who was she kidding? She couldn't just walk away—she didn't have another job lined up. How would she make the mortgage payment at the end of the month? Or buy Samantha some desperately needed shoes after her latest growth spurt?

In desperation, Kara considered turning to her parents, but they simply couldn't afford to help her out financially. Her father had been laid off last year from the job he'd held for more than two decades, and had had to take a lesser paying position with the local mall security. No, approaching them for assistance wasn't an option.

Until she found the right position, Kara had no choice but to deal with working with Jason. But for now, he didn't have to know she'd made up her mind. He could sweat it out a little while. If he thought she had alternatives, he might not take her for granted.

Eager to find a distraction, she glanced around. Her bag of knitting supplies was waiting by the front door, but Jason's invitation to explore the books in the loft was too good to pass up. She rushed over to the spiral staircase.

Their steepness forced her to slow down, having already had enough accidents for one night. At the top, she pulled on a chain hanging from a bare lightbulb, which illuminated the area. Stacks of cardboard boxes littered the floor. Surely not all of them contained books.

Like a kid on Christmas morning, she grabbed the first unmarked box and carried it to a vacant spot near the stairs. She dropped to her knees and flipped open the flaps. Inside, she found heaps of old clothes—shirts and pants that definitely had seen better days. What in the world had his grandmother been thinking, to keep this stuff?

Then a thought struck Kara. Maybe she'd stumbled across a way she could repay Jason's generosity for letting her ride out the storm here. She scampered back down the stairs and found a pen on the coffee table. Once back in the loft, she marked the box "Old Clothes. Trash."

Box after box she visually inventoried. There were old newspapers, magazines, threadbare towels and other unnecessary items. All of which she tagged for disposal.

With no more room to stack the sorted boxes, and growing tired, she pulled one last carton from the heap, hoping to at last locate a romance novel. She folded back the flaps and lifted some discolored tissue paper, to find an assortment of handblown glass balls. She grinned, feeling like a child who'd found buried treasure.

These Christmas ornaments had been lovingly wrapped and stowed away with great care. Kara vowed then and there that they would not see the inside of a Dumpster, even if it meant her taking them home.

A piece of red felt stuck between two small boxes. Intrigued, she pulled it out, to discover a stocking with white fur around the edge, with Jason's name stitched in gold thread along the instep. Her index finger traced the stitches. This had been created with love, a love she was certain Jason hadn't felt in a very long time.

He might avoid anything Christmassy, but maybe it was time he got a dose of holiday spirit sprinkled with a dash of childhood nostalgia.

Jason stared at the stack of mail on his desk with zero interest. His thoughts kept straying to the occasional sounds that came from other parts of the house. A loud thunk followed by a thump emanated from the living room. He paused in his attempt to locate where he'd placed his checkbook. Damn. What was that woman up to?

Not hearing anything else, he pulled open the left-hand desk drawer. She'd call if she needed him. He refused to accept that he was hiding from her because of the crazy things she did to his body with a mere look or a casual touch. He had responsibilities. He was a busy man with things he had to get done. He simply didn't have spare time—

Bang! He jumped to his feet. The desk chair rolled back, crashing into the credenza. With long strides, he hurried to the great room, where he blinked, unable to believe his eyes.

"Are you just going to stand there? Or are you going to help me?" Kara glowered at him as she yanked on the trunk of a pine tree that was now wedged in the doorway.

"What are you doing?"

"You told me to find something to do. I'm doing it." She gave another tug and the tree suddenly came loose, sending her stumbling back into his arms.

His heart leaped into his throat. She was soft. But her body was chilled from being outside. A longing to pull her closer and warm her up swamped his senses. This was not good. But it wasn't as if he'd done anything wrong. She couldn't hold it against him because he enjoyed the way her soft curves felt.

All too soon, she was steady on her feet. He jerked his hands away and stuffed them in his back pockets. "I meant for you to find a book to read. Not destroy my house."

She held on to the pine with one hand and turned to him. Her cheeks were rosy from the cold and begged to be warmed with a kiss.... No! Don't go there. He'd just extended her a job offer. He had to start thinking of her as an employee, no matter how much she reminded him of a sexy, tempting snow bunny.

"Since we're stuck here tonight," she said, distracting him from his errant thoughts, "I have nothing else to do...."

"We've discussed this. I don't do Christmas."

"Come on. You'll have fun stringing lights and arranging the ornaments."

His lips pressed into a firm line. "I can't think of anything I'd like less."

"Okay, Scrooge. I'll decorate the tree by myself. If you hate it, you can toss it tomorrow, after I'm gone. Okay?"

He frowned. It would keep her busy and out of his way. Ah, what could it hurt? As she said, after she left he could get rid of it. No harm, no foul.

"Just don't break anything with that bushy shrub." He started for the study.

"It's a tree—a Christmas tree," she called after him. "And where are you going?"

What could she possibly want now? He clenched his hands, his temples pounding. If she hounded him again about decorating that blasted tree, he swore he'd cut it into kindling. "I have work to do."

"Not before you help me move the table. I think the tree would look best in front of the picture window, don't you?"

He groaned. Kara smiled as though she took the utmost pleasure in his misery. With a twinkle in her eyes and a shake of her head, she turned her back on him and set to work. Once they'd moved the table, she needed a little more help. This time he had to hold the six-foot tree upright while she screwed on the base. Then the tree had to be adjusted, to make certain it was straight in the holder.

Jason clenched his jaw until it ached, holding back a string of gripes. He moved the tree this way and that way until she deemed it was in the perfect location. He knew where it would be perfect—in the burn pile. But not wanting to go another round with Kara, he choked down his sarcasm. No wonder he didn't bother with the holidays. They were a big waste of time.

"Are you sure you don't want to stay and help?" she asked, as if it was some great honor. "There's plenty to do."

He shook his head, but the enthusiastic glow on her smiling face made him wonder what he was missing. How could hanging doodads on a dumb tree make Kara glow with happiness? Although even if he didn't understand what the fuss was about, he enjoyed seeing Kara happy, he reluctantly admitted. She should definitely smile more often.

"I'll be in the study if you need me." He inwardly cringed at his choice of words. Kara could do quite well, fending for herself.

He took a few steps, then paused and turned. She'd already started digging through the cardboard boxes, lifting out smaller containers. For some reason, he was having a hard time walking away. But why? This was what he wanted: Kara occupied, so he could go off on his own. Then why did he feel he was about to miss something special?

Back in his study, Jason paused by the window and

noticed how the storm had intensified. The fallen snow was being scooped off the ground by howling gusts of wind, causing a virtual whiteout. With a disgusted sigh, he turned away.

He sank down in his desk chair and forced himself to read over the latest credit card statement. Not much later, the desk lamp flickered. At first he thought there was an electrical short, but when the light flickered again, he noticed that it affected the whole house. If they got the predicted ice on top of those winds, they'd be plunged into darkness. He raked his fingers through his hair and leaned back in the chair. Being alone in the dark with Kara, with nothing to do but snuggle in front of the fire, would be his undoing.

Her sweet voice floated through the house as she sang "Jingle Bells." Happiness rang out with each note. He could just imagine her dancing around the tree, hanging decorations here and there, a goofy look plastered on her adorable face. What he wouldn't do to watch her.

He gave his head a quick shake. He refused to let her singing draw him back to the great room. His gaze scanned the desk. Something was missing tonight, but what? His laptop. He'd left it in the other room, where Kara was pretending to be one of Santa's elves. Jason wasn't going back in there to get anything. No way. Besides, it wasn't the laptop that was bothering him.

Then it dawned on him. Sly was missing. The little black-as-night scamp usually followed him around the house in the evenings. Sometimes he wondered if the cat mistakenly thought she was a dog. He affectionately referred to her as his puppy-cat.

When he worked at the desk, she'd make herself at home on the left corner. She did it so consistently that he'd actually cleared a spot for her. Tonight the spot was empty.

Kara had not only invaded his home and his thoughts, but also had stolen his cat's affections. What was next?

Kara sorted through the open boxes scattered around the living room. Wads of paper flew. Little boxes were tossed aside. They had to be here. She started her search over again, beginning with the first box.

When her fingers at last wrapped around the crystalline icicles, she sighed. They were just what she needed to reflect the colorful lights. One by one, she attached a metal hook to the end of each ornament.

In the background, the sound of crinkling tissue paper filled the air. She glanced over to find Sly batting around a blue satin ball Kara had set aside for the garbage. The cat grabbed the small ball in her mouth and, with a jerk of her head, tossed the ornament into the air before taking off in hot pursuit.

Kara laughed at the cat's antics. If only her daughter was here to witness the shenanigans. On second thought, it was probably a good thing Samantha wasn't here or she'd start pestering Kara about wanting a kitten for Christmas—not that the subject was ever far from her daughter's lips.

Kara had started singing a round of "Deck the Halls" when the little hairs on her neck lifted. She had company. Resisting the urge to turn around, she finished hanging the icicles. She took a couple of steps back and inspected her work. Each light had been positioned with care, and then the garland had been added. And last but not least she'd used an assortment of ornaments, small at the top and large at the bottom. She'd been thrilled to find some with Jason's name on them.

"Well, what do you think?" she asked, admiring her handiwork.

Secretly, she longed for him to ooh and aah over the

trouble she'd gone to. She waited, wringing her hands together as the silence stretched out. At last Jason stepped up next to her, but he remained silent. He hated the tree. She was certain of it. Her heart sank.

She turned to apologize for overstepping, and to offer to take it down, but the wonderment reflected in his blue eyes halted her words. He stood transfixed, seemingly lost in memories. She hoped he'd gone back in time—to happier days, when his mother was alive.

Kara had never known his mother, but on the rare times he mentioned her it was always with devotion and reverence. He made her sound as if she'd walked on water. Kara used to wonder if that was what had happened to their own relationship. Had he matched her up to his mother and found her lacking?

"These ornaments," he said. "Were they in the loft?"

She nodded, but realizing his gaze hadn't moved from the tree, she added, "Yes. Do you remember them? Some have your name on them."

He stepped toward the tree and lifted an ornament of a little blond-haired boy on a rocking horse. His name was scrolled in black paint along the runner.

"I can't believe you found these."

"Surely you don't think your grandmother would have tossed them out?" He obviously hadn't glanced in those boxes to see what the woman had packed away. He was in for a surprise.

"They weren't hers. These," he said, holding the rocking horse ornament, "belonged to my mother."

"You didn't know they were up there?"

"After my mother died…my dad threw out everything. Pictures. Books. Anything that reminded him of her."

Kara's heart ached for Jason. No wonder as a kid he'd never wanted to spend time at that house. It'd been stripped of everything that was important to him. His mother. His past.

"Even the Christmas ornaments?" she asked, trying to keep her voice level to hide her astonishment.

"This was my mother's favorite time of year. She died the week before Christmas."

Her death had happened years before Kara knew Jason. At last she understood his Scrooge-like attitude.

"My grandmother must have known what my father was doing, and salvaged what she could." He turned to Kara. "Thank you for finding them."

She swallowed the lump of emotion clogging her throat. "I'm happy you were able to reconnect with your past." At least part of it. But there was one more thing he needed to do. "Maybe it isn't too late for you and your dad."

"Yes, it is."

Jason's frosty tone warned her not to go any further along this path, but being so ill, the man wasn't capable of tracking down his son and pleading his own case. Jason's father needed her help, and after he had helped her move up through the company, providing her with the means to support her daughter, she wanted to do this for him now. Somehow she had to convince Jason it wasn't too late to rebuild that broken bridge.

"Christmas is a time for love and forgiveness." She placed a hand on his shoulder, feeling his tension. "If not for your father, then do this for yourself. Forgive him for the past. Let it go."

He pulled away from her. "You don't know what you're asking."

"I'm asking for a Christmas miracle."

CHAPTER SEVEN

IN THE STRAINED silence, Jason helped hang a few last ornaments. All the while, he tried to understand why a bunch of colorful ribbon, satin and molded glass should cause a lump to form in his throat. He swallowed hard, trying to push down the sentimental pang in his chest.

Still, his mind tumbled back in time. He clearly recalled being an excited little kid going with both his parents to pick out a Christmas tree. He knew his father would rather be at home watching football, but his mother insisted they search the mountainside for the perfect tree. Through the snow they'd trudge until his mom gave her stamp of approval on a very special pine tree.

Of course, that had been before his dad lived only for his next drink. Before everything went so terribly wrong.

His father, for all his faults, had loved his wife. And he'd played along with the festive plans for the holidays, making Jason's mother very happy. Would playing along with Kara make her just as happy? Maybe in this one instance Jason should follow the old man's lead.

He turned to her. The expectant look on her face immediately had him uttering, "You did a great job with the tree."

Her smile blossomed and her straight white teeth peeked out from behind her lush lips. An urge mounted within him to cave in to his desire to sample her sweetness—once again pull her close and see if her kisses were as good as he remembered.

"You can help me with one last thing." She knelt down next to an open box. "And what are you doing in here, little one?" She straightened, holding Sly in her arms. "Guess you don't have the same aversion to the holiday as some people we know."

Jason rolled his eyes at the cat's silly expression. And Sly's purring was the loudest he'd ever heard. It seemed Kara had totally won over his cat. What was next?

After Kara placed the cat on the quilt on the couch, she turned back to the box and pulled out an elongated container. Something about it rang a bell in his mind, but he couldn't quite pull the fuzzy memory into focus.

"I found this earlier and knew it would be the perfect final touch."

She peeled back the tissue paper and reached inside. With great care, she lifted out a Christmas angel. His Christmas angel. The breath hitched in his throat. Each year, his mother had helped him put the angel on top of the tree.

"Could you help me with this?" Kara asked, holding the delicate object out to him. "I'm too short to reach."

He accepted the angel and gazed down at her painted blue eyes, graceful wings and golden halo. The white material had yellowed over the years, but she was still beautiful. His vision blurred. Damn, dust from these boxes must be irritating his eyes. He turned his back to Kara and swiped an arm across his face.

Then, clearing his throat, he rose up on his toes and placed the angel atop the tree. He took a moment to make sure it was properly positioned, just as his mother would have insisted. Then he stepped back.

"Looks perfect," Kara said.

He nodded, not yet trusting his voice.

"I'm so glad I was able to find it. Childhood mementos can be so precious."

His gaze remained on the angel. A powerful sensation came over him, as though his mother was trying to send him a message. He knew it was impossible. Ghosts weren't real. People couldn't talk to you from the great beyond. Still, there was this feeling that she wanted to get a message to him. But what?

"It's like it's a sign," Kara said, startling him with her choice of words.

He turned to her, noticing how the Christmas lights highlighted her delicate features. Here in this setting, she didn't look like someone he needed to hold at arm's length. Maybe if he let his guard down just this once...

The lights flickered. A surprised gasp crossed Kara's lips. Then they were plunged into darkness, except for the glow of the fireplace.

"Don't worry," he said. "We've got plenty of wood to keep us warm."

"You don't think the power will come back on like it did before?"

"Not with those fierce winds. We'll be lucky to have power by tomorrow."

Even though the strings of lights on the Christmas tree were darkened, the silver garland shimmered in the firelight.

"We'll need more blankets before this night is out," he said, starting for the bedroom. "I'll grab some from the closet. They might be a bit musty, but better smelly than frigid."

Not only was he stuck with an unwanted houseguest, but they'd be a lot closer as they huddled around the fire for warmth. What in the world were you supposed to do while snowed in with your ex? Okay, well, he knew what he wouldn't mind doing....

That couldn't—it wouldn't happen. His teeth ground together. *Stick with the plan,* he reminded himself. *Remain cool and detached.*

With an armful of old blankets, he headed back to the living room. "I found these to keep us warm."

"Do you really think we'll need all of those? It's pretty warm in here already with the fire."

"For now. With the winds whipping around out there, the temperatures will plummet. The house will cool off quickly and you'll appreciate some extra blankets."

He stood rooted to the spot, watching as the light danced across her porcelain-like face. Most women looked better with a touch of makeup, but not Kara. She didn't need any paint to enhance her wide green eyes, her pert little nose or those pouty lips that always drew his attention.

Not wanting to be called out for staring, he turned around to stoke the fire. Thinking it could use another log, he grabbed one from the dwindling stack.

"I better haul in some more wood to hold us over for the night," he said, not relishing the thought.

"You can't go out there. It's too cold and windy. We can make do."

"We don't have enough logs to keep the fire going all night."

"What about your knee? It won't be good having it out in the cold."

"You've certainly got that fussing and worrying bit down pat. Your daughter is very lucky to have you." Jason couldn't be sure, but by the way Kara ducked her head, he'd bet she was blushing. "Don't be embarrassed about it."

"I'm not." She lifted her gaze to meet his. "I'll fetch

the wood. You've already done enough with getting dinner and cleaning up. It's my turn to help out."

Their gazes locked and held. At first there was a challenge in her eyes, as though she was tempting him to look away first, just as they'd done numerous times as kids. But then there was something more, something deeper. His breath lodged in his throat. He should turn away, but couldn't.

He was entranced by her eyes, seeing not only their beauty but also a hint of pain. What had put it there? Was it him? Had he hurt her that deeply all those years ago when he'd taken off for the army?

He ran his hand over his short hair. His thoughts strayed back to his time in the military, with its camaraderie and the way it kept him on the go, not leaving him time to dwell on his past mistakes. Even in basic training, there hadn't been anything they could taunt him with worse than what he'd already heard from his own drunken father.

Jason had worked his butt off, proving himself to the world. As his rank rose, his bruised ego gained strength. He was a soldier, an identity that had filled him with pride. And he'd been a damn good one...until he'd lost control. He'd let his dark side out. And the price had been devastating.

But how did he explain any of it to Kara? How did he open up to her and tell her that he was still groping around, trying to figure out how to keep his unsavory side under wraps?

Anxious for some physical labor, he headed for the door. "I'm the man. I should be the one getting the wood."

"You're the man?" Her fine brows lifted. "Where the heck did that come from?"

He sighed, realizing far too late that he'd said exactly

the wrong thing. "I just meant that you'd want to stay inside next to the fire."

Her lips pursed and her eyes narrowed. Apparently that wasn't the right thing to say, either. Why did it seem as if he suddenly couldn't open his mouth without sticking his boot in it? Military life had been so much easier. He knew what was expected of him—follow orders and don't complain. Being a civilian left him grasping for the right actions, the right words.

"Does the power outage constitute us being thrown back into the dark ages?" She planted her hands on her hips. "Me woman. You man. Let me hear you roar—"

"Hey, that isn't what I meant." He chuckled at the ridiculousness of this conversation. Definitely the wrong move, as Kara's expression grew darker. "I was just trying to be nice. After your car accident, I figured the last thing you'd want to be doing tonight is stumbling around in the snow again."

When the fury in her eyes dimmed, he breathed easier. "I'll be right back."

Sly got up from her spot on the couch. She stretched, before jumping down and running past him on the way to the door, where she stood up on her hind legs and pawed at the knob.

"Oh, no," he said. "You aren't going outside tonight. You'd blow away."

"Here, Sly. Stay with me, sweetie."

Jason's shoulders tensed at the sound of Kara calling the cat by a name she used to call him.

Just let it go. That was then, this is now.

Minutes later, a thump followed by a crash sent Kara scurrying to the door. After shooing the cat away, she reached for the handle, but before she could grasp it, the door swung open.

A gust of frigid air swirled around her, sending goose bumps racing up her arms. Jason stood there with a layer of ice on his hat as well as his coat. Purple tinged his lips while his lashes and brows were caked with snow. But it was the dark scowl on his face that had her worried.

"What's the matter?"

He shook his head, then he handed over his armload of wood, before exiting back into the stormy night with a pronounced limp. She wanted to call after him to stop and rest, but she knew he wouldn't listen. Kara ran to the side of the fireplace and dropped the split wood in a heap. They continued working together until all the wood was piled on the floor. With the door locked, barring Old Man Winter, Jason limped to the chair by the door.

"Here, let me," she said, rushing over to help him with his boots. "You obviously aggravated your knee. And it's my fault. If I hadn't insisted on you retrieving my belongings from my car, you wouldn't have...done whatever it is that you did."

He reached down, grabbing her hands in his. "It's not your fault."

"Of course it is." She yanked free of his hold and continued her fight with the iced-over knot.

"Kara, you aren't listening to me. The limp. It's permanent."

This time she stopped fiddling with his laces and stared up at him. "What are you saying?"

"Remember how I told you I have a medical discharge?" She nodded and he continued, "Well, it's because of this injury to my leg."

A sickening feeling settled in her stomach. "How bad was it?"

"Bad enough."

She needed more than that. The pile of secrets and omissions between them was unbearable. She wouldn't stand for any more. She lifted his wet pant leg up to his knee, revealing an ugly red line snaking down his calf.

The breath locked in her lungs. Her vision blurred. It tore at her heart to think of him bleeding and alone in a foreign country, miles from home. He'd had no family by his side in the hospital to talk to him, to hold his hand. No one should ever be that alone.

Jason lowered his pant leg. "It's an ugly mess farther up. So much for those sexy legs you used to go on about."

She dashed her fingers over her eyes. "Tell me what happened?"

He shook his head, once again blocking her out. "Just write it off to 'shit happens.'"

Sensing he hadn't opened up about it to anyone, Kara pressed on. After seeing the sizable wound, she knew keeping the memory all bottled up inside wouldn't allow him a chance to heal. "I'd like to know, if you'll tell me."

He rubbed his injured knee as though unearthing those memories increased his discomfort. "It wasn't anything spectacular. Just a normal day in the Middle East. Our unit was out on patrol…."

He paused and his gaze grew distant, as though he were seeing the events unfold in front of his eyes. His jaw tensed, as did the corded muscles of his neck. She wanted to reach out to him, but hesitated.

Jason cleared his throat. "My buddy Dorsy was on foot patrol with me. Earlier that day, he'd spotted a Christmas card addressed to me. The return address had a girl's name on it and he jumped to the conclusion that I had a secret girlfriend."

The thought of Jason in another woman's arms left a

sour taste in Kara's mouth. But she had no claim over him. Who he chose to spend his time with shouldn't matter to her.

"Were you and this girl serious?"

He swiped a hand over his face before rolling his shoulders. "No. I didn't even know her. Besides, I don't get involved in serious relationships. Not anymore."

"I noticed," Kara muttered under her breath. His arched brows let her know her slip hadn't gone unnoticed. "Sorry. Please go on."

"The card was from a high school student whose class had sent them to deployed soldiers. But Dorsy wouldn't drop the subject. He kept pushing, wanting to know… It doesn't matter now. The thing is I couldn't take his digs any longer. I told him to shut up, but when he wouldn't, I lost control—I shoved him."

Kara placed her hand over his cold fingers. "Yelling and giving him a push isn't so bad. I'm sure he forgave you."

Jason pulled away. "He never got the chance. He stumbled into the opening of an abandoned building, triggering a booby trap."

"Oh! I'm so sorry." The words were lacking, but they were all she had. "He was lucky he had you as a friend."

Jason shook his head. "No, he wasn't. If I hadn't lost my temper, he'd still be alive. I always end up hurting those closest to me." He paused yet again, as though to pull himself together. "Now, how about you finish untying my boot?"

Kara blinked repeatedly before making short work of unstringing his laces. "Is there anything that can lessen the pain in your knee?"

The tension in his face soothed as they moved on to a new topic of conversation. "Sometimes I use a heating pad, but without power that isn't an option."

She tried to think of a substitute. "Do you have a hot water bottle?"

He broke out into a chuckle. "Do they still make such a thing?"

She shrugged. "Hey, I'm just trying to help."

"I know. And I appreciate it."

The sincerity in his eyes sent a warmth swirling in her chest. When he smiled, her heart tripped over itself. She needed some distance. Some air. Anything to calm the rush of emotions charging through her body.

"I'll be back," he said. "I need to change into something dry."

She nodded and made her way over to the mess of wood on the floor. Work was a welcome distraction, but all too soon she had the logs neatly stacked, and had no idea what to do next. She plopped down on the couch and reached for a magazine. It was a sports issue, but thankfully, not the swimsuit edition. When she lifted it, something fluttered to the floor. A photograph.

It landed upside down. She wondered what image was on the other side. His ex-girlfriend? Did he sit here at night thinking of her? The chance that she'd been letting herself get all tangled up in old emotions while he was secretly pining for another woman left Kara spinning. The old Jason wouldn't have done that, but this new Jason she knew next to nothing about.

Anxious for an answer, she snatched up the photo. Her gaze riveted to the image of two young men with similar blue eyes and brown hair, each holding a colorful snowboard. Their appearances were so strikingly similar that they'd been mistaken numerous times for brothers.

Shaun...

At that moment, the floorboards creaked, announcing Jason's presence. He joined her on the couch. "Ah, I see you've found the picture of Shaun. Do you remember that time?"

Did she remember? She was the one who'd taken the photo.

"I remember." She swallowed hard. "We were sixteen. And life was so much easier back then."

Jason took the photo from her and held it in front of him. "Never thought we'd be sitting here nearly twelve years later, and things would be so screwed up. Back then we were the Three Musketeers. Now you and I hardly speak to one and other. And Shaun's..."

"Dead." The word pierced her chest.

"I know. It's been what? Seven years since he died in a car accident."

"How do you know about it?" She turned to him. "When you left, I thought you cut off all contact with Pleasant Valley. Or was it just me and your father you cut out of your life?"

His brows furrowed together. He reached out to her, but she scooted to the far end of the couch. "It wasn't like you're thinking."

"Then how was it?"

"When I left, I vowed I wouldn't look back. It was easy to get lost in my job, my mission. In the beginning, I'd volunteer for whatever assignment came up—regardless of the risk—but as the years passed, my curiosity about what went on back here grew."

She crossed her arms and glared at him. "So who did you contact?"

"You've heard of the internet, haven't you?"

She released a pent-up breath. "Oh."

"That's where I came across the *Pleasant Valley Journal* and stumbled over the article about Shaun's car accident. Damn shame. He was so young. He had his whole future to look forward to."

She nodded. Unable to find her voice, she thought of the boy who'd always followed Jason around, from childhood through their high school days. He'd always been there for Jason and her. Trusted, funny and dependable. Those were the traits she'd loved about Shaun.

It wasn't until Jason left town that she'd learned Shaun had been harboring feelings for her. With her being madly in love with Jason, she'd never even considered that Shaun's devotion was anything more than a deep, caring friend-ship. But the night Jason broke her heart at the Christmas dance, Shaun had been the one to drive her home. And again, a couple of months later, he'd been there at one of the lowest points in her life. He'd reached out to her and...

"Kara, are you okay?" Jason asked, moving next to her.

She glanced back at the photo, seeing Shaun's sweet smiling face...so much like her daughter's.

"I'm fine." Her voice was barely more than a whisper.

"It's okay. You aren't alone. I miss how things used to be, too."

The wind howled outside, while Jason's heated gaze warmed her soul. The past and the present collided. His thumb brushed over her cheek and down her neck. Kara's heart thumped madly. Could he feel the blood pulsating through her veins, making her head dizzy with need?

His gaze dropped. His pupils dilated. He was going to kiss her. Her breath caught in her lungs. This was wrong. But it'd be only once. For old times' sake. Drawn to him in the same manner a hummingbird craves sweet nectar, she licked her lips with the tip of her tongue.

His head lowered. She should turn away.

Instead, her eyes drifted closed. His mouth pressed to hers. A moan of long-held desire formed at the base of her throat. This was crazy. Utter madness. And in that moment she wanted nothing more than to be here with him, like this.

She slid her arms over his shoulders. Her fingers stroked his short tufts of hair, enjoying the texture.

His hands moved to her waist, pulling her closer. Her chest bumped against the hardness of his. Her palms slid down his shoulders, savoring the ripple of muscles. No man had a right to feel so good. She attempted to impress every delicious detail, every spine-tingling sensation to memory. She never, ever wanted to forget this moment.

His mouth plundered hers. She welcomed him with an eagerness of her own. Her protective walls fell away, leaving her open and vulnerable to this man who made her body sing with desire.

Her breath came in rapid gasps. Her hands slipped inside the collar of his shirt. His skin was smooth and hot.

"Kara," he murmured, as his lips traced up her jaw. "I want you so much."

She wanted him, too. The years peeled away. Lost in a haze of ecstasy, she couldn't form even the simplest of words. Instead, she sought out his lips and showed him how much she wanted him.

A thundering crack sent her jumping out of his arms. Dazed, she glanced around the room.

"What…what was that?" she asked, her breathing labored.

"It's okay," he said, running a hand over her hair. "Probably a tree limb snapped in the wind. As long as it doesn't come through the roof, we're in good shape."

Satisfied they were still safe in their little bubble, away from the realities waiting for them just outside the door, she turned her hungry gaze back to him. She leaned forward, eager to taste him once more. Thirsting for him like a person lost in the desert thirsts for water, she pressed her lips to his mouth.

Yet his lips did not yield to her.

They were pulled tight, resisting her advances.

Confused, she sat back.

The flames of desire in his eyes had died out.

"This can't happen." His voice was raspy and his chest heaved. "You and me. This thing. It can't happen. Not now. Not ever."

CHAPTER EIGHT

EVERY MUSCLE IN Jason's body tensed, bracing for the firestorm brewing in Kara's eyes. She yanked herself out of his hold.

"You're right." She ran a shaky hand over her mussed-up hair, failing to smooth the unruly waves. "I don't know what I was thinking. You rejected me once. Why in the world did I think it'd be any different now?"

"It's not you. I never rejected you."

"Really? That's odd. I seem to recall you making me promises of forever, and then just leaving, with no explanation." Pink stained her cheeks as her voice rose almost to a shout. "You didn't even have the decency to tell me what I'd done wrong. You never gave me a chance to fix things."

He smothered a swear word and shot to his feet, ignoring the ache in his leg. With a pronounced limp, he moved to the fireplace. He had to tell her. He had to explain the terrible secret that drove them apart—the one that would keep them apart forever.

"It wasn't you. It was me," he said, turning to meet her glare.

"Sure. Whatever you say." Her eyes said she didn't believe him.

"I already told you how I got my buddy killed. Isn't that enough to convince you that I'm bad news?"

"That was a very unfortunate accident." She settled her hands on her hips. "It has nothing to do with this... with us."

He'd have to go into the whole sordid story to make her see that his hasty departure had been in a moment of shock—of self-defense. And it had absolutely nothing to do with anything she'd said or done.

Refusing to give in to the pain in his leg, he paced to the end of the fireplace mantel, then turned, with a precision drilled into him during his time in the military. He'd never divulged his shameful secret to anyone. At least his father had done one decent thing in his life and kept it to himself. Except for the fateful night when he'd flung the gruesome secret in Jason's face.

His gut churned as the nightmare began to unfold in his mind.

Jason paused. Looked at Kara. Opened his mouth. Then closed it.

With a jerk, he turned away. The pain in his leg was no match for the agony in his chest. He continued pacing. Where did he start? And what did he do when his worst nightmare came true—when Kara looked at him with revulsion? An acidic taste rose in the back of his throat and he swallowed hard.

"Don't do this again. Don't shut me out," she insisted. "Talk to me."

"I can't—"

"Yes, you can. Tell me what awful thing drove you from your home—from me. Or is it that there isn't any secret? Did you just chicken out when things got too serious? Instead of facing me and explaining why you wanted out of the engagement, did you find it easier to bolt?"

Did she really think him such a coward? He considered not telling her, considered holding back out of spite, but that would be childish. After everything, she deserved the truth. No matter how much it cost him.

"It all happened the night I was supposed to meet you at the Christmas dance." His voice grew uneven and he paused to clear his throat.

He searched for the right words. There were none. His palms grew moist. Puzzlement lit her eyes, as though she was trying to guess what he would say next.

"I was on my way out the door when my father stopped me."

Jason inhaled an unsteady breath and blew it out. "We started arguing about his expectations for me around the resort. I'd had enough of him criticizing my job performance, nitpicking my every move. I blurted out that I planned to enlist in the army. He was livid. I'd never seen him so angry. He told me I was an ungrateful, sniveling brat and that I owed it to him to run the place."

Jason glanced up to see the color wash out of Kara's face. Her eyes were large and round, prompting him to keep going.

"I said I was tired of being a slave to a man who lived his life inside a bottle. I didn't stop there. I also told him you and I were getting married and leaving this place. He laughed in my face. His alcohol-laced breath made me want to puke."

Jason forced another breath in, then out. "He said no woman would want to marry me when she found out the truth. I told him there wasn't anything he could say or do to keep me from marrying you."

Boy, had he been wrong.

He swallowed hard, fighting back the wave of fear over Kara's impending repulsion. He wanted more than anything in the world for her to understand, but how do you understand the incomprehensible? How do you reconcile yourself to the fact that the person you thought you'd once known was a stranger?

He just had to say a little more and then it'd be out there. There'd be no more fighting this attraction, because she'd never let him get close to her again. And he wouldn't blame her.

"My father staggered up to me. He stabbed his finger in my chest and stared at me with those bloodred eyes. He told me I was an ungrateful bastard. His words were slurred, but their point came across loud and clear."

Kara's hand flew to her mouth. Her eyes shimmered with pity.

When dreadful seconds of silence fell over the room, she asked, "Why in the world would he say such hateful things to you? No parent wants to see their child leave home, but…"

"But he was drunk, and furious at me for what he saw as betrayal, for leaving him here to deal with a resort that was losing money left and right."

After seven years, the events of that night stood out crystal clear in Jason's mind. His father's words still held the power to stab at his heart, forcing him to blink repeatedly to clear the blur in his eyes.

In his mind, he could still recall his father's last blow—the one that shattered any hope he'd had of having a life with Kara. He wasn't his father's biological son. Under the strained circumstances, that should have given him some comfort—but it didn't.

The truth about his origins was so much worse. He'd run from it for so long that now there was no place left to hide.

He was the spawn of a monster.

The breath hitched in his throat. Kara would never be able to look at him the same if he told her. The thought ripped at his gut.

"Still, you were barely twenty years old," she said, drawing him from his jagged thoughts. "How could he do such a thing? I understand why you left, but why didn't you take me with you? Or at least talk to me so that we could make plans?"

With his head hung low, Jason turned away. "I couldn't."

"Why? What aren't you telling me?"

"You won't understand," he shouted.

Frustration balled up in his gut over his cowardice to spit out the real reason he'd left, the reason he could no longer be with her. He was the son of a rapist—his mother's rapist.

"I never knew you thought so little of me." Pain reflected brightly in Kara's eyes. "I thought…I thought back then that we could tell each other anything."

His vision blurred. His throat started to close. He had to stomp down these tormenting emotions. He was a soldier. He was strong. He could get through this and be honest with her.

He lifted his head. His gaze met hers. He opened his mouth, but nothing came out. The thought of her being repulsed, or worse, being afraid, silenced him.

Besides, what did it matter now? They'd both been reminded that they weren't good for each other. Nothing more needed to be said.

"I have to get some more wood," he muttered, needing to be alone for a moment to collect his thoughts.

"Right now, in the middle of our talk?" Disbelief and frustration laced her voice.

"We're going to need it tonight." He walked to the wood pegs by the door to grab his coat.

"But you just got some—"

"Not enough."

CHAPTER NINE

THE FOLLOWING MORNING, the rumble of a snowplow signaled their freedom. Jason didn't waste any time calling the towing company for Kara's car. Learning there was a considerable wait for service, he ushered her out the door. He needed to get her home. Now. He couldn't let his thoughts become any more muddled.

The ride down the mountain, though still treacherous in some places, was a far cry from the night before. Kara leaned against the door, leaving as much space between them as possible. She stared straight ahead while an ominous silence filled the SUV.

"Turn right here. My dad said they'd be at my house, checking to make sure none of the water pipes froze during the night. I can't wait to see my little girl."

Excitement laced the last sentence. Love for her daughter had filled that part of her heart he'd broken so long ago. If only things had been different—if he'd been different—he'd have a place in her heart, too.

"You can drop me off here," she said, at the foot of the long driveway.

"That's okay. Since someone took the time to plow the drive, the SUV shouldn't have any problems making it to the top of your hill."

The little white house with deep blue shutters held his

full attention. It was so small. Not that his log home was a mansion, but he'd swear her whole house could fit in his great room. How did she live in such tight quarters—with a toddler, no less? She'd constantly be stumbling over discarded toys.

"You own this?" he asked.

She nodded. "It's cozy, but it's home."

He took note of the pride glittering in her eyes over owning this gingerbread house. "It's a real nice-looking place."

"Thanks." She grabbed the door handle. "I'm sorry for imposing last night."

"I'm glad I was there to help."

The door swung open and she grabbed her things before slipping out of the vehicle.

"Wait," he called. "You never answered me about staying on the payroll until after the first of the year."

Her pink lips pursed. Little lines formed between her brows, as though the decision was a real struggle for her. He'd thought his offer had been sweet enough. Could she sense his desperation? Was she holding out for more money? Or did she simply hate the idea of working for him?

"Come on, Kara. Don't make me beg. I've sunk everything I have into the resort. If you're worried about working together, don't be. The past is behind us."

"How can you say that when I still don't know the whole story about why you called off our engagement and skipped town?"

His back teeth pressed together and his jaw ratcheted tight. Why did she have to keep harping about the past? Nothing he could say would make it any better for her; in fact, it would make things so much worse.

He gazed into her eyes and saw steely determination reflected there. She was clinging to this need to know worse than a cat holding on to a catnip mouse.

An exasperated sigh passed his lips. "If I agree to tell you, will you stay on at the resort until we have it up and running?"

"Are you still willing to provide the severance package and reference?"

He didn't want to see her go, but he didn't have any right to stop her. If she could just help him get through the reopening, he'd be able to take it from there.

"I promise you'll get the severance package and the reference. Now do we have a deal?"

"I'm still waiting." She crossed her arms. "You owe me one more thing...?"

"You surely don't expect me to dig into my past right here in the middle of your driveway." He checked the time. "Besides, the tow truck guy will be waiting for me to guide him to your car."

She bit down on her lower lip as though weighing his words. "But you'll tell me?"

He nodded. The hum of the idling engine and the occasional gust of wintry air were the only sounds as he waited, hoping she'd see reason.

"You have a deal," she said. Before he could breathe a sigh of relief, she added, "But don't think I'll forget about your end of the deal. I expect a candid explanation from you."

"I understand."

"Then I'll see you Monday morning."

As the door thudded shut, he took comfort in the fact that there was no time limit on her request. Kara had always been persistent when it came to something she wanted, but she wouldn't be the first person he'd put off. Eventually she'd get tired of asking, wouldn't she?

A groan grew in the back of his throat. His temples started to pound. He needed a distraction. He glanced down to turn on the radio, then spotted the pink bear on the passenger seat.

With the fluffy thing in hand, he jumped out of the vehicle. "Hey, you forgot this."

Kara turned as he rushed up to her. "Oh, can't forget Bubbles. Samantha would never forgive me."

"We wouldn't want you getting in trouble."

"Mommy. Mommy," cried a child's voice. "Can we put up the Christmas tree?"

A young girl dressed in jeans and a pink winter coat ran toward them, her arms pumping. This was Kara's daughter?

Where was the baby—the toddler—he'd imagined? This little girl was so much older. She looked to be school-age. He glanced from mother to daughter. The child's pert nose, rose-petal lips and dimpled chin resembled her mother's, but there was something else. Something very familiar about her. The eyes. They were the same shade as his. So was her brown hair....

Could she be mine?

The air whooshed from Jason's lungs. The stunning suspicion bounced around in his mind at warp speed, making him light-headed.

Even though he and Kara had taken precautions when they'd made love, he wasn't foolish enough to think that accidents didn't happen.

The girl looked about the right age. His heart hammered his chest with such force his ribs felt bruised. The child had to be his.

He turned a questioning stare at Kara, but she wouldn't look at him. Did she really think she could keep his daughter a secret forever?

The little girl attempted to stop on the icy driveway and ended up sliding. Jason instinctively reached out for her. His arms wrapped around her slight shoulders and steadied her.

She eyed him tentatively with wide blue eyes. "Who are you? And why are you holding Bubbles?"

"This is Mr. Greene," Kara told her. "He helped me during the nasty storm and saved your bear from the snow."

The girl looked at him again, hesitantly at first. Then her hands rested on her little-girl hips, bunching up her padded coat. "You were smiling at Mommy. Do you like her?"

Jason choked back a laugh.

"Samantha Jameson," Kara shrieked. "Apologize."

Samantha—he liked the name. It also didn't miss his attention that the child had Kara's surname.

"Sorry, mister. Can I have my bear now?"

The *mister* part jabbed at him. She had no idea he was her father. Obviously, Kara hadn't showed Samantha any pictures of him.

He crouched down and held out the stuffed animal. "Here you go."

"Do you like Mommy?"

She was certainly a cute kid—and quite persistent. "Your mother's an old friend of mine."

Both females shot him surprised looks. Before Samantha could continue her inquisition, Kara's mother called to her from the doorway. Then, catching sight of him, Mrs. Jameson waved, a much friendlier greeting than he'd been expecting. This trip certainly had been filled with one surprise after another.

Samantha waved goodbye and ran to her waiting grandmother, oblivious to the turmoil going on inside him.

When the front door banged shut, Kara turned to him.

Her narrowed eyes shot daggers at him. "What'd you go and say that for? She didn't need to know anything about you and me having a past. Now she'll be full of all sorts of questions that I don't want to answer."

Certain Samantha was their daughter, a daughter he never knew about until now, anger bubbled up in him.

"You haven't told her about me, have you?"

Kara's brows scrunched together. "Of course not. Why would I?"

"How long were you going to keep this from me?" Betrayal pummeled him. "I'm her father. I should have been told."

"No. You're not."

"Come on, Kara. Don't lie. She's the right age and she has my blue eyes."

Kara's hands balled up at her sides. "She is *not* your daughter."

"Are you sure there's not someone else in your life?" he asked, driven to know if he'd been replaced in his daughter's life. "Someone your little girl calls Daddy?"

"No. There isn't."

Kara glared at him as though warning him to drop this line of questioning. But no amount of denials and icy stares would convince him to let go of this subject. There were simply too many coincidences to come to any other conclusion. Samantha was his little girl.

He wanted to push the topic, but backing Kara into a corner wouldn't get him any closer to his daughter. He needed a different tactic to get Kara to open up to him. And making things even more tense between them wasn't the right course of action. He needed to retreat and regroup. After things cooled down, he'd come at the situation from a different angle.

"Fine. I understand," he lied, watching the tension ease in Kara's shoulders.

What did she have to gain by continuing to deny he was the child's father?

Then it dawned on him what she was doing, protecting their daughter from him. She didn't trust him to stick around. And the fact that he was keeping the past from her was just one more strike against him.

The thought of missing out on his daughter's life overwhelmed him. For one crazy moment, he considered blurting out the awful truth. But how on earth would the revelation that he was the son of a monster—a rapist—going to help his cause? His chest tightened. The truth about his past certainly wouldn't make him a candidate for Father of the Year.

It'd be best for everyone, his newly found daughter included, if he kept his secret to himself. He'd just have to keep Kara distracted until the past was forgotten.

Besides, he wasn't the only one who'd been holding a secret. Anger simmered in his gut over being kept in the dark for so long. If the snowstorm hadn't brought them together, he might never know he was a dad.

Still, Kara thought she was doing the right thing by protecting her daughter—their daughter. The phrase stuck in his brain.

"You should get inside," he said, letting the subject drop for now. "I've got to go."

Saturday evening, after spending the afternoon scouring the internet for job opportunities, Kara sent out her résumé to five companies advertising for an office manager. Hopeful that someone would take an interest in her application, she headed to the Pleasant Valley Care Home.

After signing herself in, she paused and scanned the list of recent visitors, searching for Jason's name. No such luck.

To her utter frustration, her thoughts had dwelled on him since their winter storm odyssey. When he'd first laid eyes on Samantha, she'd noticed how he'd struggled to hide his surprise. And after he'd boldly stated he wasn't planning to have kids, she'd been shocked by his insistence that he was Samantha's father. Thankfully, he'd finally accepted the truth.

Maybe she should have explained her daughter's background, but the circumstances hadn't been right. Standing outside in the freezing cold while Samantha waited inside for her hadn't lent itself to a heart-to-heart talk. Besides, what did it matter? Kara wasn't in a relationship with him. There wasn't even a possibility of it.

After seven long years, he still couldn't face her and explain what had made him break her heart. He didn't trust her then and he sure didn't trust her now. But he did owe her the truth…and she intended to collect.

Kara's footsteps echoed through the empty corridors of the nursing home. No matter how many trips she made here, she could never shake the unease that came over her when she entered the well-kept facility. Maybe it was the idea of her own mortality—that she might one day end up here, too.

Halfway down a brightly lit hallway, in front of room 115, she stopped and gently rapped her knuckles on the open door.

"Come in," Joe's voice rumbled, followed by a coughing spell.

She stepped into the room, finding him propped up in bed with a college football game on the TV. His roommate was lying wrapped in a sheet, with his back to them and the privacy curtain partially drawn.

When Kara's gaze settled on Joe's gaunt features, her heart clenched. His thinning white hair was a stark contrast to his yellow pallor. Some people had good days dotted with occasional bad ones, but it seemed since he'd put the Summit up for sale, his days had all gone downhill.

"And how are you?" she asked, as was her habit. But she truly cared about his answer.

"Awful," he grumbled, hitting Mute on the television. "They won't let me have a cigar while I watch the game."

"You can't smoke. You're on oxygen."

His whiskered face contorted into a frown. "Didn't say I was gonna light it."

"Oh." She didn't know what else to say.

Joe had had to give up a lot of vices when his health collapsed and he'd ended up in this place. He still fussed about wanting a juicy, rare burger with fries, and the cigars, but not the alcohol. Maybe at last he realized how it'd destroyed his life.

"My boy. You've seen him?" A wet cough ensued.

Kara filled his glass with water from a plastic pitcher and handed it to him.

"I did see him. You could have warned me you sold the Summit to him." She wanted to be angry at Joe for keeping such an important fact from her, especially after all she'd done for him over the years. But it was hard to be upset with someone so ill.

He at least had the decency to drop his gaze to his bony hands. "I need you to convince him to come see me. Tell him I'm sorry."

Kara wrung her hands together. Maybe she should back out of being the go-between for these two. After what Jason had told her about what went down between him and his dad, it might be asking too much of Jason to re-establish the father-son relationship.

"I tried," she said, still not sure how to proceed. "He's very stubborn."

Joe made an attempt to reach for something on his nightstand.

"What do you want?" she asked, ready to do whatever she could to help.

"Jason's picture."

She grabbed the framed graduation photo of the boy she'd once loved with all her heart, and handed it to his father. Joe pulled off the back and yanked out a wrinkled envelope.

"Give this to him...." His words faded into a string of coughs. "Make him read it."

Her mouth gaped. How did Joe expect her to do this when Jason wouldn't discuss his father, much less have anything to do with him? But she couldn't turn her back on this man who didn't have anyone else to look out for him. She couldn't give up hope that somehow father and son would be reunited.

Joe reached for her arm and placed the envelope in her hand. His cold fingers squeezed hers. "Find a way. Jason has to know I regret what happened. Please, Kara."

CHAPTER TEN

"LET ME LICK them. Please." Samantha held out her hands for the beaters from the mixer.

"You can have one and I'll have the other." Kara couldn't resist the sweet buttery taste of cookie dough.

They were both licking at the creamy batter when a knock sounded. Sunday afternoons were notorious for impromptu visits from her parents. She continued savoring the sweet treat on her way to the door. She peered through the window, finding Jason.

Jason? What was he doing here? Maybe she'd forgotten something at his place yesterday in her haste to get home.

She yanked the beater down to her side and wiped away any evidence of her childish behavior before opening the door. When she looked into Jason's dreamy blue eyes, her heart started beating in double time. "Hi. What are you doing here?"

"Thought you might want this." He moved to the side, revealing a lush evergreen lying on the sidewalk.

"You got us a tree?"

"You said you always wanted a real tree, so here you go." He peered around her and she turned, finding her daughter lurking behind her.

"Samantha, you remember Mr. Greene, don't you?"

She nodded and moved to stand beside Kara. "Is that for us?"

"Yes, it is. Do you like it?"

Samantha's head bobbed up and down, while a huge grin showed off her pearly whites.

Kara ushered him inside. "You're letting in all the cold."

"I didn't mean to stay. I just wanted to drop this off. Unless, of course, you already put up your tree."

"We didn't," Samantha volunteered. "Mommy didn't have time. Can we have it, Mommy? We've never had a real tree. Ple-e-ease."

Kara eyed her pleading stare. "Fine. Mr. Greene, can I help you carry it into the living room?"

"I've got it," he said.

He picked it up with ease and moved forward, favoring his leg more than usual. Concern swirled in Kara's chest as she quickly ducked into the kitchen to drop off her licked-clean beater. She wanted to ask him about his leg but reminded herself that it wasn't her concern. They each had their own lives to lead, and he didn't need her nagging him about his health.

Kara held the door wide-open while he maneuvered the chubby pine through the doorway. Her living room was small and cozy. She didn't have a clue what they'd do if the tree was too big. Samantha would have a fit. But they'd cross that bridge when they got to it.

"Put it here," Samantha called, pointing to a spot in front of the window. "This is where we always put the *other* one."

Jason glanced at Kara and she nodded in approval. "Just give me a second to slide the chair out of the way."

In a matter of seconds, the tree stood prominently in front of the window, with a few inches of clearance between the tip-top and the ceiling. Kara breathed a sigh of relief. Jason had already anchored it in a red-and-green metal stand, attached to a piece of wood. All she'd have to do was add water and a tree skirt.

Samantha clapped her hands together and beamed. "Mommy, isn't it great? Now you don't have to find time to drag down that dang tree—"

"Samantha! That's enough." Kara's cheeks warmed with embarrassment. Apparently her daughter had overheard her muttering to herself in frustration at the overwhelming prospect of putting all their Christmas decorations up this weekend.

"Sorry." Samantha didn't look the least bit sorry as she grinned at the tree as if she'd never seen one before.

But when her daughter's blue eyes settled on Jason with that same ear-to-ear smile, Kara knew she was in trouble. She didn't need these two to bond. No way.

"We're making cookies," Samantha said. "Wanna decorate 'em with me?"

Jason rocked back on his heels. His hesitant gaze traveled to Kara. Working with him would be tough enough. She didn't need him befriending her daughter. She gave a slight shake of her head, praying he'd get the message.

"Thank you. That sounds great...." His gaze ran to Kara again, as though he was actually interested in spending time with a six-year-old.

Part of Kara wanted to relent and have him stay, to make her daughter happy, but she knew in the end that it'd end up hurting Samantha when he walked out of their lives. He wasn't a forever kind of guy. When the going got rough, Jason got going. *Reliable* definitely wasn't in his vocabulary.

And what was even worse was that he represented the one thing Kara couldn't give her daughter—a father. Up until this point, Samantha hadn't shown any curiosity about her dad, but the day was coming when she'd be full of questions. And Kara couldn't help but wonder if her little girl would blame her for never marrying and giving her a father figure. Still, Jason wasn't an ideal candidate.

Kara steeled herself and gave another shake of her head. Jason was a gentleman and explained that he had a previous engagement, causing her daughter's smile to morph into a frown. Kara couldn't blame her. If she wasn't careful, she, too, would get sucked in by his charms.

He walked to the door, then turned to Samantha. "I almost forgot. I have something else for you. I'll be right back."

Samantha raised her bright eyes to her mother and practically bounced with excitement. "I wonder what it is."

"I don't know." Truly she didn't, but she had to admit she was curious.

When he rushed back up the walk, he was holding a small box. It looked familiar, but Kara couldn't quite place it.

He held it out to Samantha. "This is for you, but on one condition. You have to finish baking with your mother and help with the cleanup before you open it. Can you do that?"

Her head bobbed. "Sure."

"What else do you say?" Kara prompted.

"Oh, yeah. Thank you. Come on, Mommy." Samantha pulled at her wrist. "We have cookies to make."

Jason chuckled. Kara hadn't seen him this relaxed in all the time she'd spent with him at his place. Apparently he related to little girls more easily than he did to big ones.

"Have fun baking." He waved and strolled down the walk, whistling a little ditty.

What in the world had put him in such a good mood?

"Mommy. Mommy. Look at this."

Kara closed the door and turned, to find her daughter

had ripped away the snowman wrapping paper and opened the cardboard box. "You promised to wait to open it, remember?"

Samantha shrugged, peering inside the box. "I know. But I just wanted to peek. Isn't she beautiful?"

She held up the box for Kara to get a good look at the contents. The angel. Jason's Christmas angel.

When Samantha made a motion to reach inside the box, Kara yelled, "Don't! Your hands still have cookie dough on them. Hand me the box." Samantha frowned, but did as instructed. "Now go wash up. We have cookies to finish making before we decorate the tree."

Kara carried the heirloom into the living room. What had Jason been thinking when he'd decided to give away this treasured memento from his childhood? She'd thought for sure, with the memories of his mother the angel invoked, that he'd hold on to it. This just went to prove that she really didn't know him at all.

After another quick glance at the angelic figure, she placed it atop the bookshelf for safekeeping. He might not be ready to appreciate such a fine gift from his past, but she'd hang on to it for him, until his heart was open to the joy of Christmases past and the hope of Christmases future.

Jason Greene, for all of his faults, was hard to resist when he turned on the charm. His visit today had chipped away at the hard edges around her heart. She glanced out the window, but he was long gone.

She still needed to talk to him about so many things. Not only did they have the past to straighten out, but now his father's Christmas wish was weighing on her. She prayed there was some way to broker a bit of peace between the two men. The sands of time were running out for this father-son reunion.

* * *

Jason sat behind a large, solid wood desk—the same desk where his grandfather used to hold him on his knee and tell him that one day this place would be his. That day had finally come. He'd just never imagined he'd be working alongside Kara.

His gaze lifted and met hers. He'd been doing most of the talking for the past hour, explaining his vision for the future of the resort. He'd noticed her raised brows a couple of times when he'd covered how he thought they could cut back on expenses. However, she never interrupted, just continued to take notes.

Now it was time to get to the part where she could really be helpful to him. "While I work on finding the appropriate balance between year-round and seasonal workers, I'd like you to get new quotes from all the available vendors."

"Which one did you have a problem with?"

"It isn't that I have a problem with any of them, but it's a smart business practice to periodically get quotes and make sure no one is gouging us."

She shook her head. "They wouldn't do that. We've been doing business with these companies for years now—"

"And when was the last time you received quotes from the competition?"

"Never, but—"

"Exactly what I thought. My father always did take the easy route. I'm sure that's why this place is in the red."

"I should have been on top of this. Is this really what has the business in trouble?"

He didn't want her blaming herself. "There are many things that contributed to the financial mess, but it's not one single person's fault. We're going to put into place new procedures and policies, so we don't end up in a rut again."

"Which vendors did you want me to work on?"

"All of them. From the liquor to the vegetable supplier and everything in between."

"But surely you don't want to get rid of Pappy Salvatore's."

Jason searched his memory. The name didn't ring a bell. "Who's this Pappy?"

She cast him a look of disbelief. "He's a childhood friend of your father's. He and his sons have been providing us with the freshest vegetables longer than I've been here. They're punctual and their produce is of the finest quality."

Jason paused and stared at her. Throughout this meeting, she'd accepted what he'd said about overhauling the mechanics of the place. Her occasional frown let him know she didn't always agree with his methods, but she'd kept her mouth shut. Why in the world would she pick this one particular vendor to defend? Was it possible there was more going on with the Salvatores than just business? The thought soured his stomach.

"How well do you know this Pappy? Or perhaps you're more familiar with one of his sons?"

She glowered at him. "Don't twist this into something it's not. Yes, I know Pappy. He used to come to the resort once a month to go over the order with me...and your father. He's a sweet man and his whole family is involved with the business."

Still not getting the reason for her to defend their business ties so ferociously, Jason prompted, "And..."

"And he was instrumental in convincing your father to give me the promotion to office manager. He was so impressed with how I'd reworked the various menus, giving each of our food outlets a different ethnic flair."

"Of course he was. He wanted you to swing him more business."

Her eyes narrowed and her chin lifted. "He didn't need to. Your father had already awarded him the resort's full order years ago. He did it because I impressed him with my ideas."

Jason rocked back in his desk chair. He liked this Pappy and he hadn't even met him. He also liked Kara's strong sense of loyalty. He could only wish she'd hold *him* in such high esteem one day. But how he'd manage to get there, he didn't know.

"That still doesn't put the Salvatores above review. Get the quotes. We'll talk later."

Kara's lips pursed together as her pen flew over her notepad. "Is that all?"

"There's one more thing. Could you check on the furniture we ordered for the Igloo Café?"

She nodded, got to her feet and headed for the door.

Not wanting her to go just yet, he said, "I meant to ask you if Samantha liked the tree."

Kara clasped her notepad to her chest. "She did. Depending on what time I get home, we're supposed to finish trimming it."

"There's no need for you to hang around here tonight," he said, deflated by the fact that she hadn't extended him an invitation. "I've got all the files I'll need. Go home and enjoy the evening."

Her green eyes widened. "Are you sure? The reopening isn't far away."

"Positive." He wanted this Christmas to be special for their daughter, whether Kara let him share it with them or not.

She hesitated at the doorway. Was she having second thoughts about inviting him over? Hope rose in his chest. Christmas still wasn't one of his favorite holidays, but for Samantha's sake, he could learn to like just about anything.

"Did you need something else?"

She nodded and pulled an envelope from the back of her notebook. "I need you to read this."

Disappointment hit him hard and fast. He struggled to keep his poker face in place as he held out his hand. "Is it something I need to go over tonight?"

She worried her bottom lip. "Time is of the essence."

"Pass it over and I'll give it top priority."

When he glanced at the envelope and saw the return address, he groaned. Now he knew why she was acting so strange—it was from his father.

"Kara, take this back." It'd be filled with more accusations about how he'd failed as a son. He couldn't—no, he wouldn't let that man inflict any further pain.

"You said you'd read it. You said you'd make it a priority." Her brows scrunched together as her eyes pleaded with him. "You can't pretend he doesn't exist. And you'll regret it if he dies before you have a chance to make peace with him."

Jason didn't want to hear any of this. "I'm the injured party here. My father was the one who pulled away after my mother died. He's the one who turned to a liquor bottle for comfort. He never thought of me or my needs."

"I'm so sorry, Jason. To lose your mother and then for all intents and purposes to lose your father, too, must have been devastating for you. But it's not too late to try and undo some of the damage."

"Why is this so important to you?"

"This will be your father's last Christmas." Her voice cracked with emotion. "If a person can't forgive, they can't know real love. It's a lonely life. Is that what you want for yourself?"

"You think I can't love?"

She shrugged. "Joe wasn't always a bad father. You told me."

Jason's jaw grew rigid. She was a good talker, but he just couldn't put himself out there for his father to throw all his misdeeds back in his face.

Jason held out the letter, but she turned her back and walked out of the room.

With a sigh, he leaned back in his chair as her last comment settled in. It was true. His father hadn't always been a bad man. In fact, Jason could remember a few fishing trips to the state park. They'd hardly caught a thing, but his dad hadn't seemed to mind, as the two of them talked a lot about sports. Jason had just been glad to have his father pay some attention to him.

Then his mother had gotten sick and there were no more fishing trips. It was at his mom's bedside that he first saw his father cry. That was when Jason knew his mother was never going to get better—and that was when he'd really needed a father. But his dad retreated to his study and wouldn't let anyone in. Bottles of Jack Daniel's and Jim Beam had kept him company, putting him into a numbed, drunken stupor.

"Damn." Jason threw the envelope on the desk.

Since the first night he'd run into Kara, she'd been on this blasted campaign to reunite him and his father. And no matter how much Jason wanted to please her, he couldn't do what she asked of him. Too many damaging words had been inflicted. The deep emotional wounds had festered over time, not healed. It was best to leave them alone.

He shook his head, trying to chase away the unwanted memories. His teeth ground together. This was Kara's doing—unearthing his past. She'd wanted him to remember, but it wouldn't work. This was one Christmas miracle even she couldn't pull off, with all her good intentions.

But if she truly thought he couldn't love, she was wrong. As much as he wanted to deny it, she had a permanent spot in his heart. And as for their daughter—he'd fallen for her at first sight.

Now he just had to find a way to show Kara that he wasn't the heartless creep she imagined him to be.

CHAPTER ELEVEN

MEETING AFTER MEETING about streamlining the resort's expenses kept Kara in close proximity to Jason. However, with so many other employees drifting in and out of his office, she didn't have a chance to ask about the past, and get answers to the questions that had plagued her for so many years.

If she didn't know better, she'd swear he'd planned his open-door policy as a way of keeping them from talking privately. But if he thought she'd forget about their agreement, he was most definitely wrong.

So when the phone rang on Saturday, Kara was startled to hear his voice at the other end. He was all-business, asking for her assistance in finding some pertinent paperwork. When she said that she'd have to bring Samantha with her, his tone softened and he said he had an important job for her, too.

Not wanting to give him any excuse to fire her before the holidays, Kara shut down her internet search for jobs, scooped up Samantha from in front of the television and rushed out the door.

With the late afternoon sun playing hide-and-seek behind the trees lining Greene Summit's winding roadway, she drove up to the lodge. Samantha chattered about anything and everything that caught her attention, as was normal during a car ride. Only today her conversation wasn't about school or Santa. Today her only thought was about seeing Jason.

They parked in the vacant front lot, by the main entrance. Massive timbers acted as supports for the alcove roof, while layered logs made up the walls of the lodge, giving it a natural outdoorsy feeling.

"Mommy, hurry," Samantha said, yanking on her hand. "He said I could help him do somethin' impotent."

"Important," Kara corrected, and released her daughter's hand in order to unlock the door.

Inside the newly renovated lobby, a soft pine scent lofted throughout the two-story space, thanks to the giant Christmas tree that soared up toward the skylights, lights twinkling from every branch. A musical rendition of "Have a Holly Jolly Christmas" played in the background. Since they were the only ones in the building, aside from Jason, she couldn't dismiss the fact that he'd taken time to turn on the lights and music to impress Samantha. Her daughter walked all around the tree, admiring the red and green decorations.

"Wow, look, Mommy. Think Mr. Greene did all of this for us?"

Kara smiled. "I think the decorations are for the grand reopening, but I'm sure he'd be happy if you told him how much you like them."

"I will."

As though her thoughts had summoned him, Jason strode over to them. A smile lightened the tired lines on his face. "Hi. So what are my two favorite ladies up to?"

"Waiting for you." Samantha giggled.

"I hope we didn't take too long. I had a nut roll in the oven when you called," Kara said, trying to ignore the way his smile made her heart pound.

Samantha moved to stand directly in front of Jason. "Mr. Greene, I'm ready to work. Look," she said, holding up her stuffed bear. "I brought help."

He chuckled. "Samantha, I wish all my workers were as eager as you and Bubbles."

"What are we gonna do? Is it fun?"

"Slow down," he said. "I called you and your mom here because I have a little work I need your mother to do for me."

Kara stood next to the towering evergreen, observing the way her daughter's eyes lit up as she interacted with Jason. He certainly could turn on the charm. She'd have to be careful or they'd both be vulnerable to his radiant smile and kind words—and that couldn't happen. She knew how much it had cost her when he'd changed his mind about a future with her, and moved on—alone.

Samantha's lower lip stuck out. "I thought you had somethin' impotent for me."

He chuckled, most likely at her daughter's poor grammar, or maybe the way her bottom lip sagged.

"Cheer up," he said, "I have something in mind for you. A real important job. First, would you like to see the changes we've made to the resort?"

Samantha shrugged. Kara knew she should just take care of business and leave, but she was anxious to take a look around. Since Jason took over the Summit, she'd been tucked away in the office, shuffling papers, making phone calls and attending meetings. She'd missed seeing all the renovations. What would a five-minute tour hurt?

"And afterward—" he knelt down by Samantha and whispered loud enough for Kara to overhear "—I was hoping you could help me test the machines in the game room."

"The game room!" Samantha screamed. Her blue eyes sparkled with excitement.

Kara bit back a groan. What was he up to? The last thing either of them should be doing on a Saturday afternoon was hanging out like...like a family. The thought was so foreign to her. It'd always been enough to know she and Samantha were a family unit. Kara didn't like how being around Jason filled her head with thoughts of what was lacking.

She cleared her throat, gaining the others' attention. "As kind as your offer is, we can't stay—"

"Mommy." Samantha's cherubic face scrunched into a stormy frown. "I wanna stay!"

Kara's gaze moved from Samantha to Jason's pleading look. Why was she the only person who thought this was a bad idea? Didn't he have more important things to do than play tour director?

"Please, Mommy? I already have my homework done."

That was true enough. Samantha had been an angel all week. Kara knew it had a lot to do with Santa, but she'd take what she could get, when she could get it. Her daughter had earned the right to have a little fun. Who was she to take it from her?

"Okay. But we can't stay long—"

"Yay!" Samantha cheered.

"Good." Jason smiled, setting Kara's heart aflutter. "Let's go take that tour. I think someone is anxious to begin her work."

"Uh-huh." Samantha beamed a cheery smile at them before grabbing a hand of each adult and pulling them onward.

Kara glanced past her daughter to Jason, who seemed truly relaxed and comfortable holding Samantha's hand. Letting him field the child's million and one questions about the resort, Kara took in all the recent updates.

The hallway's robin's-egg-blue walls were bare, and a faint smell of fresh paint lingered. A lifetime of memories lived and breathed inside this ski lodge. If these walls could talk, they'd spill stories of stolen kisses, tears and shared promises.

Jason pointed out the new restaurants, spa and indoor Olympic-size pool while the past continued to crowd in on Kara. She remembered how things used to be—how things might be again, if only she could make Jason understand the impossible. But her confession wouldn't fix things between them. It'd only scare him off. She doubted even this business could hold him back if he learned exactly what had happened after he'd dumped her. Not that she'd ever have a reason to tell him. He was her boss, nothing more.

The tour concluded with the game room to the left and a bowling alley to the right. A screech of joy ripped from Samantha's lungs. "There's a bowlin' alley, too."

Both of them laughed at her comical enthusiasm as she tried to decide what game she wanted to try first.

"Mister, can I really play them all?"

His smile lit up his face, making his blue eyes twinkle. "First, call me Jason."

"Jason, can we play now? Bubbles wants to bowl. Can we, huh?"

"We have a lot of games to test, so we better get started." He rolled up his shirtsleeves, then found the power switch. Lights flickered and the lanes lit up.

"Mommy, are you gonna play, too?"

"I don't think so. I can't bowl in these boots."

"Not a problem," Jason assured her. "We've got brand spanking new shoes. What size are you?"

Kara took in the expectant look on her daughter's face and then turned to meet Jason's appealing gaze. How could she turn them down? After spending way too many hours being professional, and a responsible adult, she was just as anxious as Samantha to let loose and be included in the fun.

They placed bumpers in the gutters to keep their balls in the lane. Jason and Samantha nearly doubled over in fits of laughter when in her enthusiasm Kara flung the ball too hard and too soon. It bounced over the bumper and into the next lane. Samantha, with the aid of a bumper or two, pulled off a spare, while Jason scored strike after strike.

After he soundly beat Kara, he surprised them with a takeout pepperoni pizza he'd kept warm in the employee kitchen. When he glanced her way, Kara mouthed, *"Thank you."*

He had outdone himself this afternoon. The man certainly was full of surprises. Her daughter was thrilled with the fun, and to be honest, Kara was thrilled, too.

When they finally worked their way over to the game room, Jason produced a pocketful of quarters. He handed Samantha a few. "Here you go. You can test the machines in here while your mother and I talk a little business."

"Aren't you gonna play, too?"

"In a couple of minutes." He ran a gentle, reassuring hand over Samantha's back, making Kara's heart pinch as she thought of all the father-daughter moments her little girl had missed.

Samantha, seeming satisfied to wait, moved to a claw game where the intent was to pick up one of the colorful plush animals with the shiny metallic prongs and place it in the chute. Before she could utter a complaint about being too short, Jason produced a plastic footstool. This was the thoughtful, generous guy Kara had fallen in love with all those years ago. And if she wasn't careful, the past just might repeat itself.

"Step up here," he said, holding out his hand to assist Samantha. "Better?"

"Yeah. Thanks." She surveyed the mound of colorful stuffed animals. "I want that purple monkey."

"Put your quarter in and give it a shot."

Kara swallowed back the emotional lump in her throat. No man had ever taken such an interest in her daughter. Who'd have guessed Jason's Scrooge-like heart could be thawed out by a little girl? Miracles really did happen.

With Samantha occupied, Jason approached Kara. "She's having a lot of fun, isn't she?"

Funny that he'd need her confirmation when the glowing smile and rosy cheeks on her daughter spoke volumes more than Kara could ever vocalize. "Yes, she is. Thank you for this. Since I started working overtime to prepare for the new management, there hasn't been any time to get out and have fun."

"Jason, aren't you going to play, too?" Samantha whined. "I keep droppin' the monkey."

"I'll be right there." He turned back to Kara. "Do you want to help her?"

"She wants you. But first, what file can't you find?"

He paused as though he didn't have a clue what she was referring to, then a light of recognition sparked in his eyes. "The order for the parts for the lift on the double-diamond slope. They were supposed to be here yesterday. Without a functioning lift this grand reopening is going to be a grand disaster."

He wanted an order form? On a Saturday afternoon? There was nothing he could do about the missing order before Monday morning. What had he been thinking when he'd called her? Of course, he hadn't been thinking. She'd never seen anyone work harder than Jason. He expected his employees to give their all, which she didn't mind during the week, but the weekend was for family—something he knew nothing about.

She glanced up to find he'd moved to the claw machine. His hand worked the joystick and his lips pressed into a firm line as he concentrated on grabbing the toy. Her annoyance faded. This was the most enjoyment she and her daughter had had in a long time.

"I'll be right back," Kara called out. Neither seemed interested, as the monkey hung precariously from the metal claw.

She moved swiftly to the business offices, located the purchase order and placed it front and center on Jason's cluttered desk. Her hand hovered as she debated whether to see if the letter from his father was still there. What would it hurt?

It took a little bit of searching, but eventually she located it beneath a mountain of paperwork. Still unopened. She frowned as she placed it conveniently beneath the folder Jason had requested. He would read his father's words, eventually. Hope burned strong and bright in her heart.

Jason's cheeks grew sore from smiling.

He shook his head in disbelief. Samantha hit the left bumper on the vintage pinball machine. How could this pint-size little girl clutching a purple monkey bring him such happiness?

He regretted each and every minute he'd missed of her life, but it would be different from here on out. As soon as he proved to Kara that he could keep the monster side of him at bay, and show her that he wasn't going anywhere ever again, there'd be a lot more moments like this. He'd make sure of it.

Kara strolled back into the game room. Even though she wasn't wearing anything stylish, he thought she looked positively radiant. A pastel pink sweater stretched across her chest, snuggling against her feminine curves. His mouth grew dry. And her low-slung jeans clung to her rounded hips. If he were to envision the perfect snow bunny, it'd definitely be her.

"I can see by the new stuffed animal in Samantha's arms that you two beat the claw machine."

He swallowed. "It took a few quarters but we got it."

"Samantha looks happy. Has she tried every game yet?"

"Almost." As far as he was concerned, she didn't have to leave anytime soon.

"By the way, I found the order form and left it on your desk. But the supplier won't be open until first thing Monday morning."

"Thanks. I'll straighten it out then."

"We should get going," she said. "I'm sure you've got more important things to do."

"Stay just a little longer." He reached for her hand. His thumb stroked her soft skin. "You haven't told me what you think of the remodel."

He honestly didn't care what they discussed. In that moment, he was at peace, and dare he say it, happy. Peace and happiness had eluded him for years, and he'd give almost anything for it to last just a little longer.

"You've done a marvelous job breathing new life into this place," Kara said, letting her hand rest in his. "The color scheme is cheerful and relaxing. It's a very inviting atmosphere. A great escape from the realities of life."

"Really? That's the impression you get?"

"Isn't that the impression you want to give? Don't people come to resorts to escape the pressures of their everyday lives? Aren't they here to have fun, unwind, and for some, to recapture their youth?"

Their gazes met and locked. The guarded walls around

his heart cracked. The glow of Kara's smile filtered through the crevices and warmed him. He couldn't help wondering if she was moved by the host of memories contained within the newly painted walls.

"Do you remember how we used to be?" he asked, his voice husky with reawakened desires.

A flicker of emotion reflected in her eyes. His breathing hitched as he anticipated her next words.

"I remember. How could I ever forget?"

He touched her cheek. His fingers slid down to her neck, where her rapid heartbeat pulsed beneath his fingertips. She wanted him. And he most definitely wanted her. His head lowered.

"Hey, guys," Samantha called out. "I'm outta quarters."

Jason snapped to attention. How in the world could he have let himself become so distracted that he'd forgotten their daughter was just across the room? He still had a lot to learn about being a dad.

Not willing to lose ground with Kara, he laced his fingers with hers. It felt so natural. And he noticed she didn't pull away. The pieces of his life were at last falling into place.

He glanced down at her. "Shall we go see what our daughter wants?"

The smile slipped from Kara's tempting lips and her hand withdrew from his. In that moment, he realized he'd misspoken. The shocked look on her face dug at him. How long did she intend to keep up this little charade, when they both knew the truth?

"Don't look at me like I said the unforgivable. I'm sorry I let that comment slip about her being our daughter." He paused, not exactly comfortable with apologizing. "Actually, I'm not sorry. I know you denied she's mine because

you don't trust me, but it's time we were honest with ourselves and her."

"No!" Kara's eyes were round with worry. She glanced
over at Samantha. He followed her gaze, finding their
daughter preoccupied with another pinball machine. Kara
lowered her voice. "I wish I could tell you what you want
to hear, but...but I can't. She's not yours."

He stepped back, crossing his arms over his chest. "That
can't be. She has my eyes. She's the right age. And I haven't
seen any signs of another man in your life."

"He's not in our life." Kara's eyes shimmered. "You
don't know how many times I've wished she was yours...
but her birthday is in November. You left town in December. It's simply not possible."

"You'd say anything to protect her, but I swear I'll never
do anything to hurt her." He whispered the words past the
jagged lump in his throat. "Please tell me she's mine."

Kara visibly swallowed. "I can't lie to you. And I won't
lie to my daughter. You both deserve better. I swear she's
not yours."

The thought of Samantha being another man's daughter hit him square in the gut. He didn't want to believe
Kara. But the anguished look on her face drove home the
bitter truth.

This wasn't right. This wasn't supposed to happen.
They were finally reunited and...and he'd allowed himself to care about them. He'd been so close to having something he'd never thought possible—his own family. Now,
he didn't know what to do with the tangled ball of disappointment and longing churning in his gut.

"Guys, you said you'd play with me," Samantha whined,
putting an end to this painful exchange.

"One game," Kara said, glancing over at him, and he
nodded. "Then we have to go home."

* * *

The next day, Kara's phone rang. Jason's deep voice echoed over the line, making her insides quiver with excitement. For a moment she forgot she had just filled her kitchen sink with hot sudsy water to wash up the lunch dishes.

"Kara, are you there?"

The air whooshed from her lungs. "Yes. Sorry. I was distracted."

"I didn't mean to bother you. I wanted to check to see if it'd be all right if I stopped by your house this evening?"

Her pulse kicked up a notch. After yesterday, she didn't think he'd want anything more to do with her. "Um…sure."

"I found Bubbles this morning and thought Samantha would be lost without him."

He only wanted to return the bear? Disappointment pulsed through Kara. She tried to assure herself that this distance between them was best for all concerned, but it brought her absolutely no comfort.

She twisted a strand of hair around her finger. "I searched everywhere for him last night."

"You should have called me. I would have checked around here for you. As it was, I came across him in the lunch room when I was raiding the snack machine."

"You're working today, too?" she asked, astonished at his dedication and worried that he might be pushing himself too hard.

"We're making a staggering number of changes and I want to oversee everything. I need to make sure the alterations are having the effect we anticipated."

"Do you need help?" She honestly didn't have time to spare, given the scarves she had to finish knitting for Christmas presents, and more cookies to bake for the nursing home. But she felt a certain responsibility to the business that had kept a roof over her head. Plus she didn't like the idea of Jason hiding away in the empty resort, wolfing down some unhealthy lunch from a snack machine.

"I've got it under control." His voice was cold and distant.

"Samantha will be thrilled to have Bubbles back. You'll be her hero. Not that you aren't already, after that wonderful day we had and you winning her the purple monkey."

"It's nothing I wouldn't have done for any of the other employees and their families."

Kara's heart sank. She knew he wouldn't have gone to those lengths for just anyone. He'd obviously been more hurt by the news that Samantha wasn't his daughter than he'd let on. Kara felt absolutely awful. She hadn't intended to upset him. In fact, that was the last thing she'd ever want to do.

"I'll drop Bubbles off at six."

Her heart thump-thumped at the thought of seeing him again.

He'd already hung up by the time she realized he'd be there at dinnertime. Samantha would insist he join them. How would Jason act around her daughter now that he'd accepted the truth? He was a man who had trouble forgiving people, but would he really punish an innocent little girl? Kara would like to think not, but she couldn't dismiss how he refused to make amends with his dying father.

This was her fault. She'd let him into their lives when she knew better. From here on out, she'd have to be more careful when it came to dealing with him. She'd need to keep her emotions at bay—hold him at arm's length.

CHAPTER TWELVE

HE WAS LATE.

Jason lightened his foot on the SUV's accelerator. The last thing he needed was to get pulled over for speeding, and waste more time. His delay couldn't be helped. When the mechanics he was paying double time to work around the clock let him know the double-diamond lift had experienced another significant setback, he'd dropped everything to go investigate.

With the grand reopening only twelve days away, his priority had to be the resort, but tonight was different. He knew how much the bear meant to Samantha, and he couldn't stand for her to be needlessly upset. It wasn't so long ago that he'd been a child himself. He could remember what it was like to want something so badly and to have to wait. Each second seemed like a minute. Each minute dragged on for an hour. Too bad he hadn't found the little guy sooner.

The fact that Samantha wasn't his—that she belonged to another man—still had him spinning in circles. When he allowed himself to think about it, the realization socked him in the chest, making each breath painful. He should just cut his losses and move on. That was exactly what any sane man would do.

But no one had ever claimed Jason was particularly

wise. And he was already in this thing clear up to his neck. The question was, where did he want this thing with Kara to go?

And the trickier question: Could he accept Samantha without any prejudice?

The little girl was a constant reminder of how he'd messed things up with Kara. And evidence of how quickly she'd gotten over him and moved on. His fingers tightened on the steering wheel. The thought of Kara in another man's arms—a man who'd deserted her and their baby—made him furious. Jason was thankful he'd been too shocked the other night to even think of asking for the man's name. At this particular juncture, with disappointment and frustration pumping through his veins, he didn't want to do anything stupid.

His actions had already cost him a buddy's life. Jason didn't want to make things even worse for Kara and her little girl. The man might be a waste of space, but he was Samantha's father and somehow Jason had to learn to respect that fact.

He glanced at the clock. Twenty minutes after six. Being tardy would not help his already tense relationship with Kara. And until he knew what he wanted, he didn't wish to make things worse. He could only hope she hadn't noticed the time.... He shook his head. His luck wasn't that good. With her lack of faith in him, she'd probably think he'd forgotten and wasn't going to show.

When he pulled into her driveway, he noticed how she'd decorated the edges of her roof with those white icicle lights. A glowing snowman stood front and center in the yard. And in the picture window he caught sight of the Christmas tree he'd brought them, now lit up with colored lights.

The tension in his shoulders and neck uncoiled. A smile

pulled at his lips. Maybe the decorations weren't so bad. Kara certainly was filled with holiday spirit. He'd swear she was one part Santa's elf and the other part Christmas angel.

He pushed the SUV door open and eased out before leaning back inside to grab the pink bear from the seat. He glanced down at Bubbles. For a second, he envied the stuffed animal. He wondered what it'd be like to be so loved by that sweet girl.

His knee throbbed from the cold, but he refused to let it slow his pace up the walk. He'd just raised his hand to knock on the bright blue door adorned with a wreath of holly berries when Samantha pulled it open.

She stood there in a red-and-white sweatshirt with criss-crossed candy canes on the front. "Hi." Her gaze lowered to his hand. "Bubbles!"

He held out the stuffed animal to her. She immediately scooped it up into her arms and gave it a great big hug as if they'd been separated for years. He watched in wonder at the little girl's abundance of love. How could her father walk away from her?

Jason choked down a lump of emotion. "I thought you might be missing him."

Samantha held the bear at arm's length. "Shame on you, Bubbles. You shouldn't have stayed at the resort all night by yourself."

"Hi," Kara said, making her presence known. "I thought you'd changed your mind about coming over."

"I'm sorry I'm late." He opened his mouth to say more, but then closed it. He was certain telling her he'd gotten caught up in his work wouldn't warm up her demeanor.

"Step inside and close the door. It's cold out there."

Not exactly an invitation to stay, but she hadn't told

him to leave, either. Deciding to take his chances, he did as she suggested.

Strains of "Have a Holly Jolly Christmas" played in the background. The fact he even recognized the song surprised him, but it helped that the singers repeated it over and over. He didn't foresee a jolly Christmas in his future, and for the first time since he was a kid, it niggled at him.

The scent of apples, cinnamon and various other spices lingered in the air. He inhaled again, remembering how his grandmother's house had often smelled like this when she had pies in the oven.

"Were you baking?" he asked.

"No. It's warmed cider."

So much for making small talk. By the frown on Kara's face, he was wasting his time. "I should go."

"You can't," Samantha interjected. "Mommy made us wait to eat till you got here."

"Samantha, hush." Kara's face filled with color.

She'd made him dinner? The words warmed a spot in his chest that sent heat spreading through his body. It'd been a long time since someone went to any bother for him.

"It's true." Samantha continued as though her mom hadn't spoken a word. "She said you need somethin' 'sides candy to eat."

Jason chuckled. Samantha's spunk was so much like her mother's. He noticed Kara make a hasty retreat into the kitchen. Her embarrassment only made the moment that much more touching.

"Your mother is very wise. You should listen to her."

After he shed his coat and made sure the soles of his boots were dry, Samantha slid her little hand in his. His heart grew three sizes in that moment. Maybe he'd been wrong all those years—maybe someday he could be a good father. But could he be a parent to another man's child?

Could he set aside the jealousy of knowing Kara had replaced him so quickly, so easily?

Samantha gave his hand a tug, dragging him back to the present. "Come on."

The kitchen was small, but warm and inviting. He took a moment to absorb his surroundings, noticing how Kara had painted the room a sunny yellow, giving it a pleasant, uplifting feel. Sunflowers adorned the curtains, baskets lined the tops of the light oak cabinets and a small arrangement of silk sunflowers filled a blue milk pitcher in the center of the table. Kara certainly had a flair for decorating.

"Are you sure this isn't an imposition?" he asked.

"Samantha's right. We have plenty of spaghetti and meatballs. Besides, you do need to eat a real meal if you keep pushing yourself so hard to make this reopening a success." Kara drained the noodles. "Have a seat."

He pulled out a chair at the table and sat down. He looked up as Kara bent over to rummage through a drawer, and he noticed an electric candle burning in the window above the sink. It was like a beacon, calling him home.

"Mommy, Mommy, can I have more cider?" Samantha held out an empty cup, her bottom lip protruding in a look designed to arouse sympathy.

Jason would have caved faster than a house of cards in a category 5 hurricane. So when he heard Kara tell her that she'd had enough for the evening, he was impressed by such fortitude. Before he became a parent, he had much to learn.

"Go wash up," Kara said. "It's time to eat."

"Okay." Samantha scampered away.

Soon they were all seated around the table. The more he smiled and laughed at Samantha's childlike antics, the more Kara loosened up. Jason was captivated by the easy banter and the abundance of smiles. Kara had really made a happy home for her little girl. Samantha chattered on about everything she'd asked Santa for, while he made mental notes of the unfamiliar toys so he could scout around for them. For the first time in forever, he was starting to look forward to Christmas.

But the second thing he noticed that evening struck him most profoundly. They didn't treat him like an outsider. They included him in their talk, as if he was one of them. As if he was family.

After two heaping helpings, Jason pushed aside his wiped-clean plate. Utterly stuffed, he couldn't remember a meal he'd enjoyed so much, even though he'd barely tasted the food. He was too caught up by the company. Time flew by and before he knew it, he'd helped Kara wash up the dinner dishes, while Samantha watched a holiday movie. He didn't want to leave, but he also didn't want to overstay his welcome.

After he said good-night to Samantha, Kara walked him to the door.

"Thanks for staying for dinner," she said. "Samantha really enjoyed your company. Sorry about her going on and on about her Christmas list. She gets a bit wound up."

"I didn't mind at all. It was actually very helpful. Otherwise I wouldn't have a clue what to buy her for Christmas."

Kara slipped outside and closed the door. "Don't feel obligated. Santa will take good care of her."

"I'm sure he will," he said, stepping closer. His gaze zeroed in on Kara's lips, thinking they presented him with an irresistible temptation. "I would just like to do something special for both of you."

His head lowered and he pressed his lips to her warm ones, feeling the slightest tremble in her. Not wanting to push his luck, he pulled away. He caught the softest sigh from Kara. She wasn't as immune to him as she'd like to think.

He cleared his throat. "Thank you for tonight."

She pressed a hand to her lips and glanced up at him. Their gazes held for a moment before her hand lowered. "We're baking cookies on Wednesday after work and making up trays of them to take to the care home. If you aren't busy you could help."

Things weren't running as smoothly at the resort as he'd like, but he'd work day and night if it meant spending another evening in this gingerbread house with these two lovely ladies.

"Count me in."

At last, Wednesday arrived. Jason glanced down at the bag of goodies on his office desk. He'd run out at lunchtime to buy them for tonight's cookie-baking endeavor. The jaunt to the mall had taken him most of the afternoon, but it'd been worth it.

"Here's the report on the latest quotes we have from alternative vendors." Kara set the spreadsheet on his desk and gazed at him. "So what put the cat-who-ate-the-canary look on your face?"

He cleared his throat, trying not to smile, but found it to be a challenge. "I don't know what you mean."

Her brows arched. "Okay, well, these are the latest figures we received. There's only one vendor, Biggest Wholesales, who's beating out Pappy Salvatore's prices."

"Good. I'll have a look." Jason noticed the frown on her face. "You know it's best for the Summit."

"It's not that. It's Biggest Wholesales. I've heard some things about them."

If he was thinking of switching their food services to another supplier, he was smart enough to know he had to be concerned about more than just the bottom line. Sometimes the cheapest wasn't always the best.

"What have you heard about them?"

"That's just it, I can't remember. But it's chewing at the back of my mind. I'm sure it'll come to me eventually."

"Let me know when you recall. And maybe you could do some checking around about them."

She stepped toward the door and pushed it closed before turning back to face him. "Are you still coming over this evening?"

"Wouldn't miss it for the world. I have a date with a cutie to keep—make that two of them." When Kara smiled, he couldn't hold back a grin of his own. "I'll stop by your desk when I finish up here."

"My desk—for what?"

"I thought we could leave together, as long as you don't mind stopping for dinner." He really liked the thought of ending the workday and going home with Kara. It seemed natural, something he could get used to.

"But we can't," she said, a look of horror on her face. "What would people think?"

He shrugged. "Does it matter what they think?"

The fact he'd been able to utter those words and truly mean them stunned him. For so many years he'd stayed away from here, worried about what people would think of him. But now things were changing—he was changing. With Kara and Samantha in his life, he realized he was more than just the genetics that created him—he was a man with wants and needs that surpassed any gossip.

"I care what my coworkers think." Kara tilted up her chin. "They'll start saying we're a couple. I don't want that."

Jason's chest tightened. "You don't want what? Us to be a couple? Or for people to talk about us?"

"I...I don't know. Both I guess." But her gaze didn't meet his. "We still have unresolved issues."

He hadn't forgotten. He just needed a little more time before he tested the ultimate strength of their relationship. And his invitation for Christmas-cookie detail was going to help his cause.

"What are you smiling about?"

"Uh, nothing. Don't worry. I'll be discreet when I leave in about..." he glanced down at the work on his desk "...about a half hour. Do you have a preference for dinner?"

She shook her head. "But that isn't necessary. I can throw something together."

"You'll have your hands full, baking. Dinner is the least I can do."

Just as promised, a half hour later, not caring that he hadn't responded to the last five emails in his in-box, Jason shut down his computer and promised himself that he'd be in early the next morning to deal with them.

On the way to Kara's house, he made a detour to pick up an assortment of sandwiches and side orders from a little mom-and-pop shop. The restaurant been around since he was a kid, and he loved the homemade food.

Armed with food and gifts, he pulled into Kara's driveway, his heart tap-dancing in his chest. Jason didn't know much about making Christmas cookies, so he felt a bit out of his element, but he swallowed hard and climbed out of the SUV. He'd just made it to the sidewalk when the front door swung open and Samantha appeared. With the door left wide-open and a toothy grin on her sweet face, she ran up to him.

"You came! I knew you would," she said excitedly.

"You doubted my word?"

She shook her head, swishing her brown ponytail back

and forth. "Mommy said you might not come. I told her you would."

So Kara still didn't trust him, not even to keep his promise for an evening of Christmas-cookie baking. Seemed tonight he'd have to make certain she knew he intended to stick around. The thought of making it permanent floated into his mind, but he still had his doubts about taking on the role of father.

What would Samantha call him? Jason? Daddy? Did he even want her calling him Daddy? After all, he didn't know much about being a good parent. The throbbing of an ensuing headache had him rubbing his forehead. Now wasn't the time to contemplate "forever."

"Jason, hurry." Samantha grabbed his free hand and started to pull him toward the kitchen. "We have to make the cookies."

"Not so fast," Kara said from the doorway. "We're going to eat first."

"Ah, do we gotta? Jason, are you hungry?"

He might not know much about kids, but only a fool would insinuate himself between mother and daughter—and he wasn't that foolish. "We better listen to your mother. She knows what's best."

He glanced up to catch a look of approval on Kara's face. He schooled his features to hold back a grin, but his chest puffed up just a little. Score one point for him tonight. If only he could keep it up the rest of the evening, he'd definitely be in Kara's good graces, and those kisses would become reality.

Kara ushered them out of the cold and in no time they were working their way through a chicken Parmesan sub, an Italian sub and a meatball sub. Seemed as though he'd found something each of them would eat. He sighed in relief. They were off to a very good start.

With everyone's stomach filled, he pulled out his bag of goodies. He handed a ruffled, white apron to Kara that read: Don't Mess with This Cook, I Carry a Rolling Pin… and I Know How to Use It.

She laughed. "And let that be a warning to both of you."

"Do I get one, too?" Samantha stretched her neck, trying to peer in the bag.

"Hmm…let me see." He took his time, as though unable to find anything.

"You forgot me?" she asked, sounding dejected.

Then he pulled out a smaller pink apron that read: Professional Taste Tester. It also had the picture of a chocolate chip cookie with a big bite taken out of it.

"I love it!" Samantha moved over and threw her arms around his neck. "Thank you."

Jason's heart thumped hard against his chest as he tenderly hugged her back. In that moment, the thought of forever got just a little less scary.

"You're quite welcome."

And last but not least, he dumped the bag on the table and a large assortment of cookie cutters spilled out. "I bought every single kind they had in the store. I can take them back if you don't want them."

The girls oohed and aahed over the various shapes, from Christmas trees to reindeer. He smiled broadly. He thoroughly enjoyed making them happy. Once the new cookie cutters were scrubbed up, they set to work making cookies for trays to deliver to the care home where Jason's father was staying. Jason tried to block out the image of his once strong dad, now sick and needy. Uneasiness laced with guilt churned in his gut. No. He refused to let that man steal this wonderful evening from him—he'd already missed so much.…

Kara was in charge of rolling out the already made and

chilled cookie dough, as well as working the oven. That left him and Samantha to do the decorating. Bowls of various colors of icing lined the table. In addition, there were red, green and white sprinkles of varying shapes and sizes. Kara certainly seemed to think of everything.

"What's that?" he asked, gesturing to the cookie Samantha was about to decorate. "A pony?"

She giggled. "Mommy, he doesn't know what a reindeer looks like."

"He doesn't. Well, I guess you'll just have to teach him these things."

"See? These are the antlers." Samantha grew serious and pointed to the cookie. "And if I put this red ball on its nose, then it's Rudolph."

Every time the child smiled it was like warm sunbeams hitting Jason's chest. He couldn't resist a bit more teasing. "I don't know. Still looks like a pony with a bad cold."

The sweet chimes of Samantha's laughter pealed through the kitchen. Even Kara was smiling and shaking her head. He had no idea until that moment how rewarding he found the sound of laughter from these two special ladies. So why was he hesitant to lay the whole truth on the line with Kara? Why couldn't he take the next step necessary to ensure he didn't lose her, now that he'd broken through her stony barrier?

"What's that?" Samantha scrunched up her button nose and pointed at the cookie he was currently smearing icing on.

"It's Santa Claus."

She shook her head. "Santa doesn't wear green."

He glanced down and realized his thoughts had meandered, and he'd accidentally grabbed the bowl of green icing. "Well, my Santa wants to be different."

"But Santa can't be green."

"He can't, huh?" Without thinking about the trouble he'd be in with Kara, he dipped his finger in the green icing and dabbed his fingertip on Samantha's nose.

Her mouth gaped open. Her eyes rounded with surprise. It took only a second for the shock to subside. She dunked her finger in the same bowl and reached out, giving him a matching green nose. They both started to laugh.

"What are you two up to?" Kara turned and he braced himself for a stern lecture. "You're supposed to decorate the cookies, not each other." With a smile tugging at her very kissable lips, she turned to check the oven. It appeared he and Samantha weren't the only ones enjoying this evening.

By eleven o'clock, Samantha was asleep in bed and they had just finished wrapping the cookie trays. Kara walked him to the door. "Thank you for all the help. We couldn't have gotten so much done tonight without you."

"I'm glad I could help. Samantha is a great kid. And her mother isn't so bad, either." Thoughts of kissing her bombarded his mind.

"She isn't, huh?" Kara smiled up at him and that was all the encouragement he needed.

He pulled her to him. With their lips a hair apart, he paused. When she didn't move, he brushed his mouth over hers. She tasted sugary and delectable. It surprised him when she didn't resist his advances. In fact, she sidled up against him, chest to chest, lip to lip. He moaned. This was the sweetest torture he'd ever experienced. He'd been wrong—kissing Kara wasn't enough to appease his mounting desires. In fact, it just made him want her even more.

"Let's go back inside," he murmured.

Kara's hands pressed against his chest. She tilted up her chin. "Are you ready to talk about the past?"

Part of him was willing to say anything just so this

moment wouldn't end. It'd been so many years since he'd made love to her...but tonight wasn't the right time.

If he was to stay here and make love to her, it would be tantamount to declaring that he was ready to spend forever with her, and he just wasn't there yet. Kara and Samantha were a package deal, and until he was ready for all that it entailed, he'd be left with nothing but sweet kisses at the door.

"I should go."

"You know you could stop by tomorrow and we could deliver the cookie trays to the care home—"

"I can't." He just couldn't go, knowing his father was there. Not even for Kara. "I still have a ton of stuff to do before the resort's grand reopening."

Her smile faltered. "I understand."

"But I'd like a rain check. How about Friday I take you and Samantha out to see a holiday movie?"

The smile came back and lit up her eyes. "You have yourself a date."

CHAPTER THIRTEEN

FRIDAY EVENING, KARA loosened her seat belt, allowing her to twist around in the passenger seat of Jason's SUV to check on Samantha. The little girl's head had lolled to the side and her eyes were closed. The hint of a smile still pulled at her lips, while bits of buttered popcorn dotted her chin.

It had been quite an evening, with dinner out followed by an animated Christmas movie. In fact, the whole week had left Kara breathless, from her phone interview for a promising junior management position in Ohio, to letting her guard down with Jason and remembering what a good friend he could be.

She tried telling herself that with things improving with him, she wouldn't lose her job. But she couldn't hang her and her daughter's future on wishful thinking. Not only hadn't he mentioned the possibility of her staying on at the Summit, but they still had so much left unsaid between them.

She'd put off talking to him about what had happened all those years ago, thinking that once he understood he wasn't Samantha's father, he wouldn't be back. But he'd surprised her. He'd been so thoughtful, so attentive. Now that this thing between them no longer seemed so casual, she had to tell him the whole story. Her insides shivered with anxiety.

Although it really worried her that Jason was unwilling to forgive his father. Would he be as unforgiving with her when she explained the circumstances of Samantha's birth? The soda and popcorn she'd had at the theater suddenly didn't sit so well in her stomach.

At her house, Jason carried Samantha inside.

"I've got it from here," Kara said, taking hold of her daughter.

His searching gaze went from her to Samantha and back. "I should get going—"

"No." She wanted to get this talk over with, now that she'd finally worked up the nerve. "Stay, please—unless you have someplace to be."

He shook his head.

"Good. You can wait in the living room while I tuck this little one into bed. I'll be right back."

"But Mommy, I'm awake."

Kara let her stand on her own, but made sure to grab her hand, not wanting her to scamper away. "You're still going to bed. It's way past your bedtime."

"Aw, Mom."

"No 'aw, Mom' with me. Scoot."

Samantha yawned and headed to her room. The lack of protest told Kara her daughter was beyond exhausted. She'd be asleep in no time. Once they got her teeth brushed, her clothes changed and the covers turned down, Samantha begged for a bedtime story. Kara firmly believed reading to children should be a priority, but she had really hoped Samantha would be too tired to notice tonight.

"Read me 'The Night Before Christmas.'" Samantha sent her a pleading look.

"But sweetie, Jason is waiting for me." Kara pulled the pink comforter up and tucked it under her daughter's arms.

"He can read to me."

What? Jason reading to her daughter? No, not tonight. Before they got any closer, Kara had to talk to him—had to set things straight.

"Jason! Jason!"

"Samantha Jean, quit screaming," Kara said in a stern but hushed voice.

In the next moment, she heard hurried footsteps in the hallway.

"Is something wrong?" He peered into the room.

"Will you read me a story?" Samantha held up the Christmas storybook while clutching Bubbles with her other arm. "This is my favorite."

He looked at Kara. At this point, she supposed making a fuss would only cause more problems. She nodded her consent. She took a seat at the foot of the twin bed while he approached Samantha and accepted the book.

"Sit by Mommy," her daughter insisted.

His glance met Kara's and she nodded again. She scooted over and he eased down beside her. His thigh brushed hers. The heat of his body permeated her jeans, warming her through and through.

He opened the book and cleared his throat. Samantha settled back on her pillow as his lyrical voice read each line with intensity. Kara closed her eyes and listened. His voice wrapped around her with its warm tones, like a plush blanket being draped around her shoulders.

The coziness of the situation swept over her. She longed for it to continue forever. *Don't get too comfortable.* She forced her eyes open. Tonight might be the last time they saw Jason. If he couldn't handle the truth behind Samantha's birth, he'd bolt—like last time.

When Jason flipped to the last page, Samantha let out a great big yawn. Kara peered around him and witnessed her daughter's struggle to keep her eyes open.

"The end." He closed the book. "Time to go to sleep."

Kara saw this as the perfect opportunity to put a little distance between them. She slid off the bed and took the book from him.

"Aw, one more, please," Samantha whined, but without her usual enthusiasm.

Another yawn escaped her lips and Jason chuckled. "Maybe another time."

Kara replaced the book in her daughter's abundant collection and turned to find Jason standing in the doorway, waiting for her.

She straightened the covers once more and hoped he didn't notice the slight tremble in her hands. It was time for the "talk." Time to clear the air. Suddenly it no longer seemed like such a good idea. Like her daughter, she enjoyed Jason's company—but she'd already delayed telling him for way too long.

After a kiss and an "I love you," she flicked off the light. She turned and caught the warmth glowing in Jason's eyes. Reading a story to Samantha had gotten to him, too. Kara's fate was sealed, but she had to make sure he understood about this family he was insinuating himself into. This time around she didn't want secrets or omissions to come between them.

She followed him to the living room. When he stopped to turn on the tree lights, she nearly ran into him.

He turned to her and stroked his thumb down her cheek. "Thank you for sharing the evening with me. You have no idea how much it meant to me."

Her mouth went dry and she swallowed hard. "Samantha…she likes you, too. A lot."

His finger traced Kara's jaw. Her heart pounded in a most irregular rhythm. "I like her, too." He stepped closer. "And I really, really like her mother."

Drawn into this enchanting spell, she heard herself utter, "And her mother really, really likes you."

In the soft glow of the Christmas tree, her gaze locked with his. Common sense warred with her body's desires. With her exhausted daughter tucked in bed, her plans for talking began to give way to the crazy sensations Jason evoked in her. Why ruin such an enchanting evening?

His hand slid to the back of her neck as his head lowered. His lips gently brushed hers, but the restrained eagerness was undeniable. She wanted him more than she'd thought possible. And his hungry kisses were so much better than her dreams.

Snuggling closer to him, she trailed her hands behind his neck. Her soft curves pressed to his rock-hard body and a moan escaped her lips.

Suddenly, Jason grabbed hold of her shoulders and held her at arm's length. In a passionate haze, she sent him a baffled look. He wanted her as much as she wanted him, so what was the problem?

His breathing was heavy. "Remember how I owe you an explanation about my leaving?" When she nodded, he continued, "I think you better hear it now...before we go any further."

The seriousness in his voice and the worry in his eyes sent an arrow of alarm piercing her chest. She wanted to talk to him, too, but something told her that if he didn't get this off his chest now, he might never do it.

Jason drew an unsteady breath. He'd been thinking about this talk all week. And he didn't see where he had much choice. Kara deserved to know what kind of man she was getting involved with before they took this relationship to the next level—something he'd come to desire with all of his being.

But first, he had to give Kara the facts—every last horrid one. He knew he was kidding himself. She would despise him once she knew everything, and toss him to the curb. Still, since he'd been spending time with her, he was starting to believe in miracles. He had to at least take the chance, even if it was a long shot.

Kara perched on the edge of the couch and looked at him expectantly. "It's okay. Whatever you have to say, we'll work through it."

He really wished he could believe her. With his shoulders pulled back, he said, "Remember the fight between me and my father?" She nodded and he went on. "There was more to that argument than I told you.... My father was drunk, and livid that I was leaving him to deal with the resort on his own."

She didn't interrupt, even though part of Jason wished that she would. Facing combat and his own mortality had been easier than what he was about to do.

He paced the floor, searching for the exact words. When he found them, he stopped in front of her. "He told me no son of his would abandon him like I was about to do. He yelled that I was not his son...that I never had been and never would be." Jason's voice caught and he swallowed hard. "He said I was the spawn of a monster."

Kara pressed a hand to her chest as her eyes shimmered. "How horrible."

Jason's head hung low. "There's more. He told me no woman would ever accept me as a husband, much less want me for the father of her children."

He forced himself to stand ramrod straight, his shoulders rigid. He drew on the discipline hammered into him over the course of his military career. He would complete his mission.

"My mother was raped...just after my father met her." Jason ignored Kara's horrified gasp and kept going, or he'd never get it all out. "I was the consequence of her rape. My dad is not my biological father. Some unidentified monster brutally attacked my mother and..." His voice cracked and died in his throat.

In an instant Kara was standing in front of him. Her arms wrapped around his shaking body, pulling him close. The self-loathing and pain surfaced. In her embrace, he let himself feel everything he'd kept bottled up for years.

Kara held on to him, whispering words of comfort. He desperately wanted to believe it'd be all right, but it wouldn't be. It couldn't be. There was no way to rip that bastard's DNA from his body.

But now it was all out there. In the open. Kara knew he was damaged goods, inside and out. Jason pulled back and turned away to swipe his flannel shirtsleeve over his cheeks. Now it was time to face the moment he'd been dreading for years, seeing the repulsion in her beautiful eyes.

Suck it up, soldier. Facing her can't be avoided. Get it over with and move on.

He lifted his head, pulled his shoulders back and turned. With him towering above her five-foot frame, his gaze shot over her head.

Look down, soldier. One glance and it'll be done. The damage will be evident.

He forced his eyes down over her rumpled hair—hair he'd only moments ago been running his fingers through. The air became caught in his lungs. His gaze skimmed her forehead, passed her gathered brows and settled on her eyes, which held no hint of repulsion or disgust.

How could that be?

Kara stood there, returning his stare, as though he was the same man she'd always thought him to be.

"Say something," he ordered. He wanted this over. It'd already dragged on for too many years.

"I'm sorry…"

"Sorry? For what?" This wasn't making any sense.

"For your father being so horrible to you. Obviously you were never meant to know any of that. I'm sorry that in a drunken rage he'd say such hateful words."

Jason's gaze bored deeply into hers. He had to be missing something. "Do you understand what I said? My biological father is a rapist. A monster. And I have his blood pumping through my veins."

Empathy glistened in her eyes. "You're nothing like that man. You're the son of a very wonderful and loving woman."

He recalled his mother and her eternal smile. She had always been an upbeat person. His dad used to refer to her as a Mary Poppins wannabe. Always looking for the good in people. And she'd most definitely loved him.

"Can you honestly say you don't see me differently?"

"You had no control over your conception. And your mother loved you. She never held the past against you. So why should I? You're nothing like your biological father."

Jason took a hesitant step toward Kara, watching for any sign of fear in her. She didn't budge. Her steady gaze continued to hold his.

"You really believe I'm a good guy, inside and out?" His breathing stopped as he waited for her ultimate decision.

She stepped up to him. Her gaze never wavered as her hand reached out and caressed his cheek. "Absolutely."

With a smile, he swept her up into his arms and held her tight. With her feet suspended, he swung her round and round. In that instance, he knew what he wanted—what he'd always wanted.

"Jason, there's more we need to talk about."

CHAPTER FOURTEEN

KARA NEEDED TO get this over with as soon as possible.
But before she could utter another word, Jason's lips were
pressed to hers. She should pull away so they could finish
talking, but after what he'd just told her, she didn't have
the heart. He needed to know without a doubt that he was
still worthy of love.

As the kiss intensified, desire flooded her body and
short-circuited her best intentions. For so long now she'd
been holding herself back from him, but no longer. She met
his kiss with a burning heat of her own. Her arms wrapped
around his trim waist, pulling him to her. His body was
hard and solid against hers. She could barely believe this
was happening, that he was holding her close again.

She'd dreamed of this moment for years, never believing
it'd happen. Perhaps her fairy godmother was lurking in the
shadows of the Christmas tree, waving her magic wand.

Jason sank down onto the couch, pulling Kara with him.
His lips still teased and taunted hers. He tasted buttery,
like the big tub of popcorn they'd shared at the theater.
She traced his lips with her tongue, savoring the added
saltiness.

His kisses trailed up her jaw to her earlobe, where he
probed and tickled her, sending waves of shivers down
her spine. His fingers played with the hem of her sweater,

sneaking underneath to her bare waist. More goose bumps swept over her skin.

He stopped kissing his way down her neck long enough to say in a breathy voice, "We've wasted too many years apart. Marry me?"

"What?"

She yanked herself out of his embrace. He couldn't be serious, could he? Her breathing still rushed, Kara moved to the far end of the couch, trying to gather her composure. She straightened her clothes before running a hand over her hair.

"That's not exactly the reaction I was expecting."

"You're serious?" When he nodded, she continued, "You're not just getting caught up in the moment?"

A broad smile lit up his eyes. "It shouldn't be that big of a shock. After all, this isn't exactly the first time I asked you."

"But there's Samantha to consider."

"I know. But you said the biological father isn't part of her life. We'll just petition him to relinquish his rights." When Kara didn't say anything, Jason squeezed her hand. "Will the man give us problems?"

The backs of her eyes stung and Jason's image blurred. "Not like you're thinking. But there's something important you need to know."

Jason's gut churned as it used to do when he was out on patrol in hostile territory. Right now his internal radar system was telling him to duck for cover.

Until this moment, he didn't understand how much Samantha had come to mean to him in such a short period of time. Only a couple of months ago, if someone had told him he was a father, Jason would have been in total denial. Now, he'd no more be able to deny his connection to

Samantha than he could deny his love for her mother. He was more than ready to step up and accept a role in Samantha's life—in both of their lives.

"We'll deal with it together," he said, with all the confidence in the world. "What's the guy's name?"

He'd had long enough to come to terms with Samantha being another man's child. He didn't like it, but at least now he could think about it without losing his temper.

"You don't understand...."

"I know this is hard, but just tell me his name."

Kara's face paled to a sickly white, and her bottom lip trembled. "Before I do, there's something you have to understand."

The raw emotion in her eyes ripped at his gut. Jason stood on the cusp of losing the future he'd come to dream of—the future he desperately wanted. His arms dropped to his sides and his hands clenched into tight balls. *No, this can't be happening.*

"Don't do this." The hoarse words tore from his throat.

A single tear dropped onto her cheek. She swiped it away.

"I'm sorry, but you need to hear the truth—the whole truth."

He was a man who'd been on the front line of combat, who'd faced the enemy and never considered backing down. But at this moment, he wanted to make a hasty retreat. His eyes searched out the door, yet his feet wouldn't cooperate. Running from the truth wouldn't change it.

"Whatever you have to say, I can deal with it," he said. He had to.

He loved them.

The revelation stole the air from his lungs. He wanted Kara and Samantha more than he'd ever wanted anything in his life, including restoring his family's resort.

He couldn't let this thing between them end before it had barely begun.

Surely whatever she had to say couldn't be nearly as bad as what he'd told her. Kara was just overreacting. If she could forgive and accept him, then he could do the same for her now. After all, wasn't that the foundation of a good relationship—being able to forgive each other?

"When you left—" Kara's voice cracked. She started again. "After you'd ended our engagement with no explanation, I was devastated."

She pressed her lips together and swallowed. "For a couple of months I hid in my room. I cried my eyes out, trying to figure out what I'd done wrong to make you leave. I hoped and prayed you'd change your mind and come back for me." She paused, sucking in an unsteady breath. "I even asked your father for your phone number or address, any way I could get in contact with you."

"I didn't let him know where I was stationed. I even changed my last name, to make it impossible for him."

"Your father sounded so broken up when he told me he hadn't heard from you. I was totally lost and I hurt so badly. My friends rallied around me. They said I needed to forget you and get on with my life. They insisted I go out with them to a party. But they didn't understand. How could they understand what you and I shared?"

Her words were like a sledgehammer, beating at his chest. Jason opened his mouth, searching for an apology. Unable to find words to express the depth of his regret, he closed his mouth. She wouldn't even look at him now. Her hands were clenched in her lap. He wanted to reach out to her, but his nerve faltered.

Kara had never been a partier. She'd much rather be doing outdoor sports than watching her friends get drunk.

Something must have happened at that party. His chest struggled for each breath as he waited.

The silence flowed on. Her pink lips trembled. He'd always been drawn by them. Surprised he'd noticed them now of all times, he continued to stare. The temptation to smother them in a reassuring kiss and erase the rest of this doomed story overrode his apprehension. He stepped forward. Maybe just one kiss could change this perilous course they were on, but logic told him it'd only delay the inevitable. This journey had been preordained years ago.

He pulled his foot back and took a firm stance. "Kara, whatever it is, just say it."

"At the party," she said, giving him a hesitant glance, "I found a dark corner and stayed there. I regretted going, but since I hadn't driven, I had to wait for my ride. Anyway, someone decided I needed to loosen up, so they spiked my drink. When I realized what they'd done, I hesitated. I wasn't thinking clearly, but they convinced me that the drink would take the edge off the pain."

She paused, her eyes not meeting his. One by one, each muscle in his body grew rigid, while a sickening feeling brewed in his gut.

"I was young and stupid. I don't have any other excuse for what happened next. One drink led to another and another. You know I didn't drink, so it didn't take long before I was feeling good—too good." She rubbed her hands together. "Shaun showed up. Someone had called him when they found me wasted. He took care of me...."

Jason's uneasiness ramped up to an excruciating pain, as though he'd been riddled with bullets, left on the side of the road to die a slow, agonizing death. He wanted to be there for Kara, just as she'd been there for him, but this... this was different.

"I was wrong," he said, his voice hoarse. "I don't want to hear this."

He took a step toward the door.

"You have to listen." The eerie, high-pitched tone of her voice put a stop to his retreat. "You can't run away. Not this time."

His teeth ground together. His jaw flexed. The door was in sight, but the determination in Kara's voice told him that she'd follow him this time. He summoned up the courage he'd clung to on the battlefield, and turned.

Kara stood now. Her gaze held his with a fierce determination. "You weren't there to help me—but like always, Shaun filled in. He was your lifelong best friend. We had been the Three Musketeers. I trusted him almost as much as I trusted you."

She dashed away another tear. "He attempted to sober me up. He took me to his car, intent on getting me home."

Jason felt trapped on a runaway train. His life whizzed past him and there was no way to get off. He could only hold on, bracing for the devastating collision with the truth.

"On the way, I started to cry. Shaun pulled off on one of the desolate country roads. It was late and there wasn't any traffic. He tried to comfort me—"

"Stop." Jason's voice thundered in the room. He couldn't bear to hear any more.

The stabbing pain in his chest had him glancing down, searching for blood. He took a moment to gather his shattered illusions.

"Shaun is Samantha's father?" he asked, stumbling to latch on to this fact.

Kara nodded. Silent tears streamed down her cheeks. "Yes, he is."

The brown hair and blue eyes made sense now. Jason

and Shaun had been mistaken all their lives for brothers because of their similar looks.

Shaun. His best friend.

And Kara. Kara! The only woman he'd ever loved.

How was it possible his girl and his best friend had created a baby?

Pain spanned from temple to temple. This couldn't be happening. It had to be some kind of sick, twisted nightmare. Kara and Shaun never would have betrayed him like this.

Jason's breath came in short, rapid puffs.

"This can't be right. Kara, tell me it isn't true. Tell me you're saying this to get even with me for leaving you, and none of it is true."

"I can't."

"But how? Why?" The questions tumbled through his mind. "Did you always have a thing for him?"

"No. It was a mistake. A combination of too much to drink, a deep aching loneliness and hearing that Shaun loved me."

"He loved you?" Would the blows never stop coming?

"He admitted that he loved me, but up until then he hadn't been able to do anything about it, because of you...."

Jason ran a hand over his mouth, trying to remember some sign, some hint he'd missed. "I had no idea. How could I have been so blind?"

"You weren't the only one. I didn't know, either."

Her words didn't comfort him. Inside, he was mortally wounded, worse than when his father had smacked him in the face with the truth about his parentage. Jason had thought nothing could hurt worse than that, but he had been oh so wrong.

His vision grew blurry as he looked at Kara, no longer seeing the woman he loved, but rather the woman who'd betrayed him with his best friend, and stolen away the child he'd so wanted to be his little girl.

"Why?" His voice croaked out. "Why him?"

If it had been anyone else in the world, he'd have been able to deal with it. But not the one guy he'd considered a brother.

He had been wrong.

He couldn't forgive this.

If that made him less of a man, more a coward, so be it.

Shaun being the father of Kara's little girl made Jason's stomach lurch. The thought of his best friend and the woman he'd wanted to marry clinging to each other—Shaun's lips on hers—made the bile rush to the back of his mouth. Jason swallowed hard, pushing down the sickening thought.

When Kara opened her mouth to speak, he held up a hand to stop her. "Don't answer. I don't want to hear it. I can't believe you betrayed me with my best friend."

He couldn't stay here any longer. He was going to be ill.

In a few quick strides, barely noticing his injured knee's protest, he reached the door. His hand paused on the doorknob for just a moment. With a shake of his head to clear away the image of Kara in Shaun's arms, he yanked open the door and rushed into the frigid, dark night.

He'd never been so sick or so alone in his entire life.

CHAPTER FIFTEEN

HER PREDICTION HAD come true.

In this instance, Kara hated being right. But just as soon as Jason heard about her youthful mistake, he'd done exactly what she'd worried he would do...run. Of course, part of it was her fault. She'd waited too long to tell him about Shaun, and she hadn't prepared Jason at all. The whole situation couldn't have been handled any worse if she had tried.

Days had passed since that fateful night and Jason had completely avoided her, both in and out of the office. The devastation of him turning away like this made her anxious to find a new job. She'd let herself get in too deep with him. She'd let herself trust him, rely on him. In that instant, she realized how he'd sneaked past her best defenses.

She'd fallen in love with him.

She wasn't in love with the boy he used to be, the youth of her memories. No, she loved the man who'd saved her from a snowstorm and opened his home to her. The man who'd put her and Samantha's happiness above his own by taking time away from renovating the resort to decorate cookies and read a bedtime story.

What if Kara had told him she loved him? Would he have still walked out the door? Probably. He was unable to accept that she'd had a child with his best friend. The fact that their engagement had been officially dissolved at the time seemed completely immaterial to him.

But none of it mattered now. Whatever she'd thought they were building together was over and done. She had to focus on the new job she'd been offered in Ohio. It was in the next state, not that far from her family...or Jason, not that he'd ever visit them.

"Mommy, Mommy, look." Samantha hurried into the kitchen, holding a folded piece of red construction paper.

"What do you have there?"

"A Christmas card. See?" She held it two inches from Kara's face.

A step back allowed Kara's eyes to adjust and focus on the highly decorated paper. She noticed the green cutout of a Christmas tree and the shape of an angel at the top, reminiscent of the tree topper Jason had given them. Kara's bottom lip started to tremble at the thought of never having him drop by their house with little gifts for Samantha, or just to share a cup of hot cider and discuss his day with her.

"Do you like it?" Samantha asked, jarring Kara back to the present.

"It's lovely. You did a great job. But didn't we have a long talk about you not using the glue without asking?"

"Uh-huh. But it was a surprise."

"I understand, but don't do it again." She didn't have the heart to be more assertive. "You're quite the artist. I like how you used glitter to make the garland on the tree."

Her daughter ducked her head and shrugged. "I wanted it to look just like the tree Jason gave us."

Kara swallowed the lump that formed in her throat at the mention of his name. She had yet to tell Samantha that he wouldn't be coming to visit anymore. She knew it must be done sooner rather than later, but she also knew how attached her daughter was to him. How in the world was Kara supposed to break her heart?

"I have another picture I have to finish." Samantha turned and started out of the room.

"Wait," Kara called. "Don't you want me to put your card on the fridge?"

"Uh-uh. I made it for Jason."

Kara picked up the card and opened it. *"Merry Christmas, Jason. We miss you. XOXOXO Samantha."*

This was the moment she'd been dreading. Kara backed against the counter for support. "But honey, he's really busy with the resort. I don't know if he'll have time to visit again."

Samantha pressed her hands onto her hips. "Then you can give it to him at work."

"I'll try."

"You have to. Promise?"

Unable to deny helping her daughter with this gesture of kindness, Kara said, "I promise."

"Don't forget."

She wouldn't forget the card or Jason. Although she couldn't wait around for something that obviously wasn't meant to be. She'd been down this road before, but this time she knew she had to move on—to do what was best for her and Samantha. No matter how much it hurt.

Jason leaned back in his office chair late Thursday morning. He ran a hand through his hair, not caring if he messed it up. He didn't have any appointments, just a huge stack of mail, files to review and invoices to sign. He'd spent most of the week working on the lift on the double-diamond run. It'd taken three tries to get the right parts for such an old piece of equipment, but at last they'd done it. Things were finally on track for the grand reopening in two more days.

He'd spent months working toward this moment, and now that it was almost here, he should be excited, bursting with happiness. But without Kara and Samantha around to share his accomplishment, he was empty inside. They'd provided him with the driving force to overcome unforeseen problems and the strength to push through the long hours.

He picked up the phone to dial Kara's extension, but then slammed it back down. He had no idea what to say to her. Now that he'd had time to calm down and think everything through, he realized how poorly he'd reacted to her admission. What had he expected? For her to be a saint, and loyal, after the horrible way he'd ended their engagement and left town without even an explanation?

He had only himself to blame for everything that had happened. His heart pounded with unrelenting exasperation. How could he have handled this situation so horribly? Maybe he was more like the man who raised him than he'd ever imagined—unreliable. Jason found it strange how he found himself in such a similar position to the one his dad had been in years ago, both of them loving a woman who had a child by another man.

Jason's head hung low and shame washed over him at the way he'd failed while his father had succeeded. His dad had moved past the fact that Jason's mom was pregnant with another man's child. He'd married her and raised her baby as his own. Jason had to give the man credit; he'd tried to be a good father.

Jason shook his head. He hadn't even stepped up to the plate and welcomed the woman he loved and the daughter of his heart into his life. His hands clenched. Instead, he had lived up to Kara's worst nightmares and walked away from her. Again. She'd predicted that this was how he'd react when things got to be too much for him, and he'd proven her right.

There'd be no going back this time.

He ran his hands over his face. He'd really screwed up. Anger over his knee-jerk reaction balled up in his gut. After she'd forgiven him for leaving her, and accepted him, screwed-up genes and all, he'd overreacted to something she'd done years ago in a moment of confusion and pain.

A deep, guttural groan grew in the back of his throat. He'd ruined everything. His eyes closed as he tried to block it all out. Kara's image refused to fade away. The anguished look in her green eyes ripped at his gut. He clenched his hand and slammed it down on the desktop, making everything shake. The desk calendar fell over, a pen rolled off the edge and the stack of paperwork requiring his attention teetered over, spilling onto the floor.

With a frustrated sigh, he rose to his feet, surveying the mess of files and correspondence. He placed everything in a haphazard stack on his desk. Maybe some work would take his mind off the chaos he'd made of everyone's lives.

With a sigh, he sank down on his chair and tackled the very first item on the intimidating heap of paperwork. More than an hour later, he came across a plain white envelope. Jason looked at it and frowned when he found it still sealed. It was customary for his assistant to open everything and date stamp the correspondence. It wasn't like her to miss things.

He slipped a finger beneath the flap and yanked, ripping open the envelope. He pulled out a folded piece of red construction paper. When he saw the crude cutout of a Christmas tree, he was quite puzzled. He flipped it open and smiled at the scribbled, green crayon message, with Samantha's name printed across the bottom. He blinked repeatedly as he stared at the prettiest card he'd ever received.

Was it possible Kara didn't hate him? His hands began to shake as his hopes started to mount. Was this her attempt at a peace offering? Or had Samantha merely insisted she deliver the card? Either way, he was deeply touched by the gesture.

He set it on the desk and sucked in a deep, calming breath. He couldn't go off half-cocked—that was what had led him to this mess.

He glanced down. An old weathered envelope caught his attention. It was the letter from the man who'd hurt him so deeply—the same man who had taught him to fish and how to play ball. Jason stared at the envelope, remembering his promise to Kara to read it.

Maybe there really was such a thing as a Christmas miracle. Or maybe he needed to make a Christmas miracle of his own. He needed to prove to Kara that he had changed into a man she could trust with her heart, through the good and the bad. Words wouldn't be enough. He needed to do more. Perhaps this letter was the perfect place to start.

He ripped open the envelope, bracing himself for a string of hateful words. But when he read: *"Son, I'm sorry..."* his gaze blurred. He blinked repeatedly and kept reading the heartfelt note. His father hadn't meant what he'd said in his drunken rage. Jason checked the date, finding it'd been written almost seven years ago, while he was still in basic training. He'd wasted all these years being stubborn, thinking his dad hated him. But he'd been wrong.

Jason's throat grew thick with emotion. Kara had been right all along. This was the season for hope and forgiveness.

A plan started to take shape in his mind. He'd show her

that he could embrace the spirit of the season. He knew what must be done—the most important mission of his life. Operation: Win Kara Back.

And he didn't have a moment to lose. He'd already wasted seven years. He could be a reliable, steadfast man for Kara and a father to the little girl who'd already claimed a permanent spot in his heart. He wouldn't repeat his or his father's mistakes. He'd make sure both Kara and Samantha knew how much he loved them.

Jason shoved back from his desk. With long strides he headed for the office where Kara's desk stood. When he found her chair vacant, he spun around, scanning the shelving units, file cabinets and other desks. No Kara.

What if she'd quit? His chest tightened.

"Mr. Greene, do you need something?" asked Sherry, a redhead wearing a festive reindeer sweater.

"First, it's Jason, remember?"

She smiled, then nodded.

"Do you know where Kara is?" He'd track her down to the ends of the earth if that was what it took. He couldn't lose this chance to set things right. Something told him it would be the last chance he got.

"Oh, well…"

"Spit it out," he said, lacking any patience.

"I took a message for her when she stepped out to get some coffee. When I gave her the note, she grabbed her things, said she didn't know when she'd be back and ran out the door."

Had something happened to Samantha? Jason's heart lodged in his throat. But surely Kara would have said something. Then he realized, with the way he'd left things between them, he'd be lucky if she ever spoke to him again. And he couldn't blame her after the ass he'd made of himself.

"Do you remember the message?" he asked, praying for a little help here.

Sherry nodded. "It was the Pleasant Valley Care Home."

Regret sucker-punched him. His breath hitched. Kara's prediction had come true. Something had happened to his father and Jason had been too stubborn to go to him, to hear him out. Now it was too late to give his dad some peace of mind. Or was it? Was his guilty conscience jumping to conclusions?

"What did the message say?" he asked, poised to rush out the door.

"For her to come to the home—that Joe needed her."

Jason still had a chance to make things right.

He bolted toward the parking lot, hoping he wouldn't be too late to put his father's mind at ease. Jason might not have liked the drunk he had become, but the man he used to be, when Jason's mother was alive—he owed that man a bit of peace.

And Kara shouldn't be shouldering this all by herself. She might not want him there, but he owed it to her to at least make the attempt.

Jason clung to the hope that he wouldn't be too late as he tramped the accelerator on the way to the sprawling facility. He took the first available parking spot and ran to the door.

Out of breath, he said to a small group of women behind the counter, "I'm here to see my father."

One with bleach-blond hair and blue eye shadow directed him to sign in, gave him directions to the room and buzzed him through the double doors. Though the process took only a couple of minutes, each second dragged on forever.

The muscles in his shoulders and neck grew rigid as Jason strode down the wide corridor, checking each room number, his hands balled up at his sides. At last he reached room 115. He fully expected to see a flurry of nurses shouting out lifesaving orders, but instead the lilt of laughter echoed through the doorway. Kara was laughing?

He stood there in the hallway, breathing a sigh of relief. Little by little, his body began to relax. His father had to be okay or she wouldn't be laughing.

Suddenly he was caught up in a wave of second thoughts. Neither Kara nor his father knew he was standing just outside in the hallway. He could easily slip away and nobody would be the wiser. He'd be back...soon. Once he gave this reunion some thought and planned out what to say. Somehow "Hey, Dad, how's it going?" didn't quite work in this case.

His gaze swung back to the double doors leading toward the parking lot. It'd be so much easier, and he had so much work to do at the resort.

He'd stepped back when he heard someone say, "Mr. Greene, I see you found your father's room. You can go ahead in."

A pretty, young nurse with a brown ponytail was headed down the hall, carrying a white blanket. He vaguely remembered seeing her at the reception desk.

"Thanks."

More footsteps sounded and then Kara stood before him, her face lit up with a smile. In fact, he'd say she was glowing.

"I knew you'd eventually find your way here. In your own time."

His instinct was to deny he was here for any other reason than to check on her, but he couldn't. The time had come to be truthful about the feelings he'd been running from for too long. As crazy as it sounded, if there was a chance to see the man who'd called him son, Jason wanted to take it.

"They said at the office there was an emergency." He glanced into the room, but could only see the end of a bed and a couple of empty chairs.

"Everything is okay. Your father got worked up when a doctor he didn't know tried to examine him. His doc went out of town for the holidays and the newest associate drew the short straw, pulling holiday duty."

"You were able to sort it all out?"

She smiled and nodded.

Kara shouldn't be here, dealing with his father and the doctors. She had enough on her hands being a single mother. It was time he started shouldering the responsibilities where his father was concerned.

"Kara," a gruff voice called out, followed by a string of coughs.

"I'll be right there." She moved closer to Jason and lowered her voice. "Prepare yourself. He's a mere ghost of the man you left seven years ago."

Jason nodded, still not exactly sure what to expect. He couldn't imagine Joe as anything but six foot four, with shoulders like a linebacker and a stogie hanging out the side of his mouth.

"One more thing," she said. "If you came here to settle up on an old score—don't. He can't take the strain. He isn't strong enough."

Jason nodded once more.

"I mean it." Her tone left no uncertainty about her seriousness.

"I get it."

First, he'd deal with his dad, and then he'd talk to Kara. He started for the door, letting her follow him inside. His steps were slow but steady.

When at last he saw his father's face, he stopped. A word of greeting caught in his throat. He blinked, unable to imagine someone could physically change so drastically from a vibrant man to barely more than a skeleton with yellowing skin.

Jason choked down his alarm. The pitiful sight doused any lingering resentment inside him. There was nothing he could say to hurt this man any worse than he'd hurt himself. His father had suffered enough.

"Son, you came." A round of hacking coughs overtook him.

For a moment, Jason stood frozen, bombarded by his dad's appearance, from the oxygen tube aiding his breathing to the sunken eyes and the bony hand covering his mouth as he struggled through the fit of coughing. It was the distressed look on his father's face that finally kicked him into action. Jason stepped alongside the bed and filled a glass with water.

"Yes, Dad, I'm home."

After handing over the glass, Jason peered over his shoulder to make eye contact with Kara, but she was gone. Their talk would have to wait a little longer.

"I...I was worried." Joe paused to catch his breath. "Thought maybe I'd never lay eyes on you again."

"I'm here." He placed a reassuring hand on his father's bony shoulder. Jason schooled his features, hoping to keep his pity and shock under wraps. "Whatever you need, all you have to do is ask."

"You'd do that...now...after everything?" He coughed again.

"Yes."

The one syllable said enough. Jason didn't want to rehash the bad times, knowing they'd wasted too much time looking over their shoulders instead of appreciating the here and now. Besides, the letter had already told him everything he'd ever need to know. Too bad it'd taken him all these years to read it.

"Hey, Dad, remember those days when we'd head out with our fishing poles in hand to catch dinner?"

The corners of his father's thin lips lifted. "You remember back then?"

"I remember, Dad."

"We never did catch much."

"But it was fun trying."

"That it was." This time it was his father who reached out to him, squeezing his forearm with cool hands. "I was worried you'd forget those times." Another coughing fit overtook him and Jason offered him more water. When his breathing calmed, Joe continued, "I'm sorry it all went so wrong. I couldn't handle your mother's death, and I let you down."

Knowing this was no longer about him, but about giving his father everlasting peace, Jason added, "But before that you were the best dad. I wouldn't have made it to quarterback in high school if it hadn't been for you teaching me to play ball at an early age."

A twinkle came to his father's sunken eyes just before his eyelids began to droop. Obviously, the emotional reunion and the coughing had zapped his energy.

"It's okay, Dad. You rest now."

"Son, tell Kara I still want my Christmas present."

"I will." Jason hoped she knew what his father was talking about, because he certainly didn't. "I'll be back tomorrow to check on you."

"Promise?" Joe murmured. His eyes were completely closed now.

"I promise. You don't have to worry anymore. I'll be here when you need me."

And he knew without a doubt that he wasn't going anywhere—no matter what fate threw at him. He would be here for the loved ones in his life. Now he just had to convince Kara to trust in him.

CHAPTER SIXTEEN

FRIDAY EVENING KARA'S heart hammered harder and faster the closer she got to Jason's log home. She could hardly believe he'd once again called and summoned her to drop everything, grab Samantha and come running.

This time he'd requested the vendor quotes. Of course, she couldn't blame him. She was supposed to have dropped the report on his desk on her way out the door, but a printer snafu and a phone call from her impatient daughter had left her thoughts scattered. Kara had walked right out the door with the printed report in hand.

But she also had some important information for him. After checking around with other restaurants, she knew what she didn't like about Bigger Wholesales—they undercut their competition with inferior produce, and a lot of money was lost due to waste.

As she made a left-hand turn onto Jason's road, she wondered if tonight might be a good time to let him know that she'd done a phone interview with the company in Ohio. Her background check had come back clean and now the only thing standing between her and an office manager position with benefits was for her to accept. She should be excited, or at least relieved, but she couldn't work up any enthusiasm for leaving her family, home or—most of all—Jason. It'd taken years to be reunited and now, in a blink, they were over.

A groan from behind had Kara glancing in the rearview mirror at her daughter, who was squirming in her seat belt. "Sweetie, what are you doing?"

"I dropped Bubbles." Guttural grunts sounded. "Got him."

"Maybe you should leave him in the car so you don't lose him while we're at Jason's. We won't be long."

"Bubbles stays with me."

Not in the mood for an argument, Kara let the subject drop. Jason's driveway loomed in the distance. A nervous energy made her stomach quiver at the thought of seeing him outside the office, where they didn't have to maintain a professional facade.

She glanced at the clock. Seven on the dot. They were right on time. She turned into the drive and was floored to find the entire house decked out in multicolored, twinkling Christmas lights. Her mouth gaped open.

"Mommy, look at all those lights."

"They're beautiful."

Tears threatened as she wondered if Jason's Scrooge-like view on life had at last changed. She quickly tamped down her emotions. It wasn't as if he'd done this for her. He must be planning to invite the investors to his house for a party or some such thing. He probably hated each and every one of the lights adorning his yard.

She glanced down at the gift she'd wrapped for him, wondering if perhaps she'd chosen the right thing to give him. Would he take offense? Still, she just couldn't run out and buy him any of the traditional gifts, such as a tie, flannel pajamas or a cheese tray. Those things didn't say "Jason" to her. But seeing the house all decked out with holiday fare reaffirmed her choice of gifts.

Her insides trembled as she pulled the car to a stop next to the porch. Before she had a chance to decide her next move, Santa stepped out onto the porch.

Santa?

"Mommy. Mommy, look."

When Santa moved in front of her headlights, and stared back at her through wire-rimmed glasses, Kara gaped again. Why in the world was the man she'd commonly thought of as Scrooge all dressed up like the jolliest man at the North Pole?

She swallowed hard, trying to comprehend what was going on here.

"Mommy, doesn't Jason look neat?" Samantha opened the door and scooted out of the backseat.

Too late to back out now.

He walked down the steps in his black boots and out the walk to greet them. Kara immediately noticed his lean waist had grown into a very plump tummy, with a thick black belt and a gold buckle holding everything in place.

"Ho-ho-ho." His deep voice rumbled.

"You make a good Santa," Samantha said, patting his rounded belly.

"And have you been naughty or nice?" he asked, in a Santa-like voice. "Ho-ho-ho."

Kara couldn't help but laugh. What in the world had gotten into him?

When she regained her composure, she asked, "Um... are we early?"

"You're right on time. You and Samantha are my only guests."

Her eyes opened wide. "You planned all this for us? What about the vendor report?"

"We'll go over it Monday at the office. Afraid that was just a ruse to get you here." He smiled sheepishly. "I know how much you enjoy the holidays and I thought you might appreciate the decorations. Do you like them?"

Samantha ran off to check out the various Christmassy figurines lining the porch, leaving the two adults with a little bit of privacy.

Kara gazed up into Jason's blue eyes and her world tilted off center. Giving a little tug on his cottony beard, she said, "I like Santa best of all."

"I'm so sorry, Kara. I was such a jerk the other night—"

"We've both done things we aren't proud of. I should have been totally straight with you from the beginning about what occurred after you left town."

His steady gaze held hers. "I wanted to show you just how much you both mean to me."

She bestowed upon him her biggest and brightest smile. "Well, Santa, you've outdone yourself. Especially today with your father. Thank you for making the effort."

"No, thank *you*. You finally talked some sense into me. It was way past time that my father and I patched things up. We'll never be candidates for a Norman Rockwell painting, but we've made peace with each other, and you won't have to worry about him so much anymore. I'll be there for him."

"I'm glad." She squeezed his arm.

"Let's go inside," he said, climbing the steps and opening the door for them.

When Kara stepped inside, Sly ran up to her with a loud meow, followed by a boisterous purr as she rubbed against her ankles. Kara bent down and ran her hand over the feline's satiny fur.

"Hey, sweetie. I missed you, too."

As though understanding Kara's words, Sly paused, lifted her golden eyes and meowed in agreement.

"Wow. A kitty." Samantha ran over and dropped to her knees.

Sly scampered away to a safe distance before turning and taking in the little girl with a cautious stare.

"Come here, Sly," Jason called to the cat.

Sly paused. Big, curious eyes checked them out before she sauntered over. In one fluid motion, Jason scooped up the cat in one arm and started to pet her.

"This is my friend Samantha," he said close to the cat's inky-black ear. "She's really nice." He leaned toward the little girl. "Go ahead and pet her head."

Kara smiled as Santa did his best to make her daughter feel at home. Her eyes glistened as she took in this tender moment. What in the world did all this mean? She didn't want to jump to conclusions. She was certain Jason would eventually explain.

In the background, she spotted the Christmas tree exactly as she'd left it. She couldn't stop smiling. Jason had let the joy of the holiday back into his heart. A happy tear splashed on her cheek. She swiped it away with the back of her hand.

Samantha ran over to the tree and sat on the floor next to it. The sleek feline followed, eventually rubbing against her arm.

"Look, Sly, at all the presents. There's three with my name on them." Samantha glanced over her shoulder at Jason. "Can I open them now?"

"Sure. If it's okay with your mom."

Kara nodded. As Samantha ripped into her gifts, Jason draped an arm over Kara's shoulders. "I hope I did okay. I've never bought toys for a little girl before. In fact, I've never bought toys before, period."

After Samantha unwrapped a pink plush cat, a jewelry

and makeup kit, and an electronic game, Kara said, "Samantha, don't we have a gift for Jason?"

Her daughter rushed over, removed a wrapped package from Kara's oversize purse and handed it to him. "It's your turn."

"What's this?" he asked, giving it a little shake.

Samantha shrugged.

"Just a little something," Kara stated.

He tore off the wrapping paper in much the same frenzied fashion as her daughter. "The angel." His brow crinkled. "But I gave this to Samantha."

Kara pressed a finger to his lips, stopping his protest. "This is a very precious gift, and Samantha and I enjoyed having her atop our tree. But it was time she came home where she belongs—with you." *The same place I want to be,* she almost added, but held her tongue. A heavy sadness settled in her heart as she blinked back the moisture gathering in her eyes.

Jason disappeared into the kitchen and returned with three champagne glasses. "Here's some sparkling cider. I thought it would fit the occasion." He handed each of them a glass and then held his high. "Here's to the two most wonderful ladies." He paused, clearing his throat. "May your futures be everything you want them to be."

Kara clinked her glass with his and forced a smile on her face. "And to a successful reopening."

She glanced up at him and saw the puzzled look in his eyes. He must have picked up something in her expression. Deep inside, she didn't want to move away. Living in a city meant there'd be no yard to plant spring flowers, and Samantha would have to go to an after-school day-care center while she worked, instead of staying with her doting grandparents. City life would be very different from what she'd imagined for her and Samantha.

And most of all, Jason wouldn't be around to drop by on a moment's notice. Oh, how she'd miss him, and the chance of them being more than just old friends. Sometimes life could be unfair.

Still, she couldn't discuss her reservations about the move. She had to maintain a positive front not only for Samantha but for herself. Kara stiffened her spine and swallowed down her misery. She'd wait until the day after Christmas to break the news of the move to her daughter. She didn't want to ruin the holiday.

CHAPTER SEVENTEEN

Jason took Kara by the elbow and led her to the other side of the living room, giving them a little privacy.

"Will you give me another chance?" he asked, staring deep into her eyes.

"A chance for what?"

"For us. For you and me and Samantha to be together."

She continued to stare at him. Her eyes grew shiny but her lips didn't move.

"Kara." He placed a finger beneath her chin and lifted her head so their gazes met. "Talk to me. You want that, too, don't you?"

She blinked repeatedly while worrying her lower lip, as though internally waging a deep debate. Was it really so hard for her to decide? Was he about to lose her for good?

Jason searched her darkened eyes, detecting the swirl of confusion and utter frustration in them. "Please, say something."

"Why now?" Lines of stress creased her beautiful face. Her eyes pleaded with him to be honest. "If only you'd said something sooner, maybe we could have figured out something. But I've found a new job…in Ohio."

Her words sent his heart plummeting. He'd thought this through before she and Samantha had arrived. He knew there'd be hurdles to cross. Now wasn't the time to give up. If it meant he had to meet her halfway, or more than halfway, he'd do it.

"Come outside with me," he said, taking her arm.

"Outside?" She pulled back. "But why?"

"I need a few minutes to talk to you. Alone." He glanced over his shoulder at Samantha. "Don't worry, she'll be fine sitting next to the tree, with Sly by her side and her toys to occupy her."

"All right. Just for a couple of minutes."

He grabbed her coat from the back of the couch and draped it over her shoulders. After letting Samantha know where they'd be, Jason ushered Kara out the door into the chilly night.

A few inches of snow layered the ground and dusted the trees. With the lights he'd painstakingly strung over the porch rails and small trees and shrubs, it did look magical, if you were into that sort of thing. It wasn't something he'd normally have done; he considered it a labor of love. But as he stood here, looking out over the yard and watching colored lights twinkle on the snow, he had to admit it wasn't so bad.

"I still can't believe you put up all these decorations." Kara moved to his side.

When he turned his gaze back to the woman he loved— the woman he didn't want to let go for a second time—his insides twisted with anxiety. He'd never been so nervous about anything in his life, not even making his way through boot camp or being sent into enemy territory.

"I saw the worried expression on your face when I made the toast," he said. "Is there a problem with your new job?"

She shook her head. "No. Not at all. In fact, they're anxious for me to get settled into my new position."

Not what he wanted to hear, but nothing he couldn't handle. "So you're going ahead with the move?"

"Of course. Why wouldn't I? This is an amazing opportunity."

"I'm sure it is." Jason swallowed back his disappointment.

"You know, it's beautiful here," she said, leaning her hands on the rail. "You're so lucky to have this little piece of nature."

He turned to her and she stared up at him. The gentle breeze carried with it the scent of strawberries from her golden hair. The nippy air also brought out the pink hue in her smooth cheeks. And the red of her lips intensified, drawing his full attention to them. They looked so perfect for kissing.

"*Beautiful* doesn't even begin to describe it," he murmured, never moving his gaze from her.

"The yard looks amazing with all the lights. Did you do all this for us?"

He nodded. "If it's what makes you happy, then it's what makes me happy."

"And that Santa suit… You really outdid yourself." Her gaze slid over him, and he grew self-conscious when she eyed the puffy pillow widening his midsection.

"I need to apologize for being such a jerk the other night. Seven years ago, I dumped you. You were free to do whatever you wanted with your life. And I've accepted that. I'm sorry I overreacted. Most of all, I'm sorry I put you in that position all those years ago."

Her fingers reached out and touched his cheek. "We may have not made the best decisions back then, but despite them something miraculous happened. I gave birth to the most wonderful little girl." Kara turned to the living room window and he followed suit, glancing in at Samantha. "I've never for one instance regretted her."

"Nor do I," he admitted, surprised by his own heartfelt

sincerity. "She may not have my DNA, which is probably a blessing in itself—"

Kara elbowed him. "We had this conversation already, remember? You were created from your mother's love and Joe's best intentions. A child would be fortunate to have you as their father."

Her confidence in him warmed his insides. How could he have ever doubted her and her ability to handle his secret?

"Do you really mean that?"

"Of course I do."

"Santa almost forgot. He has one more gift to hand out." He reached beneath his costume and fished out a small box wrapped in red foil and tied up tight with a bow. He held it out to her. "Here. Open it."

Her eyes grew round. Her searching gaze moved from him to the tiny present.

"Go ahead," he coaxed. "It won't bite. I promise."

Her fingers trembled as she pulled on the ribbon, but they were no match for the quivering in his stomach. The most important mission of his life had finally reached the critical juncture. He had to succeed with this part of his plan. Otherwise his heart would end up a fallen victim on the front line.

Kara deftly made her way past the wrapping to the black velvet box. As though she was afraid to stop, she quickly lifted the lid.

Her lips formed an O.

Unspoken questions filled her eyes. She stood there staring at him like a deer caught in headlights, not knowing which way to go. She didn't throw the box at him and stomp away. Nor did she squeal with delight and throw herself in his arms. He'd take her reserve as a positive sign.

He still had time to convince her that they could make this thing between them work. He *had* to convince her.

"Don't say anything," he said, pressing a finger to those delectable lips. "Just listen. We can make this work."

She shook her head, her eyes shimmering. He fortified his determination with the knowledge that she hadn't heard his proposal yet. Once she did, she'd realize the possibilities for them.

"First, I love you," he said, gazing straight into her eyes. "I've always loved you. I am so sorry for destroying our dreams all those years ago. I wasn't mature enough back then to have faith in you and me—in us—to handle the news about my biological father."

Jason reached out and took her free hand in his. He rubbed his thumb over her cold fingers. He had to speed this up so he could get her back inside, next to the fire.

"I know how important this new job is to you. I can't expect you to change your plans and drop everything to live here in the country with me."

"What are you saying?"

"I'll move with you. You, me and Samantha will be a family."

"You'll move." Disbelief rang in her voice. "But you can't! You've only just come back. Your father needs you. And you're about to reopen the resort."

He'd done some serious thinking about this and he knew what he had to do. "I'll have my father transferred to wherever we are, and I'll sell the resort."

"Sell the resort?" Her brows arched. "You can't!" she repeated. "You just restored it."

He swallowed the jagged lump in his throat. "The Summit is important to me, but not as important as you and Samantha. I can be with the two of you and lose the resort and still be happy. But having the resort without the two most important people in my life would be a hollow victory."

Kara pressed a hand to her chest. "You really mean that, don't you?"

He nodded. "I'll do whatever it takes for us to be a family. I love you more than ever. And Samantha. She may not be my biological daughter, but she's the daughter of my heart."

"Oh, Jason. I love you, too. But I can't let you do this."

He took both Kara's hands in his. "Yes, you can. I was the one who walked out on our plans seven years ago. It's only fair that I fit into the life you've created for yourself, no matter where it is."

"The thing is, I don't want to move. I want to stay right here with you, my family and friends." She stepped into his open arms, resting her head beneath his chin. "Do you really think we can make it work?"

"I do. I've changed. I've grown up. With honesty between us, we can face anything."

She looked up at him, their breath intermingling. He couldn't resist his desire to taste her sweetness. His head dipped low. His lips met hers. She was compliant and eager beneath him. A moan rose in the back of his throat. He'd never, ever grow tired of kissing her.

As much as he hated to pull back from her, they needed to finish this conversation. They still had one more thing to discuss.

"It's starting to snow," he said, remembering the last time they'd been here and it had snowed—the miraculous night when she'd made him feel love again.

She turned, leaning back against his chest as they both watched fat snowflakes drifting down. "Do you think we'll get stuck here?"

He pulled her close. "One can only hope. By the way,

my dad said to tell you he's waiting for his Christmas present. Mind explaining?"

She laughed. The sound was the most delightful he'd ever heard. "Your father won't let me forget. I promised to knit him a red scarf so he can wear it outside. He misses the snow. He wants to feel it on his face once more."

"Is the scarf done?"

She nodded.

"Looks like if this snow keeps up we'll have a Christmas wish to fulfill."

"It'll be a Christmas of miracles."

Now was the perfect moment for the last thing he had to ask her. He dropped to his knee. "Kara Jameson, I've loved you since we were kids, and you mean more to me with each passing day. Please tell me that you'll be my best friend, my lover and my wife." He took the ring from the box and held it out to her. "Say you'll be Mrs. Jason Greene."

Tears dripped onto her pink cheeks. "Yes. Yes! *Yes!*"

His heart felt as if it would burst with joy. He slipped the ring onto her finger, stood up and pulled her into his arms, then swooped in and planted a gentle kiss on her lips. Her arms slipped up around his neck. He'd never felt this deeply for someone in his life.

"I saw Mommy kissing Santa Claus…." They turned to find Samantha grinning at them, happiness twinkling in her eyes. "Does this mean I get the present I really want for Christmas?"

Kara's eyes met her daughter's. Unable to contain her joy, she smiled back. "What present is that?"

"I want Jason to live with us. He can be my daddy."

Jason smiled, and Kara draped her arm around his waist and leaned into him. "I think that can be arranged," she said.

He knelt on one knee again and held out his arms. Samantha rushed into them. "I'd be honored to be your father."

Over her head, Jason's gaze met Kara's. "I can't think of anything I'd love more than to be part of this wonderful family."

* * * * *

THE PROPOSITION

JC HARROWAY

To the DARE team for their vision, guidance and support — I have the best job, writing these stories!

CHAPTER ONE

Orla

I TAKE THE first delicious and well-earned sip of my drink with a sigh, my lip curling with satisfaction as the decadent flavour of the Macallan Scotch glides over my tongue. Not because I drink a lot of the spirit, or alcohol in general, but because it's a Scottish single malt, and therefore considered inferior by my Irish-born father. Even at the age of thirty-six, I feel the need to break free from his expectations.

The oppressive feeling that's followed me since I arrived in Monaco to pursue my latest client, Jensen's, weighs down on me once more, as if the air itself is too heavy. My intel that Jensen's are shopping around, sniffing at my father's door, adds to the pressure. Perhaps I'm burning out, pushing myself too hard to be the best, to outmanoeuvre the man who considered me unworthy to take the helm of our family business. But this deal has too much riding on it for me to blow it now; better to back off, to let the prospective client feel as if they've been wooed, but not cornered.

My fingers toy with my glass, slowly spinning it on the sleek and shiny bar. I look around the dimly lit intimacy of the casino, trying to shake off any thought of work, more determined than ever to embrace a change of pace for the evening. That's why I'm here, dressed to the nines, pretending to enjoy myself at Monaco's most glamorous club; why I left my sumptuous suite in the hotel upstairs despite its stunning views of Port Hercule in the dusk, a million lights dancing on the gently bobbing Mediterranean Sea. To let off a little long-overdue steam after a day of meetings, of waiting for the email that will tell me I've won Jensen's' business from under my father's nose.

I clink the ice in my glass, smirking at my pathetic efforts to cut loose from working, which is pretty much my entire life—a single-drink party for one.

Wow, Orla. You really know how to let your hair down...

Ignoring my snarkier side, and to distract me from ruminating on the high stakes of the Jensen's deal, I slide my stare around the casino, scanning the tables beyond the bar while I contemplate a tame gamble to liven up my rare night off. A small bet won't hurt, even if it goes against every cell of my venture capitalist's brain to risk money on a whim of chance. But it's exactly what I need—a release valve, a way to break free from my own head, my own high expectations, my endless desire to succeed.

A distraction.

I sigh, disgusted with myself. It's been ten years

since I was passed over for my younger and less qualified brother. Ten years of hard work, one successful global investment firm and one marriage casualty later and I'm still trying to prove him wrong. My father, that is.

My roaming attention is drawn to the group of excited onlookers around one of the roulette tables. Someone must be about to either lose or double a significant chunk of his net worth on a single spin of the wheel for the game to attract such interest. We're all members of the M Club here, all wealthy enough for an invitation-only membership and therefore used to top-shelf hedonistic pursuits, so this big roller must be something else.

I click my tongue against my teeth at such reckless behaviour. To me money is sacrosanct—a means to live on my own terms and a marker of success beyond being from one of Sydney's most affluent families. My entire livelihood is based on how much wealth I can generate for my clients, who trust me with their investments.

I crane my neck despite myself, curiosity winning over the distaste of witnessing someone about to gamble with daredevil abandon, if the crowd of onlookers is any indication, catching only a glimpse of the back of a blond head. His hair is a little long for the usual immaculate clientele of the M Club, but whoever it is who's providing this evening's entertainment, at least he's enjoying himself and thrilling the crowd. At least he's not moping at the bar with a barely touched drink, thinking about work. At least he knows how to have fun outside of endlessly striving to prove something to a father who happily overlooked his daughter in favour of having a son at the helm.

I finger the two-carat diamond stud in my ear, my mind dragged from the audacious stranger. The earrings were a twenty-fifth birthday gift from my father—a gift I consider a consolation prize. A gift I wear every day as a talisman, a reminder that what I've achieved in the ten years since, I've done alone and in spite of my archaic, misogynist father. A fresh layer of impotence settles over my skin, a familiar layer of prickly heat, one that drives me to be better, to aim higher, to prove him wrong...

The second sip of my Scotch fails to deliver the escape I crave. Now all I need to complete my misery is to ruminate on my failed marriage to Mark...

I release a sigh. For fuck's sake, can't I spend one evening having fun?

I glance back at the roulette table, more in need of a distraction than ever now that my thoughts have turned maudlin and focused on my greatest failure in life. The crowd around the man who seems to be causing the casino security team to sweat inside their pristine white collars parts, gifting me a full, uninterrupted view of the high-stakes gambler.

In the same heartbeat he looks up from the table, the chip he's twirling between his fingers stalling as our eyes collide for a split second.

My breath catches. I slide my parched tongue over my lips, seeking the remnants of the sip of Scotch to steady my pulse at the violent jolt of attraction. This place is crammed to the gills with wealthy, beautiful and successful people, but this guy...

Harshly masculine, from the cut of his square, stubble-covered jaw to his body's uninterested lounge in the chair, he's hotter than Hades, explaining at least half—the female half—of the attention he's assembled. But he's younger than I assumed—mid-to-late twenties—young, in fact, to be a member of the M Club, which is exclusively for billionaires.

Too young for me. But I *did* ask for a distraction, and they don't come more eye-catching than a gorgeous man in his prime.

My finger traces the rim of my glass as I watch. He's focused once more on the spin of the wheel, and yet I can't drag my greedy eyes away, even though I've seen this kind of display before, met *his type* before. Playing hard and fast, they never last long as M Club members, no doubt blowing money they have no idea how to master, allowing it to own them until they lose every cent and their membership is delicately, but adamantly, rescinded.

But despite his flagrant display, my body warms, the delicious stirring of interest kicking up my pulse as I watch the latest easy-on-the-eye hotshot from my vantage point at the bar. From his appearance, the way he's flouting the strict dress code of tuxedos for men and evening wear for women with his absence of a bow tie and his unbuttoned shirt collar, I'm surprised he was even admitted to the casino. Somehow, and for reasons I can't fathom, his devil-may-care attitude adds to his appeal. My existence must be particularly dull at the moment for me to be impressed by someone who, on the surface, seems to be intent on making himself considerably poorer. After all, I, and most of the people in this casino, are in the money-making, not money-losing, business.

The rebel lifts a glass of amber liquid to his mouth and I'm caught off guard anew by his hands: the manly size of them—serious, capable hands that look more accustomed to manual labour than they do to running an empire from a smartphone as do most of the M Club's members.

Teasing fingers of intrigue dance down my spine. What would those hands feel like holding my face as we kissed? Rough or smooth? Hesitant or demanding?

In unison the crowd around him sighs, snapping me from lusty fantasies about a younger stranger and informing me that his winning streak has dried up. But not a flicker of emotion crosses his handsome face. With less interest than if he'd tossed away a soiled napkin, he slides a stack of chips forward, placing another bet seemingly at random.

Then our eyes collide again.

I freeze, too startled to look away, although I should in case my intrigue is written all over my face, but I'm too fascinated by his expression of both boredom and challenge to do anything other than gape.

His eyes—I can't tell from this distance whether they're blue or grey—travel my face, dip lower and then bounce back up. In that second I know he's appraising me as I am him, and by appraising I mean assessing availability clues, scanning for a wedding ring and generally lusting.

And why shouldn't I lust? My sexy side is long overdue an outing; in fact, she's probably desperate to break free, she's been so neglected recently. This guy certainly looks as if he could bring a nun out of her shell…

I smooth a hand over my sleek chignon, adjusting a hairpin that's slipped a fraction in a largely unconscious gesture.

The stranger's expression shifts again, his lip curling with mild derision, telling me that *he,* with his overly long hair and his disregard for the club dress code, very much sees that I'm exactly the type of member the M Club was created for—wealthy, demanding, with an appreciation for the finer things in life. But rather than my membership earning his respect, I can tell he's somehow judging, as if he thinks he has me all figured out.

I stare a little harder, sit a little straighter, spurred on by defiance and used to fighting my own corner against the men in my life. His mouth stretches into a sinfully sexy and lazy grin that seems to burn through my designer silk dress as if it's made of cobwebs.

Perhaps professional exhaustion and sexual frustration is messing with me, because he's definitely interested, despite his judgement, our age gap and our apparent differences.

For a split second, danger and excitement zaps through my bloodstream as if he's delivered a potent shot of the Macallan directly to my system from across the room with that seductive smile. But before I can suck in a calming breath, he looks away.

My pulse plummets. What was I thinking?

I spin back to the bar on my stool, trying to shake off the uncharacteristic bout of sexual curiosity for a younger man. Curiosity for *any* man since my divorce is a rarity. If I'm not working or travelling I'm thinking about work. Yes, I wanted to blow off some steam, but not with *his* kind of distraction. I need something more forgettable, less consuming and more...fleeting.

The idea of a horizontal distraction takes root as I tap one fingernail against my glass. Why not? It would be more fun than drinking alone at the bar. I dressed and came downstairs in search of a change from the norm, a break from the long hours I habitually put in, a way to stop myself pushing my latest deal into the hands of my main competitor—my father's company.

With the reminder that, in my father's eyes, and despite my having built my own international firm, I'll never be quite good enough. I'm back to square one. Instead of celebrating the successes which have brought me this far, I'm mired in the two great failures of my life. I take another sip of Scotch, fighting the bitterness I usually harness for motivation. Hell, my entire marriage was squeezed into an unforgiving schedule of meetings, world travel and time zones, my workaholic nature almost certainly the reason it failed. Another thing to credit my father with. If he'd been a little more emotionally present, a little less professionally demanding, maybe I wouldn't be so distant, so goal orientated, so driven. Perhaps then I might have given my marriage the attention it deserved.

Come on, pull it together.

I'm not looking for another doomed relationship. I'm not looking for a relationship, full stop. Just an anonymous night of pleasure...

I look up from my drink again, scanning the patrons around me for someone more forgettable than the roulette rebel. Someone my age. Someone safe.

Then everything happens in a frenzied blur.

A commotion breaks out at a nearby blackjack table. A woman cries for help and before I've even swivelled in my seat, my sexy stranger dives from his laid-back slouch and strides towards the woman's husband, who is pale and sweaty and an alarming shade of grey.

While roulette guy commands what is clearly some sort of medical emergency—tossing off his jacket, crouching down and loosening the older man's collar— an air of panic settles over the entire room. The man clutching his chest accepts some sort of tablet from his wife, popping it under his tongue, his colour improving almost immediately. Security rallies and within seconds the blackjack table has been cleared of players to afford some space and privacy, the club's in-house nurse is in attendance and an ambulance has been summoned.

I turn away, but from the corner of my eye I see roulette guy and the nurse help the man into a wheelchair and he's wheeled from the casino, even managing a weak smile and handshake for his rescuer, who waves off the smattering of relieved applause around him as he scoops up his jacket. He returns to his table to collect his chips, passes an impressive stack to the croupier and saunters towards the bar.

A kind of forced normality returns to the room. The croupiers smile thin smiles as they resume games, the waitstaff clear already immaculate tables and members, myself included, breathe a sigh of relief that the drama was quickly and efficiently dealt with.

But then, this is the M Club.

I settle my own adrenaline surge with a shaky sip of Scotch. Then a male figure enters my peripheral vision, the space between us flooding with a spicy masculine scent and an almost palpable wall of testosterone.

I look up. Way up—sexy roulette guy is tall.

Grey—the eyes are grey. And, up close, searing and intense.

'You look pale,' he says, his confident voice distractingly deep and resonant and exactly how I imagined it would sound. 'Let me buy you a brandy—it's better for the nerves than whatever it is you're drinking there.'

I detect an Aussie twang to the accent. Although my private education rubbed the corners from my own lilt, I still have an ear for a fellow Australian.

I take a deep breath, fighting the urge to rush to the ladies' room and check if, in fact, I am pale. 'I'm good with my Scotch, thanks.'

As if deaf to my assertion, roulette guy signals the barman. 'Brandy for everyone, please—the good stuff.' He adds, although he should know the *good stuff* is all they sell at the M Club. Of course he would shout the entire casino a drink. The stack of chips I saw him tip the croupier with moments ago is more than most people will bet in an entire evening of entertainment.

But now I'm curious, although I try to affect boredom, which is out of sync with the raging of my pulse. 'Are you a doctor?' I want to blank him, to ignore the tantalising aura he seems to have around him, and return to my preconceived ideas of a privileged playboy intent on flashing his cash.

But if roulette guy wants to impress women with his affluence, he's in the wrong joint. No one crosses the threshold of an M Club establishment without a string of zeroes at the end of their bank balance.

He drapes his suit jacket over the back of the stool next to mine and unbuttons his cuffs, rolling up his sleeves to expose strong, tanned forearms in a move that hints he's dying to get out of his suit.

'No, I'm not a doctor.' The look he delivers seems to bathe me in the beam of a thousand floodlights. 'But I'm no good at sitting back and watching things unfold either. I'm used to…getting my hands dirty, shall we say?'

He looks at my mouth while he says the word *dirty*. I press my lips together, already imagining the taste of his kiss. Bold, firm, all-consuming.

What is wrong with me?

He thanks the barman for his glass of brandy with a jerk of his angular chin and tosses back the liquor in a single swallow. 'And I have some first-aid training—he'll be fine, I'm sure. He just panicked because the angina attack was worse than usual. I'm sure most people here would have helped—I just got there first.'

'I guess, although, as M Club members, we're used to everything, medical emergencies included, being dealt with efficiently and discreetly.'

His eyes swoop over the length of my body from head to toe, and I feel his scrutiny again, as if he too has made a snap judgement on our differences.

We're interrupted at that moment by a petite brunette in her twenties with a winning smile.

'Excuse me, sir, I'm Ellie Little.' At his nod, she holds up an M Club key fob. 'The key to your new supercar, sir.'

I smile at Ellie and then look back to my smug companion, my eyebrows raised in question. I passed the display of sleek sports cars in the ballroom on my way to the casino, but I paid them little attention, short of wondering who would succumb despite their hefty price tags. I guess now I know.

'Thanks.' He takes the key and pockets it, his smile for Ellie wide and engaging.

Ellie leaves us, and I spy her joining Ash Evans, the club owner, at the casino entrance. When I turn back to face my companion my expression must speak for me.

'What?' he asks, all innocence.

I shrug. 'You're having a great night, if you exclude your losses at the roulette table. Which car did you buy?' I may not know anything about cars, but I do know you can't walk into a regular showroom and drive away with a supercar. They're made-to-order, top of the range, one of a kind.

He looks away, appearing bored. 'I'm not sure…the yellow one, I think.'

'You're not sure,' I deadpan. Is he for real? Despite my growing attraction to him, I can't decide if I feel appalled or delighted.

'I bought the winning car—were you in town for the race earlier?' he asks, and I shake my head.

'No—I'm here on business.' I don't elaborate. The last thing I want to talk about is the deal that brought me to Monaco. The deal I'm trying to forget for one night.

He scoffs. 'That figures.'

I narrow my eyes. 'What does that mean?'

'You have that look about you—impatiently tapping your glass, frequently checking your phone. You look like a woman waiting for either a date or a business deal. Since no one in their right mind would stand you up, I'm guessing it's work that has you distracted.'

'Oh, nice recovery,' I say.

He flashes another disarming smile. 'So—' he glances down at my still half-full drink '—is this a party for one, or would you like some company?'

I flush that he's noticed my lacklustre attempts to let loose. Then I bristle that he's judging me. 'Are you suggesting I don't know how to have a good time simply because I'm not blowing a small fortune on a single spin of roulette or buying the latest thing on four wheels?'

I mash my mouth closed, irritated with myself for

admitting I hadn't been able to stop myself watching his little show.

He lifts one eyebrow in a look that says *if the shoe fits*, but then his eyes darken, the heat behind them kissing my skin wherever his stare trails. 'Do you know how to have a good time?'

Why does it feel as if we're talking about something more intimate than gambling or drinking? 'I… Of course I do.'

He rests one elbow on the bar. 'I assume you're here to let your hair down in a safe, luxurious space—isn't that why you're an M Club member?' He leans in. 'Or is it all about the networking? All work and no play?'

His spot-on assumption leaves me squaring my shoulders with indignation, a move that in no way combats my attraction to his particular brand of insolent swagger. 'Why are *you* a member? And why Monaco? Why so far from home?'

He shrugs, feigning boredom with my question, but I see a flash of hesitation in his eyes, a hint of vulnerability, rapidly blinked away and replaced with that roguish smile. 'Can't you tell?' He tilts his head in the direction of the roulette table. 'I'm on a bender, a pleasure spree, free and easy and hoping to broaden my horizons with luxury travel, fast cars and—'

'Let me guess,' I interrupt, 'beautiful women?' I try to laugh but I'm too attracted to him for the sound to emerge.

But *he* laughs, a deep rumble in his broad chest, and I flush hot at the power he seems to hold over my out-of-practice libido. His tongue swipes his bottom lip as he watches me more intently. 'Well, what's not to love about that combination? You're a stunning woman, intriguing, alone—what are you doing here if not seeking your own kind of hedonistic escape?'

'Arrogant much?' I try to look away, but it's as if we're pinballs, bouncing and sparking off each other. I search his eyes, if only to show I'm not intimidated. But now he's brought up pleasure it's all I can think about... How can he tell I'd been sitting here contemplating exactly the kind of distraction he's talking about? Would he be open to sex with an older woman looking to blow off some steam for the night? Isn't that what the look of intrigue in those smoky eyes is saying?

He shrugs, a mocking twist to his generous mouth. 'I saw you looking at me—you want something, and it's not to drink or gamble like everyone else in this room.'

'No, I don't make a habit of risking my hard-earned money.' I shrug. 'Perhaps the occasional tame flutter.'

He inches closer, drops his voice to a conspiratorial level. 'I'd bet the stack of chips I have in my pocket—' he shakes his jacket, the telltale rattle indicating his point '—that *you* don't even know what it is you want.' His teeth scrape his bottom lip and, despite myself, my body leans a fraction closer to his imposing masculinity.

'But I'm guessing *I* do,' he stage-whispers, his breath gusting over my exposed shoulder and sending delicious tingles down to my fingertips, which itch to reach out, to tangle in that slightly too-long hair and tug him down to my kiss...

'Is that so?' I hold my breath, trying to avoid his delicious scent, but my body has other ideas, my thighs clenching and my underwear growing damp at the mere thought of what he'd be like as a lover. Can he really see me so clearly? See what I want when I've spent the past thirty minutes sitting here trying to figure it out for myself? And do I care who's right? Wasn't I, only moments ago, contemplating what his deep voice might promise?

An anonymous night. A delicious distraction?

My heart leaps against my ribs. I wanted to unleash my sexy, playful side for the night. My ex gloried in telling me how uptight I was, that I didn't know how to be a wife, how to switch off from work. Well, I came to this casino to do just that. But with a man like him? Arrogant. Reckless. Some sort of fly-by-night success intent on brashly disposing of large chunks of his wealth...

He nods, his fingers drumming out a beat on the bar only he can hear. 'You want to let down that gorgeous but tightly leashed hair. You want to slip out of yourself for a while, loosen up a little.'

I do, not that I can admit it to the perceptive man who thinks he has me all pegged. My throat tightens, hot and achy. It's as if he can see straight through me, as if he can see that, for just one night, I want to break free of it all. But why shouldn't I have my sexy diversion with a stranger I'll never meet again?

'Why don't you sit down before you fall down?' I say, defensive. No matter how hot, how confident, how intuitive he is, I'm not rushing into something I'll only regret in the morning, for all his persuasive skills.

He grins, but his eyes harden a fraction, telling me he's fully in command of all his faculties and won't be slighted. 'I'm not drunk, if that's what you're implying. And I prefer to stand.'

'So women have to look up to you?' I might be currently captive to the unexpected revival of my hormones, but I'm not in the market for a cocky young buck, all talk but lacking in substance.

He smiles as though he knows the effect he's having on my erogenous zones, as though he can read how I'm drawn to his brand of lazy confidence simply by looking into my eyes.

'Who am I to spoil anyone's fun when I could be the source of it?' he says.

I swallow. Hard.

I'm so tempted. I promised myself a little fun. Who better to let loose with than a man who looks built for sin and seems to see what I need tonight as some sort of personal challenge? I'd bet my anticipated deal with Jensen's that his confidence is justified and he could deliver a night of hedonistic sex designed to make me forget everything but my own name.

Don't I deserve an unforgettable, anonymous night? A way to recharge the batteries? A reminder that all work and no play does not a happy Orla make?

But first I need to suss out his intentions. Make him work a little harder. 'So you have a cougar fantasy, is that it?'

I expected an arrogant shrug at best, but he leans closer, stares more intently, as if seeing deep inside me to my darkest desires. 'I'm twenty-eight, but don't get hung up on the numbers when we could already be heading upstairs.'

I scoff at his arrogance, even as my nipples turn to hard peaks beneath the silk of my dress. Do I really care that he's eight years younger than me? 'I've met your type before—'

He interrupts. 'I very much doubt that. And if by *type* you mean the kind of man who can give you the anonymous night of your life, then you're right. Admit it—you knew we'd be good together the minute you looked at me and you're even more certain now, which perhaps tells me the reason you're fighting it so hard—fear.'

'Fear?' I laugh, although the sound lacks conviction, just like my shaky resolve. He's spot-on, but really, what do I have to lose? I wanted a distraction and he's irresistible. The urge to step off the hamster wheel for a moment and become lost in the pleasure I'm certain would follow is tantalising. His challenge is irresistible, because it aligns so perfectly with the one I set myself tonight: to let go.

'There's not much I'm afraid of,' I say. My heart, banging against my ribs, proves me wrong and him right.

He nods—slow, confident, almost luring me to kiss the smooth smile from his lips. 'It's fear all right. Fear of letting go of your tightly leashed control. Fear that you might actually have a good time. Fear I'll ruin you.'

His eyes slide to one of my earrings. 'You and your four-carat-diamond, one-glass-of-single-malt life.'

Instead of the outrage I should feel at being so neatly dissected and accurately pigeonholed, even insulted, every nerve in my body fires alive with electricity.

Fight, flight or fuck? I should definitely take option one or two...

I roll back my shoulders and stare into his cool grey eyes, seeing the hint of challenge. 'Are you suggesting I'm uptight? I'm amazed you, with your devil-may-care attitude, even know what the concept means.' I should walk away, go back upstairs and check on Jensen's—but oh, the temptation to prove him wrong is overwhelming...

'Hey, princess, if the shoe fits...'

We face off, sparks flying and heat building.

I can let go. I can have fun. He's right, I do want him. I *want* to be ruined for one night.

And I always get what I want.

'The earrings are two-carat,' I say. 'And, okay. I have a suite upstairs—let's go.'

CHAPTER TWO

Cam

HER WORDS—WORDS that shatter my certainty that she'd toss her Scotch in my face—bounce around inside my head to the beat of my pounding heart as she slides her drink away, unfinished. Yes, she's my type looks-wise—tall and willowy, naturally rich red hair, and a body whose every inch I want to acquaint with my tongue. But, by the earrings, the immaculate hairdo and the general air of class around her, I assumed she was way too buttoned-up to take our flirtation to the next level.

She reaches for her clutch and prepares to slide from her stool.

Eager, now she's stopped fighting herself. Another fucking awesome surprise.

'Wait.' I stall, my dick throbbing in revenge. 'I think we should at least introduce ourselves so you know whose name to scream later.' I hold out my hand. 'I'm Cam.'

She purses her delicious-looking full lips and strokes her hand over her sleek chignon as if mildly annoyed by the interruption of formal introduction. She takes my hand in hers, her greeting as firm as I'd expected.

'Orla.'

'Irish Australian?' I say, prolonging the handshake, deliberately sliding my roughened thumb over the back of her hand to gauge her reaction to my touch, because I'm certain that under normal circumstances, in our everyday lives, she wouldn't give a man like me the time of day. She's too polished, too precise and undoubtedly super-high maintenance. There's not a hair out of place or a wrinkle in sight, but I have the driving urge to see her all dishevelled and undone. She'd look twice as sexy rumpled and satisfied, those sea-green eyes pleasure-drunk...

'Yes. I'm from Sydney.' She looks down to where my thumb swipes across the delicate skin of her inner wrist, her small smile masking a look bordering on aversion while her free hand toys with the diamond stud in her ear.

In spite of my work-roughened skin, there's excitement drawn all over her ethereal face, but her eyes say she's all too aware I'm not her usual type. No doubt she's used to the type of man who belongs in this club. The type who's certain of everything in his life, especially where he comes from and where he's going.

'I grew up in Sydney, too.' If only she knew that we came from opposite sides of the tracks before I inherited enough money to be thrust into her sphere. I look down at our joined hands, the sick slug of satisfaction at my rough and calloused hand swallowing hers, which is by comparison as delicate as a bird's wing and impeccably manicured, adding to the thick desire humming through my veins.

Prior to my current fucked-up predicament—the very reason I'm here in this club for the elite and obscenely wealthy, having earlier this evening bought a supercar I'll likely never drive and gambling as if I'm spending Monopoly money—I worked in construction.

And now?

Now I'm frittering through as much of the unwanted inheritance my no-good asshole of a father left me as I can. Oh, how he'd hate to see me now, wasting the money he sacrificed his family for, travelling the world in a private jet, gambling, bedding beautiful women in the most exclusive club in Monaco.

The familiar nausea I get whenever I think about my father takes hold, a part of me repulsed at becoming his puppet. I focus on the exquisite woman in front of me, a strong urge flaring up to push her out of her buttoned-up comfort zone until I know exactly how far she'll go for her night with a stranger.

She glides from the stool, her hand still in mine. Instead of pulling away, she sidles up close until I see the golden streaks in her green irises, streaks that perfectly match those in her silky auburn hair, and I'm overwhelmed by how fantastic she smells. Classy and expensive.

She presses a fingertip to my mouth. 'Don't tell me any more. Anonymous, remember.'

I nod, dislodging her soft fingertip from my mouth

while I wrangle the thick thud of my desire under control. She may as well have kissed me for the effect that simple touch from a solitary fingertip has on my body.

Yes, she's way too rich, too straitlaced for my blood, but damn is she sexy. I want to haul her slender frame up in my arms, press every inch of her against my body until those eyes glow with the desire I see lurking in the shadows.

But could she let go enough to embrace this fierce chemistry?

'Give me your phone.' My voice is low but firm enough to encourage a frown of defiance from her stunning face. She likes being challenged, but wants to be in control. She's clearly used to giving the orders.

I can handle that.

'Why?' She purses perfect lips. Lips I'm dying to taste.

'Because I'm a stranger you're about to invite into your hotel room. I'll take a photo of myself, and you can send it to someone you trust, giving them your suite number and mine, too, if you like—two-seven-six-six.'

She nods, hands me her phone and I snap a quick selfie before handing the device back. I watch as she fires off a text, fascinated with the way her lips press together when she's concentrating and how, despite the safety-conscious turn of the conversation, her nipples are hard peaks beneath the tight-fitting, backless black dress that hugs her toned frame and caresses the gentle flare of her hips.

'So, shall we?' She looks up, her chin tilted and face

relaxed, but there's vulnerability in her eyes, and I wonder what her *real* story is. Not the sanitised version she probably tells herself every day as she peruses her markers of success. But the version deep inside, hidden vulnerabilities which, if probed, wobble the confidence she wears like a tiara balanced on her regal head and perhaps the reason she's alone in a bar in Monaco, far from home, toying with a drink she barely touches in the first place.

But then, who am I to judge? I swallow a bitter lump in my throat. Fuck knows what I'm doing here apart from running, hiding, while dispensing of the blood money I can't stomach even thinking about.

I want to form a fist as the anger that chased me from Sydney swells inside. But I've tried and failed to keep things normal for six months, tried to ignore the inheritance sitting in my bank account accruing more interest daily than I formerly made in a year of building houses with my bare hands, but somehow my life, who I am and what's important to me have still changed beyond recognition.

I swallow down the acidic taste and focus on beautiful Orla and her mesmerising eyes. Perhaps we're both hiding from something bigger than us, and that's perfect. Perhaps we'll succeed in fucking it from our systems, a perfectly timed distraction, and tomorrow go our separate ways, usual service resumed...

Damn, if only it were that simple for me. My stomach rolls at the reminder that normal is a distant memory. I ignore the gnawing pain, the yearning for my old life, and nod. I grab my jacket and follow her towards the bank of lifts. When we're inside the empty car and she's selected the correct floor I move closer, my restless body demanding action and the need to touch more of her than her wrist driving me hard.

I expect her to back up as I invade her personal space, but she holds her ground and simply levels bold eyes at me while her chest rises and falls with the excitement I want to see.

I keep my hands by my sides. My reward is waiting for me and I want to string out the anticipation for as long as I can, knowing the moment will be twice as sweet when we both, finally, surrender.

But neither can I stay away.

I look down, loving how small she is in comparison to me and the way it defies her bold and confident manner. Damn, I bet no one ever says no to her. I bet she's always had things exactly on her terms.

That part of me, the part that wants to test her, rears up.

'How do you want this to play out, beautiful?' I suck in an Orla-scented breath, my blood pumping harder. Despite our chalk-and-cheese differences, I wanted her the minute I saw her walk into the casino—a beautiful woman, composed, alluring and sexy as fuck. But the fact she tried to fight her obvious interest…well, that simply added another level of challenge. I'm a scrapper who's spent every day of his life until six months ago earning his honest, comfortable place in life, earning every cent of what he deserves—beautiful women no exception.

She takes a shuddering breath and licks her lips, the first hint of hesitation. 'You know, just the usual...'

She clearly doesn't do this often—sleep with a stranger—and for some reason she's decided tonight's the night and I'm the lucky guy. But there'll be nothing usual about our night together.

I nod, noting the slow ascent of the lift and deciding we have time to start this right here, because I'm done waiting. She knows what she wants and I plan on giving it to her. That and more.

'Ask me to touch you.' Her full, kissable mouth draws all my attention. I've wanted to taste those lips since she spotted me at the roulette table, her mouth twitching with intrigue. And why shouldn't I taste? Now, when I can have anything I want in life, is not the time to begin denying myself a damned thing, beautiful Orla included.

She too glances at the digital display and back, and before I can ready myself for the impact she grabs the back of my neck and drags my mouth down to her kiss.

The first taste is rich and decadent, just like Orla, the hint of Scotch lingering on her soft but demanding lips. While she seems too prim and proper for a simple, spit-and-sawdust kind of guy like me, my body clamours for more, because I can already tell there's another level to this woman, a tightly leashed wanton ready to be coaxed to reveal her uninhibited side. And I'll take as much wildness as she's willing to give, in my current mood—anything to stop the endless feeling I'm trying to outrun something while wearing lead shoes.

Her lips part and she slides her tongue to meet mine with a throaty little moan that screams *woman*. My pulse roars with triumph, centring me with the assurance sex brings. In this moment, I'm me and in control.

I walk us back to the wall, and she drops her clutch and hikes up her dress so she can spread her thighs to accommodate my hips, which pin her in place. She tugs my hair and moans as if she wants to be fucked right here in the elevator, and bloody hell, I'm tempted.

We part for breath and she reaches for my fly, her teeth trapping her bottom lip as she rubs my cock through my trousers. Then her eyes roll closed and her head hits the wall behind her. 'Oh, I knew you'd be good, exactly what I need.'

I clench my jaw, fighting the rush of pleasure her palming my cock brings. I can be what she needs for one night—easy. Our backgrounds don't matter for what we have planned.

I lift her thigh and press closer until my dick and her hand are crushed between our bodies. She looks at me then, and I grin.

'I'm happy to be your man toy for the night, gorgeous.' I scrape my mouth up the soft, silky column of her neck, sucking in her scent as I reach her earlobe and the massive rock sitting there, a beacon to our stark differences. My hand on her thigh slides north as I tongue the stone, tugging her earlobe, complete with earring, into my mouth. I finger the lace of her underwear, which is stretched across the gorgeous handful of ass cheek I have in my hand, while I press my erection between her legs, where she's hot and damp and grinding against me.

'Your hot little clit is hungry for what I can give you.' I slide my hand forward, finding her underwear drenched. 'Question is, can you take it?'

'Yes…oh, yes.' She doesn't flinch at my candour or deny my assertions, simply tugs my mouth back to hers with a frustrated yelp.

Her *yes* thrills me. We might be from different worlds, but tonight our goals are aligned and all about pleasure.

The lift pings and we quickly straighten our clothing to perform the hurried walk to her top-floor suite. Inside, a quick glance confirms it's a carbon copy of mine—the best money can buy—but then, I'm too focused on the woman in front of me to care about décor or square footage.

While I shrug out of my jacket, she tosses her bag, turns to face me and begins to undo the clasp of her dress at the back of her neck, but before she gets anywhere, I grip her waist and back her up against the wall once more—I have plans for Miss Buttoned-Up and they don't involve staid missionary position with the lights off.

Let's see how much she wants to let go.

I kiss her, coaxing more of those greedy little whimpers from her throat as my hand travels under the dress once more to find her drenched and scorching hot.

I break free from the kiss as I slide my fingers past the crotch of her underwear to the silkiness beneath. I rub one fingertip over her clit, watching her eyes grow unfocused.

My other hand grapples with the tiny, frustrating clasp at the back of her neck. It feels like a bra clasp but the hooks may as well be welded together for all the luck I'm having. I reluctantly remove my hand from the delicious, soft slickness between her legs and try with two hands, my frustration to see what the dress conceals building and making my fingers clumsy. On my third attempt, while she's given up waiting and is clearly intent on driving me insane with the kisses she's pressing over my neck, jaw and mouth, I say, 'Are you particularly attached to this outfit?'

Confusion registers, chasing away the lust, but she shakes her head. 'No, why?'

I press my mouth back to her arched neck—I can't seem to get enough of her taste and scent. 'I said I'd ruin you.' I look up. 'I wasn't joking and I'm afraid this dress is going to be the first casualty.'

'I don't care. Hurry!'

I grip the low neckline of her dress, tearing the fabric clean in two from neck to waist so her fantastic, bra-less breasts spill free.

She gasps, but the sound turns to a low moan because I cover one bare breast with my mouth, sucking hard on the firm, pink nipple. While she twists hand-fuls of my hair between her fingers as she cradles my head and watches my mouth devour her breast, I hoist up her skirt and perform the same trick with the crotch of her underwear, tearing it in two so I can access my reward unhindered.

I pull back, surveying my handiwork while my knees grow weak. She's perfect. Mouth red and swollen from our kisses and the three-day scruff I couldn't be bothered to shave earlier; her clothing bunched around her waist so all that creamy skin dotted with golden freckles is on display; my hand wedged between her pale thighs, the strip of reddish hair on her mound a beacon guiding me to paradise.

Fuck, I'm not sure who will ruin whom. Her willingness to ride this storm with me spurs me on to keep pushing... Perhaps I'm wrong about her being strait-laced.

'Put your legs around me,' I say, my strangled voice gruff. But she doesn't seem to care that I'm giving orders, any more than she cares that I've torn what must be an obscenely expensive outfit. I fully intend to replace it, of course. In fact, tomorrow I'll buy her a whole new wardrobe in compensation.

I carry her the short distance to the suite's living area to a wide armchair, where I deposit her delectable ass. She tries to tug me down on top of her but I resist. I want to look. To gorge my fill of this incredibly sexy woman, who's smashing all my assumptions to bits.

She's still debauched, her hair mussed as I wanted it and spilling free of the uptight chignon she wore, her eyes glassy with desire.

'Fuck me,' she says, still in control.

I quickly strip off my shirt while she watches, her tongue wetting those lush lips as her eyes trace the ink on my shoulder and across one side of my chest. But she can't have everything her own way.

'All in good time.' I drop to my knees and spread her thighs wide open so she's completely exposed to me and my own greedy stare. 'First I want a little taste.'

She nods, then her head drops back. 'Oh, my God, yes.'

I chuckle at her enthusiasm. 'Cam will do.' But then I'm done talking because her pink, wet pussy calls to me and I dive in.

The erotic scent and taste of her drags a growl from deep within my chest, but it's her thighs clamped around my shoulders and her hands tugging at my neck and head as if trying to urge me closer that thrill me. If I wasn't already there, she'd bring me to my knees with her passion and honest desire.

My dick is dying to be buried in the tight, warm haven greedily sucking at my fingers, but she's fully embracing this, watching me eat her out, her mouth slack with pleasure as she rides my face. Orgasm number one is going to have to happen right here for Orla, and I'm going to enjoy every second of watching this woman detonate. She may not remember my name, but I'll make it my mission to ensure she'll remember every orgasm of our night together.

I add another finger and suck down on her clit, grinning when her thighs begin to judder and eyes widen with ecstasy.

'Cam, yes…oh.'

So my put-together princess is not above begging or riding my face to get what she wants. She comes, her sex squeezing my fingers and my name a protracted cry on her lips. I milk every spasm from her and then withdraw, leaving her sprawled and spent on the chair while I loosen my belt, unzip my fly and take a condom from my pocket before lowering my trousers and briefs. All I want now is to be buried inside her, to forget my woes for a few mindless minutes, and just be the old Cam.

She sits up and takes my cock in her hand, tugging my length and then helping me with the condom. When I'm sheathed, I take her hands and yank her to her feet, spin her around and bend her over the wide arm of the chair.

'Hurry,' she says as she braces her arms on the cushion and spreads her feet wide, staring back at me over one shoulder. My knees weaken at the exquisite sight, her red hair splayed down her pale back, her post-orgasmic flush staining her cheeks and her ruined clothing bunched around her waist—a sign that neither of us had the patience to do this primly or properly.

Who knew the poised woman delicately sipping her drink hid such a sensual being? Such an unexpected siren?

I position myself at her entrance and grip her hips, every cell urging me to rush while my brain clamours to go slow and enjoy every second.

But we have all night.

Patience spent, I surge forward, my cock swallowed

by her tight pussy. I fist the fabric of her dress and thrust in the last inch until our joint moans tell me I'm as deeply seated as possible. For a few glorious seconds I suck in calming breaths and simply enjoy the view. Her skin is like porcelain, her pale ass cheeks round and her hair a wild, tousled mess across her bare shoulders. The dress ruched around her waist gives the impression of bonds, a reminder that, despite being the most put-together woman I've ever met, Orla was as impatient to let go as I was to help her.

I grip the dress and her hip tighter and begin to thrust, every slap of our flesh together and every gasp of her pleasure riding me harder until sweat stings my eyes.

'Touch yourself,' I say, because I'm not going to last much longer and I want her coming with me. I want to make her come all night. I want to prove to her that we're the same on one level. That, like this, we fit together perfectly.

She whimpers but complies, her hand disappearing between her thighs, where I feel her stroke my balls before she sees to herself. I grit my teeth, the drugging pleasure sucking me down. 'Are you close?' I grit out.

She cries out but doesn't answer, and I'm running out of time.

I widen my feet, still thrusting at a punishing pace, abandon my grip on her dress and slide my finger along her crack to tickle her asshole. That does the trick, and as she screams a hoarse cry, her muscles clamping around me, I let go, fiery heat rushing down the length of my cock as I fill the condom.

We slump forward over the chair, although I'm careful to take my own weight and not crush the fantastic woman under me as I catch my breath.

She recovers first, wriggling free and turning to cup my face and smatter hot kisses over my lips.

'Wow.'

My chest burns but I grin.

'Glad you had a good time.' I just didn't know she'd embrace it so thoroughly, so honestly and so fucking sexily.

'I hope you didn't plan on getting any sleep, because we'll be doing that again.' She tugs me towards what I know is the bathroom, and as I watch the sway of that gorgeous ass, I concur.

Yes; yes, we will.

CHAPTER THREE

Orla

I RISE FROM the desk chair in my hotel suite, a triumphant smile making my cheeks ache while a surge of adrenaline leaves me searching the bed for Cam. I want to share my news with someone. With him. Jensen's made up their mind and signed on the dotted line this morning.

Then I remember that he's gone. After the sex marathon, I spent half the night working while he slept. He woke around six, crept up behind me where I worked and kissed me goodbye. Such a gallant, old-fashioned gesture, I practically swooned...

As I look at the debauched but empty bed, my sense of achievement dwindles a fraction. It shouldn't matter—I don't need to share my success in order to feel its validation, but a celebratory orgasm might have been nice...

I stretch out my back muscles, frowning when I realise how long I've been sitting in one place. I've hustled this deal for the past three months, a deal snatched from under the nose of my main competitors—the firm now run, rather sloppily, in my opinion, by my younger brother under the critical tutelage of my father. A firm that should have been mine to run by rights after my years of hard work and the long hours that cost me my marriage. Another casualty of my father's expectations...

Thinking of my ex, and how he bailed after seven short months because he couldn't handle a wife who worked harder than him, sours my mood further.

I ignore the well-worn path of anger and rejection that courses through my body every time I think about how I was overlooked, passed over on the basis of my sex, as if my years of commitment and my qualifications counted for nothing in the eyes of my old-school father. What century does he even inhabit? I'm the eldest. I put in the most work. I'm the best qualified—the company was mine by rights.

When the sting in my lip tells me I'm taking out my frustration with my own teeth, I relax my jaw and sigh. Even this success with Jensen's feels somehow tainted by the past. No matter how hard I work, I can never quite reach the finishing line.

Casting a look of longing at the empty bed, I head for the shower, recalling the pleasure I shared with a stranger to sweeten this morning's professional victory.

Cam—my reward.

Yearning builds in the pit of my stomach. He claimed my body, used it and his to drive us both mindless with desire. His obscene stamina. His wicked, inventive challenges and almost impossible positions... I've never experienced anything like it. He effortlessly brought out the sexy side I wanted to embrace the minute we stepped into the lift.

Who even was I with him?

I ache, aware of every step I take, every muscular twinge—all Cam's fault...

But he was gentle too. Thorough and attentive and considerate. My breath catches as a feeling of invincibility courses through me. After a night like that, I can accomplish anything. Alone and without validation.

The hot water spray buffets my skin, reminding me of Cam's rough, calloused hands gripping and possessing. The water on my breasts and between my legs mimics the glide of his demanding tongue, the caress of his dirty mouth, and when I press my fingers to my clit, trying to banish the renewed flutter of hunger, I relive every single orgasm of our decadent night together.

This is what well-fucked truly feels like.

I sigh a happy, sated sigh, the emotional impulse as unexpected as the man himself. Perhaps he's a good-luck charm, if I believed in luck. Perhaps letting loose, embracing my wild side, is good for me, allowing me to achieve some much-needed work-life perspective. Either way, I can't deny I feel more alive, more enthused for the months ahead than I have in years.

I shampoo my hair, hair that Cam wrapped around his fist as he pounded us both to oblivion that last time, sometime in the dark early hours. He fell asleep soon after, splayed on his stomach, his muscular back and tight buttocks a visual feast I struggled to tear my eyes from. I was so energised, my mind so focused, I worked through the rest of the night. Even now I'm in no way tired, although pulling all-nighters isn't that unusual for me. When you run an international firm, sleep is an expensive luxury.

But could I afford another luxury, one in the form of a sexy Australian with grey eyes who reminds me I have needs? I slide my soapy hands over my skin, an idea forming. He said he was free and easy. No work commitments, money clearly no issue. The way he threw it around last night, almost as if trying to offload as much as possible, perhaps he'd be up for a whirlwind tour of the globe with stopovers at all the international M Club establishments? We could continue this arrangement for a few weeks… A way to explore the sexy side he's unleashed in me. A way for me to keep this feeling, this newfound perspective, alive.

My proposition takes form in my mind as I towel dry and comb through my hair. A month, six weeks ought to be enough time to work my *man toy*, as he put it, from my system. I'd have to make the sex-only proviso crystal-clear. My one trip down the aisle confirmed that relationships and I definitely don't mix. I have no desire to repeat *that* mistake. I don't need a relationship, which in my experience is just another way to fall short of someone's expectations.

If Cam agrees, if he too wanted more than just one fantastic night, he could accompany me while I toured my international offices to ensure everything is as I like it—ticking along like clockwork and expanding on our year-by-year profits.

A sex-only arrangement.

'Amazing sex,' I say aloud, catching my laughing reflection in the fogged-up mirror—eyes bright with excitement, hair tousled and damp the way it was last night after our first shower, when Cam fucked me from behind in this very spot, ordering me to tweak my nipples hard until I saw stars right before I came.

The man was some sort of sex god, a G-spot genius, and I his willing, eager-to-excel pupil. But I didn't simply want to excel. I wanted to be top of the class.

I smile at my reflection—a feline smile.

I'd show him I could let go.

I'd ruin *him.*

Dressed in my favourite floaty Capri pants and a silk spaghetti-strap top in deference to another stunning Monaco day, I make discreet enquiries at Reception for Cam's whereabouts. There was no answer when I knocked on the door to his suite, just down the hall from mine. Even if he hadn't made a splash in the gaming room last night, he's pretty unforgettable—his height, his commanding presence, not to mention his *fuck you* air of flouting convention and living the good life.

I find him in the club's gym, the sole occupant. He's ignoring the *Shirts must be worn at all times* sign, performing chin-ups on a bar facing a wall of mirrors. And I don't blame him. If I had his body, every inch cut slabs of muscle draped in golden skin, a gorgeous, intricate tattoo covering one shoulder, I'd watch myself move too. I'm instantly damp between my legs just from one glance at his sweaty torso.

In fact, there's no reason I can't enjoy the show for a few hedonistic seconds. My pulse throbs through my sex while I watch, hypnotised. His back muscles flex in unison to drag his long, built frame up the foot or so required to place his chin above the bar. Sweat runs in rivulets down the bumps of those muscles. My tongue darts out to wet my lips, keen for another taste of the skin I sampled last night.

That happy sigh is back, thankfully silent and in my head, but again it strikes me I haven't felt this rejuvenated in years. Cam's the kind of man who makes a woman feel feminine. It's effortless for him—his sheer size, those calloused hands, the formidable sexual prowess I've now experienced, plus his nurturing, caring side and impeccable manners.

Enough looking.

I'm on a plane out of here shortly. Time is money. I want his answer.

I approach with confident steps, although my belly twists with uncharacteristic nerves. What if he turns me down, or has a life to get back to in Sydney, or thinks I'm too old for him beyond one anonymous night? The pinch of disappointment speaks of the calibre of Cam's brand of fucking. But I'm a big girl. A grown woman. I tell myself his refusal would be no big deal, that there are plenty of other Cams in the sea, although the shaky quality of my breathing confirms it's a lie.

But I'm not giving up yet. I'm used to getting what I want, and this will be no exception.

I meet his eyes in the mirror, and just like last night

the eye contact feels like a physical waveform buffeting me with his aura. With all the eye contact we've shared since, the physical intimacy, I should be over the starry-eyed phase by now. Bloody hell, I'm not sixteen.

Cam drops to the ground, not a hint of surprise on his face, as if he'd been aware of me staring from the doorway. He's probably used to women hounding him for more sex the morning after.

My brain scrambles to recall exactly why I'm here, other than to watch his ripped body work out while I drool.

'Has working all night refreshed your appetite?' he says, grabbing a towel. He wipes sweat from his face and chest and then slings the lucky piece of towelling around his neck. 'Women don't usually hunt me down before breakfast.'

I drag my eyes away from the bulge of his cock, visible through the thin fabric of his workout shorts, all but panting at the memories of that spectacular part of his anatomy. 'I only worked *half* the night. The other half—'

'I remember what you did the other half,' he interrupts, flashing that grin that reminds me he's in his twenties.

'And I didn't need to hunt you down,' I say, stepping closer. 'After your antics at the roulette table last night, purchasing a bright yellow supercar, you're something of a celebrity—all I did was ask for your whereabouts at Reception.'

He tilts his head in acknowledgement of my statement, his own stare taking a similar swoop of appraisal down the length of my body. 'Did you receive the replacement dress and lingerie?' I can tell that, like me, he's remembering what he did while my ruined dress and torn panties shackled my waist.

I free a groan in my head, the remembered sound of fabric ripping sending delicious spikes of pleasure to my core. I fight the urge to kiss him in that way that seems to drive him crazy—my tongue surging against his, a scrape of my teeth along his decadent lower lip.

'I did. Thank you.' At the crack of dawn this morning, shortly after he left, there was a knock at my door. I rushed to open it, secretly hoping to find Cam on the other side, but it was a hotel porter delivering a garment bag. 'The replacement wasn't necessary—how did you even do that? It's Sunday morning.'

He arches one brow in that noncommittal way of his. 'I have my methods. As you know, money opens doors.' His mouth flattens, a hint of cynicism in his expression.

'So, did we leave something unfinished? Did I leave my boxers in your room...?' He laughs and I join him, more certain than ever that spending time with him will be good for me and therefore good for business. It's been an age since a man made me laugh, since *I* laughed full stop. I deserve to celebrate such a landmark victory over my father's firm, and I want to celebrate with Cam.

'I have a proposition for you,' I say, letting him have it straight between the eyes. Now I've seen him again in the flesh, I'm even more set on my course of action. I need the next few weeks to run as smoothly as clockwork, professionally speaking, and, with Cam around as an after-hours distraction, my mind would be clear, my focus sharp and my energy restored.

Bloody hell, Orla, he's not a multivitamin!

'Oh? Sounds intriguing,' he says. 'Why don't we discuss it over breakfast? I'll just jump in the shower and meet you in the restaurant.'

My body clamours to join him in the shower, my mouth parched for another taste of his talented, thick cock. I swallow, suddenly ravenous. 'I don't eat breakfast, and I'm flying out to Zurich in—' I check my watch '—ninety minutes.'

He's not remotely disappointed with this news. My stomach plummets. No woman wants to be so easily forgotten.

'Okay—well, shoot, then.' He leans one hip against a nearby weights machine, the fabric of his shorts stretching across his crotch leaving nothing to the imagination, and grips the ends of the towel around his neck. A perfect pin-up pose for a raunchy, get-you-wet calendar. And I don't need my imagination—I have fresh and vivid memories to keep me warm.

Of course, I'd rather have the real thing…

'You said last night you were on a pleasure spree of luxury travel. Does that mean you're free of other commitments at the moment?' We haven't talked about what we do for a living. We haven't talked about anything.

'I'm free as a bird. What do you have in mind?'

'I wondered if you'd like to join me on a tour of some of the other M Clubs. I'll be travelling for work for the next five-to-six weeks… Perhaps we could have some fun along the way…?' I trail off from my perfect sales pitch, concealing most of the desperation from my voice, and I silently thank every single business proposition I've ever made for getting me through this sexy proposition without so much as a voice wobble.

'Well, that's intriguing.' His eyes glow. 'So you enjoyed your walk on the wild side, huh?'

I arch my brows. 'And you didn't?' He couldn't keep his hands off me. I have the soreness between my legs as a trophy of his insatiable stamina.

'Fair point.' He grins. 'But aside from the obvious pleasures,' he looks me up and down, 'what's in it for me?'

I splutter. Gape. I didn't expect him to play hardball. I'm used to telling people how high to jump.

'You said it yourself—you spent half the night working. Have you even slept? You don't have time for breakfast…' He shrugs, his point illustrated.

I roll my shoulders back, defensive—his censure reminds me a little too closely of my ex-husband's complaints. 'I don't need more than a couple of hours' sleep.' But he's right; my work habits do make me rather a dull travelling companion.

'As good as last night was,' his eyebrows flick up in that roguish way, 'I'm not interested in spending the next six weeks watching you working in between snatched naps only punctuated by the odd fuck. I prefer my dates—'

'We wouldn't be dating.' My temperature soars. How dare he see me so...clearly?

He ignores my interruption. 'I prefer my hook-ups to have a pulse, to have the energy to offer me a few scraps of attention and to be awake long enough for us to have a good time.' His lip curls in that playful way he's so good at. 'I'm old-fashioned like that.'

I bristle, lifting my chin. 'I know how to have a good time. You just said so yourself about last night.' It wouldn't sting quite so much if his assumption wasn't true, but I'd never admit such a thing.

He steps closer, his beautiful eyes holding me captive. 'You're right,' he looks me up and down in a way that makes me feel naked again, 'you look too put together to be as hot as you are, but once you let your hair down the sex part was great.'

'But...' I say, because I know it's coming, despite his compliments.

'But, when I woke up and reached for you because I wanted more, you weren't there.'

I fist my hand on my hip. 'I work odd hours because of international time zones.'

He nods, but continues. 'And when I found you working before dawn this morning, I assumed we were done, that the sexy woman I'd spent the night with was safely tucked away, normal service resumed.'

'Normal service? What does that mean?' Didn't I prove I could have a good time with the right incentive?

'It means this.' Cam waves a finger at me. 'You're back to being immaculate and untouchable. Perhaps last night was a one-off. Don't forget I saw your idea of fun yesterday—until we left the casino it was hardly thrilling. But perhaps I'm judging you harshly.' He folds his arms behind his head and stretches out his back. 'Why don't you help my decision-making process by coming to a party?'

My stomach drops with disappointment. This should be in the bag by now. 'I told you, I fly out soon, and what kind of party happens at ten in the morn—' I break off mid-flow, realising my mistake with a full-out blush.

No. I grind my teeth in frustration. He's wrong. I can have as much fun as the next person...

His twisted mouth tells me he finds me amusing, but then his face turns sincere, eyes alight with that flicker of challenge I recognise from when he was buried inside me, instructing me to fondle my nipples or touch my clit.

'The kind on a superyacht—the Monaco Yacht Show is in town. That's one of the reasons I'm here. And it's party time twenty-four-seven on board those things. How else can prospective buyers fall in love with the benefits of owning a floating luxury hotel?'

The depth of my irritation catches my breath even as I long to project a go-with-the-flow attitude. I can't go to some debauched gathering at ten in the morning— I have to work, vet a press release cementing my deal, catch a plane...

I grip my temples. Listen to me. He's seriously considering my proposal and I never concede this easily. I remind myself of what happened when I cut loose last night, of my elation this morning when I opened my emails to find Jensen's was on board. Relaxing the reins a little had paid off then; why not now? Plus, I can't have sexy, carefree Cam thinking I'm a decrepit old dullard.

'Tell you what,' he says, gripping the ends of the towel once more and buffing his astounding pecs, 'you come to the party so we can discuss this proposition of yours further, and I'll ensure you get to Zurich today— I have a plane.'

I almost roll my eyes—of course he has a plane— but stop myself in time. 'I have a perfectly adequate first-class ticket...' But isn't this what I hoped? That he'd consider my outlandish plan?

He shrugs. 'That's the offer on the table—take it or leave it. What's it going to be, princess? Party or goodbye?'

The desire to have things go exactly my way shunts my pulse higher as I stare, while he simply grins. But I *can* have things my way. All I have to do is go to his stupid superyacht party, drink some champagne and take his private plane to Zurich, with or without him—I can get some work done on board, have a decent sleep in a proper bed.

'Come on, you know you want to.' He winks.

My annoyance builds at his self-assured smile—he knows he has me over a barrel. Not a position I've previously enjoyed. But with Cam... My head spins with all the sexy ways I can make him pay. Ruinous ways...

'Okay,' I sigh, 'I'll come to the party.'

His eyes light up. 'I'll meet you out front in ten minutes, after I've showered,' he says, pushing away from the weights machine, all male swagger.

'Great.' My tone is sarcastic. I can't believe he's playing hardball.

But he didn't say no...

He keeps walking in my direction, slow and studied like a panther. I'm hit with a wave of his body heat, the scent of his fresh, manly sweat and undertones of pure, sexy Cam. Damn, he's worth waiting for and he knows it.

He grips my chin, his thumb swiping my bottom lip, and then he tilts my face up to his kiss, which is slow and thorough, as if he's relearning how our mouths slot together. I suck in a breath—unbelievably I'd forgotten how good he is at kissing, how it's almost a full-contact sport—all strong, demanding lips and probing tongue. How he dwarfs me, one hand practically swallowing my entire jaw and half my face, and how, when he pulls away, his eyes glassy with that now familiar desire, I want more. Want it never to end.

How can I crave him again? How do I have any more orgasms left in me? How can I convince him to say yes?

He pulls away, not unaffected by our chemistry— I see it in his eyes—and now I'm looking forward to this party, to proving him wrong, to showing him I'm worth his time.

'Give me ten.' His voice is husky, his breath warm on my wet lips.

I nod, too scared to trust my own voice because of the lust raging through my bloodstream.

* * *

I'm not surprised to see him driving the low-slung, sleek sports car he bought last night, even if it does look as if it belongs in some futuristic movie. The sight of him behind the wheel makes me wish I was someone who employed dirty tactics. I want to ride him right there in the front seat.

'So this is your new car?' I say as he lifts my suitcase into the back. My stomach sinks a little when I see his solitary brown leather messenger-style bag next to it. No suitcase.

'Yes. It's a supercar, remember, a Python—custommade.'

'Is everything super-sized with you?'

He waggles his eyebrows and I laugh.

'I'm glad you appreciate the finer things in life,' he says. He's talking about himself, so I shake my head in mock disgust, although I'm smiling.

'So what are you going to do with it?' I ask about the car.

'We're going to take it for a little test drive.' He opens my door, and I slide in.

'Shouldn't you have done that before you made such a rash purchase? What if the wheels fall off?'

'I'll get it fixed,' he shrugs. 'You wouldn't worry if you'd seen the race yesterday. It hugs the road like a dream, and wait till you hear the soft purr of the engine.' He winks as if nothing fazes him and a pang of longing shoots through me at his easygoing outlook.

I watch him stride around the front of the car, wondering anew at how he amassed such wealth at such a young age. I had my trust fund to help me out when I first started my own company. But I take full credit for what I've built since. I may not be any good at relationships, I may not have the belief of my father, but money I can make.

He joins me in the car, and, as if he's read my mind, starts the conversation. 'So, what do you do that sees you travelling for work?' he asks as he guns the engine, pulls away from the M Club and heads towards the harbour, Port Hercule.

I love the way he drives, the way he handles the wheel with the same masculine self-assuredness with which he handled my pleasure last night, everything about him exciting new areas of my body and mind until I'm aching for him to agree to my proposition. 'I'm in finance. I'm CEO of an investment multinational.'

He shoots me an assessing look, something akin to disbelief in his eyes.

I lift my chin and try not to take it personally.

'So you make money for people?' he says.

'Yes, lots of money, otherwise I'd have no clients. I'm very good at what I do and it's true what they say— money makes the world go round.'

He shakes his head and I wonder what's upset him about my profession. Most people I meet ask me for investment tips, but Cam looks as though I've said I drown puppies for a living.

'What is it? Do you think women can't be at the top of their field?'

He shoots me an incredulous look. 'Of course not—that you would suggest such a ridiculous thing shows how little we know each other. I was merely wondering just how good you are at your job.'

'Come to Zurich with me and we can work on getting to know each other,' I push, ever the opportunist. 'I'll even give you some free pointers—the markets are in flux at the moment, but there are always opportunities if you know where to look.'

'Mmm...' he says, sounding bored. 'If you were good at *losing* money for clients, I might be tempted.'

I can't tell if he's joking—he looks a little annoyed, his jaw thrust forward, lips pressed together. But he can't be serious. His gambling last night, the large tips, shouting the entire casino a drink...that was one thing. But losing money?

'Why would anyone want to lose money they'd worked hard for?' I could understand my brother's casual attitude to the company's turnover, having stepped into our father's ready-to-wear shoes, but not even he would willingly risk his affluent lifestyle. I wince at my spiteful thoughts. It's not my brother's fault our father has old-fashioned values that make no sense and are completely disloyal.

'They wouldn't,' says Cam. 'Not real hard work—blood, sweat and tears.' He's still borderline hostile at this turn of the conversation.

I should steer clear of anything personal. Clearly my mention of money is some sort of issue for him, perhaps explaining why he didn't seem to care about his losses at the casino last night.

'What's the difference between *real hard work*, as you put it, and what *I* do?' His comments skate too close to my own touchy subject. No one works harder than me. 'Everyone wants to be successful, and putting in the hours is how it happens. Isn't that how you made *your* money?'

His beautiful mouth twists in earnest now, a sneer of disgust. 'Of course, there's nothing wrong with that—I apologise if I offended your work ethic earlier. I've always worked hard, too, until recently. I...' He swallows, seeming to battle with something momentous, but then he recovers just as quickly.

I hold my own breath, waiting.

'Six months ago I came into an obscene inheritance—more money than anyone needs, to be honest.' He pulls into a parking spot, flashes me his live-for-the-moment smile and kills the engine as if closing down the line of conversation.

Intrigue sharpens my vision. Easygoing Cam has hidden depths. Demons. He hides them well behind that carefree persona. For some reason, he seems to be doing his best to offload the money he inherited, even lose it. It seems preposterous to someone in my field.

But this new information certainly explains the chip he seems to have on his shoulder, explains his casual attitude to gambling and extreme acts of generosity—the drinks, the car, replacing my outfit with the best money can buy.

'I'm sensing you don't want to talk about this any more than I want to drink shots off someone's stomach aboard this yacht, but is it a problem for you…the inheritance?' Prying lies outside the terms of my proposition, but I can't help myself. Perhaps I can help him with some investment advice. Of course, he hasn't said yes, so the point may be moot. I might never see him again.

He ignores my question, jumps out of the car and swings open my door. Reaching for my hand, he guides me from the low seat.

I ignore the sinking feeling in my chest and press on. 'Most people would embrace such a life-changing gift.' But I'm quickly coming to understand Cam isn't like most people, in many respects—his two-fingered gestures at convention, the way he sprang from his seat last night to assist a stranger in need, the fact he's even entertaining my proposition; most—no, all the men I know are way too rigid and full of their own importance to contemplate what I'm proposing. But with Cam it's as if normal rules don't apply, or perhaps it's just the age difference, or perhaps he's just exactly what he seems, killing time and enjoying his *bender*.

'Let's just say it's more the origin of the gift that's a problem, that and the terms…' He locks the car and heads towards the marina, reaching back to take my hand.

I try to conceal my flinch, because despite our kiss back at the hotel, despite what we shared last night, my hand in his feels alien in its intimacy.

Alien, but thrilling every nerve in my body.

I swallow the surge of lust and longing. 'Well, I'd

be happy to advise you on how to manage your wealth beyond gambling it all away and buying impractical fast cars, if that's of any interest to you—I have been known to make a savvy investment or two over the years.' I'm over-talking to cover my reaction to the hand-holding.

His head snaps in my direction, his smile almost maliciously bright. 'You think I'm frivolous.'

'No… I didn't mean—'

He comes to a halt. 'Why would you want anything to do with a man who wastes money—is the sex that great?' He delivers this with a smile, but there's pain in the tension around his mouth.

I look down at my feet, stung but also ashamed that he's spot-on—I have judged him, thinking only of what he can do for me, how he makes *me* feel, rather than what he might be hiding from, because years of swimming in the corporate shark tank have honed my instincts, so I know it's something.

He didn't get those calloused hands tapping computer keys. He's hinted that we work in very different worlds. He has an inheritance he doesn't seem to want. But he's more than the clichéd playboy I pegged him for on first impressions, just as, despite my age and my hard-won success, there's a little girl inside me still seeking her daddy's approval.

Who is the real Cam? And who left him an obscene amount of money he doesn't seem to care about?

I look up, regret that I can't see into his beautiful eyes, which are hidden behind sunglasses, stealing my breath. 'I'm sorry—making money is what I do. Pretty much all I've done my entire adult life—first for my father's firm, and then for my own. It's a hard habit to break. I didn't mean to judge, but you're right. I don't know anything about you beyond the fact that, yes, the sex is pretty sensational. That doesn't mean I don't want to know more, so why don't we rectify that? What's your surname, Cam?'

He lifts his sunglasses. 'North. Cameron North.' He smiles then, a belter of a smile. I release a shudder, appalled at how absurdly we've behaved—sharing a night of incredible sex without even knowing each other's surnames.

I smile too.

'And you are?' he asks, his hand outstretched in my direction for the formality of a handshake.

'Orla Hendricks. Nice to meet you.' We grip each other's hand, the fresh start unspoken but welcome.

'So, Orla Hendricks,' he says, guiding me towards a waiting speedboat, which will take us out to the yacht. 'Let's go have ourselves some fun, and then we'll talk about this proposition of yours.' He jumps ahead of me into the speedboat and then swings me after him, his hands gripping my waist. I want to kiss him again, but now I'm unsure of where we stand, the easy pleasure-seeking vibe we shared last night long gone.

We're taken to the biggest yacht in the harbour, the *Abella*—sleek, at least seventy metres, her pristine hull gleaming in the sun. I hear the music before I see the throng of people on deck—most of the women bikini-clad and many of the men wearing shorts. I grind my teeth in frustration—I have a swimsuit in my case back on the dock. Why didn't I think to put it on?

We disembark the tender and climb aboard the *Abella*. Cam takes a glass of bubbles from a member of the smartly dressed welcoming crew and hands it to me with a smile. Every inch of the stunning vessel is packed with beautiful people in a full-on party atmosphere. I grip Cam's hand as we head to the upper deck, which features an infinity pool, a hot tub and the best views of Monaco.

We wind through the partygoers and head towards the rail. My phone vibrates in my bag, and I pull it out, scanning the message from my assistant but checking the time. Despite Cam's promise to deliver me to Zurich, I'm aware of every second he delays. Perhaps this was a mistake. I certainly didn't get to where I am by making many of those.

Cam spies my phone and I shove the device back into my bag. 'So, are you thinking of buying this?' I want to caution him against making such a rash investment, but then, boats like this are more about hedonism and status than sound returns and I don't want to sound like a killjoy. But really, most people who own one of these spend a few weeks a year actually enjoying the lifestyle. Who has the time to take a year off work?

People like Cam, I guess, deciding to ask him about his inheritance if he agrees to come to Zurich.

'She's beautiful,' he says. 'Who wouldn't want to own her? You could permanently live on board. She's fully equipped—a cinema, a gym, a spa. And you should see the stateroom.'

'But?' We might be here so I can prove I'm not a stick-in-the-mud workaholic, but I can sense that sailing around the Mediterranean in the *Abella* isn't his dream, despite her charms.

He smiles as if I cracked a code no one else has. 'But I prefer bricks and mortar, preferably something I've built myself.' He holds up his calloused hands in proof.

I nod, impressed. I want to get to know this side of him more but stop myself, remembering what happened when we steered too close to personal. 'Blood, sweat and tears?' I say.

'Bingo,' he says, his easy smile wider.

Then I spoil the moment by handing my untouched glass of champagne to a passing waiter.

'You don't like champagne?' he asks.

'I have work to do later—I need a clear head. And you're not drinking.'

'I'm driving you to the airport after this.' I sense his disappointment, feeling as if I've failed the first test.

At his reminder that I'm on probation, I seize the change of topic to push my agenda. 'So, will you come to Zurich?' I want his company. I want the way he makes me feel, what he brings out in me, to be that woman who remembers how to enjoy herself, remembers that it's allowed, even beneficial.

'You're very direct, aren't you, Orla Hendricks? Direct, not afraid to proposition a stranger, and very driven.'

'That's a fair assessment, given we don't know each other very well.'

He tilts his head in acknowledgement. 'No, we don't know each other. So, here's what you need to know about me beyond the fact I'm a sensational lay,' he says with a wicked grin that tells me he's teasing me again, so I can't help smiling along. 'I'm a decent bloke. I'm not harbouring any sexually transmitted infections, so you can shag me with complete peace of mind, and if you want my company for the next six weeks I have two conditions.'

My pulse leaps with excitement, warm, syrupy heat forging through my blood as my lips twitch at his forthright declaration. 'Thanks for the honesty and the practicality. What are these conditions?' I say, my blood roaring through my ears with anticipation.

His eyes darken in that sexy way that reminds me of last night's Cam. 'One, you name the destinations and leave the rest up to me—*I'll* foot the bill, the transport...' he waves a dismissive had around at our current luxurious location '...the off-the-clock itinerary.' One eyebrow lifts above the rim of his sunglasses in that self-assured way. 'Even the wardrobe—I have a feeling I might ruin a few more of your outfits now I know what's hidden underneath. All you have to do is come and come and come...'

My current underwear goes up in flames at the very idea of him being impatient enough to get to me that he goes all caveman. He's sufficiently evolved that he sought my consent first. I hold in a smile and offer a droll, 'I get the picture.'

I'm woman enough, secure enough, to concede a little control to this man. After all, I hold the advantage in terms of age and life experience, and it's not as if we're entering into a relationship—this is about pleasure, and he's proved he can deliver. And, while I'm not used to relinquishing control over my life—it's why I'm successful—do I really care if he wants to pick up the travel tab?

'Okay, but I want it known I'm happy with more… frugal methods of transportation than supercars and private jets.' It's not as if I need his money or run any risk of becoming a *kept woman*—I almost splutter a laugh at the absurdity of that thought. My days of trying to play wife ended in disaster.

He shakes his head. 'Noted, but it's my call. You can be frugal on your own time.' He winks and I capitulate. For his own reasons, reasons he's already hinted at, his generosity and extravagance are motivated by more than altruism, but is his request any more outlandish than my proposition?

'And two?'

'Two—you won't like this one.' He pauses.

My pulse hammers in my neck.

'You have to loosen up a bit more. If this is about us having a good time, I'm going to want to see a whole lot more of last night's Orla.'

My jaw drops. 'What do you mean? It's eleven a.m. I'm at a superyacht party. How loose do I have to be?'

His head drops back and he looks at the sky as if seeking inspiration. 'Ah, Orla, you have so much to learn...' He smiles, perfectly pleasant, his tone teasing. But then he turns serious. 'You're at a party, checking your phone and thinking about work, probably biding your time until you can get back to it.'

My shoulders tense in defence. I heard similar criticism a hundred times from my ex.

'Actually, I was checking the time. I have other places I need to be, so let's wrap this up. Are you joining me in Zurich or not?' My patience is stretched to the limit.

Instead of answering, he sidles up close to my side and stretches his arm along the rail at my back. He leans in close, his mouth inches from mine, and my irritation evaporates in anticipation of being kissed.

'No need to get defensive,' he says, his voice low, seductive. 'Last night was fun. Fun that could have continued into this morning.'

I watch his lips move, reminded that I had the best sex of my life.

His hand slides between my shoulder blades and he urges me closer. 'Instead I woke up in an empty bed to find you working in the dark.'

My head spins, confused by the contradiction in the way he's looking at me, the way he's touching me, and the censure of his words. 'I'm not going to apologise for working—'

'Of course not, but when you're not working hard, where's the harm in playing hard?' He looks over his shoulder to where the most enthusiastic partygoers are climbing from the pool or hot tub and diving into the sea from a diving platform. 'Now, they look like they're really letting loose, wouldn't you say?'

I hear his subtext loud and clear, even as my body sways closer to his. He thinks I'm too straitlaced to let down my hair to that degree. He thinks because I work long hours, I don't know how to enjoy myself. Adrenaline floods my blood, my pulse leaping with defiance.

He turns back to face me and I touch my lips to his in a barely-there caress as I say, 'You're right, that does look fun.' I'm not wearing a bikini, but what better way to show Cam that not only can I be as outgoing as the next person, but also that I'm up for any challenge—in or out of the bedroom?

I hold his stare for one beat, two, my belly tight with anticipation, but I don't kiss him as I want. Instead I step away and slip off my sandals.

His eyes grow wide and then wider still as I slide my Capri pants over my hips. I'm wearing a black cotton thong and a strapless bra—no more revealing than half the bikinis here.

'What are you doing?' Excitement and awe war in Cam's eyes and I roll my shoulders back, the fact that I can impress him spurring me on to exhibit my best assets.

I scoop up my pants and drape them over his arm and then add my camisole top.

'I'm letting loose.' I press a kiss to his startled mouth, ignore the stares I'm attracting, stride to the swimming deck slowly and confidently and dive into the cool Mediterranean.

The water is warm after the initial shock. I break the surface and look up, expecting to see Cam's impressed face looking down at me, but he too is on the deck, stripping off his T-shirt and shorts and then following my lead by executing a perfect dive.

I have a split second to register the jealousy that heats my blood at the way some of the women ogled his spectacular physique, but then he surfaces not far from me and swims my way with long, confident strokes.

We tread water face to face, both grinning.

'Is that loose enough for you?' I ask, splashing him in the face.

He grips my waist and presses a kiss to my mouth with a growl that promises retribution. 'You're fucking irresistible, Orla Hendricks. There are a couple of guys up there I thought I might have to resuscitate—this gorgeous body is much too hot for general consumption. I can see I'm going to have to be on hand to protect the male population from your hotness.'

The air leaves my lungs in an excited rush, the familiar taste of triumph. 'Does that mean you'll be joining me in Zurich?' I mentally tsk at the flare of euphoria— a stupid, girlish reaction for which my libido is totally to blame.

He grins wider and then drags my body against his so I feel his hard cock pressed against my stomach. 'As long as you accept my conditions and you're happy to travel in style.'

'My first-class ticket was style,' I say, rubbing my lips against his, tasting salt and Cam.

'You'll like my style better; now let's get going before I change my mind and buy the *Abella* just so I can watch you do that again.' We break apart, laughing, and swim to the yacht's stern, where a crew member is helpfully waiting with two fluffy white monogrammed towels and our neatly folded clothes.

I dress quickly, driven by the heat in Cam's eyes, as if he's already mentally undressing me, almost promising the minute we're on board his private plane I'll be crying out his name.

By the time we reach the marina, my pulse pounds with excitement. 'What about your luggage, and what will you do with your car?' I slip into the leather passenger seat, eager to get in the air before he can change his mind.

He dons his sunglasses, guns the engine and pulls out of the parking spot. 'I have everything I need.' He indicates the leather messenger bag on the back seat. 'And I'm shipping the car to Sydney—I bought it for my cousin.'

I gape, my mind reasoning that we have sports cars in Australia. But by the time we get to Monaco's private airfield and I see the cute little Cessna on the tarmac, I'm grinning—there is something to be said for Cam's travel-in-style sense of hedonism.

CHAPTER FOUR

Cam

MY EYES STING with the trickle of sweat, but I can do nothing about it while I'm braced on both hands over Orla, who is close to climaxing. The minute we boarded the plane she jumped me, and I only too happily obliged, stripping us both while I headed for the craft's king-sized bed.

I know she's close because she clutches my arms until her nails dig into my skin, her staccato breaths becoming trapped in her throat. I've watched her come so many times in the last twenty-four hours that I've lost count. And this time is just as addictive. She lets go, her release real and joyful and noisy as if she's not expecting it, as if it creeps up on her, as if she's embracing this sex-only proposition with both hands.

I ignore the needs of my own body and dive once more for her nipple—she loves it when I give her just a scrape of my teeth. Orla likes a hint of rough with her pleasure. Who'd have guessed this passionate, sexually adventurous woman and the serious, put-together financier I met at the bar are the same woman? If it wasn't for our differences outside of sex, she could be made for me.

'Cam... Oh, my...'

She comes with her beautiful eyes on me and I follow her—bareback. She's too fucking tempting and my control was shot to pieces the minute she suggested we ditch condoms for the duration of this sexy little interlude she proposed.

I collapse on top of her, spent for now, and then roll to the side as I slip from her body, my dick still half-hard. How could I be anything else? She's incredible. She blew me away with that stunt on board the *Abella*. I'll never forget the sight of her clad only in the skimpiest of underwear, her lithe, toned body glowing in the sun as she dived into the sea. I wanted to run around scouring the image from the eyes of everyone there, male and female.

My breathing slows and I rest my head on my hand, wondering, who is the real Orla? The siren or the CEO? Perhaps neither.

She's certainly the most ambitious and driven woman I know. But what about life? Relationships and family and the future? What does the real Orla want beyond global domination of the financial sector? I'm not even going to pretend to understand what she does for a living outside of the fact I'm certain my father would have used her wealth-building services.

She turns to face me, one thigh slung over mine, sliding the wetness we've both left between her legs over my skin. I hold in a groan because I want her again, and I've barely caught my breath.

She wriggles until she's comfortable, using my shoulder as a pillow. I kiss the top of her head, the scent of whatever shampoo she uses filling my senses. I breathe her in, congratulating myself on the impulse to accompany her. I was tempted the minute she asked in the hotel gym, but I wanted to push her, to see how far she'd go for my company, and boy, has she surprised me.

My first impressions of her were all wrong. Yes, she carries the poise and polish of her wealth, but with a little encouragement, when she's not glued to her phone or her laptop, she's more than willing to let loose and embrace this thing between us—two people who couldn't be more different united in a pretty constant need to slake our fierce attraction.

Who knew a woman so tightly controlled could be so hot, insatiable and demanding? Thank fuck she suggested a continuation of the sex, otherwise I might have resorted to some unflattering trawling of the M Clubs in search of another chance encounter...

Her small hum of contentment vibrates through my chest. I grip her closer, holding her wet dream of a body closer.

'Glad you said yes?' she mumbles from under her cloud of dishevelled hair.

'Too right.' She's become my favourite distraction technique from my personal predicament, fucking her the only thing that switches off the constant feelings of fury and futility. Better than hiding, drinking, gambling and pounding my body to exhaustion at the gym combined.

I snort a short laugh. Perhaps that's the answer to my father's legacy—to immerse myself in a sex coma so profound I'm numb to the sheer audacity of the man. How dare he think he can control me from the grave with his last will and testament and make amends with money for a lifetime of indifference and absence?

Orla shifts, mashing her breasts to my side. If only dear old Pa could see me now—sprawled beneath a beautiful woman on board a private jet, blowing my unwanted legacy in the most debauched way I can.

I swallow bile and focus on the light glinting off Orla's beautiful hair. No, her proposition of pleasure couldn't have come at a better time.

'Are you okay?' She sounds sleepy and guilt pricks at my skin. I should let her sleep—she's been up most of the night.

I mutter something affirmative and try to keep my body still and relaxed in case she wants to nap.

'You're so good at that. Sex.' Her fingers stroke my abs and my dick perks up—greedy fucker. 'I'm so glad you decided to come.' Her voice vibrates where her head rests on my sweaty chest, strands of her hair tickling my chin.

'Thanks.' I laugh, my restless fingers drumming a rhythm on her back. She's so honest and forthright. She knows what she wants—damned sexy traits. 'But you wouldn't have brought me along otherwise, right?

Unless you make a habit of seducing younger men and luring them to be your sex-slaves.'

She sees the joke in my words, and laughs, then raises her head to press a kiss to my mouth. 'You're free to leave any time,' she says, even as she entwines her legs with mine, preventing my immediate escape.

'Mmm...' I press my thigh between her legs, loving her scorching wet heat. 'But then I'd miss your delicious cunt and your tempting mouth.' I trace her full lips with my fingertip, dipping my head for one more kiss while I evaluate the chances of me being ready for another round, versus heading for the on-board shower.

She pulls back, mock censure on her face. 'So you wouldn't miss my scintillating, fun-loving personality?'

I love this sassy, playful side of her; I can imagine her wearing cut-off shorts and a bikini top, hanging out and drinking beer on the balcony of my place in Sydney while we enjoy the spectacular sunset over the harbour.

'I'd miss every fuckable inch of you,' I say, slipping my hand over her hip to caress her ass, watching with mounting excitement as her slumberous stare widens, heat banked behind her eyes.

'And I don't know you well enough to miss your personality. Why don't we rectify that—we have a few hours to kill?' And, second only to fucking, verbal sparring with this sharp, witty woman is the best distraction technique. Left to its own devices, my brain would try to problem-solve, freaking me out with thoughts of forgiveness for a man I detest, acceptance of his final bequeathed gift and ways I can use his money—because it will never be *my* money—to make a difference, to do some good. But only danger lies ahead of those insane thoughts. The danger that I'm becoming just like him—a man who chose the pursuit of wealth over love, over his family.

Over *me*.

'Mmm, I really should work…' Orla's contented, half-hearted excuse draws me back to the present. Despite using this trip as the perfect antidote to my predicament, and despite my jokes about being her man toy, I really do want to get to know her better, the real her, to work out which of the two awesome versions of Orla Hendricks is the real deal.

I cup her ass cheeks in both hands and roll her on top of me, pressing my hardening dick between her legs so she gasps. 'Work *schmirk*—haven't you made enough money for today?'

'Is that a thing? Can you ever have too much?' She indicates our luxurious flying bedroom. But I can't concede that point without divulging my father issues, so I change the subject.

'Come on. I promise no deep, searching questions.' I tilt my hips, rubbing her clit with the head of my cock. 'Just a quick-fire quiz so I can get to know you before I fuck you again. Stop me feeling like a gigolo and you like a cougar.'

She laughs from her belly—deep and throaty—and it's such a beautiful sight and sound, one that makes me forget my troubles, that I'm determined to make it happen as much as I can while we're together.

'Tell me,' I coax, pushing her hair back from her face, 'favourite animal?'

She doesn't hesitate. 'Well, they're just so cute-looking, I'd have to say wombat,' she says, choosing an Australian icon, embracing the game even as she grinds her hips, sending fresh blood to my already hard dick.

'Do you have any pets?' My voice grows husky. The shower will have to wait—she knows what she's doing to me, her tongue darting out to wet her lips. Perhaps she hates talking about herself. Perhaps, despite her willingness to embrace a challenge, there's nothing in her life besides work, after all. Her degree of professional success requires sacrifices; I would know. I'm a prime example—I refuse to think of myself as a victim—of such single-minded focus.

'No, I travel too much to own one.' She sighs, her eyes turning wistful with longing. 'I used to have a Labradoodle called Talia when I was growing up.'

I nod. 'You could have one if you wanted. It could travel with you on its own passport. I had a golden retriever who used to come to work with me every day until she died about a year ago. Her faithful company made the days fly by, and I always had someone to talk to.'

'I'm sorry.' She presses her mouth to mine, and again I forget. Forget that I started this game, forget that we're getting to know silly things about each other. But, now I've seen a flicker of the woman behind the trappings,

I'm intrigued anew. I pull away. 'Okay, what's your dream job?'

'Mmm… That's tricky. I've only ever done what I do now, and I've never wanted to do anything else. I started working for my father on the weekends at sixteen, joined the family company after university and left ten years ago to start my own firm.'

So she'd always been career-focused, even from a young age. 'I spent most of my weekends surfing or drumming at sixteen,' I say. 'What happened to the family firm? Didn't they miss you when you left to strike out alone?'

She snorts, her face hardening. 'I doubt it. My brother can, apparently, do my old job as well as me, despite working half as hard.' She shakes her head and changes the subject. 'What about you, what's your dream job?'

But it's too late. That single sentence tells me exactly what motivates her: she's competitive and wants to be taken seriously. I sanitise my answer, reluctant to confess I need never work again, if only I could reconcile dear old Dad's dying wish. Because the truth is it's ruined everything. *He's* ruined everything. In my life before, working hard, striving and grafting and being proud of where a poor boy from Sydney had dragged himself gave me purpose, a sense of accomplishment. It made sense.

But now…? When I could buy the construction company I once worked for outright a hundred times over and barely notice the cost…

I swallow, hedging how much to reveal. 'I used to

work for a construction company back in Sydney before the inheritance, but I'd say I have the perfect job right now—enjoying myself and everything that money can buy.' I hold her closer. 'Travelling in style anywhere in the world. And, of course, meeting a beautiful woman who only wants me for sex is an added bonus.' I wink, bringing out her throaty chuckle.

But then she turns serious. 'Do you miss construction?'

I shrug. 'Sometimes. I love building things, always have, even as a boy. I like to be active and use my hands. There's nothing better than a day of graft and sweat and getting splinters followed by relaxing with an ice-cold beer.'

I catch the curl of her lip, the wrinkle of her nose that reminds me we're still very different. 'Well, almost nothing better,' I say, sliding my hand over her hip to caress her backside, steering us back to the reason we're here: the sex. She may not be the straitlaced princess I first had her pegged for, but that doesn't mean she'd be happy hanging out with the real me—the me without the money and the jets and the cars and the billions in the bank.

'You miss getting splinters?' she asks, her voice mildly incredulous. She comes from wealth, her family own a business; she's probably known it her whole life, despite whatever sibling rivalry sent her striking out alone.

I nod, breathing through the urge to defend how I once made a modest but sufficient living with my own two hands. How I didn't need more than savings in the bank and the pride of being able to look after my mother.

Not like *him*.

My sperm donor. Because he didn't stick around long enough to earn the title of father. A man who thought he could come back into my life from the grave and dictate how I live.

I choose my words carefully. 'Before the money I lived an average life.' I try but fail to shake off the memories of going to school hungry, of having to fake a stomach ache to get out of gym class because I was ashamed of my trainers, of having to stay late at school to do my homework on the computers in the library because, try as she may, my single-parent mother couldn't afford luxuries.

I force my muscles to relax when they scream with tension. I don't want Orla to know the turn in this conversation highlights how different our worlds are. But she doesn't have to fit into my life, my *real* life, the life I had six months ago. All she needs to do is to fit in my bed, temporarily. She wanted sex. She's already stated she's happy I can deliver what she's looking for and she's willing to embrace a challenge.

'So, next question,' I say, moving on. 'What's the most sexually adventurous thing you've done?' My mind ruminates on the infinite possibilities we could cram into six weeks of sexual exploration.

She laughs, but doesn't falter. 'I'd say proposition-ing a stranger for sex is pretty adventurous.' She kisses me, eyes open, her tongue pushing against mine until I forget the question I asked.

'It's up there,' I say when she allows me up for air. Yes, she owns her desires; she's almost as insatiable as she makes me, and I'm damned well determined to enjoy every second of testing her boundaries, extending her comfort zone, pushing her buttons. Something tells me not only will she do her best to rise to the challenge, but we'll both reap the rewards as she continues to surprise me, to allow her outer shell to crack, revealing the real, uninhibited Orla inside.

'What about you? Threesomes? Bondage? Sex with an older woman?' Her eyes twinkle.

'Ah, a gentleman never tells.' I roll onto my side, taking her along, curious as to what led her to proposition a stranger. 'So why am I here? What do *you* need from this that you don't already have?'

Her mouth flattens as if she wasn't expecting the question, but then she sighs. 'As you've already pointed out, I work hard for long hours. I travel a lot. I'm divorced and have no desire to enter into another relationship. Why shouldn't I have the kind of sex-only fling I want with a gorgeous man who wants the same thing?'

'No reason at all,' I concede, fascinated for details of her failed marriage. But because I want to steer us back from the supremely personal, I say, 'What kind of sex are we talking about here? Threesomes? Bondage? Sex with a virile younger man?'

She throws her head back on a delighted, throaty laugh. 'Fishing for compliments?'

'I'll always take compliments, but how can I give you what you want if I don't know what that is?'

Her fingers trail through my chest hair, her eyes growing lazy with mounting desire. 'Hot sex. Frequent hot sex with a man who pushes all my boundaries.' Her hips begin to gyrate as she rubs her pussy over the head of my cock once more.

'You like having your boundaries pushed?' A slug of heat scorches through me at the idea of testing her limits, although the experience might just kill me, she's that hot.

'I'm happy to keep up with you.' She tilts her hips, aligning her pelvis so just the tip of my cock slips inside her.

I stifle a groan, my hand dragging her hip closer, my fingers flexing into the deliciously round cheek of her ass until I sink in another inch. 'So, sexual adventures are on the cards?'

'Anything is on the cards.' Her pupils dilate, swallowing the emerald of her exquisite irises.

'Really? Anything?' It's hard to think straight when her pussy sucks at the head of my dick.

'If you're asking if I've ever done anal, the answer is no, but...' Her breasts rise on a breathy sigh.

Excitement builds in my chest at the idea of taking her somewhere previously forbidden, of guiding her to explore something new, of extending her comfort zone.

Ruining her.

'So that's something you'd be open to—excuse the pun—not that I'm in any way pushing?'

She bites her lip and straddles me, sinking back on her heels until her hot sex swallows my length to the hilt. She stares down, levels me with that look—the one that reminds me she's driven, successful, older and, outside of anal sex, perhaps more experienced. 'I wouldn't *let* you push me, but I'm not into pain.'

I clasp her rocking hips, trying to force words out past my tight throat as pleasure grips me. 'Me neither, but pleasure…?'

She leans forwards, kisses me, her tongue surging against mine until I've not only forgotten my own question, but I'm also close to losing my mind. 'Perhaps,' she whispers. 'But we'd have to start off small. There's no way I'm ready to take this bad boy.'

I slip my hand between us, my thumb finding her clit, because all this talk about pushing sexual boundaries, the way she's riding me, means I'm close and there's no way I'm coming until she is.

I don't miss the gush of moisture bathing my dick as she gasps her pleasure against my mouth. 'I'm happy to explore anything, but only if you're as accommodating…' She trails kisses across my chest as she scoots back. 'Let's start with the bondage.' She smiles, the expression wicked and self-satisfied.

I grip her hips, guiding her rhythm, but she untangles my hold and pushes my arms above my head. 'Nuh-uh. I want to be in charge this time.' She reaches for her discarded bra and binds my wrists with it before securing them loosely to the headboard.

'Yes, ma'am.' Before I can speak another word she

starts the rocking again, this time cupping her breasts and rolling her nipples between her thumbs and fingers as if she's determined to drive me insane, even more insane than the idea of testing her, taking her on an unexplored journey of pleasure, showing her that nice boys from nowhere can rock her tightly controlled world.

But I can't enjoy it for long. She gasps as she rides me harder, sinking so deep there's nowhere left to go. I hold still, splayed beneath her, watching her pleasure her breasts, my eyes drawn to the way she tugs her lip under her teeth. I want to move. To suck on that sensitive lip until she begs me to take her places no one else has. To see my dick rest there before she takes me to the back of her throat. To buck up into her and take us both over the edge into mindless oblivion, where I'm just a man and she's just a woman—no differences, no complications, no expectations beyond finding the ultimate pleasure.

Her rounded hips undulate, finding the rhythm and angle she wants, that make her moan and start to chant my name. She looks down at me, her face rapt with pleasure and the hint of a feline smile on her lips. 'I'm intrigued now. You have my mind thinking dirty thoughts, Cam North. You're bad for me.' She rocks back and forth, her head thrown back and her cries telling me I'm nothing but good for where she wants to go.

I'm speechless at her astounding willingness to embrace this, although my mind fills with all the filthy words I could use to describe such an amazing sight as this woman riding me while she fantasises about other pleasures to which I'm going to introduce her.

And then she fumbles with my restraints, her hands jerky in their desperation. 'Do it. Do it now.' She guides one of my hands to her ass, her fingers over mine slipping between her cheeks to lead the way. 'Touch me like you did last night.'

She resumes her rocking, her hands returning to her breasts, and I grip both cheeks, thrusting up into her with her every down-stroke while my fingers explore her rear.

'Oh, Cam, yes…'

Fuck, she's incredible. How did I ever think she'd be too straitlaced for the kind of sex I enjoy? The kind with a woman who isn't afraid to own her pleasure, to claim it, to heighten it any way she chooses? She's glorious, a woman in her prime, taking her pleasure and then demanding a little more.

Her glazed eyes open, looking down at me through heavy lids. 'I'm going to come.'

I grit my teeth, bucking harder underneath her and pushing the tip of my finger, which is wet from the arousal slicked between her legs, inside her rear.

Her orgasm tears a scream from her arched throat and I come seconds later, the thought that, sexually at least, Orla Hendricks could have been made for me filling my mind.

CHAPTER FIVE

Orla

I DON'T RECOGNISE the hotel suite, although I've only been away for a morning, on the second day of meetings at my Zurich office. The bed is covered with shopping bags and parcels, the floor littered with stacks of shoeboxes, and there's a clothing rack filled with garment bags. I shake off the fatigue I felt when I found Cam absent and open one, my curiosity burning out of control; I find a beaded ballgown the colour of peacock feathers, the iridescent hues catching the light and changing colour before my eyes.

My first instinct, to roll my eyes at Cam's extravagance, fades, replaced by awe. My fingers trail along the exquisite fabric. It's exactly what I would pick out for myself, and I can't believe his thoughtfulness. He hasn't just mindlessly bought a year's worth of clothes. He's personally selected these, and I know because yesterday he told me how pretty I looked in my favourite green silk blouse.

With jittery fingers I open one of the parcels on the

bed, the delicate tissue paper parting to reveal a filmy wisp of lingerie—sexy but comfortable and the right size. With the shoes—my one weakness—I'm a little less restrained, flipping off the lids to reveal pair after pair of exquisite, barely practical heels from all the biggest fashion houses. Just how I like them.

I catch my wide smile in the mirror, Cam's gifts, no matter how excessive, forcing an ache to my cheeks. Cam never does anything by half measures, whether it's making me come or reserving the best suite money can buy—the suite we're currently occupying at the M Club, which has views of Lake Zurich with the Alps in the distance.

My phone pings, drawing my attention from Cam's gift, which is enough haute couture to make a supermodel weep. I scan the message and fire off a quick response to one of my assistants, my gaze returning to the outfits with longing. When will I even have the opportunity to wear most of these? We've been in town two days, and despite my assurances that I can play as hard as the next person I've had no time to explore.

I sit on the bed and kick off my shoes, my tired toes protesting. I've promised I'll take tomorrow off to go skiing—Cam has planned a day on the slopes. I try to recall the last time I had an entire day off. It's been at least a year.

I glance at the exquisite gowns with longing. Why have I allowed my life to become so…insular? And why has it taken meeting a sexy Aussie guy to bring me out of my self-imposed shell?

I text him my thanks and let him know I've arrived back at the hotel.

Thinking of Cam, I feel my pulse pick up, delicious fingers of anticipation curling around me.

Where is he?

I slip off my jacket and flop back on the bed, part of me wishing I'd been with Cam on his shopping spree— I rarely have time for visiting actual stores these days, preferring to purchase from my favourite designers on-line, but it's not the same. I used to adore shopping, the thrill of finding something I loved, the reverence of bringing it home in a pristine bag.

The door clicks and in he walks, casually dressed, unlike me, in worn jeans and a black T-shirt. I sit up, hit with his delicious, freshly showered scent seconds before he leans over me on the bed, his mouth finding mine, and I'm lost in his now familiar, demanding kiss.

'Good morning,' he says, pulling away, his smile wide and warm and filling me with regret.

I laugh while I wrestle my heart-rate back under control. 'It's afternoon.' I stand and wrap my arms around his neck, wanting to be closer.

He shrugs, holding my hips to his. 'Well, you were gone when I woke, so I missed my good-morning kiss.'

I fight the urge to sweep the parcels from the bed and drag him back there so we can have a do-over— this morning was the only one since I met him that my day hasn't begun with my waking to find him raising an eyebrow of enquiry before wedging himself between my thighs, coaxing my clit equally awake with his tongue.

'Yes, I had a seven a.m. meeting.' The only way I would be able to squeeze in what I needed to work on and spend tomorrow skiing the Zermatt with him before we leave the day after. 'I see you've been shopping…'

He shrugs, one corner of his mouth kicking up at my gross understatement. 'Just a couple of things. An extension of my apology for tearing your dress.'

'A dress you already replaced. This is too much, Cam.'

His mouth twists in that sexy way of his, one usually preceding some sexy command or request. 'I noticed that you travel light, so I thought you might need a few things, especially for the opera tonight.'

'Cam, I'm a woman, a woman who loves shoes, but even I wouldn't go this far.' I look around the room, my financier's brain totting up a dizzying sum.

'That's because you're frugal. Indulge me,' he says before I can take umbrage. 'And remember the rules— you get to have your wicked way with me as often as you like, and I dictate the after-work itinerary and cover the costs.'

I nod, breathless because now I want to have my way with him once more. I could use a dose of Cam's special magic after the morning of meetings, of hustling, of living up to my reputation as one of the industry's global trailblazers.

A strange and unfamiliar restlessness infects me; it was there when I walked through the door. I probe the feeling so I can label it.

I'm jealous.

Jealous of the time he spends without me, even though *I'm* the one who's leaving *him* to work. I'm jealous that he's doing who knows what, while I have the same meeting over and over, only in different countries and different languages. And I'm jealous that living the high life seems to come naturally to him; wherever we are, he hunts out something fun to do. This is my sixth trip to Zurich, and I've never been to the opera.

I stroke Cam's strong arms. He's becoming an addiction—the more I have, the more I want. An edge of panic grips my throat. It wasn't supposed to feel this way...

'So what else have you been up to while I've been at work?' I hadn't thought about how he keeps himself busy when I'm not around—I guess I assumed he works out at the club gym or goes for a swim.

His expression turns shifty, pricking my curiosity. 'You won't approve.'

'Why? Did you elbow an elderly lady out of the way to get to that ballgown?'

He laughs but his eyes stay wary. Then he sighs. 'I visited a music store—I still play the drums.'

'So that's why you're always tapping something?'

He pulls me in for another kiss and I sink into it, grateful he made the first move because the urge to kiss him is pretty constant. I'd practically zoned out during one of my meetings this morning, fantasising about him, what he might be doing, whether he was naked, in our bed, perhaps jerking off because he couldn't wait for me to get back.

I'm drawn back to the present when he pulls away. 'I bought a drum kit.'

I look around in confusion. 'There's no room here for a drum kit.'

He shakes his head. 'More's the pity. No, these weren't for me.' He turns serious and I hold my breath, certain he'll show me a little piece of himself if only I'm patient.

'There was a kid at the music shop. The sales assistant told me he comes in every week to pay off some money towards the kit he wants.' He shrugs, his eyes taking on a faraway look. 'I remember what that was like, how hard I saved for my first set—I worked surf lifesaving all summer.'

I smile and slide my fingers through his glorious hair. I can picture a teenaged Cam, all tanned, his hair bleached by the sun.

'I couldn't resist—I paid off the kid's balance and had the kit delivered to his house.' Suddenly he scoops me around the waist, hoists my feet from the floor and swings me in a circle. 'You should have seen his face.'

I squeal and laugh, and then my feet touch down and I sober as I look hard into his eyes. 'Cam, that was such a kind thing to do.' I try to picture the man I know doing that, the one who tips everyone he meets and spends money with reckless abandon. It makes my stomach hurt.

He downplays his generosity with a shrug, but I can see that this means something to him, something more than purchasing exquisite gowns he thinks I'll like.

'Playing drums helped me through my teens. Music is a great hobby.'

He looks uncomfortable and I squeeze his biceps, because I'm still holding on to them as if I'm scared he'll disappear. Were his teens difficult? Did he go through a rebellious phase? Butt horns with his father? My chest aches with questions but I bite my tongue, not only because it's clearly a soft spot for him, but also because it's personal. I know from the haunted look in his eyes that he once struggled and strived to buy things I would have taken for granted. I want to ask, to know this side of him, but it's not what we're about.

I take a shuddering breath as the restlessness returns, twice as fierce. I think about the meeting I have this afternoon with my Zurich chief financial officer and head of investments. I'd much rather spend time with Cam, break my own rules and get to know the drum-playing, sexy Santa side of him better.

'Anyway,' he says, releasing me and walking to the bed. 'I see you haven't had time to unwrap everything,' he picks up a black box I hadn't noticed and holds it out in my direction, 'but I want to watch you open this one.'

I accept the change of subject, shelve my curiosity and take the box, which is heavier than it looks, black velvet, monogrammed with the M Club logo and slightly smaller than a shoebox.

'What is it?' I ask, the look of heated challenge in his eyes leaving me nervous and so turned on I'm hyperaware of every breath I take.

'It's for you—I couldn't resist.' His voice is deep,

dark, and his eyes gleam, that sexy secret smile of his firing every pleasure centre in my brain so I want to abandon my own curiosity as to the box's contents and jump him, to drag us both back to the safe place where we lose ourselves in each other, in pleasure.

'Open it.' It's a husky demand, just like the ones he issues in bed.

I prise open the lid and gasp, and then laugh, locking eyes with his in time to see the excitement dancing there. Inside the box, nestled in deep maroon satin, is a matt-black vibrator, the base bearing an M Club logo encrusted with tiny diamonds.' I finger the two rows of sparkling stones on top of the *M*.

'Are these real?' Pressure builds in my chest, as if I'm oxygen-deprived. Only Cam would buy such an extravagant and intimate gift.

He nods, slow, confident, sexy, and then he watches my tracing finger.

With a breathy shudder I can't hold inside, I slide my fingertip up the length of the sex toy as slowly and sensually as I can, tracing the realistic ridges to the very tip, and then meet his stare with a challenging one of my own. 'It's not as big as you.'

His eyes darken with sexy promise and that hint of challenge he seems to love where I'm concerned, one I'm only too happy to meet head on. Can't have him thinking he's besting me in our little arrangement.

'No, but it's big enough. I thought you needed a sex toy for when I'm no longer around.'

Lust is a tangible aura around us, impossible after

the amount of sex we've had this week, but there all the same. Lust and something else. Perhaps trust. A deeper awareness. I focus on the lust because that's the only feeling I'll allow myself, although Cam's reminder that this is temporary dampens some of my excitement.

Because you want it to be temporary.

I latch on to Cam's eyes to stop my head spinning with what-ifs. I see my own desire reflected. He too is turned on.

We're both fully clothed, no longer touching, but his need is there in the husk of his deep voice and the avid way he's watching my every move, like a predator about to strike.

And now I'm desperate to reschedule my afternoon and break in my new toy with Cam. Mmm… Perhaps I could make time for that.

I know exactly what I'm doing to us both when I abandon the vibrator and lift the second item from the box, holding it up between us with a questioning brow, because all I want to do is laugh, kiss the self-satisfied delight from Cam's handsome face, and then drag him to bed and force him to introduce me to these gifts.

'What's this?' I say, my voice low. 'A butt plug?'

He nods again. 'You wanted to experiment.' He steps closer, grasping my hips and grinding his erection between our bodies as he kisses me with his trademark thoroughness.

My hands are occupied with his over-the-top provocative gifts—who even knew diamond-encrusted sex toys were a thing?—but I embrace the kiss as always, my pulse galloping to keep up with my filthy mind. When I'm panting, the tops of my thighs slick with arousal, I pull away, now determined to reschedule my meeting and forget. Forget that my life is so work-focused and that it no longer feels like enough. Forget that I'm sleeping with a man I hardly know but I'm too scared to change the status quo. Forget everything apart from the way he makes me feel invincible.

'Show me,' I whisper against his mouth. Everything else fades, as if nothing is as important as losing myself in my addiction to Cam.

I hear the sharp intake of his breath.

His pupils are so big I can no longer see the grey of his eyes. His hands fist in the fabric of my skirt over my hips, and he hisses between his teeth, leaning down to rest his forehead against mine and scrunch his eyes closed with obvious regret.

'I will—hell, I will.' He breathes hard, his sincerity pouring from him in waves of intensity I've only seen when he's turned on, battling his control to push me into that final, exhausted orgasm before he allows himself to follow. Cam takes my pleasure incredibly seriously, perhaps as if he sees *me* as some sort of challenge be-yond the challenges he sets for me, the ones my com-petitive nature demands I embrace.

He grips my hips tighter before pushing me away and groans, clearly getting himself under control. 'But, for now, we have a delivery to make. Are you done for the day?'

My high plummets, the expectations of being immediately gratified and chasing off this edgy feeling hitting a brick wall.

'No.' I pout, my disappointment as effective as a cold shower, to be replaced with a flush of shame at the deflated look on his face. Whatever he had planned means something to him, perhaps as much as purchasing a drum kit for a stranger, and it's clearly more important than getting naked and trying out his newest extravagant purchase.

I fight the heat rising in my face; I was willing to cancel my meeting for sex, but not for whatever Cam has planned? My priorities confirm we're still very much on different wavelengths where the pursuit of pleasure is concerned. But I can give him time after everything he's given me.

I mentally reshuffle my schedule so I can spend the afternoon with him, in or out of bed, because I want to see more of the look he wore when he told me about the drums. I want to see more of the real Cam.

'But I can be free—I'll just need to make a few phone calls. What did you have in mind?'

Cam smiles and my decision feels right. 'I'll make it up to you, I promise.' He takes the butt plug from my hand and places it back in the box, snapping the lid closed with a frustrating finality. 'Want to go on an adventure?'

His excitement infects me with a feeling of lightness, of possibility, of freedom. It's heady and terrifying all at once. 'What kind of adventure? I thought you'd planned skiing for tomorrow?' I breathe through

the feeling that I'm escaping my comfort zone emotionally, because I just don't do this—cancel work commitments, play hooky for the afternoon, do something just
because I'm overcome with the heady urge.

'I have. Heli-skiing—it's the best way to ski.'

'Of course it is. And the most expensive, no doubt.'
I smile, because I know by now that Cam lives to the
max. And how do I live? I love to ski. Despite all my
visits to Zurich, I've never taken the time out for one
of my favourite pastimes.

My earlier shame intensifies. I don't have time for
pastimes. All I do is work. Mark was right. Not only
was I emotionally distant, but I was also absent most
of the time.

What is Cam doing to me, and why does it feel both
naughty and liberating? 'So where *are* we going?'

He must sense my residual petulance, that I'm not
entirely happy about postponing my orgasm, because
he kisses me, his lips firm and coaxing and his smile
both hot and indulgent, as if he's already thinking about
what we'll do when we return from our fully clothed
adventure. 'It's another surprise.'

'I hate surprises.' I exaggerate the pout that earned
me one of his delicious kisses.

'Because you're a control freak.' He softens his rep-
rimand, giving me the kiss I wanted. 'Trust me, you'll
love this surprise.'

Still, I wheedle. 'As much as I love the sex toys?' I
lick my lips and watch the flare of heat in his eyes with
satisfaction.

Such a low blow…

He laughs and looks down at my outfit: a sharp business skirt and a silk blouse. 'I can't promise that. But you might want to change into something more casual.'

Defeated for now, I change, choosing my favourite pair of soft denim jeans and a simple white T-shirt for any eventuality, trying to embrace the surprise Cam has arranged.

With my phone calls made, my meeting rescheduled for seven the following morning, we leave the hotel hand in hand. I'm eager to get whatever this is over with so I can persuade Cam out of his clothes, and Cam is just plain eager, because he knows where we're going and, to him, life seems to be one big adventure.

When we approach a covered truck instead of the sleek sports car I'd been expecting, I skid to a halt. 'We're going in this?'

He said we had a delivery to make, but I was expecting…well, I don't know what I expected. Nothing Cam does is expected.

Cam nods, climbing up on the footrests to open the passenger door for me.

'Can you drive this?' I hide the scepticism from my face, certain he'll surprise me with his answer.

'Of course. I'm a jack-of-all-trades.' He winks. 'Come on, up you go.' He guides me up into the cab, his hands helpfully shoving me in by the backside so my core clenches and I can't wait to get whatever diversion Cam has planned out of the way and head back to the hotel so he can make it up to me, as he promised.

When he's sitting beside me, his big hands expertly wielding the power-assisted steering to direct us on our way, I ask, 'So where are we going?' It's certainly not lunch on the shores of Lake Zurich or a boat cruise, otherwise why would we need the delivery truck?

'I want to make a donation. A personal delivery to some very deserving recipients. I thought you might enjoy helping.' He looks over to gauge my reaction. 'Don't worry, I promise I'll make it up to you later—those toys won't be staying in the box.' He chuckles at my obvious exasperation, so I shove him in the shoulder and then slide my hand over his thigh, grinning. His excitement is palpable, infectious, so I almost don't mind that we're not back in the hotel room trying out his gifts, and now I get my wish to play Santa with him. I can be his naughty elf…

I'm still none the wiser as to our destination, but I've learned that Cam can be bull-headed, so I let it drop—I'll find out soon enough.

'You know the M Club organises many charitable events throughout the year, right?' I say. 'There are plenty of opportunities to make sizeable donations. That's one of the beauties of membership, and it's what I do.' His extravagance shows no signs of letting up; in fact, he seems to go out of his way to best himself day by day. He said his inheritance was *obscene*, and, short of giving it all away, he seems at a loss to know what to do with his newfound wealth.

He nods, his mouth tight, which tells me it's something of a touchy subject. 'I know. I already give as much as I can, but this donation is a little more personal—you'll see.'

We pass the rest of the journey in companionable silence, which is laced with curiosity on my part and what looks like knowing glee on Cam's. My mind wanders back to my cancelled meeting with my Zurich team. I have hordes of people I delegate the small things to, but I've never fully let go of the reins and simply watched the profits come rolling in. I'm not built that way. I'm too much of a control freak, as Cam pointed out.

I check my phone, pulling up my itinerary for my time in Dubai, which is where Cam and I are heading after Zurich. It's a packed week—after London, Dubai is my second largest office, my clients among some of the wealthiest people on the planet, but even so, Cam's filled all the gaps with 'must do' activities—dinner in the tallest building in the world, an Arabian Desert safari, our own private yacht tour of Dubai Creek.

My head spins, already exhausted. But I promised him. Perhaps this is his first world trip.

'Have you ever been to Zurich before?' I brush a speck of lint off my jeans, keeping my tone light and conversational rather than nosy and intrusive.

He shakes his head. 'Until I left Sydney for Monaco, the furthest I'd been was New Zealand.'

'So you've never been to Dubai either?' No wonder he wants to cram in as many tourist attractions as he can, although surely he can return any time he wants.

'No. Construction isn't the best paid work in the world, but I had a comfortable life.'

'Why not go back to your job, if you love it so much?' My scalp crawls—if someone told me I couldn't do my job, I'd be lost. Perhaps that's why he's struggling with his inheritance. But just because he never needs to work again, it doesn't mean he can't do what he loves. I do.

'My boss looked relieved when I told him I wanted to take some unpaid leave. I think the company is struggling. And in theory, I no longer need the work.'

'In theory?' My probing is hesitant because I'm in the same position. I choose to work, because I love it. It's my life. It's what I'm good at.

'It's complicated.' He keeps his eyes on the road, but his jaw is bunched, telling me he doesn't want to elaborate. I've already suggested financial advice, so I don't repeat the offer. But I want to help him.

The questions I want to ask clog my throat, because he's hinted that he hasn't always known modest or even comfortable wealth. That perhaps he has more in common with the boy at the music store than he does with me or any other M Club member; that none of this, the luxury, the charitable donations, the escapist hedonism comes naturally to him.

After ten minutes, he pulls the truck to a halt. I look out but all I can see is what appears to be an animal-welfare facility—not that my German is very good, but the logo of a cat and dog give it away. I'm even more confused, but Cam's already hopped out of the vehicle to open my door. I slide from my seat in the cab and he helps me down, his lips still tight. At least the haunted look has disappeared from his eyes.

I follow him to the back of the truck. 'Where are we?'

He opens the rear doors and I get my first glimpse of our cargo—sack after sack of dog biscuits. 'Dog food?'

Cam nods with a smile, tossing one giant bag up onto his shoulder. 'Yep—enough to last them at least a year.' With his free hand he grasps mine and tugs me towards the entrance as if he can't wait to get inside.

I want to tell him he's the only billionaire I know to be this hands-on, that if he loves dogs this much he could buy the pound or become a lifetime sponsor, but since that first day in Monaco I've learned that the quickest way to shut Cam down is to mention his wealth.

'What about the rest? We're not emptying the entire truck ourselves, are we?'

He shoots me that indulgent smile, the one that tells me he thinks I'm a bit of a princess. 'No need—I'm donating the truck too. Come on.'

'Wait.' I can't have him thinking I'm too precious to get my hands dirty or break a nail. I hoist a bag of dog food from the back of the truck and lift it onto one shoulder, as he did.

He stares, his eyes full of something that looks like respect and the smouldering heat I'm used to seeing. 'Let's go.' I walk ahead of him towards the shelter, my back burning with the knowledge of how easy it is to impress Cam North.

We're greeted by the manager, a man named Klaus, who speaks perfect English as he thanks us for the generous donation. Cam places his sack of dog food down on the counter in the small foyer and I follow suit.

'Is it okay if we look around?' asks Cam, addressing Klaus.

'Of course,' says the manager, all smiles for his generous new benefactor. 'This way.'

We're led to the rear of the facility, following the sound of barking.

'All of the dogs here are up for adoption,' Klaus tells us. 'We usually rehome around ninety-five per cent of our dogs, but sadly, there are always one or two we find it impossible to place.'

Unease grips me, drying my mouth. Does Cam expect me to walk away from here with a new pet? Is that why he brought me here? I know I told him I had a soft spot for dogs, but that doesn't mean I want to own one. Panic settles in the pit of my stomach like a rock, even as my pulse flutters at the extreme sweetness of Cam's gesture. Once the door is open and I see those expectant canine eyes, it will be harder to stay strong.

I tug Cam to a standstill and speak to him in a hushed whisper. 'What are you doing? I can't adopt a dog. I told you my life is completely unsuitable for pet ownership.' My phone buzzes in my pocket but I ignore it. It's important Cam understands me, that my resolve is rock solid before Klaus opens that door and we're greeted with a hundred pairs of puppy eyes, including Cam's. This is why he's so irresistible, why I can never say no to him. He's full of contradictions— big and sexy and manly on the outside with a heart of gold and a massive soft spot for the underdog, human or four-legged.

He takes both my hands and squeezes my fingers. 'I know. I don't expect you to adopt one, although how awesome would that be?'

At my stunned silence he continues. 'You just said you liked dogs, so I thought it might be nice to hang out with a few for the afternoon. Pets are the perfect stress reliever.' He looks down at my pocket, where my phone is happily buzzing again.

My fingers, nestled in his, twitch to answer the phone, even as I acknowledge the thoughtfulness of his surprise and that it means for him we're not just having sex. He's listened to me. He remembers my favourite colour and the fact I miss owning a dog.

My throat grows tight at his show of consideration. When was the last time someone, anyone, did something like this for me? Something simple. Just because.

'I'm not stressed.' I flush hot with guilt. I sound ungrateful, but I'm too busy to be stressed. I think of the stack of work requiring my attention back at the hotel, my crack-of-dawn meeting tomorrow and the next month of travel, all to ensure my firm is the biggest, the best, and ticking along like clockwork.

Because *I* need to be the best? Because work is all I have?

I sigh—how can I be such a mess? A week ago I had everything sorted, my life engineered exactly the way I want it. What has changed?

Cam.

I know an afternoon off won't do me any harm. In fact, I know I'll feel refreshed and energised by his infectious energy. But at what cost? I shake my head, trying to assess why I'm overthinking this so endlessly, another new trait I seem to have acquired.

Cam clearly feels I need a little more persuading. 'Look, you work hard, and you said you can play hard, too. Isn't that why I'm here? Why you invited me along? So we could have a good time along the way? Will one afternoon off really make that much difference? I find it hard to believe your empire will crumble that easily—you're too good to allow that to happen.' His argument is a recurring one and he doesn't really need to coax me. He's right. This is what I wanted when I propositioned him. A distraction, a way to unleash my playful side. To find some balance. I'm worrying needlessly.

'We'll just stay an hour, and then I'll take you back to the hotel and run you a bath before the opera. What do you say? Will you come meet some Swiss dogs?'

My mouth twists as I attempt to hide my smile, my lips drawn back to his for another kiss I can't deny myself. He's so open, so generous, not just with money, but also with his time, his enthusiasm and the easy way he sucks every scrap of enjoyment from any activity, simple or grandiose. How can I refuse him?

'Okay.'

He blasts me with his dazzling smile, and we follow a patient Klaus to the kennels. The inhabitants of the shelter are so excited to see us, I'm immediately overcome with feel-good emotions, all thoughts of work forgotten.

We're taken to a large garden behind the shelter where we can throw balls for the dogs, who without exception seem to want nothing more than to be close to us. I know how they feel; I'm developing quite an attachment to Cam myself. I watch him use his superior athleticism and strength to toss the ball to the far corners of the garden, his T-shirt riding up as he throws to reveal a tantalising strip of skin that snares my attention.

There's a beagle cross that seems to feel a particular affinity for me, returning time after time to my side and obediently dropping the ball and sitting, patiently waiting for me to throw it again. I stroke the dog's silky head, an uninhibited giggle bubbling up. Funny how you don't realise the toll something takes until you're forced to stop and pay attention. Perhaps I am stressed. Perhaps the burn-out feeling I had in Monaco wasn't temporary. Perhaps that's why the triumph over my father doesn't taste quite as sweet as I'd expected.

I glance over at Cam, who is with Klaus examining some partially constructed storage sheds along the far wall. He gestures to the other man, pointing at the roofline and indicating for a hammer left on the ground by the builders.

Before I know what's happening, he's knocked out some sort of upright and is repositioning the wood with the absolute authority of a man who knows what he's talking about. I take a seat at a rickety table and chairs and relax back to watch the Cam show. He wields the tools with proficiency, but what did I expect? He tackles everything that way. Confident, taking control, but with enough humility he's in no way arrogant. I watch the way his back, shoulder and arm muscles move and bulge while he works, my eyes glued to his spectacular physique.

In some ways he's a conundrum, in others an uncomplicated man—no agenda, what you see is what you get.

What am I doing with him and why do I feel as if I'm in over my head when this was my idea?

My phone pings for the umpteenth time and I pull it from my pocket with a sigh of regret that I have to look away from Cam's sexy show-and-tell.

It's from my number two back in Sydney. I quickly scan the message, my equilibrium returning at the good news. The lawyers have finished with the paperwork, and the Jensen's deal snatched from under the nose of my father has hit the international financial headlines, the ripple effect so predictable, I can almost see the zeroes at the end of my net worth multiplying. The kick of satisfaction I always feel at a job well done is there, but today it's muted, its potency somehow diminished, as if making money, being the best, proving I, a mere woman, can do anything my brother and father can, no longer holds the same all-consuming appeal.

Perhaps the news would taste sweeter if shared. Perhaps the shine of my success would return if I had some of Cam's balance. Perhaps he's right about me, after all—I don't know how to have fun...

My head jerks up from the screen of my phone in search of him, my good-luck charm. He's striding my way with a Jack Russell in tow. The dog has abandoned the ball and seems content to simply follow him to the ends of the earth.

I swallow hard. I know that feeling. It's the same feeling—dangerous and terrifying—that I get when I open my eyes and find him asleep next to me in the morning.

Cam sits opposite me at the rough wooden table and the dog settles at his feet. 'I'm sorry I'm neglecting you. I got carried away. Some cowboy builder has left the sheds half built and they're not sure if he's going to come back to finish them.' He spots my phone. 'Is it work? Do you need me to take you back into the city?'

I shove my phone away and try not to focus on the attention Cam lavishes on the delighted Jack Russell's ear rub.

Nice one, Orla. Jealous of a dog.

'No, I'm sorry—breaking news in the financial world—money never sleeps.' My attempt at humour, designed to cover my embarrassment that I can't even enjoy half an hour off to be in the moment, falls flat and a chasm opens up between us across the scarred and weathered tabletop.

His quiet scrutiny makes me wince, not that he's judging, but I see acute awareness in his intelligent eyes. He sees me all too thoroughly. And even before he asks, I know his question is coming.

'Can I ask you a personal question? I know we've avoided too many details up to now, but I'm…curious.'

As if sensing the tension radiating from us, my own new doggy friend curls up against my foot and promptly closes her eyes, as if all she's needed this whole time was a warm leg to lean up against while she sleeps.

'Sure, although I reserve the right to not answer.' I keep my voice light-hearted, although my tummy is tight with nerves for what he might ask and, worse, for what I might expose.

One of his big hands stretches across the table and covers my hand, his thumb rubbing back and forth over my knuckles, and I want to curl into him and admit that, just like these dogs, I'm a little lost and in need of a new direction.

But he's not my rock. I don't need a rock. He's not even my boyfriend. I'm just using him for sex.

I shudder inside—I can almost see the grins on the faces of my married girlfriends, hear the cackles of excitement over cocktails and the names they would bandy about if they could see me now—*toy boy, man toy, cougar.* A protective streak slices through me, even as the words *it's not like that* ring hollow in my head. Because it *is* like that—that's what I wanted. Sex on tap. No feelings. No personal details. No consequences.

Was I naive, or just deluding myself, because sex, even sex as hot and liberating as the sex I share with Cam, is bound to come with consequences? And they've already begun. I feel it. He's changing me. Just by knowing him I'm different, more open to new experiences, wanting to challenge myself and emulate the person I'm beginning to admire.

'I just wondered why.' Cam's voice is low, gentle,

as if he doesn't want to spook the slumbering dogs. Or perhaps he's worried about spooking me.

'Why what?'

'Why you work so hard. Why you put in the hours you do. The travel, the lack of sleep. I…' He looks down at the table as if embarrassed. 'I looked you up on the internet. I wanted to know more about you without prying into personal stuff.'

'And what did you discover?' I've been tempted to do the same myself and research him, only every time I open my laptop, work snatches my attention.

'That you're worth a fortune. That you probably don't need to work ever again,' he says.

'Just like you, then.' I wince, scrunch my eyes closed for a second to block out the wounded look on his face, because I already know that was a low blow. He told me it was complicated. He told me his inheritance came with conditions and I know he's come from a very different background.

'Sorry. I didn't mean that.' I try to lift the atmosphere I've created with levity. 'I was kind of hoping you hadn't noticed that I get up in the early hours to work.' I stroke the dog's silky head as I formulate my answer, because for once it doesn't come easily. Cam wants the real answer, not the throwaway flippant version that rolls off the tongue.

No, it's not a crime to be driven. But that's not what he's asking. He wants to know the motivation behind my success beyond wealth and status and security, and that's harder to define or admit, especially when examining too closely what pushes me to be where I am brings up painful emotions.

'I've always worked hard, just like you.' I turn his hand over and rub at the calluses across his palm. He looks up from our hands, answering my smile with a watery one of his own.

He wants more. And, while it's not what we're about, I can't help but give him a piece of myself I don't normally share. With anyone. He's given me so much—his time, his generosity, his joie de vivre. It's as if his energy is contagious.

'When I joined my father's firm after university I felt like I'd found my niche. The work was exciting and everything I wanted in a career, but it was never about the money. I was lucky. I've always had a privileged life. But my father is old school. When he talked about succession planning I felt confident I'd be the next CEO. I'm the eldest. I worked hard for him for five years.'

I look away, watch the dogs roam and sniff, the remembered betrayal tightening my throat. 'When he overlooked me in favour of my younger brother I realised I had no choice but to leave and start my own firm from scratch. Ever since then, I've put in the hours, but the difference is I'm doing it for myself.'

It sounds so shallow, so single-minded, that a new wave of defensiveness courses though me, although he's in no way attacking, just asking in his gentle, insightful way. But I rear back from the vulnerable place I've exposed with my confession, bringing my motivations back to general rather than personal drivers. 'And it's a competitive field—I didn't get to the top without working harder and longer than anyone else.' I shrug. 'Some sacrifices are inevitable.'

He nods, his mouth a flat line, and even though he's still I sense the tension coiling in him. His thumb resumes its hypnotic swiping. 'You mentioned you're divorced. Was your marriage one of those sacrifices?' There's no censure in his expression, but his eyes are hard and the reminder of my failure forces heat to my face.

'For my part, I rushed into that marriage without loving Mark. For his part, Mark thought he was fully evolved, but at the end of the day he didn't want a wife who worked as much as he did, and I can't say I blame him. I guess he expected I'd change after the honeymoon. Perhaps he wanted his shirts laundered and a prop on his arm to make him look good.'

'Don't you know? Didn't you ask?'

I swallow hard, admitting, not for the first time, that my emotional distance, a trait I learned from a lifetime of trying to meet my father's standards, likely contributed to the breakdown of my marriage. 'No, I guess I wasn't any good at being the kind of wife he needed.'

Cam's fingers flex into mine in silent support. 'Couldn't he launder his own shirts?'

I shrug and laugh at the image of my ex working a washing machine or an iron. 'He's happily remarried now.' I swallow hard, old bitterness foul-tasting. Perhaps if I hadn't been so caught up in proving my worth to my father, in trying to project an image of having it all, I might have evaluated my relationship with Mark more thoroughly. 'I'm happy with my decision. He's happier married to someone else. And I learned a valuable lesson—I'm good at what I do. That's nothing to be apologetic for.'

'Absolutely not. Mark sounds like an asshole who didn't know what he had, if you don't mind my saying.' He smiles that secret smile he uses in the bedroom, the one that makes me forget I'm older than him.

'Thanks, but I played my part. I'm sure I wasn't easy to be married to. You said yourself, I'm always working.'

He shakes his head. 'You're not working now, and it sounds like he had expectations you had no desire to fulfil—good on you. You're a person, not a puppet. No one likes to feel they're being controlled.' He's more animated now, his eyes ablaze with defiance, as if my confession has pricked some wound inside him. Easygoing, carefree Cam has his own demons.

Who doesn't?

'You were probably that way when he met you, right?'

I nod.

'So he was arrogant enough to want to change you, to squeeze you into some mould, to try to make you perform to his expectations.'

'I guess, although I have to take my share of the responsibility—I'm pretty stubborn. As you've witnessed, I push myself hard, without compromise, something I learned from my upbringing. And at the end of the day, marriages—the ones that last—are about compromise. I guess Mark and I both failed. If you know anything about me already, it's that failure doesn't sit well with me, which is why I'm single. That's why what we're doing suits me perfectly—we get all the good bits of a relationship like spending time together, having fun, amazing sex, without all the heavy stuff.'

'Lucky me,' he says with a wink, and I know he's letting me off the hook. That my confession is enough to satisfy his curiosity about the woman he's sharing a bed with, for now.

'Lucky me, too.' I look down at our hands, moved by his solid, refreshing presence in my life, albeit temporarily. I want him to know that I appreciate him and everything he does to enrich our time together, even if I'm not always present in the moment.

'Thanks for this. The dogs. For taking the time to organise everything—the clothes, the opera, the skiing.'

'Wait until you see what I have planned for Dubai.' He winks.

'I'm serious, Cam—thanks for bringing me here. You were right. It was just what I needed.' I bend down to stroke the coat of the sleeping beagle cross, wishing I could take her home, to a home I'm hardly ever at myself.

'Want to go back to the hotel and remind ourselves how clever we are to have come up with such a perfect situation?' I ask, shying away from pressing him for his own secrets, telling myself that, despite my confession, this is still about sex.

'Absolutely. Sounds like the next best plan short of adopting all these dogs and transporting them home to Sydney in the jet.' He grins and tugs me to my feet, slipping his hand into the pocket over my ass as we head inside, a trail of dogs in pursuit.

I laugh nervously. Knowing Cam, he just might do something that awesome.

CHAPTER SIX

Cam

I LOOSEN THE bow tie around my throat and roll up my shirtsleeves. I went all out tonight with the full tux. For Orla. I reserved the M Club box at the Zurich Opera House, and just as I predicted she looked sensational in the green beaded gown, so I felt compelled to play my part, even if it meant dressing like a trussed-up penguin.

I pour a glass of chilled white wine and loosen the top few buttons of my shirt, tempted to strip off completely and join her in the bath. But she looks beat. Perhaps I'm pushing the after-work agenda too hard. Now I understand why she's as driven as she is, everything makes sense. She pushes herself, almost as if she still has something to prove to her traditional father and perhaps even her ex-husband. Neither of whom seem to have any concept of her true worth.

She made light of it but she's proud. I understand the emotion. Her failed marriage bothers her, not for the man himself, but in the sense that she sees it as a black mark on her track record, perhaps even uses it as a reason to avoid getting involved in another relationship.

Not that I should care outside of the fact some asshole might have hurt her, although it seems I need look no further than her own father to find the source of *that* damage. Who behaves that way in this day and age? Fuck, I thought my father was bad, but at least he simply took off. At least he didn't stick around to inflict daily damage on my self-esteem. At least I don't have to prove a damn thing to the man.

Of course she's driven by success, of course she needs the success. Somehow it's all tied up in her self-validation. But to what degree? Could she loosen the reins, live a more balanced life and still be herself?

I scrub a hand through my hair, gutted that my instincts about her, about our differences, were spot-on the money. I proved myself correct at the dog sanctuary. I'd expected her to be more delighted. Of course, she embraced the visit, even hefting in a sack of dog food like it weighed no more than the designer handbags she loves. But I spied the sneaky looks at her phone, the way she checked her watch as if she had somewhere else to be. She couldn't relax, couldn't take off her CEO hat for even a couple of hours.

Not that it should matter. I should focus on the end game, focus on the trip we're taking together, focus on having a good time at my father's expense. Isn't that why I agreed to come along for the ride?

But my aimless bender no longer holds the same appeal, not now I've met Orla.

I snag a beer for myself and return to the bathroom with her glass of wine, my own personal dilemmas tucked neatly away behind my smile. Orla looks more relaxed than I've ever seen her, and I suffer a sharp pang of regret at how hard I pushed her to divulge personal details earlier, especially when I'm such a closed book, literally changing the subject every time she probes a bit too close.

I place the glass on the side of the bath and pull up a chair, taking a long draw of my ice-cold beer.

'Cam, stop spoiling me. I might get used to it and chain you to my bedpost.'

I grin—I wouldn't put it past her. At least we work sexually. No problems on that score.

'I wouldn't complain, as long as I get to see this sensational body naked every day.'

Without moving from her relaxed wallow, she holds out her hand for my beer. I hand it over, my eyebrows raised in mock censure. She's taken to stealing a sip every time I open a bottle.

'What?' she asks, tilting the bottle to her pursed lips for a swallow. 'I'm just trying them out until I find one I love. Don't be stingy.' She takes a second swallow and hands the beer back with a contented sigh.

I grin, my insides on fire for her and the way she makes me feel, like the best version of myself. 'I don't care. You can drink all my beer. It's just…funny.' Funny, sexy, comfortable. 'Who'd have thought when we met in that casino that the stunning, classy woman drinking single malt alone would like a regular old beer in the bath?'

'You should never judge a book by its cover, Cam. Haven't I proved there's more to me than the uptight princess I know you had me pegged for the first time we met?'

I laugh, heat for her burning out of control. She gets me as much as I get her. I want to be a better man when I'm around her. I want us to fit outside the bedroom. But could we? Seriously?

I place the beer bottle on the floor. 'Drink your wine, princess.' I wink, trailing one hand along her soapy thigh, down her slender calf. At her soft sigh, I lift her foot from below the surface of the water so I can press my thumbs into the sole of her foot, one after another in a slow, rhythmic massage, because I want to touch her. All the time.

Her head lolls back on the edge of the bath, and her toes curl. 'Mmm...you are so good at that—another skill to add to the list. Is there nothing you can't do?' she says without opening her eyes.

'I feel the same way about you.' Having her by my side, persuading her to travel in style and play hard, and the way she's embracing the sexual adventure too—we understand each other. Just her presence makes me feel like I'll figure out my own dilemma over the money. Like it's not as big a deal as I'd fanned it up to be. Like anything is possible.

The pretty constant resentment and bitterness I've

had since the summons to the solicitor's office back in Sydney wanes. If only I could bottle the Orla feeling.

'A good foot massage will help you sleep,' I say, my mouth twitching because I know as soon as she leaves this bath I'm getting lucky, despite her long day. When we returned from the dog shelter she was visibly deflated to find all the purchases I'd made, including the intimate M Club gift, cleared away, out of sight. She mentioned twice at the opera that I'd promised her a reward for her patience. She's so fully embracing her sexually adventurous side; I wanted to strip her there and then. But I promised her a night at the opera and a relaxing bath, and I'm a man of my word.

She looks up, her eyelids heavy but in that turned-on way that tells me she has other plans before sleep. 'What if I'm not tired? What if I feel like squeezing a little more enjoyment out of the day?'

I hide my smile. I've created a monster.

'I thought you'd rescheduled your meeting for seven a.m. I don't want you to be too exhausted to enjoy the slopes tomorrow.'

'Cam…' Her eyes stray closed as if she's enjoying my foot massage, but there's a hint of warning in her voice. 'You'll be using that vibrator on me before we sleep. No getting out of it. Or I'll use it myself and force you to watch.'

'Yes, ma'am,' I say. 'Such hardships I have to endure as your plaything…' I release her foot and lift the other one from the water, subjecting it to the same treatment.

After a few seconds she reopens her eyes, which had fluttered closed on a contented moan the minute I pressed my thumbs to her instep.

'Cam?'

'Yes, Orla.'

'Have *you* ever been in a serious relationship?' She takes a sip of wine and watches my face from over the rim of her glass. This is payback for my bout of curiosity earlier. But I couldn't stay silent any longer. She works practically twenty-four-seven. Her travel schedule is punishing—I know she's allowed me to add a few days here and there for extras, but what's the point of visiting all these countries if you're too busy to enjoy what they have to offer? What's the point of earning the kind of money she makes when she's never in one place long enough to spend any of it?

I allow her foot to sink back below the surface of the water and reach for a sponge and a bottle of body wash. 'Not really. I've had girlfriends off and on. But I'm in no hurry to settle down.'

'So you've never been in love, then? Never met your perfect woman?' With any other woman I'd assume she was fishing. But not Orla. She's made it clear she's done the marriage thing. Done it and failed. Effectively crossed it off her list.

'Not sure I believe in love—I watched it all but destroy my mother, so, like you, I'm pretty sceptical.'

Her smile is small, her eyes searching. 'See—I told you we're perfect for each other.'

Yeah, perfect but temporary. The clock is ticking

on our arrangement. By the time we reach Sydney I need to have some sort of definitive plan outside of using our sexual relationship to help me forget, because going back to pretending the inheritance doesn't exist isn't an option and spending it will take three lifetimes...

Orla sobers, her eyes searching. 'What happened with your parents?' Her voice is low, whispered, as if I'm already giving off an injured-animal vibe.

I suck in a deep breath and stand, moving behind her to slide the soapy sponge over her shoulders and the back of her neck, which is exposed, her hair piled up in a messy topknot.

I'm literally hiding, but I need cover. Talking about my mother, the grief and anger when I think about how she pined for my father, still tightens my throat so I feel like I can't breathe.

'My father left her for greener pastures. I was three.'

I hear her gasp, but I ignore it and slide the sponge around first to her clavicle and the top of her breast, and then I sweep it down one arm.

When I reach the back of her hand with the sponge she grips my fingers, squeezing. She's silent for a beat or two and I think I'm out of the woods. No such luck.

'That must have been really hard on her. And you.'

'Not really. I don't remember him ever being there.'

She releases my hand, as if she can sense my discomfort. It's hard to feel her touch, something I associate only with pleasure, and think about the worst parts of my past in the same heartbeat.

'Was it another woman?' she asks.

I really want to distract her, to drag her from the bath and make her forget her inquisitiveness, pleasure her into silence. But she's relaxed, and she deserves some answers after my days of vagueness, hedging and changing the subject.

'No—he remarried eventually, but money was his mistress. He bought a tech company at the right time, invested heavily and got lucky, making lots of what he loved—money. And, as you know, money makes money.' I sigh, my anguish over his last will and testament undoing what an evening with Orla had accomplished. 'At the end of the day he loved money more than he loved his wife and kid.'

'Did your mother remarry? Did you have a stepfather? You talked about how the drumming helping you through your teens.'

'No. It was just the two of us.' My answer sounds harsh, echoing around the tiled room. But further explanation sticks in my throat. Does she really want details? Is she truly longing to hear that my mother worked two jobs to make sure I was fed? That she pawned her wedding ring to buy me my first bike? That she never stopped loving a man who chose the pursuit of wealth over her, so much so that she never once chased him for a single cent towards raising me?

As if sensing the rage building inside me, coiling my muscles to snapping point, she doesn't press for more details. 'Well, she raised a fine man in you. Are you still close to her?'

'She died a year ago. Cancer.' I deflate. What is the point of harbouring hatred for a man when they're both gone? What's the point of my regret? It won't bring either of them back—him so I can toss his damned money back in his face and her so I can try to convince her he wasn't worth her love.

'I'm sorry,' whispers Orla.

I've stopped washing her, too caught up in useless emotions. I move around to the other side of the bath, performing the same moves with the sponge down the opposite arm. But now she's probed, the words come a little easier. 'To that day I think she still loved him. That's why I can never forgive him.'

'I don't blame you—it must have been very hard for you to watch. Hard for you to grow up without a father. I'm so sorry to hear about your mother, Cam.' This time when she grips my hand she tugs me forward and sits up in the bath, so I have to slap on a mask to hide the resurgence of resentment from my face.

'You know, it's not the same, but my father was pretty absent too. He worked long hours, and even when he was home he never seemed interested in me, what I'd done at school or that I'd passed a piano exam or joined the school choir.' She laughs, a humourless snort. 'He always made time for my brother's sporting events though. Funny, that.'

We stare, fragile threads of memories and the emotions they bring connecting us.

'Have you told your father that you feel that he wasn't

there for you growing up?' she says, her voice barely above a whisper.

Every muscle in my body tightens. Even if I could reach out, there's no room in me for forgiveness. Not for what he did to my mother, or for how he tried to control me from the grave with his beloved money.

'Have you told yours?' I say, the venom in my voice shocking us both.

She looks down and I swear under my breath, tilting her chin back up so she can see the sincerity of my apology. 'I'm sorry. Look... I...I never really cared that he wasn't around for myself. If my mother had been happy, I doubt I'd have given him a second thought.'

Ah, the lies we tell ourselves...

I focus my anger. 'He treated my mother worse. And anyway, it's all in the past. He's dead too. Six months after her—ironic, right?' I take a deep breath, too close to every feeling I've battled to contain these past six months—my entire adult life, if I'm being honest. And, despite her relationship with her own emotionally distant father, we're different enough without my tales of woe, my sad little poor-boy-turned-billionaire sob-story.

Her intelligent eyes latch on to mine. 'Is the inheritance from—'

I cover her mouth with my fingers. 'Enough.' Of course she would make the leap. She's smart. But I don't want to talk about my father's legacy. The legacy I'm working day and night to forget because of what it represents.

'I thought we were keeping the details out of this—just sex…?' The words taste jagged because I'm a hypocrite. I care about her—why else would I take her to see rescue dogs, worry about her burning herself out with work and lavish her with gifts? Because I like the way she looks in green? Because I enjoy seeing her sensational figure clothed in everything from a simple T-shirt to the sexiest lingerie?

But caring isn't allowed. More than sex is a fool's game. She knows that and so do I.

My own reminder of our boundaries helps me back to safety. This is sex. No matter how she makes me feel, or how much I enjoy her company outside of the bedroom. No matter how her stare seems to penetrate, her intelligent eyes stripping me bare. I'm here for one reason only—enjoyment. Well, two if you count my own personal goal to spend as much money as I can, a goal on which I should refocus my attention and forget about crazy ideas like testing Orla's suitability as a potential partner. Because she's not mine. She's not interested in anything beyond the good time we have together.

It's a dream scenario for any guy…

'Ready to get out?' I ask, because she wants this to be about sex—on-tap sex—and right now that's the only thing that will chase away my demons.

At her nod, I tug her hand and she rises from the water, rivulets of foam sliding over her perfect skin. She meets my eyes and I see empathy in the depths of her stare. She knows I'm hiding something bigger than me. She knows I'm a coward, but she sticks to our nothing-personal rule and offers me an out clause.

My hand still holds the sponge. She guides me to wash her breasts and her stomach, only releasing my hand when she's pressed it between her legs so she can grip both my shoulders while she rides my hand and the sponge with undulations of her hips.

'Cam,' she whispers, her eyes on mine. 'Let's get lost together.'

I don't need a second invitation. I toss the sponge and lift her from the bath, snagging a towel on my way out of the bathroom. In the bedroom I deposit her on her feet and slide the towel over every inch of her skin until she's dry, by which time my erection is painfully hard and straining behind my fly. But I don't touch her, nor do I give her my mouth, which is what she wants, her head lifting to mine every time I move close, her lips seeking the kisses that make her moan.

I hold my own body taut to prevent me from swaying her way. I've got this. I'm here for the sex. I can control the sex. She likes being nudged to explore her sexual boundaries, but beyond that...

There is no beyond.

'Go to the wardrobe and get the M Club box,' I say, my voice tight with longing. Yes, the urge to be close to her, to be buried inside, to kiss her into silence, is as strong as ever, but there's a new driving force in me tonight. A dangerous force—to be more to her than her sex toy. To gain her trust, to hear her acknowledgement that I'm not like the men of her past, men who've betrayed her, underestimated her, overlooked her. That I'm different.

I swallow hard. It's just sex. That's all she wants from me.

Her eyes flare with excitement and she sashays to the wardrobe, loosening her hair from its messy bun as she goes. I'm momentarily lost in the sight of the sway of her heart-shaped ass, but then she's back before me, a sexy smile of challenge on her face. 'Now what?'

I take the box. 'Lie on the bed.'

She obeys, her movements slow and sensual as if she wants to put on a show for my eyes only. As if she knows she's driving me mad, pushing me every inch as far as I push her. Because she's right. Maybe we do both need to get lost, and this is the best way.

With hands that could tremble from the adrenaline surging in me, if I wasn't wound so tightly, I deposit the box beside her feet and strip my shirt overhead, tossing it onto a nearby chair. Her teeth scrape over her bottom lip and her eyes follow my every move. I retrieve a bottle of lube, watching every subtle nuance of her reaction when she sees what it is.

She's excited, her chest rising and falling rapidly, and like the impatient, self-sufficient woman she is, not content to wait, she slips her hand between her thighs to touch herself.

I place the lube next to the box and take off my dress trousers and boxers, my eyes glued to her hand working her clit. 'Don't come. Not yet.' I stand over her, scooping her head up from the bed by the back of her neck so

I can angle her mouth up to mine. I kiss her until we're both panting and then I break free.

'Fuck, you're so sexy. I want to take you to a place no one else has. I want you to remember me, just like, when this is over, I'll never forget you.'

I have no idea where that comes from, but I accept its truth. It's too late to take it back anyway.

'Yes. Cam, yes.'

So she feels it too, that we're skirting dangerous territory. That, if we're not careful, our feelings could become all snared up in this thing we've started. But neither of us has room in our lives for that complication.

I flip the box open and reach inside for the vibrator. 'Tell me to stop if this gets too intense, okay?' I flick the hidden switch so the device emits a barely audible hum. 'Lie back.'

She listens, abandoning pleasuring herself to sprawl back on the satin bedspread with her arms slung casually over her head.

Perfect.

Splayed out for our pleasure.

I lean over and kiss her, my tongue duelling with the push and slide of hers until she's panting and writhing once more. Then I touch the tip of the vibrator to one of her nipples. She arches off the bed, a ragged moan torn from her throat. I break free from the kiss to watch my handiwork, sliding the toy to the other nipple in order to drag out another whimper.

'Open your mouth.' I trail the black phallus over the

curve of her breast and along her breastbone. Her lips part and I slide the tip past to her waiting tongue, which she laves seductively over the toy before wrapping her mouth around the shaft.

The sight is so erotic, I take my cock in my free hand, offering it a few lazy tugs in appeasement for the torture I'm putting us through. Orla watches me, her eyes widening, but then she abandons the toy and reaches for my hips, tugging me forward and over her so she can take the head of my cock into her mouth in place of the vibrator.

I grit my teeth, grunt a few unintelligible curses and then slide the now wet toy back to her nipple. But I'm done teasing us. With a groan of protest I pull back and position myself between her thighs. I lap at her clit, sliding the vibrating toy up and down her inner thigh as I do to stimulate as many nerves as I can.

Orla grips my head, her fingers twisting and tugging. I keep the suction on her clit slow and subtle while I work the head of the sex toy inside her tight pussy, plunging and mimicking what my own body is desperate to do. But not yet. I have plans. Plans I hope will lead us one step closer to our end goal.

While I keep up the tonguing of her clit, I discard the vibrator and reach for the lube and butt plug.

Sensing my movements, Orla lifts her head from the bed and looks down.

I pull back, needing to hear her confirmation. 'Do you still want this?'

'Yes.' No hesitation, just a blaze of challenge burning through the desire in her beautiful green eyes.

'Do you trust me?' I'm a fool, I know, but her answer matters more than just physical oblivion.

'Yes, oh, Cam, yes.'

I slide my tongue over her opening back to the tight bud while I slather the plug with lube. But Orla's not content to lie back and simply feel. She settles on her elbows and watches me, her mewls and moans of encouragement a guide to her pleasure.

When her hips begin to buck and her hands grow greedy, tugging on my hair as she rides my face, I press the tip of the plug to her rear. It's small and she's so close, it slides in with minimal resistance, but her moans grow to cries of pleasure and my beautiful, sexy Orla starts to chant my name like a prayer, filling my head and my chest and the parts of me that want more than her body with euphoria.

I keep up the suction on her clit, adding slow twists of the plug, while I watch her face with rapt attention, seeing every streak of pleasure. That she trusts me with her body, with her act of sexual exploration, resets my priorities. I can be myself with her; like this we're just a man and a woman enjoying our near violent chemistry.

No amount of money, extravagant spending or working can re-create this feeling. This is real.

She may have had her fingers burnt in the past, she may not want a relationship, but now she's embracing her sexy side. Hell, I've lost count of who's challenging whom here, because she's almost more woman than I can handle.

With one last twist, one last flick of her clit, she comes, her neck arched back on a long cry that I'm worried will cause complaints. But then I'm past caring because she collapses back onto the bed, tugging me down on top of her and spreading her legs wide to accommodate my hips. She holds my face between both palms, pressing kisses to my mouth as I hold my weight on my arms, braced over her.

'Thank you.'

I smile. 'What for?'

'You know what for. That was…oh…incredible.'

My ego inflates. I press a gentle kiss on her lips, overcome by tenderness for this dauntless, exceptional woman. She lifts her legs and crosses her ankles in the small of my back, her eyes widening with renewed sensations as she moves with the plug in situ.

The tip of my cock slides between her lips and I wince at the sharp burst of pleasure. 'Want me to take it out?'

She shakes her head and tilts her hips so I'm engulfed in her heat. 'No. I want you, Cam, now.'

I roll my hips forward, working my way inside, the tightness enough to make my eyes roll back, but I find her slick, swollen clit with my thumb and rub out any discomfort she might feel at the dual penetration.

'You okay?' I bite out, taking it as slowly as humanly possible. And I am only human, never more so than when I'm with this woman, who makes me feel exposed, and vulnerable, and ten feet tall all in the same heartbeat.

'Yes, better than okay. You?'

I groan against the side of her neck, placing a tender kiss there where her skin smells fantastic—pure Orla. 'You have no idea.'

She presses her mouth to mine, a strange intensity on her face, and she doesn't stop kissing me until we come, me seconds after her, wondering how in the world I'm ever going to get enough of Orla Hendricks.

CHAPTER SEVEN

Orla

I LOOK AWAY from the view of the Persian Gulf from my office window in Dubai's International Financial Centre and try to refocus on the business proposal on the computer screen when all I can see is Cam's face, his sexy, playful grin and his sparkly eyes, which always seem alight with animation.

Somewhere between leaving Zurich after our thrilling heli-skiing trip and arriving in Dubai, I've experienced a seismic shift—I can't seem to get Cam off my mind, as my current daydream proves. It's almost as if my mind is sick of numbers and craves the intrusion. As if he's there because he belongs. Because I want his presence in more than my bed. But that's crazy…

Is it because he finally opened up to me, telling me about his loss and his childhood, which must have been far removed from my own? Is it because seeing his pain, filling in the gaps, makes me desperate to help him overcome the issues holding him back? I'm certain it was his father who left him the inheritance. The timeline fits, and the fact that he doesn't seem to care if he loses every cent. That money represents more than a life-changing windfall. For him, it's tainted, tangled up in rejection and pain and resentment. Even when he seems to be enjoying it, living a lifestyle most people would jump at in a heartbeat, deep down I'm certain Cam would be equally happy to return to his life before.

Cam's in pain. He's hurting. The big-spending gambler I first met is far removed from the real Cam North. The real Cam gives a wicked foot massage. The real Cam takes the time to talk and, more importantly, to really listen. The real Cam is a roll-up-your-sleeves kind of man: a man who loves the simple things in life—an ice-cold beer on a sunny day, a view of the sunset, throwing a ball for a delighted dog.

As fascinating and addictive as he is complex.

I push away from my desk in self-disgust, admitting my productivity is done for the day, and head to the hotel for a shower. As I turn on the water, tie up my hair and strip off, I berate myself further. It's one thing to care about the wonderful, thoughtful and capable man I'm sleeping with—after all, I'm not a robot, despite what my ex-husband thinks—but to allow it to interfere with my work?

I've never once struggled with focus before, so why now? And why to this degree? There could be any number of explanations: jet lag, too much of what Cam likes to call *playing hard*, the pesky burn-out, which seems to be getting stronger, not lessening as I'd hoped.

But I suspect it's just Cam. Clearly I underestimated

how much of a distraction a man like him could be—stupid, stupid Orla.

Thinking about him has an inevitable effect on my body and I turn the water to cool to douse the reaction. Perhaps there's such a thing as too much sex? If we're not screwing, which is at least a twice-a-day occurrence, we're teasing each other, whispering, sharing stolen secret glances, a torturous form of foreplay.

I step under the spray and lather my body with divine-smelling body wash. If only I could wash my confused and intrusive feelings away with the suds. Because they have no place here. This was never for keeps. Thanks to my father, my ex and my own high expectations, I'm just not emotionally built for relationships.

Why is this so hard, when I've never before struggled to compartmentalise sex? I can blame physical exhaustion. Between my own punishing schedule, the inability to keep our hands off each other and always exploring somewhere Cam deems essential, it's no wonder I can't think straight.

The last few days have been a whirlwind. An ice bar on our last night in Zurich, dinner last night on the one hundred and twentieth floor of the Burj Khalifa, the world's tallest tower, and, as today is opening day at the Meydan racecourse, we're due to spend an evening at the races.

Despite my cold-shower distraction technique, waves of anticipation move over my skin—he'll be here any minute. It's as if my body has a sixth sense: Cam detection. Perhaps he'll look for me and join me in the shower. But even as I feel the flutter of excitement low in my belly, I probe my feelings deeper. Yes, the sex is amazing. Yes, he brings out some sort of lust-craved wanton in me—who could resist such virile and enthusiastic attention? But he's more than that; he puts my life into perspective. When I'm with him I almost forget that I'm Orla Hendricks, CEO. The bitterness I feel towards my father seems irrelevant and trivial. I don't care about proving myself worthy. I don't care about being the best. I can simply exist. No need to strive to be anything other than myself.

A woman to his man.

My sigh is shaky, tinged with fear.

Oh, no… No, I can't do this. I can't feel the things I'm feeling. Not for him, not for anyone. I swallow, forcing myself to be brutally honest. Despite the age gap and my determination to avoid relationships, Cam is exactly the sort of man I could fall for, and that's bad.

B.A.D.

I freeze, the realisation of how dangerous Cam is to my resolve a shock, as if the water had turned instantly icy. Then I laugh aloud, although the sound is hollow and unconvincing. We're too different. Cam would no more think of me as a relationship candidate than I would think of him, in our normal, everyday lives. He's twenty-eight years old. I'll be thirty-seven in a few months.

It's ridiculous.

Even if I *wanted* a relationship, we'd never work. Deep down he's a solid, steady, dependable man who says it like it is. I'm a hustler. I always need to be moving, striving, ticking off the next goal.

I try to visualise introducing Cam to my Sydney girlfriends over brunch, or picture him being content to see his woman once in a blue moon, if the stars align. My washing movements become slow, automatic, as I'm lost to the pictures my imaginings paint, as if they're tantalising in their reality. I've never asked him, but surely Cam wants a wife and a family one day. I've long since sworn off such trappings, finding contentment in the one thing I'm good at: my career, making money for my clients and for myself along the way.

But is that enough any more? Can I go back to my sad, workaholic existence after Cam?

I slam off the shower spray, my irritation directed at my flights of fancy.

Of course I can. I'm set in my ways. This is my life, a great life I've built—self-sufficient, independent, successful. I'll move on from my fling with Cam, just as I moved on from my marriage to Mark.

With my equilibrium restored by my harsh mental pep talk, I dry off and put on the modest green silk dress with buttons down the front that I've chosen for the races. I apply light make-up and slip on nude strappy sandals with a low heel.

When I emerge from the en suite bathroom, Cam is sprawled over the leather sofa near the window. I come to an abrupt halt, my eyes sucking in the sight of him, as if they know time is running out and one day he'll only be visible in my memory.

He too is dressed in smart-casual attire for the races—chinos, a shirt and tie, and a blazer. His hair is tamed, slicked back from his handsome face with product, and he's focused on the screen of his phone, his brows dipped in an act of concentration that should make him look adorable, if he wasn't too much man for that particular adjective.

My stomach clenches at the sight of him, sexy, suave and in his prime, the epitome of masculinity. I tug my bottom lip under my teeth and close my eyes for a decadent second, remembering the way he woke me this morning before my alarm. Sleepy, warm and demanding, he'd dragged me close with one strong arm, spooning me from behind. As I nodded and smiled in agreement, his hot mouth had found my nipple and I'd arched against him until he'd seated himself inside me from behind—a perfect position for Cam to toy with my clit until I climaxed and he'd achieved the unforgettable wake-up call he'd wanted.

For some reason I kept my eyes closed throughout, and we didn't speak, because it somehow felt different—slow, sensual, reverent—almost as if we were making love.

I shake the alarming thought from my head and clear my throat to alert Cam to my presence.

He looks up. A grin stretches over his face, but his eyes are hot, just like every other time he looks at me: full of promise, provocative, and deeply piercing, as if he sees me to my soul.

I approach, my legs shakier than they should be,

given the stern lecture I'd only moments ago administered to myself. Cam stands, the perfect gentleman. I accept his hungry kiss, returning it with my own. It's as if we've been separated for years, not hours, but with his mouth on mine it's hard to overthink, so I simply surrender to the moment.

When we part, the exposed, unfocused feeling I've experienced for the past few days intensifies, so I reach for his phone to distract myself.

'What has you so absorbed that you didn't hear me come in?' I expect to find a list of statistics for today's thoroughbreds, but instead I see pictures of a shabby-looking cottage, the paint peeling, the steel roof warped and the veranda partially collapsed where the boards have rotted.

'What's this?' I flick through the pictures. The views are enviable, but the house is a mess.

Cam shrugs, his expression wary. 'A cottage. I bought it a while ago. Before the money. To renovate.'

It can't be larger than a hundred square metres. And the ceilings are low. 'Do you plan to live here? You'll be constantly bumping your head.' He's already told me he owns a Point Piper penthouse with harbour views back in Sydney.

At my confused expression, he takes the phone from me and scrolls through the pictures, as if showing off a prized possession. 'I'm not sure. Perhaps. It's in an amazing location. Look at the views.'

I nod. He's right—this cottage commands an enviable spot on Sydney's North Shore.

'My mother grew up close by. After she moved away, we'd go back to her favourite spots for picnics or to the beach. She always admired this cottage, and when the elderly owner passed away I purchased it. For her.' His face falls and he tucks the phone into his breast pocket. 'She died before I could make a dent in the work it needs.'

My heart clenches, the urge to hold him and chase away the defeat in his eyes intense. 'But you're going to finish it anyway? Earn yourself a few splinters and build up a sweat?'

He grins because I understand him. It's almost a tribute. My chest burns with empathy. I touch his arm, wanting to do more, but too afraid of the feelings I've battled all day.

'Yeah, once I'm back in Sydney. Mum was right—it could be perfect.'

I take his hand and lead us back to the sofa, where I tug him down at my side. 'How much work have you done?'

His enthusiasm falters. 'Not that much. I bought it before the inheritance with my savings. It made Mum's last weeks happier to think of me one day living in the cottage she admired from afar.'

My throat aches for his loss, the desire to be there for him building until I confess something I rarely allow myself to think, let alone say aloud. 'You know, I often wonder what it would be like to live somewhere like that.'

Surprise flitters across his face. 'You do...?' A small, almost delighted smile kicks up his mouth.

'Yeah. How peaceful it would be to wake up to the sound of the sea every morning. To step outside before the sun is fully up and drink coffee on a quaint old veranda like that, taste the salt in the air. Simple. Everything I need. To be...content, I guess.'

His silence and the frown that steals his smile and draws his thick eyebrows down over his eyes make me feel self-conscious. He stares, as if seeing me for the first time.

My face grows hot. I've revealed something from deep inside, a place I hardly ever delve. I want to stuff the telling words back inside my mouth. Instead I stand, collect my bag and the wide-brimmed hat that matches my outfit, and breathe my emotions back under control. What is he doing to me? Where did that insane and impractical confession come from? I have a perfectly adequate penthouse in Sydney with its own enviable views. Not that I spend much time there.

I wait for him to join me near the door, my shoulders tense as if I'm anticipating his next words.

'You know, you could live like that, Orla. There's nothing to stop you.' His words are predictable, his tone mild, but the subtext is loaded with the unspoken. If I were that content woman, then perhaps there'd be a chance for us, or perhaps that's just what I want to hear because maybe the appeal of that cottage, that life, is that it would include Cam.

But I can't want that, to be his woman. It's a dead-end fantasy.

'I know.' My clipped tone closes down this alarming conversation, but I soften it to say, 'You should finish the cottage, Cam. I can tell it's going to be beautiful. Shall we go?'

He accepts my change of subject, although there's an undercurrent of unease between us on the journey to the racecourse in another of the sleek sports cars Cam loves. It's as if we're both wearing armour on top of our clothes. As if we need protection from each other, when prior to today everything was easy and open.

We park in the VIP car park and enter the grandstand, which is over a mile long and houses not only the immaculate racetrack, but also a trackside hotel and entertainment venue. I'm relatively well-known among Dubai's business community, so I introduce Cam to some clients and local dignitaries. I'm deep in conversation with a former client who wants to talk shop when I sense Cam's edginess. The unfamiliar taste of guilt makes me wince as I try to fight my first reaction to become defensive. I'm not used to having to explain my actions to anyone. But I'm supposed to be off the clock. This is supposed to be a social event.

He's right; I never stop. I'm never off the clock. My stomach twists, a strange mix of resentment for the life I chose and longing for something more. I shoot him an apologetic look and wrap up my consultation as politely as I can, reassuring the sheikh I'll see him before I leave Dubai.

'I'm sorry,' I say when I've escaped. 'He's a very good customer and he prefers to work with the top dog, not the very competent minions.'

Cam's expression is free of judgement, but I hear the censure from inside my own head. *Don't you want more than work?*

'I'm not surprised. She's beautiful and talented—it's almost a shame there's only one of her...' He smiles, and I slip into the comfort of his arms, because I'm less sure of my life plan than I was yesterday.

We head to our private suite with a terrace overlooking the racetrack. It's a perfect day for the races, although I'm glad for the air-conditioning of our suite. As it's the first race of the season, the grandstand is packed with spectators. We can't bet, but our waiter informs us there are several competitions running for correctly guessing the place-getters. I choose the three horses with names that appeal the most—Desert Haze, Buyer Beware and Human Condition—knowing nothing about their pedigrees, owners or trainers, but Cam seems more interested in the pre-race action at the edge of the track.

'There he is.' He hands me a pair of binoculars and points in the general direction of the milling jockeys and horses.

'Who?'

'My horse—number seven.' He slips his arm around my waist and tugs me close, his enthusiasm a distraction I need.

I focus in on the thoroughbred—a magnificent chestnut stallion—the jockey bedecked in red and gold. 'Did you place an offshore bet?' Of course Cam would find a way to offload some cash in a country where gambling is illegal.

'No.' He sounds so pleased with himself, I take a good hard look at his face, which is wreathed in smug excitement. 'I bought him. He's mine. Contempt of Court—isn't he perfect?'

Unease dries my mouth as I take another look at Cam's latest purchase. It doesn't matter. I should let it go. I don't want to spoil our evening, but really? A racehorse?

'How long have you owned him?' I hedge, hoping to discover it's a lifelong dream of his or a regular hobby. But the hair rising at the back of my neck tells me I'm unlikely to be comforted by his answer.

'A week. When I knew Dubai was on your itinerary, I put out some feelers. He was already registered for the race, the name is perfect, so I offered the owner a number he couldn't refuse.' He takes two glasses of champagne from our waiter and hands me one, clinking his glass to mine with a grin.

I stare, a shudder passing through me at how much a thoroughbred already registered for one of the world's richest races must have cost. It's none of my business, he's hardly bankrupting himself, and I'll damage the fragile mood between us, but I can't stay silent. On the surface he's enjoying his inheritance, yes, but deep down it's because he doesn't care about the money, which makes sense if it's from his father.

'So you bought an expensive racehorse just for his name?'

He sees the disapproval I'm trying, and clearly failing, to hide. 'I bought him because I could—the name was an added bonus. And I knew you wouldn't approve.'

'You're right, I'm…cautious with my money, but it's not that I don't approve.'

'What, then? We're here to enjoy the races. Having a horse in the race will add to my enjoyment. I'm just making the most of this moment in a way I can afford.'

The unspoken is there again, hanging in the air between us like a swarm of irritable wasps. A dig, a rejoinder, aimed my way. *What's the point of having it all if you don't take the time to enjoy it?*

'So what will you do with him? He's not a homeless dog. Do you plan on shipping him back to Australia too, like the car?' I can imagine why he's struggling with his father's legacy, since the money came from a man who abandoned him, but can't he see that the excesses won't help him deal with his anger and resentment? I can no longer ignore the two sides of Cam's personality and the inconsistencies that tell me he's hurting, despite his live-for-the-moment attitude and his hedonistic pursuits.

'I told you, the car was a gift for my cousin. And I haven't thought what I'll do with him beyond today.' Another shrug, but his body is tense, defensive. 'He'll pay his way, I guess, or I'll sell him.'

'So why buy a racehorse for a single race if it's not a particular hobby of yours or a dream to fulfil?' I can't let this go. The dog food was cute, the drum kit for the boy heartbreaking but understandable, given what he's hinted at about his own spartan upbringing with his single-parent mother. But this? It's deeper than lavishly throwing around money.

'Why does this bother you so much? I can afford to buy ten racehorses if I want them. I'm living the high life.'

I ignore the jibe I could interpret as some sort of comparison. 'Are you? Or are you running from something?' I sigh and touch his arm to show him that, although I'm crossing a line here, I'm doing so because I care. 'I'm sorry, I don't want to upset you, I just… I can't stand by and watch you struggle with your inheritance. There are ways I can help.'

I see the look on his face, an expression I've never seen before on easygoing, laid-back Cam—cold, hard anger. 'Well, thank you for the unsolicited financial advice but I know exactly what I'm doing. I'm not some schoolboy with a winning lottery ticket.'

'No, but you don't care about the money either, do you? It's because it's his, isn't it? Your father's?' I'm walking a fine line here, but I ache for him. 'That's why you're blowing it with private planes and racehorses and fast cars. You're not at peace with it.'

He's still angry, malice glittering in his beautiful, expressive eyes. A desecration. 'What makes you think I'm struggling? I'm having the time of my life, aren't I? World-class luxury, every hedonistic pursuit known to man, and a beautiful woman on tap, for whenever I want a good fuck.'

My hand curls into a fist and I'm tempted to slap him, but he's clearly hurting, lashing out. I've backed him into a corner and he's fighting for his life. I step closer, when I'm certain he expected his harsh words to drive me away. 'One minute you're passionate about the underdog, tipping the hotel staff, making some kid's drumming dream come true, even taking time to play with abandoned dogs, and the next you're blowing millions of dollars with a cavalier attitude. We're all complex beings, but this,' I wave a hand at the racehorses, 'isn't you.'

His eyes dart, some of the anger leaving him, as if he's warring with some internal demons.

The race is about to start, so I'm aware my timing sucks. But is there ever a good time to feel exposed? Don't I feel the same way every time he pushes me to talk about my father or brings me to account over my workaholic tendencies? Every time we've been intimate this past week, as if with each searing look he peels away another layer of my armour? Every time I peer into the future and see a terrifying glimpse of a life I thought I was long past craving?

I lean up against the rail, pretending to watch the race I'm no longer interested in. I feel his struggle in the tense air between us, and regret makes my posture deflate. I want to close the gap. To touch him again. To offer physical comfort if he won't accept my emotional support. He's there, right beside me, but may as well be miles away.

'You're right.' His sigh carries in the dry air, my

hearing highly attuned to the strain and defeat in his voice. 'The inheritance was from my—' he makes a fist and then relaxes it as quickly '—my father.'

I hold my breath, desperate to hear what he's finally decided to tell me, but feeling every blade of his pain. It's my penance for pushing him, for caring this much, for breaking my own rules.

'I didn't want it. Why would I? From a man I never knew? A man who considered my existence irrelevant, who held little score in the values of integrity and family commitment.'

A man so unlike him.

He turns to face me then, both of us deaf to the starter gun and the roar of the excited crowds as we hold each other's eye contact with brittle and fragile force.

'I'm sorry, Cam. I understand. I can see how you might harbour resentment for your childhood, but your anger won't make a difference to what's done. There are other ways to compensate.'

He presses his lips together, but I see in his eyes that he's heard. He's a smart man; he's probably told himself the same thing a thousand times.

I plough on. 'Perhaps he was sorry. Ashamed. Perhaps leaving you that money was his way of apologising. The only way he knew how to reach out to you after having left like he did.'

I'm shocked speechless by the venomous expression souring his face. 'Well, neither of us knew him, did we? Maybe he just wants to control me from the grave. To disrupt my life, which by the way was pretty near perfect before all of this, and dictate how I live. Just because money was the most important thing in his life. I'm not him.'

'Of course you're not him. You're wonderful. I'm just trying to point out that there are other things you can do with your money.'

'*His* money. You know, Orla, you more than anyone should understand what it's like to have a manipulative parent.'

I ignore his reference. I've laid him bare and he's lashing out again. And, of course, he's right. My father has done his fair share of damage. My shoulders slump. Am I still jumping through my father's hoops? Is that what drives me still? Yes, maybe in the beginning…but now, when I'm more successful than ever, more even than he is?

But this isn't about me.

'Why are you so convinced your father wanted to control you? Why isn't it just a gift? A way to make amends?'

'Gifts are yours to do with as you please. They're not conditional. They don't chain you.'

I think about my earrings, the gift designed to send me away, quietly and without a fuss, from a role that was mine by rights. A gift I wear to remind myself that we don't always receive what we deserve, and that not everyone, even those who should do, sees the real us.

'I know that.' My voice is small, because Cam's touched a nerve.

'Without conditions I could do what I like with it,

but he put a clause in the will which prevents me from giving more than twenty-five per cent away. I couldn't even donate the entire sum to the hospice that nursed my mother through her last days. Even from the grave, he still cares more about that money than he does about me or his ex-wife and mother to his only son.'

His smile is so vengeful, my stomach turns. 'I'd stake my life on the fact that he would detest what I'm doing with his billions,' he says. 'Frittering it away with a cavalier attitude, as you called it.'

A brittle silence settles between us. He's right. Neither of us knows his father's intent.

I grow hot under Cam's focus. I want to rewind, to start over, to hold him until I've chased away the distress I've put in his eyes. But how do I repair the damage? We're not a real couple. We only have a few weeks of shared history to fall back on, most of that superficial and impersonal, at my insistence. Why would he seek comfort from me of all people? And I shouldn't offer it, not after admitting that my feelings are dangerously ensnared.

But…

I glance down at the racetrack. The race is over. 'I'm sorry, it looks like Contempt of Court lost.' I turn back to face him, seeing him, understanding him in a whole new light. 'You're right though—it's a perfect name.' A two-fingered gesture to a man he can't confront any other way.

All the energy drains from my body. I've messed up. I should have known Cam would never do anything frivolous or erratic. He's the most thoughtful and considerate human being I know. This is what happens when I forget my rules. This is what I hoped to avoid by keeping things purely physical. This feeling of failure. That I can't do this. That relationships just aren't my strength.

I should stick to what I know.

'Do you want to get out of here?' I want to touch him, to show him my regret for both his situation and for drawing out his secret pain. I want to get back to where we were this morning. Restore my own equilibrium and his in the only way I can allow: physically.

But not here.

His struggle to let go of the things I've dragged up passes over his face, but he finally nods and I gather my bag and hat.

The journey is tense, quiet, stomach-churning. Back at the M Club in Dubai's downtown, I assume we're heading for our room, but without comment Cam takes my hand and leads me to the basement club, which is alive with the insistent beat of some dance track. The last thing I want to do is dance, to pretend that everything between us is okay. But perhaps that's exactly what I need to do. Pretend. Pretend this is still about no-strings pleasure.

I follow him, weaving through the crowds of clubbers.

'Let's get a drink,' says Cam, his voice hard, all that lovely deep and sexy resonance rubbed away. 'I've reserved one of the private rooms.'

I nod, my heart heavy, but I follow him to the club's perimeter, where discreet private booths are located.

The interior is decorated in signature M Club black—a womblike space, a fully stocked bar, a wide and sumptuous sofa, an adjustable PA system so the volume of the thumping music can be altered to personal taste or allow conversation, and a wall of one-way glass, to ensure absolute privacy, even as the occupants feel part of the club's vibrant atmosphere with a view of the dance floor.

Cam hands me a Scotch, knocking back his own in a single swallow. He doesn't adjust the volume of the music, but I don't think we're here for conversation.

I take a mouthful of my drink, my mind scrambling for something to say. I want to make things right between us. I shouldn't have pushed so hard. I shouldn't have lowered my guard enough to care. But I do.

'Cam, I'm sorry.'

His fingers settle against my mouth. He hushes me as he glides the pad of his fingers across my sensitive lips.

He takes my glass and drains what's left and then replaces his fingers with his mouth, parting his lips to allow a trickle of the liquor to pass from his mouth to mine in a decadent, provocative kiss.

I swallow, my lips clinging to his in silent apology. His kiss turns demanding, his tongue probing while his eyes burn into mine as if begging for something. Silence? Understanding? Escape?

He pulls back. 'I don't want to talk any more.' His hands settle on my hips and his body starts to move to the pounding beat of the dance track. I move with him, lost in the intensity in his eyes, deep, dark desire concealing the earlier pain. I clutch the lifeline. The desire. It's easier to chase because I want him, despite my other, harder-to-name feelings. Our need for each other is the only stability left now everything else feels as if it's shifting underfoot.

He wants to hide. To retreat behind what we do, what we know—how to make each other feel good. I do too. Haven't I done the same myself, more than once? Used him in the same way? Isn't a part of me doing exactly that now? Avoiding the treacherous thoughts of us being more than this?

This whole proposition began because I wanted a distraction, and now so does Cam.

I loop my arms around his neck and kick off my sandals, my hips matching his rhythm, which is confident and inherently sexy—like everything else about him. He bends so low, our lips brush as we move, not quite a kiss, but somehow more, a presence, a reminder that the other person is there, breathing the same air.

His hands curve over my backside, his fingers curling and bunching up the silk fabric of my dress as he grinds me against his hard length. 'Turn around,' he murmurs against my mouth, his hard stare glittering with now familiar challenge.

I obey, pulse leaping. When I'm faced away from him, his big hands on my hips and my hands looped around his neck behind my head, I push my ass back to torture him some more. Him and myself. Because he's hard and ready for me and I want him, as always.

We dance on, my back to his front, one of his arms

around my waist and the other hand on my hip as we sway together in a way that's more foreplay than choreography and would be completely prohibited in any other establishment in this country other than here in the privacy and decadence of the M Club.

The track changes, seamlessly blending into one that's more sensuous. No longer content to merely tease, I drag Cam's hands north to cup my breasts through my dress. He gives me a hint of friction, his thumbs and fingers rolling my nipples, but it's not enough. I want more. I always want more of the way he makes me feel.

But can this, just this, ever be enough?

To switch off my mind, I tangle my fingers in the hair at his nape as I rest my head on his shoulder and turn my face to his, begging for his mouth.

'Cam.' His name sounds like a plea and it is. A plea to drag me with him into oblivion, to guide us both until we're lost in sensation. Because otherwise I'll think, and thinking about this man, and the way I am with him, is as addictive as it is foolish.

Cam presses his mouth to my neck, below my ear, and judders wrack my body—he knows how sensitive I am in that spot, knows it turns me on to feel his scruff against my skin and hear his breath panting because he feels the same need.

'Let's go upstairs,' I say, twisting so I can capture his mouth, touch my tongue to his, swallow the sound of the low groan he lets free. I want to ensure everything is right with us after our fight. I want to know he's still with me, still happy to travel to Singapore and then on to Sydney, our hometown, where this heady whirlwind will come to a natural end.

As if it's still part of our dance, Cam nudges me forward, following close behind until I'm only inches in front of the wall of one-way glass that gifts us a panoramic view of the club. Before I can repeat my desire to take this upstairs to our suite, his hands slip to the button between my breasts and he slowly undoes one after another.

I gasp, the rational part of my brain tricked into believing the people dancing only a few metres on the other side of the glass can see us.

Can I do this? Here?

The answer is as clear as the window in front of me. The same answer as every other time Cam's challenged me, or I've challenged myself.

Yes.

'Tell me to stop.' Cam speaks against my throat, his lips a sensual glide and his chin prickling my nerves alive.

Stop is what we should do. Not just this display of exhibitionism, but also the arrangement we made. Before I slip any deeper into the building feelings and before we push each other to expose more than we can recover from.

'Tell me to stop.' He presses his erection between my buttocks and I brace my hands flat on the glass, pressing my lips together to hold in the words. Because I want him. In any way. All the ways it's possible to want someone.

I ignore the racing of my heart and the spike of adrenaline warning me to pull back. His hands continue with the buttons, his hips still swaying to the beat behind me, where I'm too turned on to do more than hold my body upright and glory in the decadence of his touch. While he scrapes kisses up and down my neck, he scoops the cups of my bra down, exposing my breasts.

The cool air hits me and I gasp at being naked here, in front of strangers.

With a grunt, Cam presses up even closer so I'm shunted forwards the last inch and my bare nipples touch the frigid glass. I groan at the foreign sensation. But I have no time to absorb the pleasure, because Cam slips one hand between my legs and delves inside my lacy thong to stroke my swollen clit, which is aching and ready.

'Tell me to stop,' he says, gruff, his face buried against the side of my neck. I hear him inhale deeply, sucking in my scent, and I almost smile, because I've done the same thing a hundred times, sniffing his sweater left on a chair or his tousled hair while he's asleep.

At my answering moan, he taps my foot with his and bunches my dress around my waist from behind, his intentions clear. He's going to do this, right here. And I want him with equal desperation.

I spread my feet wide, excitement rising when I hear the clink of his belt buckle and the rasp of his zip. I can't believe we're doing this, but it's as if we both need the reminder of why we're here and only this—hot, demanding sex—will reset the boundaries.

His hand shifts from between my legs, and I cry out at its loss, only to press my mouth up against the glass to stave off the pleasure of his fingers, which he plunges inside me from behind, as if testing my readiness.

'Cam, yes. I'm ready. Do it.'

His fingers disappear and I feel the fat head of his cock nudge my entrance. I tilt my hips back to allow him access, my palms pressing against the glass for leverage. He's going too slowly. I want to control the pace. To chase away our fight and my own confusion.

I feel him enter me, just an inch or so, and it's not enough.

'What are you doing to me, Orla?' he grits out, his fingers digging into my hips. 'Tell me to stop.'

'I don't want you to stop,' I cry. As to what we're doing, I have no answers, because whatever I'm doing to him, he's doing to me tenfold. I'm more alive when I'm with him, more myself than I've been in years, so long I've almost forgotten how it feels.

He surges inside with a protracted groan. I brace my palms against the glass as he drags my hips back to meet the thrust of his hips. His possession fills me and in that moment I want to be more to him, although I can't define in what way. I just know that if he walked away tonight, after our fight, I'd grieve more than his company and the regular, earth-shifting orgasms. I'd grieve his loss.

As if he's already decided to leave and I'm determined to give him something to remember, I lock my arms and push back from the glass, the illicit scandal of what we're doing in such close proximity to the other club members and the thump of his hips against my backside making me cry out with acute waves of pleasure.

Cam grips my hips with punishing fingers, clearly battling control himself. 'Touch yourself, Orla. Touch that greedy little clit that wants to be mine.'

His words thrill me, because all my body is his. I rush to obey, slipping one hand between my legs to rub myself while he pounds into me from behind.

It's carnal, uninhibited and glorious. But it's also communication. We've strayed from the path this evening, and this is a reminder that we can't do that again, not without sacrificing something more. Something bigger than both of us. Something so good, we'd be fools not to enjoy it for whatever time we have left.

Just when I think he's close to finishing, he grunts, pulls out and spins me around. He backs my ass up against the window as he kisses me and hoists me around the waist so my feet leave the floor.

'I want to watch you come. Hold tight.'

I nod, his puppet, willing to have my strings pulled, because I know this man. I know his values and his desires and he sees what I need.

He grips my waist in one arm, his other hand pressing our entwined fingers against the window, and I wrap my legs around his hips. With my free hand I guide him back inside, and we groan together, as if it were the first time all over again.

Cam's thrusts turn fast and shallow, his fingers pressed hard into the back of my hand as if he never wants to let me go. I grip his shoulder and tunnel my hand into his hair and hold on tight with everything I have. 'Cam...'

His eyes lance mine and his thrusts knock the breath from me, but I need to say this. To make things right between us. 'I'm sorry for what you've been through. Sorry for bringing up painful memories.'

His face twists with emotion. He drops his forehead to mine as he says, 'Hush...'

His kiss tells me I'm forgiven, and then I can't speak another word because he stops holding himself back, his hips powering into mine as he sinks as deep as he can go and we're finally lost together.

CHAPTER EIGHT

Cam

As I PULL up outside Orla's Raffles Place office in Singapore's financial district a few days later, my phone rings. I slide the car into park and answer on the Bluetooth. It's Orla.

'Hi. I'm just outside,' I say, already grinning with anticipation.

'I figured you wouldn't be far away. I'm on my way down. I just wanted to say I'm ready and I've cleared everything on my desk—no interruptions tonight. I promise.' She's mildly breathless, as if she's talking on the move. 'Perhaps I should even wear one of those glasses and moustache disguises so I don't get cornered by someone who recognises me.'

I throw my head back and laugh. 'There's no need to go that far. But I appreciate the gesture.' Since the evening at the races, where we had our first fight—although I'm not sure you can have a fight if you're not a couple—Orla and I haven't spoken about my inheritance. In fact, we haven't spoken about anything that could be considered real, only travel arrangements or her work schedule, or where we'd like to eat that evening. But every time I pay for a meal, tip a waiter or add drinks to my M Club tab, I feel her eyes on me, as if she wants to say more but is holding back.

I understand the impulse. For days now I've been fighting the urge to ask where this is going. Where we're going, because time is running out. Our trip will soon be over and we'll be back in Sydney before we know it.

What then?

Do we shake hands and walk away without a backward glance? Will we hook up every time she's home long enough to give me a call? Cam's dial-an-orgasm? Will we date other people in between? Fuck, of course we will, because we won't be dating each other—she made that clear from day one. I check my feelings, the roll of my stomach confirming without a doubt that I want more from Orla than a goodbye the minute we touch down in Sydney or an occasional booty call.

I want everything.

But what does she want? Probably nothing more than she's wanted from the start. A good time. But surely we've moved past just physical pleasure? Surely she feels the same stirrings to explore this further, back in the real world?

But whose real world?

I wince, remembering the woman tying my insides into knots is still on the line. 'Okay...well, hurry down. I've got a surprise.' Two if you count the box in my pocket.

I'm taking her to the Singapore Grand Prix, which just happens to be in town this week. She's spent a gruelling four days working, leaving the hotel suite before I'm awake and returning late in the evening, pale and about to drop. The humidity here is draining and she's been visiting a technology satellite manufacturing company on one of the islands. It's all I can do to encourage a few mouthfuls of the delicious room-service menu into her before turning on the shower and tucking her into bed.

At first I thought her drive, work ethic, and independence made us incompatible, but it's true what they say—opposites do attract and we slot together well.

But could we take this chemistry, this astounding connection, and translate it into something real once the travelling and the hedonism stop? On my turf, my *real* turf, would her enthusiasm dwindle? Would she decide that we just don't have enough in common after all?

As to her feelings…

I swallow bile—I have no clue. I'm only just waking up to my own…

I grip the steering wheel, hoping to dislodge the lump in my throat threatening to cut off my oxygen. Time is running out. The real test will come back in Sydney, on home ground. I already have plans to throw myself into finishing the cottage renovations, but I still have no definitive solution for my financial woes. Do I return to work at my old construction firm and ignore the money in my account? Will they even have me back? When I said I needed some unpaid leave to get my head around things, they didn't put up much of a fight. I knew the company was struggling; as with most Sydney-based construction companies, the building slump had taken its toll. But could I simply slot back into my old life as if none of this—the money, meeting Orla—had happened?

More importantly, could a woman like Orla—so driven, so intent on making her business the best—be happy to come back down to earth with me? Live that simple life in a cottage by the sea?

I try to picture her there, both in its current state of disrepair and once finished. I'm so used to seeing her in glamorous, decadent surroundings that the image doesn't quite gel.

There's a tap at the window. I look up to find her beautiful, lit-up face smiling down at me and I'm struck with the force of a baseball bat to the skull that I want that reality. Me, Orla, simple moments in a cottage by the sea.

Fuck, I'm falling for her. Actually falling.

I clamber from the car, my heart pounding.

I scoop one arm around her waist and pull her in for a kiss. Our first of the day and all the sweeter because I've had to wait and because each kiss we share is better and better.

'Hi,' I say after she releases me.

She laughs. 'Hi, yourself. So where are we going? I'm excited.'

My chest grows tight with nervous energy, the box

in my pocket burning a hole through the denim of my jeans. I wanted to wait, to give her the gift at a suitably romantic moment, but I can't help myself. In view of my lightning-bolt revelation, I'm impatient to start.

'I have something for you first—a gift.' I tug at the box, which is snagged on my pocket.

'Cam. No more gifts.' She covers my hand, the hand struggling to release the box. 'I know you don't want to hear it, but I can give you a list right now of a hundred sound investments to absorb your disposable income.'

'Investing is the last thing I want to do.' She's only trying to help, I see that, but perhaps because I've already had similar thoughts myself, my stance on the money I neither wanted nor asked for softening, I dig in my heels.

'Enjoying myself at my old man's expense is one thing, but touching that money in any meaningful way feels too close to forgiveness, and I'm not sure I'm ready for that.'

'I understand what you mean about forgiveness. I've struggled with that myself. But I'm not talking about making money,' she says, and my ribs pinch because she sees me, understands my struggles and, as much as I don't want to hear it, she's right. I need to find a way to come to terms with my new life. To build a new future for myself, because even if I want to return to the old life, it can never be the same.

'There are lots of ways to invest thoughtfully and with a social conscience. You're already doing it in a small way. But I can help you get around the restrictions in the will, too. Why don't you let me put together some proposals?'

I want to say so much in that second that I can't speak at all. Would she want to help if she didn't care about me? About us? And I'll take any future contact with her I can get, even if I have to sit through a million financial proposals.

'I do have something I'd like your advice on.' Since thinking about my old construction company, an idea has taken shape. She may not know anything about the building industry, but I'm certain she can advise me, let me know if my plan is feasible. But I don't want to have this conversation now.

'But right now I want to give you my gift.' I kiss away her pout and tug the box free. 'This gift is different.' I hold her stare so she understands my meaning. I know technically all my money is my money, but some of it I earned. 'I bought it with my *own* money. My savings before the inheritance.' Part of my cottage renovation fund, but she doesn't need to know that.

Her eyes widen. 'Oh, well…thank you.' She presses a kiss to my mouth, and I know she gets me. She understands the distinction and what it means to me.

I hold the box up at eye level, flat on my palm.

I know she wants to berate me for my extravagance, but she takes the box without further comment. Inside is an intricate pair of traditional Singapore gold earrings, their beauty and delicacy reminding me of her.

'I notice you always wear these,' I touch one diamond stud, 'and I thought you might like a change, so…'

Why am I so tongue-tied? It's a gift. I've given her hundreds of gifts over the past few weeks. Perhaps it's because I want to say more, to tell her that I want to see her beyond the six weeks we agreed, but I clamp my jaw shut, because I'm not sure she's ready to hear that yet.

'They're beautiful, Cam, exactly what I would choose myself.' Her mouth is back on mine, and her arms scoop around my neck so I hear when she snaps the box closed.

I guess she's not going to wear them tonight. I swallow down my disappointment. It's no big deal. 'Let's go. It's not far, so I thought we could walk.'

She tucks the earrings inside her bag and loops her arm through mine. It's a short walk to the premier grandstand, which has the best views of the street circuit's more challenging turns and spectacular views of Marina Bay, the focus of the post-race fireworks.

I take Orla's hand. 'Do you like Grand Prix?'

'Yes. It's so exciting. Is that where we're going?' She smiles her dazzling smile, and I nod, no longer interested in the motor racing. I want to take her back to the hotel and strip her naked, save for the earrings I bought. I want to drag a confession from her of how she truly feels about me. If she wants to see me once we're back in Sydney.

'Not long until we're home. It's going to be a struggle after all this adventure,' I hedge, testing the water.

'Yes. I'm sort of dreading it, to be honest. I'll have

to see my father and he's going to be pissed about Jensen's.'

I squeeze her hand in solidarity. 'Tell him to stick it. You did nothing wrong apart from being the best.'

She nods, but her eyes appear far away. 'You know, he bought me these earrings for my twenty-fifth birthday.' She touches one of the diamond studs she always wears. 'At first I was incredibly touched. We weren't that close while I was growing up—I always felt second best because I didn't have a Y chromosome. But after he'd given me a second to open his gift and thank him, he chose that moment to tell me I wouldn't be the next CEO, but Liam would.'

I stare, because I don't know what to say. I don't even know how to feel. 'I'm sorry he treated you that way.' What does it mean that she wears them every day without fail? I try to recall if I've ever seen her without them, instinctively knowing the answer is no.

'It's silly, I guess, but I wear them every day to remind myself that I don't need him or his company. That I'm perfectly capable of running my own firm. That I can be just as successful as him and Liam.'

'Probably more successful, if you think about Jensen's,' I say, and she nods. The idea she still wants to prove something to the man after all these years depresses me. I hide the heavy feeling dragging at my feet with an unconvincing smile. 'A two-fingered gesture, eh? I get it.'

Her nod is hesitant, as if she's remembering our fight over Contempt of Court, but four-carat diamond earrings…a racehorse… They may as well be the same. She squeezes my hand, because now she knows I've made enough of my own two-fingered gestures while we've known each other. 'My father never gave me anything—not a birthday card, or a pat on the back, or even a phone call. Trust me, you know I understand the impulse.'

She looks down and then tucks herself closer to my side as we walk. 'I'm not bringing that up again. I just wanted you to understand why I wear these.' She touches a stud, which may as well be a padlock to the cage she's constructed around herself.

A daily reminder. There every time she looks in the mirror. A reminder she has something to prove.

I've never met her father, but I already know the guy is an asshole. She's worth ten of him, except somehow, despite all her success, all the billions, she still feels she needs to prove to him that she's worthy.

I tug her to a standstill, the exotic scents of Singapore around us reminding me we are far from home. But we're together, and I want to be there for her. 'You know you don't need to prove anything to me, right?'

Her eyes dart. 'Of course.' She lifts her chin, the way she does when she's cornered and comes out fighting. 'What do you mean?'

'I don't care if you don't wear *my* earrings, but isn't it time you took these off?' I touch the stud with one cautious fingertip. 'You're the most driven and successful woman I've ever met. You've already bested him, made it on your own, won a major client from him. You have nothing to prove.' I hadn't planned the serious turn in the conversation, but as I see it, we both need to face our fears, to conquer our demons and move on. How else can we focus on what's really important in life? How can we focus on any sort of a relationship?

'I know that.'

'Do you? Really? Because from what I've seen you'll never stop. Ten billion, twenty, thirty. When is enough enough, Orla?'

'That's different—I...don't do it for the money. You know how frugal I am. I love my job. I'm good at it. I'm happy.'

Her statements feel like blows. I want to dismiss them, to call her a liar. But part of me is scared that if she's right, if she has everything she needs, life all figured out, completely self-sufficient, is there any room for an ordinary guy like me?

'Would you ask that question if I were a successful man?' she says, her guard now fully up.

I grip the back of my neck in frustration. 'I'm not some sexist idiot. It's got nothing to do with your gender.'

'So despite saying I have nothing to prove, you're trying to change me. Is that it?'

'No.' I cup her face. 'I wouldn't change a thing. I just... I care about you. I see how hard you work, how hard you push yourself, and I'm just worried that you feel you have something to prove, which you absolutely do not.'

Some of the anger in her deflates. She places her

hand over mine, pressing it closer to her cheek. 'I care about you too, Cam. That's what I tried to say in Dubai. That's why I'm offering to help you invest, to help you see that perhaps your father had no other choice, no other way of apologising than to leave you that money, the money he abandoned you and your mum for.'

The tables turning knocks the wind from me. 'You're talking about forgiveness again.' I tug my hand away and shove both in my pockets.

'Perhaps it might help.' She crosses her arms over her chest.

How did we get here? And why can't she see that she's enough, just the way she is? Enough for me, at least.

'I'm not sure I'm ready for that. What about you?'

My question, my challenge, falls on deaf ears. We complete the walk in silence, but it turns out that race cars and fireworks aren't as thrilling when you've glimpsed the finishing line but find yourself somehow right back at the start.

CHAPTER NINE

Orla

CAM'S PENTHOUSE IS the crowning jewel of Sydney Harbour's Darling Point. Even I'm impressed with the spectacular bridge views. I park at the top of a long, steep driveway and let myself inside with Cam's security code.

Tonight is the club's Masquerade Gala and, as we're going together, I prefer to arrive together, so I've had my outfit delivered here. Not that the tension between us is completely resolved, but since our exchange in Singapore we've called a truce, as if we're both aware time is ticking and there's no point wasting the days and hours we have left fighting.

It doesn't matter who's right.

Cam and I had our fun, and soon it will be time to say goodbye.

With that certainty weighing me down, my heels click as I make my way upstairs from the ground floor. I glance around his home, looking for clues of the real Cam. While luxurious, the whole space seems cold and cavernous, every sound echoing off the bare walls. Hardly any colour, no personality, and no sign of the warm, compassionate, vibrant man I'm lucky enough to know.

When I reach the second floor and the main living areas, my adrenaline pumping as it always does in anticipation of seeing Cam, there's still no sign of him. Neither in person nor in any evidence that he even lives here, although he told me he only bought the place four months ago. A single solitary leather armchair and a telescope face the wraparound windows, which open onto a spacious veranda and give almost three-hundred-and-sixty-degree harbour views. But there's no character, no life anywhere to be found, certainly no sign of the fun-loving, energetic Cam, a man who's entirely occupied my head since we landed in Sydney twenty-four hours ago.

My throat grows tight. This isn't Cam. This flashy, modern residence that screams status. Then it hits me. It's another of his revenge purchases against his father. I'm no more likely to find the real Cam here than I am searching the moon. Not that I should want to find the real Cam, because I have to give him up. And soon.

I pace over to the window and grip the back of the armchair, my nails digging and my heart clenching as I imagine him sitting here. Alone, trying to work out a way forward. Trying to be himself in a world that's shifted on its axis.

But then, what do I know about having everything all worked out?

I thought once we arrived back in Australia, things would fall into place. We'd share a parting kiss, perhaps laugh as we recalled the highs of our adventure, and part with only a modicum of regret. Instead, I found myself inviting Cam to the gala even before his private plane touched down.

I can't want him, but I can't do without him.

I sigh, my nerves and my need demanding I find him when I'm fully aware that all I've done is prolong the agony, drawn out the final farewell, which must come. Because my stance on relationships hasn't changed. The past week of disagreements proves my theories are correct: I'm no good at emotional entanglements. I'm better off with my single life and my shocking work-life imbalance.

My breath catches, my insistence no longer carrying the same certainty. In practice, within the limitations of my proposition, Cam and I work. But outside of that? Despite his struggles to come to terms with the inheritance left to him by a man who let him down, I know he'd be content to return to his simple, hard-working life. And I know he's going to be just fine.

We spent most of the flight from Singapore brain-storming his ideas for a construction school that teaches vulnerable and underprivileged young men and women valuable skills they can take into the workforce. Young people who need a break in life because of the path they've found themselves on. Young people like Cam might have been without his hard-working mother and his own determination to make something of himself.

With some financial guidance from me, and with Cam's passion, their lives could be rich and fulfilling in all the ways that matter.

And me?

I fight the hot tears threatening, swallowing them down. Cam needs a woman who can share that life. A woman who shares his goals. A woman free to walk and sleep and love by his side. It's what he deserves.

But I'm not that woman.

He was right about me. I need to work. It's who I am.

With a gnawing feeling in the pit of my stomach, I go in search of him. As I walk towards a corridor lined with what I assume are bedrooms, I hear a series of low, rhythmic thuds. Some sort of bass-heavy music.

My pulse leaps. He told me the penthouse has a gym; perhaps I'll get another show of Cam working out—half naked, sweaty, a visual feast. My mouth dries in anticipation, and a surge of acid burns behind my breastbone, jealousy I'm going to have to get used to if Cam gets the happy-ever-after he deserves with some other woman.

The beat builds. I open the room the noise seems to be coming from and freeze in the doorway.

The sound is deafening. Cam sits at a massive drum kit facing a floor-to-ceiling window with ocean views. He's stripped to the waist, his back slicked with perspiration and his muscular arms almost a blur as he creates the rapid drum loop that goes on and on, as if he's pounding out the rhythm of my regret.

I'm frozen. I want to watch. I want to go to him. I want to run away and sob myself into oblivion. Without making a sound I cast a quick glance around the room. Like the rest of the house, the furnishings in this room are sparse—a large bed, a sofa and some sleek Bluetooth speakers, but there's more of Cam's personality in this room than the rest of the house combined, as if he's carved out a sanctuary inside this cavernous shell. A place he can be himself.

I watch and listen from my spot by the door, indulging myself for what will likely be one of the last times. The last grains of sand are sliding through the hourglass, and any day now I'm going to have to give him up.

The thought traps my breath and sends shards of pain between my ribs. How can I walk away from someone who makes me smile without effort? Who brightens my mornings and competes with the constant draw to stay at the office? How can I go back to boring, burnt-out Orla when all I want to do is stay in our bubble with Cam?

He must see my reflection in the glass because he stops, the sudden silence ripping me from the insanity of formulating ways I can continue to see him now the proposition has run its course.

He's panting, his chest heaving as he drags in air and looks at me from beneath his brows. I'm instantly damp—hell, I was damp before I entered the house, because I know him. I know how good we are together. I've always known that, from the moment our eyes met across the roulette wheel in Monaco.

I don't speak a word.

As if he too knows this is close to finishing and he's as desperate as me to keep the illusion alive, he simply stares.

Waiting.

I saunter over, slowly shedding my blouse, skirt and heels as I approach. My need for him hasn't lessened since our first time together. If anything it's stronger, because I'm alive when I'm with Cam, but never more so than when I'm in his arms, his heart thudding against mine, our breath mingling.

I reach him and I almost chicken out, flee. I extend a shaky hand to skim his shoulders and back as I round him. His skin is warm, his muscles tense under my touch. I stand between his spread legs and he pushes back his stool to accommodate me in the small space between his body and the drums.

I twirl my fingers in his hair, holding his handsome face, tilting his mouth up to my kiss. He groans, dropping the drumsticks so he can slide his hands up my thighs and around to cup my buttocks with possessive fingers.

'Orla, what are you trying to do? Kill me?' he mumbles against my lips.

I smile, but nothing inside me feels light enough for humour. It's as if I'm weighed down by my feelings, as if there are too many of them for me to even contemplate lifting my feet from the sumptuous carpet.

'I want you. I've missed the way you make me feel.' I almost gasp at the stark honesty of my words.

He grips my hips tighter, his hands so big they span

half my lower back. He drops his head to my chest, where he nuzzles my cleavage, his breath hot. 'And how do I make you feel?' His hands slide up my back and he unhooks my bra without looking up, while he presses kisses to the tops of my breasts and my breastbone.

My head drops back as I absorb the heady sensation of Cam's touch. The words spring from nowhere, or perhaps from that tightly guarded part deep inside. 'Alive. Free. Invincible.'

It's as close to a declaration of my feelings as I dare.

I sense his smile, but when I look down his expression is bittersweet. 'You were all those things before you met me.'

The burn is back in my throat. My beautiful, broken Cam. But I know he'll be all right. He's young, he's resilient and he has so much to give.

'Well, perhaps you make me appreciate them more, then. Perhaps playing hard has put working hard into perspective.' I press my finger to his beautiful mouth, shushing him. 'I want to play hard now.'

I slide off my bra and lean over to kiss him. I want to forget that this is almost over. Forget that life after my adventure with Cam will go back to pre-Cam predictability. But I'll never forget how he unleashed this sexual being I neglected for so long. How he challenged me and then cherished me.

Slipping my thong off, I straddle his thighs where he sits. My hands push down his shorts just enough so his erection is freed. I take him in my hand between us and pump him while we kiss, and then I angle him back and sink slowly onto him, inch by glorious inch.

He holds me so tight to his chest that I fear I won't be able to draw breath, but then I stretch up on the balls of my feet and lower myself into his lap and we groan-gasp together at the depth of the penetration. This feels so right I never want to give it up, but despite the journey we've travelled, I'm still me.

We rock together, clinging tight while we kiss and move just enough to stay balanced on the stool but also to give and take what we need from each other. But it's not enough. I want him to know how much he's meant to me, to understand that, while I can't give him commitment, or the kind of future I see for him, the kind he deserves, I can give him all of me, physically.

I pull back, my lips swollen. 'Cam. It's time.'

He knows what I mean. Ever since Zurich we've skirted this issue. I want him every way I can. He'll know that I was his, briefly, but completely.

He grips my waist and stands without slipping from my body. In two strides we're on the bed, me on my back and him taking charge of our pleasure by thrusting above me. He clasps my hands, his fingers locking with mine, his beautiful face tight with pleasure, and then he dives for my nipple, sucking hard so I cry out and arch my neck.

I get lost, so lost I think he's missed my meaning or has changed his mind, but when I'm close to climaxing, my body drunk on the pleasure Cam delivers without fail, he finally withdraws and guides me onto all fours.

He takes my hand and directs my fingers to my drenched and swollen clit. 'Rub yourself.'

I hear him tear into a condom and then I feel the thrilling chill of lube between my buttocks.

'Don't stop.' He handles me like I'm made of glass, his rough hands sliding over the skin of my back and shoulders and hips, even as I feel him push against my opening for the first time.

I want this. I want what only he can give me. And I want it on my timescale, not Cam's, which I'd bet my entire wealth is in deference to my comfort. But there is no more time. There's only now. Us. This moment of trust and forbidden intimacy.

I push back, the feeling foreign and thrilling but not uncomfortable after all his care and preparation. And just as I know I can trust him with my body, that he'd never hurt me, I also know he needs convincing. 'Cam, I want this. I want you this way. Every way.'

I hear his groan, feel his fingers digging into my hips as the pressure of his possession increases. I rub my clit faster to counter the slight twinge of discomfort but then I'm full and he leans over me with a long moan, his sweaty chest plastered to my back.

'Fuck, Orla. I'll never get enough of you.'

It's as close to any sort of declaration as we've come, dangerously close. And it electrifies me even as I try to block it out by rocking my hips to distract us both back towards pleasure. My ploy works because Cam's hand joins mine between my legs, our fingers working in unison on my clit until I start to see stars and need both my hands to brace for the impact of my inevitable orgasm.

Cam arches over me, taking his weight, but I want it, I want it all. To be smothered in him, to forget where I end and he begins, to be his completely, just in this moment. Not Cam and Orla. Just a man and a woman, lost together.

'Cam, I'm close.' I struggle to get the words out, but I want him to know what he does to me, how he's changed me, enriched my life, made me feel impossible things I thought were long past. But I can't confess anything remotely as vulnerable, so I focus on the sensations that wash my body.

'Come for me, then, squeeze me, show me the real you, and what you like.'

His words liberate me and I fly, every convulsion a tribute to him, every cry his name until I'm certain that I know I've made the biggest mistake of my life inviting Cam North into my world.

When I'm fully spent, he surprises me by easing out of my body, allowing me to collapse onto my back to catch my breath. He tears off the condom and repositions himself between my thighs, his fingers spreading me open so he can guide himself back inside me. He looks up, a million emotions written in the depths of his grey eyes, before they roll closed with pleasure and he whispers one word.

'Orla.'

I know then that I've ruined him, that he's developed feelings for me, because it's there in the tenderness of his touch as he uses both hands to push my hair back from my face. It's there in the possessive and agonising eye contact he pins me with and the reverent way he kisses me time after time. He's making love to me. He's given me everything I wanted and now he's showing me what *he* wants.

I struggle to breathe, although I crave his weight on me pressing me into the mattress as he seeks his own climax. He groans, pushes his face against the side of my neck and I breathe in his familiar scent, as if committing it to memory.

His hips start to buck, his rhythm stalling as he reaches his orgasm, and I grip him tight, holding him even though I know the pain will come as soon as I have to let him go.

The Masquerade Gala is held in the lavish ballroom of Sydney's M Club, a dazzling waterfront location with harbour views featuring the iconic Opera House and Harbour Bridge.

As dinner is over, most members have removed their masks, Cam and I no exception. Not that he needed the simple black mask to look dangerously handsome—he was that the day I met him. I just didn't anticipate the end would be quite so hard.

On the dance floor, I look up at Cam, determined to enjoy tonight as it's likely to be our last date. He's been uncharacteristically quiet since our arrival, although he was attentive and charming at dinner, and as soon at the music began he asked me to dance, dragging me away from some long-time business associate and saving me from talking shop. And he's kept me here, for song after song. It's as if he doesn't want to let me go, as if he too wants to live in denial for as long as possible.

Like me, apparently, because I ask, 'How is work on the cottage coming along?' I steer the conversation away from the inevitable train wreck I can sense approaching from the haunted look in Cam's eyes.

He takes the bait with a small indulgent smile. 'Good. I ripped out the old kitchen today and knocked down a wall.' His arms grip me a little tighter and I feel cherished, as I always do in his arms. 'I'd like to show it to you sometime, if you're free.' His hand presses between my shoulder blades and I rest my head on his chest, sniffing him, inhaling deeply and hiding from his searching stare.

'I'd love to see it.' It's not a lie. He's so passionate about his beloved cottage, so committed to undertaking all the renovations with his own two hands...

'Tomorrow?' I feel the enthusiastic thudding of his heart under my cheek and my stomach tightens with a reminder that I'm going to have to end this sooner rather than later, before Cam develops crazy ideas of attachment or worse...

I look up, real regret pinching my eyebrows in a frown. 'I'd love to, but I can't tomorrow. I'm required at that family barbecue I told you about. I'm dreading it, to be honest.'

'Still?' he asks.

I sigh. I thought I wouldn't have to think about this

until tomorrow, but it's a perfect distraction from wondering how and when to end the incredible journey with this man. 'Well, things between my father and me are strained at the best of times. I'll have to tolerate his snide remarks that I stole Jensen's' business out from under his nose, for the sake of family harmony and for my mum.'

He glances down before he says, 'Why go at all if that's how he's going to behave?'

'What do you mean?'

His jaw clenches in the way I've learned means business. 'I mean, if your father is going to make things awkward because he's a sore loser, why put yourself through that?'

'Cam...' I say, a hint of warning in my voice. I know he means well, but someone telling me what to do is almost as bad as someone telling me what I can't do, and guaranteed to make me dig in my heels.

'What? I'm serious. You owe him nothing. You said yourself he was distant while you were growing up, and then he overlooked you for CEO. He's had enough chances. If you're good enough to steal a client from him, perhaps he should have valued you more when he had you on his team—it's too late for sour grapes.' His face grows sombre and I wonder if he's making comparisons, thinking about his own father. And he's right. My father has always made me feel as if I'm not good enough, probably the reason relationships and I don't work, but I told Cam those things in moments of shared intimacy, not to have them thrown back in my face.

The storm that's been brewing all day strikes, my hackles rising. 'Perhaps he has had enough chances, but just because you're carrying resentment about your father doesn't mean I have to do the same.'

He frowns, his eyes sharp with anger. 'I wasn't suggesting you should. This isn't a competition, Orla. We're not talking about me. I'm simply suggesting he doesn't deserve you if he's going to disrespect you.' He grapples his frustration under control and I hold him closer, each of us stepping back from the edge.

I ignore the warning bells sounding inside my head. I want to rewind. I want to go back to the start, diving from that yacht in Monaco, seeing the delight and awe on Cam's face. But there's no going back. I've had my six-week proposition, and although our differences didn't seem to matter at the start they're still there, bigger and uglier than before.

Cam drops his mouth to the top of my head, presses an apologetic kiss there and says, 'Just let me know when you have time to visit the cottage.'

A wise woman would offer a non-committal smile. I shrivel, thinking about my week ahead and the week after that... I can't commit, even to a brief visit to the cottage I so long to see in person because it's important to him.

This is what I've told him from the start.

My throat burns, but I swallow, resolved to be honest, not to drag out the inevitable pain of us ending. 'I will, but it won't be for a while—I'm flying to London the day after tomorrow.'

Cam says nothing. His feet stop shuffling around the dance floor. The air around us hisses with awkward tension.

He leans back so I'm forced to lift my head from his chest and look up. 'But you've only just returned to Sydney.' He presses his lips together, disappointed. 'Do you absolutely have to go again? Don't you have people all over the world, people who can do everything for you?'

I feel weighed down by sadness. I wanted to do this in a thoughtful way, perhaps over coffee. But Cam's invested. Hell, *I'm* invested, and the time for thoughtful is long gone. 'I do have people, but this is my life, my job—you know that. Nothing's changed.'

Liar. Everything's changed...except me.

His expression hardens, his jaw tense.

I feel trapped, his arms, which only seconds ago were comforting, now feel like chains. 'Why am I defending myself, Cam? It's not a feeling I like.'

He rubs one palm down his face, hurt and defeat lurking in his expression, and my stomach lurches with nausea. 'I'm not trying to make you defensive. I just... Look, you don't need to explain your actions or defend them, never with me.' His hands find my waist and he tugs me close again, as if trying to re-create the intimacy of earlier. 'I'll just miss you, that's all.' His voice is low, heartfelt, torture to my ears, because I believe him. I want to be able to return the sentiment but it's as if my tongue is stuck in my throat.

He presses a kiss to my forehead and whispers, 'I'll wait. Come and visit the cottage any time you can.'

I don't want to hurt him so I say nothing, simply nod, foreboding churning in my head. Wonderful, considerate Cam… I can't make any promises. Nor can I admit that it's business as usual for me. Or exactly where this relationship is on my priority list. But I must. This is the moment I've been dreading. This conversation proves I've allowed this to go on too long, that I've been selfish.

I look up, my heart pounding. I see hope and passion and understanding in his expressive eyes. And he must see the opposite in mine.

His body stiffens.

I lock my knees, my legs fully absorbed with keeping me upright. I know what he wants. He showed me earlier when he made love to me. He wants some fairytale, happy-ever-after future for us. But I'm a realist. I know my limitations. I know my strengths. And I know Cam and what he deserves.

'I don't want this to end,' he says, his mouth a grim line, as if he's already anticipated my refusal.

Perceptive.

I look away. I never wanted to hurt him, but it's pointless taking this any further. 'Cam, we agreed this was temporary.'

My throat is so crushed, I can't breathe.

'I...I have feelings for you and I think you have them for me too.'

I do, I do, my beautiful, caring Cam. How could I not?

I shake my head as if I can shake out his words from my memory. 'I can't... I told you. I'm no good at relationships.'

'Why, because you had one bad experience?'

Another shake.

'Why do you have to be good at it? Why can't you just give me a chance and see how this goes?'

The lure of his words, so simple in theory, makes my head spin. 'Because I'll fail and we'll both get hurt. Why put ourselves through that?'

'Just because your marriage failed doesn't mean we will. He tried to change you and I'd never do that. Why should I suffer because of his actions?'

I step out of his arms, his touch now claustrophobic. 'Aren't you doing that right now? Trying to change me? Suggesting I ditch my family barbecue so I don't have to face my father, encouraging me to delegate more work so I can be around more to play...girlfriend?' I snort. 'Even the word is ridiculous. I'm thirty-six. I'm not cut out for the commitment of a relationship.' I lower my voice. There are people all around us. Happy, relaxed, smiling people.

I move away and he reaches for my hand. 'Where are you going? We need to talk about this.'

'We do,' I say with a sigh I feel to the tips of my toes. But this is more about me than it is about him, and if I have to tell him that, I'm going to need Dutch courage.

'I'm going to get a drink. We can talk more privately.'
I head for the bar, which is relatively quiet now that the
after-dinner dancing is in full swing.

I'm almost there, my mind racing with suitable let-
downs that sound trite and hurtful and make me feel
sick to my stomach, when I spy a woman I've met
before, the M Club founder and entrepreneur Imogen
Carmichael. The usually composed blonde seems flustered. I'm stalling, sidestepping my own impending disaster, but it will only take a few minutes to say hello
and check she's okay.

'Imogen.' I snag her attention and she smiles, a flash
of relief on her face. I'm aware that Cam will be right
behind me, that we need to finish this, but something
has the normally unflappable Imogen nervous. And it
will give me a few precious minutes to gather my wits
and compose myself for what I need to say to Cam.
Otherwise I'm at risk of caving, of throwing myself
into his arms and agreeing to try…

'Are you okay?'

'Oh, I'm fine,' she says, her eyes darting around the
ballroom. 'I'm sorry, I can't stop and chat. I have an
appointment. It was good to see you again, Orla. I hope
we can catch up properly in New York next month at
the Christmas Gala.'

'Yes, I'd like that.' I watch her leave, and then I continue to the bar, where Cam is waiting with two glasses
of the Macallan.

'Was that Imogen Carmichael?' he asks, his body
language wary and distant, as if he's sorry he lifted the

lid on any discussion of a future for us. But it's too late now. We've come this far.

I swallow, my head pounding and my chest hollow and aching. 'Yes. Have you met her?'

'No.'

One-syllable answers…

I didn't want it to be like this—awkward and full of recrimination. But then, what did I expect, just because my heart is made of stone?

'You'd like her—she runs several charities,' I say. 'I'll introduce you sometime.'

He hands me my drink, his eyes glittering, all friendliness gone. 'When? Next time you're in Sydney long enough? Next time we bump into each other at an M Club function? And will we just pretend none of this ever happened?'

I have no answer, but I say, 'I don't know when. Look, Cam, I didn't want things to go this way. I…I heard what you said about trying, and I want you to know I'm flattered that you think we could be…more. But you knew from the start—'

'I get it, you don't do relationships.'

I ignore him, the reasons almost crushing my chest as I verbalise them, forcing them out. 'You know my hours. My commitments. I clock up tens of thousands of air miles. I'm hardly ever home in Sydney. I'm just not relationship material. And you'd soon grow to resent me for it. It's already started.'

'I don't resent you,' he bites out, and I shrink, shame at how cowardly I'm behaving blotting out the other feelings like panic and grief that have no place, because this is what I wanted all along.

'You're the most amazing woman I've ever met—smart, inspiring, accomplished. I celebrate you.' He sighs, runs his hand through his hair. 'As long as you work the way you do because it makes you happy and not because you're still trying to prove you don't need your father's, or anyone else's, approval—including mine.'

'I know you think that's what motivates me, and maybe once...in the beginning... But this isn't about my father. It's about me not being right for a relationship, not being right for you. Look, you'll find someone you have more things in common with, someone with time for a relationship, someone your own age.' I wince because I can hear what's just emerged from my mouth and I couldn't sound more patronising if I tried.

Fury flits across Cam's face. He swallows the Macallan in a single, knocked-back swallow and then places his empty glass on the bar. 'I've never cared about our age gap and the fact you're bringing it up now, when you've nowhere else to run, tells me what a bullshit excuse it is, and you know it.'

He steps closer, one hand finding my hip, his fingers flexing in a way that reminds me of when he's turned on and about to undress me. But I can't succumb to the touch my body craves so badly; even now I feel my resolve wobbling. It would be so easy to forget this fight, like the ones that have gone before, to mend what's broken the best way we know how. With sex. But it's not just sex any more and I can't risk another dose of the searing intimacy we share.

My eyes burn and I blink hard. The longer we draw out the goodbye, the worse it will feel. For both of us. Because we've both been stupid. Both allowed feelings to creep into what should have been a simple transaction of pleasure. I can't toy with him, now I know what he wants, know that his feelings are involved. I should never have toyed with him in the first place.

'Look, my job is my priority. I thought you understood that.' The words scratch at my throat like tears, but I hold myself in check, wound too tightly to surrender to the emotion that will make me weak enough to confess that yes, a part of me wants to believe in a future for Cam and me.

'Oh, that's crystal clear, believe me.'

'That's a low blow. Just because you were handed your fortune instead of earning it, like I've had to, it's not fair to make me feel bad for making a living while you fritter away an inheritance you don't even appreciate.' As soon as the words are out I want to suck them back in.

He's so angry, his eyes glow, his beautiful mouth flat. 'Well, it's good to know how you really feel.'

My chest collapses, squashed by the weight of my regret. I make a move to touch him, but before I make contact he says, 'I can see you're not prepared to give us, to give me, a chance after everything we've shared.'

I gape, because I'm stunned at his insight, his maturity, his quiet delivery after I've verbally slapped him in the face. I've been blind or simply hiding because I'm too scared to be emotionally vulnerable.

'You know, Orla, your father isn't worthy of the amazing woman you are. You're ten times the human being he is. You're probably smarter than him, a daughter to be proud of, whose successes should be celebrated.'

'I know that.'

'Do you? Because you seem to need a daily reminder.' He touches my diamond stud with one gentle fingertip, and I want to curl into a ball.

'Every day you push and strive and work to the point of near collapse, to prove yourself to a man who'll probably never see you, the real you. I might not be worthy of you either, but at least I see you. And I want you, I want us to have something real like I thought we've had these past weeks, but you can't even give me one single chance.'

I want to tell him he's wrong, that I want to give him everything, that I already have, but until five minutes ago it would have been a lie. 'Cam, I—'

He stands tall, slides his empty glass away on the bar. 'Perhaps I was right about you all along. We *are* too different. Because I refuse to dance to my father's tune, to be his puppet. You showed me I don't have to see the money as a bond, that I can use it for good, to make a difference. You said it yourself, Orla. It's how we live our lives that defines us. How do you want to live? If you're happy making money every second of every day, then that's fine by me, but do it for yourself. Not for him. I wanted you in my life because you're enough for me just as you are, but now I see that's never going to happen because you need to work out what is enough for you. And I see now that that isn't me.'

I sway towards him, my stomach in my throat and his whispered name ringing in my ears. But I'm frozen by the choices I've made. Trapped, when all along I believed the illusion I was free to live on my terms.

Cam hands me his phone, his face now devoid of emotions. 'Text my driver when you're ready to leave.'

He turns on his heel and heads for the exit.

I stop him. 'Wait—where are you going?'

He pauses. 'I'll walk home.'

I watch him leave, my eyes burning into him, but he never once looks back.

CHAPTER TEN

Orla

I PARK MY Mini Cooper in the garage of my parents' Point Piper mansion and head into the house, my stomach hollow and my muscles clenched, ready for a fight. It's been weeks since I've seen my family, but as I step out onto the terrace, donning my sunglasses against the glare of another fantastic Sydney day, I want to switch off the sun and hide. Not from my family, although gatherings these days are usually fraught with competitive undercurrents and entrenched dysfunctional dynamics I could do without, but from myself. From the decisions I've made. The mess. The knowledge that the mistakes I made before are minuscule in comparison to this one—losing Cam.

Holding on to the torrent of emotions inside, I wave to my mother, who's in the infinity pool with my nephew, and head for the barbecue, where, typically, the males of my family congregate, as if grilling a steak requires testosterone. Before I even arrive

I can sense an argument brewing between my brother, Liam, and my father.

I sigh, every bone in my body aching with self-inflicted grief. What am I doing here? I could have made any number of excuses—I have tons of emails to catch up on, six weeks' worth of laundry to organise…damn, even airing my own long-neglected penthouse would be preferable to this, although I'm mostly here for my mother's sake. But what I really want to do is lick my wounds while I try to work out if I've just sabotaged the best thing that ever happened to me.

My hollow stomach gripes again—ever since I arrived home last night after the gala I've wanted to throw up and it gives me a sick sense of satisfaction. I got what I wanted and it hurts like hell. It's over, the end not neat as I'd hoped, but then when is anything ever neat when matters of the heart are involved?

Something inside my chest lurches.

It's grief, just grief.

It will pass.

I force my face to conceal everything I'm feeling and greet my brother, accepting his kiss on the cheek. I pour myself a drink and take a tiny sip of the iced water, but even that gets stuck in my throat. I put it down and tune in to the argument to take my mind off Cam and the gaping hole he's left in my life, although this is the very drama I was dreading.

Cam was right. Why am I putting myself through this? I'm a grown-ass woman, not a dutiful child. And today there's only room inside my battle-sore body for one fight: staving off tears.

If I weren't afraid of bursting into those unheard-of tears, I'd join my mother in the pool, because I'm too heartsick to deal with family drama, but perhaps Liam needs my support.

'Have I interrupted a fight?' I say, watching my father stab at a steak on the grill with barbecue tongs.

My brother is uncharacteristically annoyed. 'More of an ongoing discussion of how badly I'm running the ship,' says Liam. 'You know, sis, you did well to bail when you did.' He stares at the back of my father's head as if daring him to contradict this in front of me.

I'm shocked speechless. This is the first time I've heard of any discontent between my father and his golden boy, not that the fault lies with Liam.

I try to keep the bitterness from erupting, from saying something I'll regret, but then it hits me.

I really don't care.

I'm thirty-six. I've just lost a man with whom I suspect I've fallen in love. I have bigger problems than causing a scene at a family barbecue. Massive problems. Insurmountable problems…

What have I done?

I focus on my brother. 'Well, I wasn't given a choice. As I recall, my services were no longer required.' Sympathy for Liam wells up inside me—so he's not good enough either, in our father's eyes. 'Is this about Jensen's?'

I have no desire to be the source of tension between

these two men, but really, where does my father get off with his expectations and constant criticism? I shouldn't need to impress this man, and shame, hotter than the November sun, licks at me that I even tried. I'm his daughter. His pride should be automatic. His love un-conditional. Like Cam's…

Cam—the only person whose opinion matters.

The pangs of longing twisting my stomach into knots grow stronger.

Liam's clearly more pissed than I've ever seen him, because he ignores my question and puts down his beer at the nearby table.

'You know, Dad, Orla bested us because she's just better. Perhaps you should have thought of that when you were succession planning.'

Liam turns away from our father in disgust and squeezes my shoulder. 'You look great, sis. It's been years since I've seen you look this relaxed. Whatever you've been doing these past few weeks suits you. If you want my advice, you should keep it up.'

He moves away to the other side of the terrace to join his wife, presumably to calm down so he too can get through a simple family gathering. I watch him kiss my sister-in-law and wave to his son in the pool, pangs of jealousy slicing through me, not for his position as CEO that I once coveted above all else. But because he has a life. A rich and balanced life. A life like the one I could have tried to create with Cam, if I wasn't so caught up in my fear of failure.

I close my eyes, clarity arriving like a smack in the

face. What is failure but evidence that you've tried your best?

Cam's already said I'm enough for him, just the way I am. No changes, no expectations, no conditions. I touch an earring, the earrings Cam gave me in Singapore, hoping somehow to connect with the man who's taught me how to love. Properly, unconditionally, and without fear. I located the box last night when I returned home to my dark and empty home. I fell asleep clutching it, the only part of him I had access to. The first thing I did this morning was change my earrings.

Even if I've lost Cam for ever through my own stupidity, I need a fresh reminder every time I look in the mirror. A reminder of everything he gave me. A reminder I'm more than Orla Hendricks, successful CEO. I'm also Orla Hendricks, woman, and I can have a fulfilling, complete relationship as long as I'm prepared to work just as hard at it.

Not that loving Cam would be hard.

I gasp. I love him…

For once my head is as clear as the cloudless blue framing Sydney's famous skyline in the distance.

He sees me. The real me. Despite our differences, he wants me. Or perhaps, in all areas that matter, we're not that different after all. I was just too scared to believe in those qualities. But Cam's shown me balance. He's shown me that I can have it all—a job I'm good at and a relationship I want to work equally hard at. For the first time in my life, I want the commitment. I want to devote my time and energy and everything that I am to making us work.

I want him. In every way.

My father's voice interrupts my thoughts. 'I hope Jensen's isn't more than you can handle.'

I open my eyes with new resolve that has nothing to do with justifying myself to this man. 'Really? Talking business? This is family time.'

I look down at the steaks. There's no way a single mouthful of the delicious-smelling lunch is going to make it past my throat, now I've acknowledged my feelings for Cam. But have I left it too late? Have I ruined the only thing in my life that I love more than my work?

Him.

'I've spent the past ten years building my firm,' I tell my startled father. 'It's a well-oiled machine, and even if it wasn't, it's only a job, so don't you worry about whether I can handle Jensen's. But while we're on the subject, I'm going to be taking some time off—my personal life is a mess and I'm hoping to rectify that.' The barest surge of hope wells inside me, in no way diminished by my father's dismissive grunt.

'I'm not hungry and I have somewhere else to be. Tell Mum I'll call her later.' I kiss my father's cheek and for the first time in years truly see him, see the stress lines, the grey hair and the near perpetual scowl he wears as the toll of his ambition. I want better than that for myself. And, like always, I can have what I want; I just pray I'm not too late to have it with Cam.

'You know, Dad, you should try to find greater work-life balance and support Liam in doing the same.'

I expect some scathing retort or splutter of anger, but his jaw actually drops and I wish Cam were here to witness the look on his face.

'Oh, and by the way,' I add, 'your steaks are burning.'

I pull up outside Cam's cottage as the sun kisses the horizon. When I climb from my car and hear the faint, rhythmic sound of hammering, I know I've found him at last, my body flooding with chills of relief.

It has taken the rest of the afternoon for me to track him down. He wasn't at his cold and sterile penthouse—no surprise. I checked the local beach, knowing he likes to surf. I even reached out to the construction company he used to work for, my mounting frustration turning to panic. I finally called a contact in the real-estate industry, someone I made obscenely wealthy last year, begging him to flout the law and provide me with the address of the cottage Cam purchased a year ago.

I collect the cool-bag full of Cam's favourite beer from the passenger seat of my car and head down the driveway towards the sound of banging, every nerve in my body firing like the cascade of fireworks we watched over the bay in Singapore only a week ago. As I round the property, ducking under an overhanging eucalyptus tree in desperate need of a hearty prune, I'm temporarily blinded by the last rays of the setting sun.

Then my vision clears and I'm blinded anew, only

this time it's the sight of the man I love, shirtless, with a tool belt hugging his hips, that scorches my retinas.

The rear of the property boasts the enviable sea views he showed me on his phone that day in Dubai. A newly constructed deck extends the width of the cottage, and Cam is busy framing up what appears to be a perfect sunroom off the existing living area. I can smell the sawdust before I approach, my head spinning with hopes and fears and what-ifs.

He'd have every right to turf me off his property. He's spent the past six weeks building me up, pushing me to be the best version of myself. A whole version. Not afraid to let go, to loosen the reins that have trapped me inside my own beliefs and expectations for so long.

But can I be whole without him now that I know I love him?

I must have stepped on a stick or piece of sun-scorched bark from the eucalyptus, because he hears the crack and spins. Sees me.

His arms fall to his sides, the hammer hanging in his hand. A million emotions pass over his face in the few seconds of silence that we spend staring. If I could stop the wheel spinning on the love I saw yesterday at his penthouse I would, but there's no sign of it.

Did I kill it for good? Am I too late?

I hold out the cool-bag, my arm trembling. 'I thought you might like a cold beer. It's your favourite.'

Still he stares.

I swallow, my throat parched.

He sniffs, tucks the hammer into his work belt and looks back my way. 'Why are you here, Orla?'

I try to un-hear the accusation and hostility in his question. It's not unreasonable after the way I treated him. As if he didn't matter. As if he wasn't important. As if he isn't the very reason my heart beats.

'You invited me.' My voice is small. Where is my smiling, devil-may-care Cam?

He smirks, shakes his head, but it's an expression of disbelief. 'That was before.'

Before I hurt him. Before he tried to tell me how he felt and I shut him down.

'You threw my invitation back in my face, along with my dreams for us.'

His words are like shots from the nail gun I see on the new deck. 'I know, and I want to apologise. You were right about me. My life isn't enough.'

I take a shuddering step forward and then halt when the expression on his face stays blank and cold. I put the cool-bag down on the grass.

'I want those dreams, Cam. I want you.'

He looks away to the horizon and I crumple a little more. I'm blowing this, allowing my one chance to slip through my fingers. I lift my chin, willing him silently to look back at me with every cell in my body.

Our eyes meet, just like that first time in Monaco, only now I love this man about whom my first impressions were so wrong. 'I want this dream, Cam. The cottage, waking up to the sunrise, sitting by your side on that deck to watch the sunset. I know I said I didn't want a relationship, but that was because I was scared that I had some vital emotional piece of me lacking. Scared to try. Scared to fail. Scared that I'd be nothing without my career because that's all I've had, all I've been able to control for so long.'

'So what's changed? I'm still the same me I was yesterday. The same me you didn't value enough to give a chance.' He hooks his thumbs into his worn leather tool belt in a way I'm certain he's done a thousand times, and my body jolts, because I want to be there to see him do it a thousand times more. To watch him build this cottage, his dream, and to help him build many more dreams of our shared future.

'Nothing's changed, or everything.' I twist my hands together. This isn't going well. 'I know I'm not making sense. But I spoke to my father earlier, and I realised something. Well, I realised lots of things, actually. But the most important ones were that I don't care what he thinks. I only care about proving something to you.'

'I told you last night. You never have to prove anything to me—'

'I do.' I step closer, urgency driving me, although his sphere of personal space vibrates around him like a force-field, keeping me at a distance. 'I need to prove that I love you, because I know I've hurt you and it's my biggest regret—that and letting you go in the first place. Thinking I could live without you.'

He still looks wary, even as his eyes latch on to mine, penetrating and searching.

'I know you won't believe that I love you for a while,

but I'll keep trying, keep showing you until you're convinced.' I pop one hand on my hip and push my sunglasses up onto my head so he can see I mean business.

'I mean it, Cam—you know how driven I am when I want something. You, multi-billion-dollar deals...it's all the same to me. I won't give up.' My weight shifts from one foot to the other, despite the confident spiel. I wish he'd say something, even if it's *Get off my property.* Anything to break the tension.

I'm about to turn away in defeat when he says, 'You're wearing the earrings.'

I'm so focused on breathing so I don't collapse that it takes me a moment to understand. 'What? Oh, yes.' I touch the earring again, the intricate gold filigree reassuring under my fingertip. 'I wanted a new reminder. Every time I touch these, every time I look in the mirror, I want to remember you, remember all the moments, incredible moments we shared. Because that's the life I want, Cam. A life filled with incredible, joyous, sexy, fun-packed, simple moments. With you.'

My pulse roars in my ears.

He stares, unmoving, his beautiful eyes expressionless.

And then, with his strangled grunt in my ears, I'm dragged into his arms, his big, strong, comforting arms. I'm pressed against his bare, sweaty chest, which is all dusty with sawdust, and I've never felt more at home. His mouth covers mine, and I curl my fingers into his hair, never wanting to let him go ever again.

I pull away from the kiss, keeping a hold of his face.

'I'm sorry. Thank you for challenging me, showing me I can be whoever I want to be. I can re-invent myself and break free of my own cage.'

He grips my shoulders. 'You're wonderful, just the way you are. I love you.'

I kiss him again and he pushes me back by the shoulders. 'Thank you for putting everything into perspective. You showed me I'm not defined by my inheritance, that I can rule it, rather than it ruling me.'

'You're not your father, Cam. It's just money. It's this,' I wave an arm in the direction of the cottage, his labour of love, 'and this,' I press my palm flat on his chest, over his heart, 'how you live your life, how you use your inheritance to make a difference—that's who you are.'

We kiss again and this time when we pull apart we're both laughing, joyous, thrilling laughter I want to hear and feel every day for the rest of my life.

'So are you going to show me the cottage or not?' I put my arms around his waist and rest my head against his chest, feel the steady thump of his heart.

My heart.

His voice rumbles from deep within his chest. 'Sure, but there's nowhere else to sit apart from here.' He points to two dusty, paint-splattered deckchairs on the lawn, perfectly positioned to watch the sun rise and set.

I look up, lift my eyebrows, new pangs of envy making me pout. 'Two? Had company, have you?' The thought of anyone looking at my man while he's shirt-less makes me form fists. I might have to erect a privacy fence until he's finished the cottage.

He tucks me under his arm, kisses the top of my head and leads me towards the house with a chuckle. 'My cousin's been helping me.'

'The one you sent the car to?'

He nods.

'Good, because from here on in, that second deck-chair has got my name on it—I'm going to enjoy spending the summer watching you sweat shirtless and get splinters I can kiss better.' I lift his hand to my mouth and press a kiss over his fingertips.

'Is that right?' he says, his mouth twisted in that way that makes my blood sing and my insides clench in anticipation. He leads me through the demolished kitchen and down the hall to the cooler rear part of the house. He kicks open the last door. It's a bedroom, a single camp bed is pushed up against one wall, and Cam's tuxedo from last night hangs from a rusty nail on the back of the door.

I turn, already mentally undressing him as I undo the buttons of my blouse, making it clear what I propose we do with the rest of the night.

'What about my beer?' He pops open his fly and heels off his work boots, his heated stare tightening my nipples to hard peaks.

I smile at my man. 'It'll keep. Let's take a moment.' And I kiss him, flopping backwards onto the narrow mattress and tugging him down on top of me.

EPILOGUE

Cam

THE NEW YORK M Club's ballroom is packed with party-goers, every member dressed to the nines and in festive spirit. It's the biggest gathering of immense wealth and beautiful, glamorous people I've ever seen—twice the size of the Masquerade Gala in Sydney—but I only have eyes for one woman.

My woman.

I watch her talking to Imogen Carmichael, her exquisite face animated and her eyes dancing with the reflection of a million fairy lights scattered throughout the ballroom. She carries herself with the same grace and poise as the first time I saw her, perched on a stool at the casino in Monaco, only now she's relaxed. She smiles more, laughs more, and waking up with her every morning is a privilege I'll never take for granted.

She's taken her first holiday in five years. As promised, she's spent the summer sitting on that tatty deck-chair watching me work on the cottage while she drinks my beer. She even comes surfing with me sometimes.

The only time she complains is when I put my shirt back on. She told me yesterday that my working semi-naked helps her to think.

She catches my eye, winds up her conversation with Imogen and slinks my way, so by the time she reaches my side the only thoughts in my head are how quickly I can get her out of here so I can love her the way I want to.

'What are you thinking about?' She slips her arm around my waist and tucks her body into my side. 'Tell me now, because I think I know that look on your face.' She presses her lips to my neck with a sexy little hum.

I smile down at her and bend low to press an all too brief kiss on her lips. 'I was wondering what *you* think about when I'm shirtless.'

Her eyes dance. 'Well, duh, the same thing half of Sydney thinks about—ways to get you out of the other half of your clothes, of course.' She laughs, rises up onto her tiptoes and kisses me back. 'You know you're becoming quite the celebrity, right?'

She's talking about the changes I made to the construction company I once worked for after I bought it and the training school I set up to give apprenticeships to youngsters who need a break in life.

'Well, you showed me how to let go of my resentment. I think he'd approve of how I'm using it,' I say of my father, the remorse in my voice causing Orla's eyes to shine with love and support.

'Of course he would. Opening new hospital wings you've sponsored, delivering brand-new equipment to the local surf lifesavers, planting trees. You're always splashed on the front of some newspaper or magazine these days, usually shirtless. I think he'd prefer it if you wore a shirt though.' She pouts, mock censure on her beautiful mouth.

I roll my eyes but I can't help smiling at her teasing. 'I was shirtless one time, Orla. One time. And that was only because I was trying out the surfboards.'

She laughs, a lovely tinkling sound I never grow tired of hearing. 'Oh, don't worry. If I had this body,' she runs her hand over my abs and up to my chest, 'I'd want to show it off all the time too.'

I put my arms around her waist and hold her close. 'You're doing just fine with the body you've got. Trust me.'

Our exchange turns heated, X-rated, non-verbal communication passing between us in that way couples do when they know exactly what the other is thinking.

'Want to get out of here?' she asks, her voice smoky with lust. 'I have a surprise for you.'

'Yes.' It's a no-brainer. The chemistry, the bond we share, shows no signs of letting up; if anything it gets stronger every day. And I have a surprise for her too.

My Christmas present.

The cottage is almost finished and it's hers. I signed over the deeds today and the key feels heavy in my pocket. Excitement joins the slug of potent, almost incapacitating desire I always feel in Orla's company, desire made stronger by whatever is putting that gleam in her eyes, because I know she'll always keep me on my toes.

We make our way out of the ballroom, stopping briefly to say goodnight to one or two friends. Instead of heading for the exit, she leads me towards the club's private rooms.

'Where are we going?'

She unlocks one of the doors, her small smile knowing. 'I thought we could spend the night here.'

Inside, the room is intimate and romantic and exactly what she deserves after weeks of sleeping at the cottage with me because she knows I'm more comfortable there than at the penthouse. Of course, we upgraded to a double camp bed, but she deserves a little luxury after weeks of sawdust, dodgy plumbing and unreliable electrics.

She reaches for me, her hands coming around my neck, and I kiss her once, twice...but before I get carried away I pull the key from my pocket. 'I have a surprise for you too. Merry Christmas.'

Her hand covers her mouth and she gasps, because she knows what it is I'm giving her. She understands me. She shares my dreams as I share hers.

'Cam... Oh, I don't know what to say. Thank you.'

Her reaction, her obvious delight, makes me feel ten feet tall. My heart pounds, but I plough on with the second part of my surprise. 'Say you'll wake up by my side every morning to the sound of the sea. Say you'll sit next to me on the veranda, drinking my beer. Say you'll marry me?'

I present the ring I bought earlier today, my insides twisting with nerves. 'I know it's quick, but I want to live dreams and make moments with you for the rest of our lives.'

'Yes.' She jumps up and I catch her around the waist, staggering towards the bed so I can deposit her under me and kiss her the way I want to.

Her smile, when we part for air, fills my chest with joy and love and too many euphoric emotions to name.

'Of course, you know what this means, don't you?' I say between her kisses.

'What?' She lies back on the bed and looks at me with such love in her eyes that I struggle to breathe. Struggle to believe that she's mine.

'Well, not only will I be able to offload half my fortune onto my new spouse...' I wink because only she understands how far I've come that I can joke about something as serious as my inheritance.

She cups my face, her eyes swimming.

'But I also get to keep you for ever.'

She nods.

'And I get to keep you.'

* * * * *

COMING SOON!

We really hope you enjoyed reading this book.
If you're looking for more romance
be sure to head to the shops when
new books are available on

Thursday 21st November

To see which titles are coming soon, please visit
millsandboon.co.uk/nextmonth

MILLS & BOON